Dangerous Regency Rogues

Tall, Dark &
Irresistible

Two fabulous novels
from international bestselling author

CAROLE MORTIMER

CAROLE MORTIMER'S
TALL, DARK & HANDSOME COLLECTION

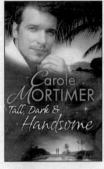

August 2013

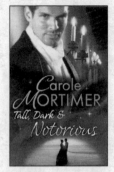

September 2013

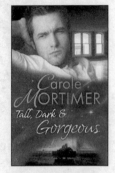

October 2013

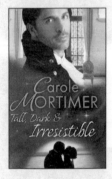

November 2013

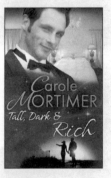

December 2013

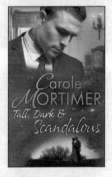

January 2014

A beautiful collection of favourite Carole Mortimer novels.
Six seductive volumes containing sixteen fabulous
Modern™ and Historical bestsellers.

Carole MORTIMER

Tall, Dark &
Irresistible

Published in Great Britain 2013
by Mills & Boon, an imprint of Harlequin (UK) Limited, Eton House, 18-24 Paradise Road, Richmond, Surrey TW9 1SR

TALL, DARK & IRRESISTIBLE
© Harlequin Enterprises II B.V./S.à.r.l. 2013

The Rogue's Disgraced Lady © Carole Mortimer 2009
Lady Arabella's Scandalous Marriage © Carole Mortimer 2010

ISBN: 978 0 263 91025 4

024-1113

Carole Mortimer was born in England, the youngest of three children. She began writing in 1978 and has now written over one hundred and eighty books for Mills & Boon. Carole has six sons, Matthew, Joshua, Timothy, Michael, David and Peter. She says, 'I'm happily married to Peter senior; we're best friends as well as lovers, which is probably the best recipe for a successful relationship. We live in a lovely part of England.'

The Rogue's Disgraced Lady

CAROLE MORTIMER

For Karin Stoecker

Thank you for listening to me when the idea for the
St. Claire family first entered my imagination!

Prologue

Banford House, Mayfair, late July, 1817

'It *is* you, Sebastian!' his hostess greeted him warmly as he was announced into her drawing-room. 'When Revell informed me that Lord St Claire had come to call I thought… But of course Lucian is newly married, and most probably still upon his honeymoon. It is so good to see you!'

Sebastian, Lord St Claire, was, as usual, dressed in the height of fashion, in a perfectly tailored brown superfine over a gold brocade waistcoat and snowy white linen, with fawn pantaloons and brown-topped black Hessians. His fashionably overlong teak-coloured hair was shot through with natural streaks of gold.

He gave a roguish smile as he crossed the room to where Dolly Vaughn reclined graciously upon the raspberry-red sofa in the drawing room of her town house. Except she was no longer Dolly Vaughn, of course, but Lady Dorothea Bancroft, the Countess of Banford.

Eyes the colour of warm whisky laughingly met her teasing blue ones as Sebastian took the hand she offered and raised it to his lips. 'Please do not shatter all my illusions and tell me that you were once acquainted with my brother Lucian,' he drawled.

'Intimately,' Dolly assured him mischievously. 'Stourbridge too, on one memorable occasion. But that is another story entirely…' She gave a delighted laugh as Sebastian's eyes widened at this mention of his eldest brother Hawk, the aristocratic and aloof tenth Duke of Stourbridge. 'Poor Bancroft has the devil of a time pretending not to be aware of the names of any of my past lovers,' she added with an unrepentant smile.

William Bancroft, Earl of Banford, should, and did, consider himself the most fortunate of men in having Dolly as his wife for the last three years. Before her marriage she had been the discreet paramour of many a male member of the ton—both of Sebastian's older brothers amongst them, apparently!

Sebastian's own relationship with Dolly was based purely on a platonic friendship that had developed when he first came to town at the tender age of seventeen, still a virgin. Dolly had found Sebastian a less experienced young lady than herself to introduce him to all the carnal delights.

'Please do sit down, Sebastian,' she invited warmly now as she patted the sofa beside her, still a golden-haired beauty, though now aged in her mid-thirties. 'I have ordered tea for us both. It is a little early as yet for me to offer any stronger refreshment, I am afraid,' she added derisively as he raised dark brows.

Sebastian could remember a time when it had never been too early for Dolly to take 'stronger refreshment', but out of respect for her role as the Countess of Banford he did not remind her of those occasions. 'You are looking very well, Lady Bancroft,' he complimented her as he sat down beside her. 'Marriage obviously suits you.'

'Marriage to my darling Bancroft suits me,' she corrected him firmly. 'And I refuse to allow you to behave so formally with me.' She tapped his wrist lightly with her fan. 'When we're alone like this, I insist we be as we always were—simply Dolly and Sebastian.' She turned as the butler returned with a tray of tea things, informing him, 'I am not at home to any more visitors this afternoon, Revell.' She waited until the servant had vacated the room before speaking again. 'I am afraid, even after three years, the servants still find my refusal to follow the rules something of a trial,' Dolly explained airily as she sat forward to pour the tea, the blue of her high-waisted gown a perfect match for her eyes.

She had given Sebastian the very opening in the conversation that he had been hoping for. 'But the ton are a little…kinder to you now than they used to be, are they not?'

'Oh, my dear, I have become quite the thing!' Dolly assured him laughingly as she handed him one of the delicate china teacups. 'An invitation to one of my summer house parties at Banford Park has become famously exclusive.'

Sebastian nodded. 'It is concerning this year's house party that I have come to see you.'

She gave him a look from eyes that had become

shrewdly considering. 'Surely you and several of your friends have already received this year's invitation, Sebastian? An invitation, if my memory serves me correctly, that you have always refused in the past.'

They were both aware there was absolutely nothing amiss with Dolly's memory. 'I am thinking of accepting this year…'

Her gaze became even shrewder. 'If…?'

Sebastian gave a husky laugh as he relaxed back on the sofa. 'You are far too forthright for a man's comfort, Dolly!'

She arched blonde brows. 'For *your* comfort!?'

When Sebastian had come up with the idea it had seemed perfectly straightforward. A simple request for Dolly to include another woman—a particular woman—in her guest list for the two-week summer house party to be held at the Banford estate in Hampshire in two weeks' time. Unfortunately, Sebastian had overlooked the sharpness of Dolly's curiosity…

'You wish me to add another guest to my list. A female guest,' Dolly guessed correctly. 'What of your affair with the widowed Lady Hawtry?'

'Not much escapes your notice, does it, Dolly?' Sebastian said ruefully. 'That relationship is at an end.' As any of his relationships were, whenever the lady began to talk of marriage!

'So who is it this time, Sebastian? Is your reluctance to tell me her name because she is a married lady?' she prompted, at Sebastian's continued silence. 'I assure you, after three years amongst the ton, I am beyond being shocked by anything any of them choose to do behind closed doors—even when it includes my own!'

'The lady was married,' Sebastian admitted. 'But is no longer.' Despite his attraction to the lady in question, Sebastian would never have considered seducing her if she were still married—after all, even a man who was considered a rake of the first order by both the male and female members of the ton must have *some* principles!

'Another widow, then. But which one, I wonder…?' Dolly looked thoughtful as she considered all the widowed ladies of her acquaintance. 'Oh, do give me some clue, Sebastian, please!' she begged a few minutes later. 'You know how I have always hated a mystery.'

Yes, this had all seemed so much easier when Sebastian had sat at home alone, considering how he might gain an introduction to a woman whose very reclusive behaviour this last eighteen months represented something of a challenge to a seasoned rake!

He grimaced. 'Her year of mourning her husband came to an end six months ago, but unfortunately for me—and every other man who relishes being the widow's first lover—she has not as yet returned into Society.'

'Hmm…' Dolly tapped a considering fingertip against her lips. 'No!' She gave a disbelieving gasp, her gaze suddenly guarded as she turned to Sebastian. 'You do not mean—Sebastian, surely you *cannot* be referring to—'

He gave an acknowledging inclination of his head. 'She was one of the few who were kind to you three years ago, when Bancroft first introduced you to the ton as his wife, was she not?'

'You *do* mean her, then!' Dolly breathed softly. 'I

would never have thought…!' She eyed him speculatively. 'Sebastian, you must be aware of the unpleasant gossip that has circulated about her since the untimely death of her husband?'

'Of course I am aware of it,' he said dismissively. 'It only makes the lady more…intriguing.'

The Countess of Banford frowned. 'There is often some truth to such rumours, you know.'

Sebastian shrugged. 'And what if there is? I told you—I intend seducing the woman, not marrying her!'

She chewed on her bottom lip. 'I am just concerned for you, Sebastian…'

He gave a grin. 'There is no reason to be, I assure you.'

'Your intentions really are not honourable, then?' Dolly gave him another of those shrewd glances.

'I have just told you they are not,' he reiterated. 'I am a bachelor by choice, Dolly—and I assure you, no matter what a lady's charms, I intend to continue in that enviable state!'

Dolly nodded. 'You do realise this particular lady has not been seen at *all* since moving to the estate left to her in Shropshire?'

'I would not be asking you to issue this invitation to her if I thought there were any other way in which I might be introduced to her,' Sebastian reasoned wryly.

Dolly's eyes widened. 'The two of you have never even been introduced?'

'Not as yet.' Sebastian grinned wolfishly. 'Her husband and I, for obvious reasons, did not share the same circle of friends.'

'He was rather a pompous bore, was he not?' Dolly conceded. 'So, the two of you have never actually met….'

'I have merely gazed at her once or twice from afar,' Sebastian admitted.

'And now you wish to gaze at her more intimately?' Dolly teased. 'Poor Juliet will not stand a chance!'

'You flatter me, Dolly.'

She shook her head. 'What woman could not be flattered by the attentions of the handsome but equally elusive Lord Sebastian St Claire?' She eyed his roguish good looks and the strength of his leanly muscled body appreciatively. 'It so happens, Sebastian, that I have already issued an invitation to the lady in question.'

'Better and better,' Sebastian murmured appreciatively.

Dolly gave an elegant inclination of one eyebrow. 'We were friends before her husband's death, and despite the gossip I have decided she cannot continue to languish in Shropshire.'

'Has she accepted the invitation?' Sebastian asked eagerly.

'Not yet. But she will,' Dolly assured him with certainty. 'Really, Sebastian, how could you possibly doubt my powers of persuasion?' Dolly rebuked as she saw his suddenly sceptical expression.

Indeed…

'What do you make of this, Helena?' Juliet Boyd, Countess of Crestwood, finished reading the printed invitation she had just received before passing it frowningly to her cousin as the two of them sat together in the breakfast room at Falcon Manor.

Helena gave Juliet a quizzical glance before taking the invitation. Her pale blonde hair was pulled back from her colourless face, her figure thin as a boy's in one of the dull brown gowns she always wore. A frown marred her brow when she looked up again. 'Shall you go, Juliet?'

Ordinarily Juliet would have left the Countess of Banford's invitation, and its envelope, on the table to be disposed of along with the other debris from breakfast. She hesitated now only because there had been a letter enclosed with the invitation. A handwritten letter that she also handed to her cousin to read.

'"My dear",' Helena read. '"You were always so kind to me in the past, and now I take great pleasure in returning that kindness by the enclosed invitation. It is only to be Bancroft and myself, and a few select friends.

'"Please, please do say you will come, Juliet!

'"Your friend, Dolly Bancroft".'

'It is very thoughtful of her to write to me so kindly, but of course I cannot go, Helena,' Juliet said softly.

'But of course you must go!' Her cousin contradicted impatiently, the sudden colour to her pale cheeks giving a brief glimpse of the beauty that was otherwise not apparent in the severity of her hairstyle and dress. 'Do you not see that this could be your door back into Society?'

A door Juliet would prefer to remain firmly closed. 'I want no part of Society, you know that, Helena. As Society has made it more than plain this past year and a half that they no longer wish to have any part of me,' she added dryly.

Her time of mourning had been difficult enough for

Juliet to bear when she felt relief rather than a sense of loss at Edward's death. But the cuts she had received from the ton as early as those who had attended Crestwood's funeral, had only served to show her that Society now felt well rid of her.

She sighed. 'It is very kind of Dolly Bancroft to think of me, of course—'

'And were you not kind to her before she became Society's darling?' her cousin reminded her tartly. 'Before Banford's connections and his prestige in the House caused them to forget that she was nothing more than a mistress who married her lover before his first wife was even cold in her grave!' Helena added, in her usual forthright manner.

It had been her cousin's down-to-earth practicality that had helped Juliet endure this past year and a half of virtual ostracism, and she smiled at Helena now. 'It was a good nine months after his wife's death, actually. And Society was not so kind to me either twelve years ago, when Miss Juliet Chatterton married the retired war hero Admiral Lord Edward Boyd, Earl of Crestwood, member of the House of Lords, and adviser to the War Cabinet. I felt offering my friendship to Dolly Bancroft three years ago was the least I could do if it helped to ease her own path into Society even a little.'

Juliet had only been eighteen when she had married a man thirty years her senior. As was customary, the match had been made and approved by her parents, but nevertheless Juliet had begun her married life with all the naïve expectations of lifelong happiness that were usual in someone so young and unknowing.

She had quickly learnt that her husband had no interest in her happiness, and that in the privacy of their own home he was not the same man his peers and the country so admired.

Juliet's only consolation had been that her parents had not been alive to witness such an ill matched marriage as hers had turned out to be, Mr and Mrs Chatterton having drowned in a boating accident only months after Juliet had married the Earl of Crestwood.

The unhappiness of Juliet's marriage had been eased a little when her cousin Helena, then sixteen years old, had escaped from France six years ago and come to live with them, becoming Juliet's companion. Crestwood, it seemed, had been coward enough not to reveal the cruelty of his true character in front of a witness.

'Then you must let her do this for you, Cousin.' Once again Helena was the practical one. 'You are still far too young and beautiful to allow yourself to just wither away in the country!'

'I assure you I am not yet ready for my bath-chair, Helena!' Juliet gave an indulgent laugh, revealing straight white teeth between lips that were full and unknowingly sensual.

Now aged thirty, Juliet knew she was no longer in possession of the youthful bloom that had once caught Crestwood's eye. Instead, she had become a woman of maturity—and not only in years. Her time spent as Crestwood's wife had left an indelible mark upon her.

Thankfully, she had borne Crestwood no children to inherit their father's cold and unforgiving nature, and so her figure, although more curvaceous now, was still slender. The long darkness of her hair was healthily shiny, loosely confined now at her crown, with wispy curls at her nape and temple as was currently the fashion. Her complexion was still as creamy and unlined as it had ever been.

But there was a lingering shadow of unhappiness in the green depths of her eyes, and Juliet smiled much less often now than she had been seen to do during her single coming-out Season twelve years ago. Before over ten years of marriage to the icy Earl of Crestwood had stripped her of all that girlish joy.

'Anyway, I will never remarry,' she added fiercely.

'No one is suggesting that you should do so, silly.' Helena reached out to squeeze her clenched hands affectionately, having been intuitive enough within months of coming to live at Falcon Manor to know of Juliet's unhappiness in her marriage. 'Two weeks at Banford Park, to gently introduce yourself back into Society, does not mean you have to accept a marriage proposal.'

Juliet had been softening slightly towards the idea of a fortnight spent in the congenial company of Dolly Bancroft's 'few select friends', but this last remark made her bristle anew. 'Nor any other sort of proposal, either,' she stated, only too aware, after years in their midst, of the behaviour of some of the ton at these summer house parties, where it seemed to be accepted that a man would spend his nights in the bedchamber of any woman but that of his own wife.

Helena shook her head. 'I am sure, as she has said in the letter that accompanied her invitation, that Lady Bancroft just means to repay your earlier kindness to her.'

Juliet wished that she could be as sure of that. Oh, she did not for a moment doubt Dolly's good intentions. She had come to know the older woman as being kind and caring, as well as deeply in love with her husband. Juliet only feared that her own idea of good intentions and Dolly Bancroft's might not coincide....

'Oh, do say you will go, Juliet!' Helena entreated. 'I can come with you and act as your maid—'

'You are my cousin, not a servant!' Juliet protested.

'But your cousin is not invited,' Helena pointed out ruefully. 'Think on it, Juliet. It could be fun. And you will be all the fashion, with your French maid Helena Jourdan to attend you.'

Fun, as Juliet well knew, was something that Helena had not had much of in her young life. Her parents, the sister of Juliet's own mother and the Frenchman she had married twenty-five years ago, had been victims of the scourge that had overtaken France during Napoleon's reign, both killed during a raid on their small manor house six years ago, by soldiers in search of food and valuables.

Helena had been present when the raid had occurred, and reluctant after her escape to England to talk of her own fate during that week-long siege. But it had not been too difficult to guess, from the way Helena chose to play down her delicate beauty and dressed so severely, that she had not escaped the soldiers' attentions unscathed.

The two of them had lived quietly and alone except for their few servants this past year and a half, at the estate Crestwood had left his widow, and whilst Juliet had not minded for herself she accepted that at only two and twenty Helena would probably welcome some excitement into their dull lives.

The sort of excitement a two-week stay at Dolly Bancroft's country estate would no doubt provide....

Chapter One

'I have no idea why you felt it necessary to force me from my bed at the crack of dawn—'

'It was eleven o'clock, Gray,' Sebastian pointed out as he expertly handled the matching greys stepping out lively in front of his curricle.

'As far as I am concerned, any hour before midday is the crack of dawn,' Lord Gideon Grayson—Gray to his closest friends—assured him dourly as he huddled down on the seat beside him, the high collar of his fashionably cut jacket snug about his ears despite the warmth of this August summer day. 'I barely had time to wake, let alone enjoy my breakfast.'

'Kippers, eggs and toast, accompanied by two pots of strong coffee,' Sebastian said cheerfully. 'All eaten, as I recall, while you perused today's newspaper.'

'My valet was rushed through my ablutions, and…'

Sebastian stopped listening to Gray's complaints at this point. He was too full of anticipation at the prospect of

the challenge of seducing Juliet Boyd to allow anything—
or anyone—to shake him out of his good temper.

'…and now my closest friend in the world is so bored
by my company that after dragging me forcibly from my
own bed and home he cannot even be bothered listening to me!' Gray scowled up at him censoriously.

Sebastian gave an unrepentant grin as he glanced
down at the other man. 'When you have something
interesting to say, Gray, I assure you I will listen.'

'Could you at least try to be a little less cheerful?'
his friend muttered sourly. 'I do believe I am feeling a
little delicate this morning.'

'A self-inflicted delicacy!' The two men had done the
rounds of the drinking and gambling clubs yesterday
evening—Sebastian had won, Gray had not—after
which his friend had left to spend several hours in the
bed of his current mistress, before returning to his home
in the not-so-early hours.

'You are in disgustingly good humour this morning,
Seb.' Gray gave another wince. 'Have you taken a new
mistress to replace Lady Hawtry?'

'Not yet.' Sebastian grinned wolfishly. 'But I intend
doing so in the next two weeks.'

'Oh, I say!' Gray's interest quickened. 'I hope you
are not intending to try your luck with Dolly Bancroft
during your stay at Banford Park? I warn you, next to
your brother Lucian and yourself, Bancroft is the best
swordsman in England!'

'You may rest easy concerning both my interest in
Dolly's bedchamber and Bancroft's prowess with the
sword,' Sebastian assured him dryly. 'Dolly and I are no

more than friends and never will be.' Especially now that he knew Dolly had been bedded by both his brothers!

Gray arched a dark brow. 'But you admit there *is* a lady involved in our uncharacteristic behaviour in attending a summer house party?'

'Of course,' Sebastian drawled, but he had no intention of sharing his particular interest in bedding the newly widowed Countess of Crestwood.

'Tell me I do not see the parson's mousetrap snapping at your booted heels…' Gray mocked.

Sebastian gave a humourless laugh. 'You most assuredly do not.' He was even more determined to avoid that state after seeing both his brothers succumb over the last year.

'I must say neither of your brothers seems to mind it so much.' Gray's thoughts travelled the same path. 'I am not sure that I should mind, either, if I had one of their wives for my own!'

'In that case, feel free to find your own wife, Gray,' Sebastian jeered. 'But for goodness' sake, do not attempt to find one for me.' His interest in any woman, Juliet Boyd included, did *not* include marriage!

'Yes, Sebastian, she has arrived.' Dolly answered his silent question once the greetings were over and Gray had departed to the library to share a glass of reviving brandy with his host. 'She has asked for tea in her bedchamber, however, and has every intention of staying there until it is time to come down for dinner. But I have given you adjoining bedchambers. The balconies of your rooms are connected also,' she confided warmly.

Sebastian smiled his satisfaction with the arrangement. 'I trust I will be seated next to her at dinner too?'

'Sebastian, I am not sure your interest in the Countess is altogether wise…' Dolly suddenly looked troubled.

'If it were "wise", Dolly, I doubt I should wish to pursue it!' he teased. 'Now, if I have your permission, I believe I would like to retire to my own bedchamber and rest a little before dinner.'

'Rest?' His hostess's brow arched speculatively.

'I assure you I have no intention of intruding upon the privacy of the lady before we have even been formally introduced,' he pointed out.

'That will come later, one assumes?' Dolly teased.

'Hopefully, yes,' Sebastian murmured.

There had been many rumours circulating about the Countess of Crestwood since her husband's sudden death—most of them unpleasant, to say the least. But none of them had even hinted at her ever being involved in a liaison with another man, either before or during her marriage. Or, indeed, since her marriage had ended….

So Sebastian spent the hours before dinner resting in his bedchamber, all the time aware that the beautiful but elusive Juliet Boyd was in the room adjoining his. All was silent behind the closed lace curtains at the windows, however, and the French doors into her bedchamber from the balcony remained firmly shut against the warmth of the day.

But she *had* accepted the invitation, as Dolly had said she would. And Juliet could not remain in her bedchamber for the whole of her stay here….

* * *

Juliet had never felt so nervous as she stood hesitantly in the cavernous hallway of Banford Park, delaying her entrance into the drawing room, where the other guests of the Countess and Earl of Banford could be heard chattering and laughing together as they gathered before dinner.

Dolly Bancroft had been very welcoming upon Juliet's arrival that afternoon. William Bancroft had been equally charming.

No, it was not her host and hostess's lack of welcome that Juliet feared, but the reactions of their other guests, once they realised that Juliet Boyd, Countess of Crestwood, was amongst their number. For Dolly's sake, Juliet sincerely hoped that none of those guests decided to depart once they realised they were to share their stay here with the 'Black Widow', as Juliet was all too aware she had been cruelly labelled after her husband's death.

She should not have agreed to come here, Juliet told herself, for what had to be the hundredth time since accepting the invitation. Much as she might have wanted to give Helena a little treat after their long period of enforced mourning, Juliet knew she should not have allowed herself to be persuaded into believing that these two weeks at Banford Park was the means by which to do it.

Perhaps she would have felt differently if she had been able to have the fiercely protective Helena at her side. Instead Helena had done as she had said she would, and accompanied Juliet as her maid—a role her cousin seemed to be enjoying immensely. She had cheerfully left Juliet's bedchamber a few minutes ago, after first dressing her hair and helping her into her gown, to go upstairs and gossip with the other maids.

'Will you allow me the honour of escorting you into the drawing room, Lady Boyd?'

Juliet turned sharply, relaxing slightly when she saw that it was her host who stood solicitously beside her, proffering his arm. A tall and handsome man in his fifties, who now looked down at her with shrewd hazel eyes, the Earl reminded Juliet very much of her father.

'I was just admiring this portrait.' Juliet glanced up at the painting upon the wall which she had, in truth, only just noticed.

'My great-grandfather—the seventh Earl of Banford.' The Earl nodded. 'A singularly ugly man, was he not?' he drawled disparagingly.

Juliet could not help the chuckle that escaped her lips; the seventh Earl had indeed been a very unattractive man!

'Shall we…?' His great-grandson, the tenth earl, offered her his arm a second time.

'Thank you,' Juliet accepted shyly, and placed her gloved hand on top of that arm.

She had chosen to wear a fashionably high-waisted gown of dark grey silk this evening, with only the barest hint of Brussels lace at her bosom and around the edges of the short puffed sleeves. A row of pearls was entwined amongst her dark curls, her only other jewellery matching ear-bobs and the plain gold wedding band on her left hand.

Juliet would have liked to remove even this symbol of Edward's ownership of her, but knew that would only add to the speculation that had followed so quickly after Edward's death and still remained rife.

Although she very much doubted that the wearing of her wedding band or the demure style of the grey silk gown would make the slightest difference to the gossip that was sure to ensue the moment her presence here was known!

'My wife always maintains that it is best to do exactly that which pleases oneself. On the premise, I believe, that it is impossible to please all people all the time,' the Earl confided.

Juliet turned to give him a startled glance. 'It has been my experience that it is impossible to please any of the ton any of the time!' Juliet murmured, some of the tension easing from her slender shoulders. 'Did your wife also suggest that it might be beneficial if you were to wait out here in the hallway this evening in order that you might gallantly offer to escort me into the drawing room?'

The Earl gave a inclination of his head. 'I do believe she may have mentioned some such thing, yes.'

Juliet gave a husky laugh. 'You are too kind, My Lord.'

'On the contrary, my dear, I consider myself deeply honoured,' he replied. 'Now, let us go into the drawing room and set the tongues a wagging, hmm?' He encouraged her almost as gleefully as his wife might have done.

It seemed to Juliet as if all eyes suddenly turned in the direction of the doorway as she entered the room on the arm of the Earl of Banford, the conversation faltering. Then Dolly swiftly filled that silence by engaging in conversation with the handsome and fashionably attired young man standing beside her.

A young man who stared boldly at Juliet, with unfathomable whisky-coloured eyes....

* * *

Sebastian was barely aware of Dolly's conversation as, along with all others present, he stared across the room as the Countess of Crestwood entered on the arm of their host.

She was incredibly beautiful—even more so than when Sebastian had last seen her, at some ball or other a couple of years ago, and his interest in her had first been piqued.

He became aware of the finer details about her. Such as the rich darkness of her hair and the entwined string of pearls. The smoothness of her brow. The thick lashes that edged eyes of the deepest green. Her small, perfect nose. The pouting bow of her sensuously full lips. The proud and slightly challenging uplift of her little pointed chin.

Her breasts were as full as ever, and they spilled creamily against pale grey lace, but her waist and hips appeared more willowy than when he had last seen her across that crowded ballroom, and the skin at the swell of her breasts, throat and arms was as translucently pale as the pearls in her hair.

'I advise that you close your mouth, Sebastian—before the drool threatens to spoil the perfection of your cravat!' Dolly whispered beside him in soft mockery, bringing a dark scowl to Sebastian's face as he realised Dolly had a point. He had been staring intently at Lady Boyd for several minutes.

Had anyone else but Dolly noticed his marked interest? he wondered, disgusted with himself. A quick glance at his fellow guests assured him that their interest was as engaged on the lady as his own had been.

'It is time for us to go into dinner,' Dolly informed him as she received a nod from her butler, where he stood discreetly in the doorway. 'Bancroft will be escorting his mother, the Dowager Countess, of course. Might I suggest, as the two of you are sitting together, that you offer your own arm to the Countess of Crestwood?'

Having been staring so intently at Juliet Boyd, Sebastian now found himself momentarily disconcerted by Dolly's suggestion. But only momentarily. Was he not the rich and eligible Lord Sebastian St Claire, brother of a Duke? Moreover, at the age of seven and twenty, had he not been considered by all the female members of the ton—debutantes and matrons alike—as the foremost catch of the Season, since both of his brothers had proved themselves unavailable by taking a wife?

More importantly, meeting Juliet was the only reason he had come here—so what was he waiting for…?

Despite the Earl of Banford's presence at her side, Juliet's appearance in the drawing room had been as dramatic as she had feared it might.

Following that initial stunned silence a muted conversation had been resumed by the female guests, at least, as they gossiped in whispers behind their spread fans. The male guests had been less quick to hide their surprise at her appearance here, and for the main part had just continued to openly stare at her.

One man in particular…

An arrogantly handsome man, dressed in the height of fashion in tailored black evening clothes, a grey waistcoat and snowy white linen. The same man with whom Dolly Bancroft had endeavoured to make conversation when Juliet first entered the drawing room.

The very same man who had made absolutely no effort to disguise his inattentiveness to that conversation as he'd continued to stare at Juliet with narrowed, enigmatic eyes. Rather beautiful long-lashed eyes, the colour of the mellow whisky her father had once favoured, Juliet couldn't help noticing admiringly.

She had expected the frosty disdain of the ton this evening. Had been prepared for that reaction. To find herself being regarded so familiarly by a man she did not even know, and who was obviously nothing more than a fashionable rake, did not sit well with her. It did not sit well at all!

Juliet's already ruffled calm deserted her totally as she saw Dolly take a firm hold of the man's arm and push him slightly in her direction. Was her intention to have him cross the room and offer to escort Juliet into dinner? An intention, for all the previous familiarity of the man's gaze, that he surely could not welcome!

Juliet snapped her fan open in front of her before she turned her back on the pair to engage the Earl in conversation. 'It seems that we have succeeded in creating something of a stir amongst your other guests despite your efforts, My Lord,' she bit out tartly. The humiliation of having a man forced to escort her into dinner burned beneath the surface of her emotions.

No matter how kindly meant Dolly Bancroft's invitation had been, Juliet knew she should not have allowed herself to be persuaded into coming here! She should not have exposed herself to—

'Would you care to introduce me, My Lord?'

Juliet felt a quiver down the length of her spine at the first sound of the man's smoothly cultured voice. That quiver turned to a shiver as she turned to find that Dolly's rakishly handsome companion had acceded to her urgings and was now standing in front of Juliet, looking down the length of his arrogant nose at her, the expression in those whisky-coloured eyes hidden behind narrowed lids....

Only Juliet did not need to see the expression in those beautiful eyes to know that this man felt the same contempt towards her as every other person here. Nor did she care to guess what leverage Dolly had exerted to persuade this man into doing her bidding....

Until this moment Juliet had believed Dolly to be totally devoted to the Earl of Banford, but it would have taken more than a simple request from their hostess to persuade this young rake into committing possible social ruination by showing a preference for the noto-rious Countess of Crestwood. It led Juliet to wonder, with inner distaste, if this young man were possibly the Countess of Banford's current lover...

'Lady Boyd, may I present Lord Sebastian St Claire?' the Earl said, doing as requested and dutifully making the introductions. 'Lord St Claire—Lady Juliet Boyd, Countess of Crestwood.'

Sebastian knew by the gleam of interest in the Earl's eyes as he made the introductions that Dolly must have confided to her husband Sebastian's intentions towards the Countess. His mouth tightened in displeasure at the breach of confidence even as he gave her an abrupt bow. 'My Lady.'

'My Lord.' The Countess made a graceful curtsey, but made no effort to extend to him her gloved hand.

Sebastian scowled at the omission. 'Will you grant me the honour of escorting you into dinner, Lady Boyd?'

'"Honour", My Lord?' She raised dark, mocking brows.

He inclined his head. 'I would consider it so, yes.'

Her laughter was light and derisive. 'Then you are singular in your preference, My Lord.'

Damn it—this first conversation with Juliet Boyd was not going at all as Sebastian had hoped it might!

In his imaginings she had been as instantly taken with Sebastian as he already was with her. To such an extent that he had envisaged them talking alone together. Walking alone together. Sitting alone together. Most definitely being alone when they made love together…!

A muscle flickered in Sebastian's tightly clenched jaw as he imagined first removing the pearls from her hair, before releasing the glossy curls so that they tumbled down the length of her slender spine. Next he would remove her gown, turning her so that he might unfasten— slowly—the row of tiny buttons from her nape down to her bottom, lingering, after releasing each button, to kiss the smoothness of the silky skin he had just exposed. When the last button had been unfastened he would then allow the gown to fall about her ankles, leaving her wearing only her chemise and stockings, with the fullness of her breasts pouting temptingly beneath the thin material, her nipples a dark delight that Sebastian would taste and possess until he'd had his fill…

'It would appear we are the last to go into dinner,

Lord St Claire,' Juliet prompted sharply. He seemed lost in thought. Perhaps contemplating that social ruination, if the pained expression on his face was any indication!

He drew his thoughts back to his surroundings with an obvious effort. 'I apologise for my preoccupation, Lady Boyd,' he murmured huskily as he extended his arm to her.

'Do not give it another thought, Lord St Claire,' Juliet assured him as she placed her gloved hand lightly upon his sleeve. She was aware of the muscled strength beneath her fingertips. 'After all, it is not every day that you are asked to act as escort to the notorious Black Widow!' she added waspishly.

'I— *What* did you call yourself?' he exclaimed.

Her smile was completely lacking in humour. 'I assure you I am well aware of the unflattering names I have acquired since…since the death of my husband,' she told him. 'Do not fear—you will have done your duty to our hostess once I am seated. I will not be in the least offended if you then ignore me for the rest of the evening.' Rather, she would prefer it!

Juliet now recognised Lord Sebastian St Claire as being the youngest brother of the aristocratic Duke of Stourbridge. A young lord, moreover, who had long been considered by the ton to be one of their most eligible—and elusive—bachelors. As such, his presence here was attracting as much attention as her own, making their belated entrance to the dining room together all the more sensational.

A puzzled frown marked his brow. 'Why should you imagine I might wish to ignore you?'

Juliet smiled slightly. 'To save yourself from further awkwardness, perhaps…?'

For the first time Sebastian considered that perhaps it had *not* been kind on Dolly's part—or indeed his own!—to invite Juliet Boyd to Banford Park for these two weeks. That after all the talk and speculation this past year and a half, concerning her husband's unexpected death, this woman would obviously be uncomfortable at making her first public appearance in some time.

Just as she was obviously aware of the unkind things that had been said about her following Crestwood's death—cruel and malicious gossip, for the most part, which, even if it were true, could not have been at all pleasant for the lady to hear….

He fleetingly touched the hand that rested on his arm. 'I assure you I feel no awkwardness whatsoever at being seen in your company, Lady Boyd.'

Her glance was scathing now. 'And I am just as sure, as the Duke of Stourbridge's youngest brother, you would consider it impolite to admit to such an emotion even if you did.'

'On the contrary, My Lady,' Sebastian countered. 'If you know anything of the St Claire family at all, then you must know that we prefer—in fact, go out of our way—*not* to bow to the dictates of Society.'

Yes, Juliet had heard that the St Claires were something of a law unto themselves. Even the head of that illustrious family, the aristocratic Duke of Stourbridge.

After years of being considered the biggest catch any marriage-minded mama could make for her daughter, the Duke had caused something of a sensation almost a year ago by choosing to woo and marry a young woman the ton had had no previous knowledge of.

Juliet moved to sit in the chair Lord St Claire drew back for her. 'Be assured, My Lord, in this circumstance you are in the company of one guaranteed to help you succeed in doing exactly that!'

She had been so busy settling herself into her seat that for a moment she had not realised he had taken the chair beside her.

'Oh, dear,' she said now, as she looked up and found herself between the Earl of Banford, seated at the head of the table, and Lord St Claire to her right. 'Have you succeeded in inciting Lady Bancroft's ire in some way, Lord St Claire?' she asked.

He raised brows the same unusual teak and gold colour as his hair, laughter gleaming in those whisky-coloured eyes. 'On the contrary. Lady Bancroft—Dolly—and I have always been the best of friends.'

Juliet continued to look at him for several long seconds. 'Indeed,' she finally murmured enigmatically, before turning away to indicate, she hoped, a complete lack of interest in the subject.

Sebastian would have liked to pursue the conversation further, to know the reason for that enigmatic glance, but he was prevented from doing so as his first course was served to him—by which time Lord Bancroft had drawn the Countess into conversation, giving Sebastian no further opportunity to talk, but every chance to study Juliet Boyd from between narrowed lids.

For all that she must know she was still attracting

more attention from their fellow guests than was polite, the Countess of Crestwood stoically ignored that interest as she continued to converse and smile graciously with their host between sips of her soup.

Did she have any idea, Sebastian wondered, how enticing her mouth was, with its top lip slightly fuller than the bottom? How seductive the deep green of her eyes? How the translucent paleness of her skin begged to be touched?

Sebastian longed to feel the slender coolness of her hands upon his own heated flesh….

To Juliet's dismay, her discomfort had only increased once she was seated at the dinner table, and she felt her every move being avidly watched by her fellow guests. No doubt with the intention of gossip and comments later. Nor was she as unaware of the man seated on her right as she would have wished to be!

Lord Sebastian St Claire was without a doubt one of the most handsome men she had ever seen. A few years younger than her, of course. With that dark, unusual-coloured hair and the mellow flirtation of those whisky-coloured eyes. A sensual mouth that could either smile with derisive humour or curl back in contempt. A square and firm jaw that spoke of a determination of character that was only to be expected from the brother of the arrogant Duke of Stourbridge.

More disturbing, perhaps, his black evening clothes had been tailored perfectly to display the width of his shoulders, his tapered waist, the strength of his muscled thighs and his long, long legs.

Juliet had been out for barely one Season before her husband had offered for her, but even so she could appreciate that Lord St Claire was that most dangerous of men—a rake and a libertine. A man, she felt sure, who felt absolutely no qualms in availing himself of a woman's charms. All women, of any age. Whilst remaining free of any emotional entanglement himself.

After years in a miserable marriage, Juliet could only envy such an emotionally carefree existence as Sebastian St Claire's.

Envy, but never emulate.

She was aware that many widowed ladies her age took advantage of their freedom from the encumbrance of a husband and marriage to indulge in affairs that gave them either satisfaction in the bedchamber or the heart. After being the wife of Lord Edward Boyd, a cold and merciless man, Juliet had no desire for either!

'…care to go boating with me on the lake tomorrow, My Lady?'

Her eyes were wide as she turned to St Claire. 'I beg your pardon?'

He smiled in satisfaction at her obvious surprise. 'I enquired if you would care to go boating on the lake here with me tomorrow?'

Exactly what Juliet thought he had said!

Chapter Two

'**O**r perhaps,' Sebastian amended smoothly as he saw the way the Countess's eyes had widened incredulously at his suggestion, 'you would prefer it if we were simply to stroll in the gardens?'

Those green eyes narrowed now, and the tension in her body was almost palpable. 'I have no idea what incentive Dolly has offered you in exchange for your being pleasant to me, Lord St Claire,' she hissed beneath her breath, so that neither their host—or the other guests should overhear, 'but I assure you most strongly that *I* do not appreciate such attentions!'

Sebastian was so taken aback by the accusation in her tone that for a moment he could make no reply. She actually believed that he and Dolly were lovers!

His own gaze narrowed to steely slits, his jaw rigid in his displeasure. 'And *I* assure *you*, Lady Boyd, that you are mistaken in your assumption concerning my *friendship* with Dolly.'

She adamantly refused to back down from his disapproval. 'Mistaken or not, your—your forced attentions to me are most unwelcome.'

No, this evening was not proceeding at all as Sebastian had hoped it would!

Neither was he accustomed to having his temper roused in this way. The St Claire family always maintained control over their emotions, whether it be boredom, amusement or anger. Not so for Sebastian, it appeared, when it came to Lady Juliet Boyd.

Sebastian suddenly realised what she'd said, and removed the tension from his body and the anger from his gaze. '*Forced* attentions?' he repeated quietly.

'Of course they are forced,' she said scornfully. 'Do you imagine I did not see the look of distaste on your face earlier when I entered the drawing room?'

Distaste? Sebastian remembered being dazzled by her exceptional beauty. But distaste? Never!

He shook his head. 'I believe you are mistaken, My Lady.'

'I do not think so,' she maintained stubbornly.

'You are calling me a liar?' His voice was dangerously soft.

'I am merely stating what I saw,' she retorted.

'What you *think* you saw,' he corrected firmly. 'Am I to infer from these remarks that you would prefer *not* to stroll in the gardens with me tomorrow?' he asked dryly.

The Countess glanced at him quizzically, a frown between those mesmerising green eyes. 'My preference, My Lord, is for you to leave me in peace,' she finally murmured. 'Coming here at all was a serious error of judgement on my part. In fact, I am seriously thinking of making my excuses and leaving in the morning.'

Sebastian had only subjected himself to the tiresomeness of this house party because he was intent on seducing this woman—he certainly had no intention of allowing her to escape so easily!

'Are you not being a little over-hasty, Lady Boyd?' His tone was pleasantly cajoling now. 'I believe Dolly told me that this is your first venture back into Society since your time of mourning came to an end. Is that so?'

After the awkwardness of this evening it was likely to be Juliet's *last* venture into Society, too!

She liked Dolly immensely, and had always found the other woman a complete antidote to the formality of the stuffy rules that so often abounded at any occasion attended by the ton. But if Dolly believed she was doing Juliet a kindness by casting one of her own lovers into Juliet's path, then she was under a serious misapprehension. The attentions of a man such as Sebastian St Claire—a renowned rake and a flirt, and moreover several years her junior—was the last thing Juliet needed to complicate her life. Now or at any other time.

'I do not consider my decision any of your business, My Lord.'

'No?' He quirked mocking brows. 'You do not think it would cause embarrassment for Dolly if you were to leave so soon after your arrival?'

Juliet raised a cool eyebrow of her own. 'On the contrary, My Lord, I believe I will be saving Dolly from further embarrassment by removing myself from her home at the earliest opportunity.'

'So your intention is to run back to the safety of your estate in Shropshire at the first hint of opposition?' Sebastian needled.

Juliet gasped. 'You go too far, sir!'

He appeared completely unruffled by her anger. Instead he leant forward to place his hand on her gloved one as it rested on the tabletop, his lips a mere whisper away from the pearl-adorned lobe of her ear as he whispered, 'My dear Countess, I have not even begun to go too far where you are concerned!'

Juliet felt the colour come into and then as quickly fade from her cheeks as she looked up and saw the flirtatious intent in that whisky-coloured gaze. How *dared* he talk to her in this familiar way?

'You are causing a scene, sir,' she snapped as she deftly extricated her hand from beneath his. 'I believe it might be better, for both our sakes, if you were to refrain from talking to me for the rest of the evening.'

He gave a wicked smile. 'Will that not look a little strange, when we have seemed to be getting along so well together?'

'*Seemed* is the correct word, sir,' Juliet assured him frostily. 'This conversation is now at an end.' She moved slightly in her seat, so that her shoulder was firmly turned against him, and began to converse with her host about the expectations of the weather for the forthcoming week.

She had never before met a man such as Sebastian St Claire. A man so forthright in his manner. A man who refused to listen to or accept the word no.

Juliet had always accompanied Edward to London in spring for the Season, attending such parties and balls with him as he had deemed necessary, and giving a ball herself towards the end of the Season, to which all suitable members of the ton had been invited. Lord Sebastian St Claire had *not* been amongst her guests.

St Claire's eldest brother, the haughty Duke of Stourbridge, had several times been invited to dine privately with them, and Juliet could see a certain resemblance between the two brothers in colouring, and in that inborn air of arrogance. But young rakes such as Sebastian St Claire had not entered into Edward's lofty circle of acquaintances, nor consequently, Juliet's own.

Even as she continued to talk to the Earl of Banford, their conversation soon including his mother, the Dowager Countess, Juliet found her attention wandering as she wondered what Edward would have made of the young Lord St Claire.

He would not have approved of him.

No, he was too young. Too irresponsible. Too rakish. Too everything that Edward had disapproved of.

Suddenly that realisation was enough for Juliet to want to make a friend of St Claire, in spite of her own reservations!

The candle was still alight in Juliet Boyd's bedchamber when Sebastian stepped out onto his balcony to enjoy a last cigar before retiring to his bed, but the lace curtains once again made it impossible for him to see the occupant of the room, and whether or not she was already abed.

It had certainly been an interesting evening, if a frustrating one. That frank, almost intimate conversation with the Countess had been enjoyable, but it had been followed by the irritation of having her completely ignore him for the rest of the meal—as she had stated she intended doing. Even more frustrating, she had disappeared completely by the time the gentlemen had rejoined the ladies in the drawing room, after enjoying several glasses of excellent port.

Would she carry out her threat to leave in the morning?

Sebastian had come to realise this evening that in her acceptance of Dolly's invitation, and by placing herself at the very centre of Society, which had judged and condemned her a year and a half ago, Juliet Boyd was being an exceptionally brave woman—but he had not expected her to be quite such a stubborn one, too!

Yet, if anything, that stubbornness—the way the sting of her anger had brought the colour to her cheeks and given her eyes the appearance of glittering emeralds—had only succeeded in deepening Sebastian's interest in her….

Dolly would have to talk to her, somehow persuade her into staying….

The faint click of a door catch warned Sebastian that he would soon cease to be alone. He dropped his cigar and ground it beneath his shoe, then moved back into the shadows mere seconds before the doors of the Countess's bedchamber opened and she stepped out onto her balcony.

Sebastian's breath caught and held in his throat as she moved forward to stand next to the balustrade and look up at the bright starlit sky.

This venture out onto her balcony before retiring had been one of pure impulse, Sebastian had no doubt. She was prepared for bed: her hair—those glorious dark curls that he had earlier imagined cascading over her creamy shoulders and down her back when it was released—actually reached the whole length of her spine to rest against her shapely bottom. It was stunning—so thick and dark, and bathed with silver by the moon shining overhead. She wore a robe of pale green silk over a matching nightgown, but with the moonlight shining down so brightly even the two items together could not disguise the fullness of her unconfined breasts beneath, nor the gentle curve of her waist and temptingly rounded bottom above long and slender legs.

She was desire incarnate.

A goddess…

'Who is there?'

Sebastian had no idea what he had done to give himself away. Drawn in an unconscious breath at the sight of her beauty? Or perhaps made a movement forward towards the temptation she offered so innocently?

Whatever it had been, it had alerted Juliet Boyd to his presence, and she turned in the moonlight to look at the exact spot where Sebastian stood so silently, watching her from the shadows of the house behind him.

Knowing further concealment was now ridiculous, Sebastian stepped forward to make her an adroit bow. 'My Lady.'

Juliet gave a gasp, and raised a startled hand to her throat as she easily recognised the man standing so large and formidable on the balcony. 'What are you doing here?' She sounded breathless.

And indeed Juliet *was* breathless! She had already

had cause to remark upon this man's audacity once this evening, but even so she had never suspected that he would later attempt to enter her bedchamber uninvited!

She stiffened in outrage. 'How *dare* you presume to invade my balcony in this way, My Lord?'

He gave every appearance of being completely unruffled by her displeasure as he drawled nonchalantly, 'You are mistaken, My Lady.'

Juliet drew herself up indignantly. 'I cannot mistake the evidence of my own eyes, sir!'

He gave a twisted smile. 'That was not the mistake I was referring to.'

She eyed him frowningly. 'What, then?'

He shrugged those broad shoulders, instantly drawing Juliet's attention to the fact that he appeared to have removed his black frock coat and cravat, revealing a silver brocaded waistcoat that was tailored to the flatness of his stomach. His billowing shirt was now unfastened at the throat, revealing a light dusting of dark hair upon his chest.

Juliet quickly averted her gaze from this glimpse of his bared flesh, even as she became aware of her own state of undress. Helena had come to Juliet's bedchamber earlier, to remove the pins from her hair before helping her into her night attire—the pale green silk and lace gown and robe that were all Juliet was wearing now, as she engaged in conversation with the disreputable Sebastian St Claire!

Sebastian could almost see the panic of thoughts rushing through Juliet's head as she gathered her robe about her and prepared herself for flight. 'I merely meant to point out that the door behind me leads into *my* bedchamber, and therefore I am standing upon my own balcony rather than yours.'

She hesitated. 'Your own balcony…?' Her gaze moved to the open doors behind him, before lowering to the space between them, her eyes widening as she obviously saw the low ironwork that separated the two balconies but was concealed amongst the potted plants placed either side of it. Her throat moved convulsively. 'It appears that I owe you an apology, Lord St Claire.'

'Do not be over-hasty with that apology,' Sebastian drawled, before stepping lithely over the ironwork that separated them. 'There. You see. An apology is no longer necessary.' He gave an unrepentant grin as he now stood only inches away from her.

Juliet trembled slightly. Despite being married for so long, she had little experience upon which she might draw in order to deal with this man's outrageous behaviour!

St Claire had stared at her so boldly, so familiarly earlier this evening, when she'd first entered the drawing-room on the Earl's arm. After their introduction he had chosen to bandy words with her, before proceeding to flirt with her during dinner—until Juliet had made a sharp end to it.

Finding herself alone with him now—on the balcony of her bedchamber, the hour late, the moonlight shining overhead, wearing only her night attire—could be considered scandalous!

No, it *was* scandalous, Juliet recognised with a sinking feeling—and it was exactly the sort of behaviour the ton were so avidly seeking in order that they might condemn her all over again.

She put out a shaking hand. 'You must return to your own balcony this instant!' she ordered.

'Must I?'

He was suddenly standing much too close to her. So close that Juliet could smell the freshness of his cologne and the faint aroma of cigars that clung to his clothing. Worse, his eyes, those warm, whisky-coloured eyes, were gleaming down at her in the moonlight as he easily captured and held her gaze.

Nevertheless, she must stand firm against all temptations… 'Yes, you most certainly must!' Juliet averred firmly.

He gave her a considering look. 'Why?'

'Because we cannot be seen here alone together like this!' she gasped.

'That is hardly likely, now, is it, Juliet?' He gave a pointed look at their surroundings, to indicate that no candles glowed in the other bedchambers to show that any of the other guests had yet retired to their rooms for the night.

No doubt they were all still downstairs in the drawing room, Juliet surmised impatiently, discussing the scandal that the presence of the notorious Countess of Crestwood in their midst represented!

'I have not given permission for you to address me by name.' Her chin rose challengingly. 'And I trust you are aware, *Lord St Claire*, of the reason the ton labelled me the Black Widow?'

Sebastian frowned slightly at the mention of that name once again, discovering that he took serious exception to it. 'For the main part, I choose to ignore malicious gossip.'

The Countess arched dark brows. 'And what if on this occasion it is not merely malicious? What if it is true?'

His gaze became fixed on those clear, unblinking green eyes as she continued to meet his gaze in challenge. 'Is it?' he asked quietly.

She gave a humourless laugh. 'I have no intention of answering such a question!'

'I am glad of it,' he replied simply. 'It really does not signify what I or anyone else believes about your husband's death.'

'It—does—not signify?' she repeated incredulously, those green eyes now flashing angrily.

'No,' Sebastian reiterated, and he reached out to lightly clasp the tops of her arms and pull her slowly, purposefully towards him. 'As I have absolutely no interest in becoming your second husband, it is doubtful you will ever have a reason for wanting me dead.'

He was wrong—because Juliet had never felt more capable of inflicting physical retribution upon another person in her life as she did at that moment! 'There you are mistaken, Lord St Claire.' She snapped her indignation as she attempted to pull away from him. 'At this moment I can think of nothing I would enjoy more than to see you consigned to the devil, where you so obviously belong!'

He gave a husky laugh, refusing to release her despite her struggles. 'You believe my past misdeeds are serious enough to send me to the pits of hell?'

'You do not?' Juliet gave him a scornful glance.

'It is a possibility, I suppose,' he conceded, after appearing to consider the matter closely. 'Drunkenness.

Gambling. Debauchery. Hmm, it does seem more than a possibility, does it not…?'

The lowering of his head towards hers slowly blocked out the moonlight overhead, and Juliet became very still as she stared up at him. 'What are you doing?' she breathed unsteadily.

He raised an eyebrow. 'As you seem to believe I am going to the devil anyway, I cannot see that one more indiscretion is going to make the slightest difference to my hellish fate!'

'You—' Juliet had no more chance for protest as Sebastian St Claire's mouth laid claim to hers.

That arrogantly mocking mouth, which never seemed far from a smile. That firm, experienced mouth. It parted Juliet's lips to deepen the kiss even as he pulled her closer against his body, in order to mould her much softer curves to the hard contours of his muscled chest and thighs.

In the whole of her thirty years Juliet had never known any other man's kisses but Edward's. And they certainly hadn't prepared her for the warm seductiveness of Sebastian St Claire's lips as they parted hers, or for the way the tip of his tongue delicately moved in exploration against them before sweeping into the heat beneath as he deepened and lengthened the kiss.

Was this arousal? Juliet wondered, slightly dazedly.

There was an unaccustomed warmth between her thighs as his mouth continued to plunder and claim hers. Her breasts had firmed, and the nipples tingled achingly where they were pressed so firmly against his brocade waistcoat. His hands caressed the length of her back, the movement causing the tips of her breasts to stroke against his body, and Juliet groaned low in her throat at the sensation that this caused throughout her body.

What was happening to her? Juliet wondered wildly.

She had never experienced any of these sensations on those occasions when Edward had pushed her nightgown up to her chin before he thrust the hard thing between his legs painfully inside her, his member so long and thick that the first time he had taken her Juliet had actually fainted as Edward ripped through the barrier of her innocence.

It had been the same every time Edward had come to her bed—he took her in a cold, silent way—and Juliet had always had to fight to keep the tears from falling, knowing that her tears would only anger Edward into making her suffer even worse degradation.

So Juliet had suffered the pain as Edward had thrust himself between her thighs, eventually giving a grunt and collapsing heavily on top of her, rather than suffer the verbal and physical retribution that would rain down on her should she attempt to refuse him.

Thankfully Edward had not come to her bedchamber quite so often during the last few years of her marriage, but on the occasions when he had done so no amount of pleading on her part had succeeded in softening his demands. She was his wife, he had told her coldly, and as such it was her duty to lie back, open her legs, and give satisfaction to his physical needs—whenever and whatever they might be.

The memory of those miserable nights with Edward was enough to kill any possibility of Juliet ever finding pleasure in any man's arms—even Sebastian St Claire's!—and she wrenched her mouth free of his before pushing him away, her hands held out defensively in front of her as she backed away from him.

Edward was dead, Juliet reminded herself desperately. She was free of him at last. Not just free of him, but of *all* men. Juliet had promised herself after Edward's death that she would never again suffer the torment of belonging to any man.

'Do not come near me again!' she warned harshly. She knew by the raising of his hand that St Claire was about to do exactly that.

Sebastian had meant only to cup the side of Juliet's face, to lay the soft pad of his thumb soothingly against lips slightly swollen from his kisses. But his hand fell back to his side, and his gaze became searching as he saw the wildness glittering in the deep green of her eyes. Like those of a rabbit cornered by a bigger and stronger predator....

Who was responsible for causing this look of desperation in such a lovely and delicate woman?

Chapter Three

Sebastian had no idea quite what he would have said or done next, as a loud knock on the outer door to Juliet's bedchamber preventing him from doing anything.

'Perhaps you should go and answer that,' he advised softly, as Juliet continued to stare up at him rather than respond to the persistence of a second knock.

'Not before I am *sure* you understand it is my wish for you to stay well away from me in future!' Her hands were clenched.

'I understand.' He gave her a terse inclination of his head.

Juliet gave him one last narrow-eyed look before turning sharply on her heel to enter her bedchamber, the softness of her slippers making little noise as she hurried across the room to open the door.

Sebastian stepped back into the shadows. No matter what Juliet might choose to think of him, it had never been his intention to involve her in the sort of scandal that his being found with her on the balcony of her bed-chamber was sure to incur.

His brows rose as he saw that her late-night visitor was Dolly Bancroft….

Juliet's legs were still trembling as she quickly opened the door, and her breasts were quickly rising and falling in agitation from her time in Sebastian St Claire's arms—on her balcony, of all places! So disorientated did Juliet feel that she could only stare blankly at Dolly as she stood in the dimly lit hallway, still dressed in her evening finery.

Her hostess looked slightly flustered. 'I am sorry to disturb you, Juliet, but there has been a slight accident.'

Was it Juliet's imagination, or had Dolly Bancroft given a swift glance behind Juliet before speaking? As if she had suspected—no, *expected!*—that Juliet would not be alone in her bedchamber?

Dolly Bancroft was the person responsible, Juliet felt sure, for giving Sebastian St Claire the bedchamber next to hers. With those adjoining balconies!

Still in that spirit of 'kindness', perhaps…?

Her mouth thinned. 'An accident?' she enquired.

'Your maid.' Dolly reluctantly drew her attention from the bedchamber back to Juliet. 'Her name is Helena, I believe?'

Juliet drew in a sharp breath at this mention of her cousin. 'What has happened?' she asked anxiously.

Dolly sighed. 'The silly girl seems to have fallen on the stairs and injured her ankle.'

Was her cousin in pain? How badly was she injured? More importantly, had a doctor been called?

'A footman has carried her up to her room, and one of my other guests—Mr Hallowell—is a physician. He has gone up to examine her even as we speak,' Dolly Bancroft answered Juliet's question before she even had the chance to voice it.

'I must go to her,' Juliet said.

'I am sure there is no need for you to trouble yourself, Juliet.' Dolly frowned at the suggestion. 'Mr Hallowell is perfectly competent, I assure you.'

'Nevertheless, I intend to go and see my—Helena for myself.' Juliet turned to pick up a candle to light her way up the stairs to the servants' quarters. 'Surely it would have been better for you to have sent one of the servants to inform me, rather than abandoning your other guests?'

Dolly pursed her lips and her gaze no longer quite met Juliet's. 'I thought it best, in the circumstances, if I came and informed you myself.'

'Circumstances?' Juliet repeated dryly. 'What might those be, Dolly?'

'I—You—' Dolly Bancroft looked uncharacteristically flustered. 'I simply thought it best,' she repeated briskly.

'Dolly?'

The other woman was suddenly every inch the Countess of Banford as she paused to turn in the hallway and look at Juliet down the length of her pretty nose. 'I really must return downstairs to my other guests now, Juliet.'

'Of course.' Her own manner was just as haughty. 'In that case you and I will speak again in the morning, Lady Bancroft.'

Some of the starch left Dolly's expression. 'Why all

this fuss, Juliet?' She gave a conspiratorial smile. 'Surely you must agree that St Claire is devilishly handsome?' She laughed softly. 'And, not only that, he is the lover that all the women of the ton secretly wish to have as their own!'

Juliet drew herself up to her little over five feet. 'Then they are welcome to him!' she announced.

'Most of them would be only too happy if they could get him. Unfortunately they are not the object of Sebastian's current interest.' Dolly gave her a knowing look.

Juliet's gaze faltered a little and her expression became wary. Was Dolly saying that it was she, in particular, whom St Claire desired? That actually, it was *he* who was the instigator of their adjoining bedchambers?

Of course Dolly was not saying that, Juliet instantly chided herself; she and His Lordship had not even been introduced until this evening, and the allocation of the bedchambers for the Bancroft guests would have been made long before that.

'Lord St Claire's interest in me is not particular,' she informed the older woman frostily. 'He is simply an opportunist. A man who sought to use my—my discomfort earlier this evening to his own advantage.' Juliet's eyes flashed as she recalled the way the young lord had invaded her balcony only minutes ago and dared to kiss her.

And he was probably on the balcony still—no doubt listening to every word of this conversation!

'Lord St Claire is a renowned rake. Nothing but a seducer of women!' Juliet added for good measure.

Sebastian was eavesdropping on the conversation between the two ladies with increasing displeasure. But he'd had no other choice than to remain, trapped as he was outside on the balcony of Juliet's bedchamber. Any attempt to step back over the dividing ironwork would clearly display him to Dolly's gaze. Yet this last accusation of Juliet's was almost enough to make him step forward in protest—and in doing so give away his hiding place to the already suspicious Dolly.

Something Juliet would definitely not thank him for!

But the captivating Countess had to know that Sebastian was still outside on her balcony. Just as she must also be aware that he would overhear her every word. No, her every *insult*…

Sebastian had no idea at that moment whether he wished to soundly spank Lady Juliet Boyd's delectable bottom, or just kiss her until she was weak and wanting in his arms! Or whether doing either of those things would bring that trapped look back into her eyes. The same expression Sebastian had seen and questioned a few minutes earlier….

'Sebastian is usually too busy avoiding those avaricious women to rouse himself into seducing any of them,' Dolly continued.

'Then I wish he would stop avoiding them and let himself be caught!' Juliet snapped. '*I* certainly have no interest in knowing Lord St Claire any better than I already do!'

Dolly gave a rueful shrug. 'I fear, Juliet, that you will have to inform Sebastian of that yourself.'

Sebastian knew that she just had….

* * *

Juliet, reluctant as yet to go downstairs to breakfast and face any of the other guests, requested that the maid Dolly had sent to help her dress return downstairs once this task had been completed, and bring a tray up to her bedchamber.

She had not slept well, and a single glance in the mirror earlier had shown her that this was all too apparent in the dark shadows beneath her eyes and the pallor of her cheeks. Both those things seemed all the more noticeable once her hair was secured on her crown in loose curls.

Juliet had told herself that her restless night was because of her concern for Helena and her badly twisted ankle, but inwardly Juliet knew her insomnia had been for another reason entirely.

Because of another person entirely.

Lord Sebastian St Claire.

Juliet had half expected that he might still be on her balcony when she'd returned from visiting Helena's room the previous evening. Or, worse, actually awaiting her in her bedchamber. But she had found both her bedchamber and the balcony empty, and a surreptitious glance onto the balcony adjoining hers had shown her that it was also empty, the doors firmly closed, and no lighted candle visible in the bedchamber itself. Indicating that Lord St Claire had either gone to bed or he had rejoined the men downstairs playing cards. Juliet strongly suspected the latter.

One thing she knew for certain: she would not be able to leave today as she had planned. Helena's ankle was indeed very badly swollen, and Mr Hallowell had advised that she must stay in bed for the day, and perhaps tomorrow, too, to allow for the swelling to go down. More importantly, he'd stated that Helena should not travel any distance for at least the next few days, to aid her recovery. And Juliet could not—would not— depart Banford Park without her.

Another reason for her disturbed and sleepless night.

For if she could not leave Banford Park, then she could not escape seeing St Claire again, either….

'Is there enough tea in that pot for two?' A familiar voice interrupted her unwelcome thoughts.

It seemed that Juliet could not escape the persistence of Sebastian St Claire even in her own bedchamber!

Her eyes were wide with disbelief as she stood up to turn and find him standing in the doorway that opened onto her balcony. 'My bedchamber is *not* a public thoroughfare, sir!'

'I should hope not.' He grinned unrepentantly as he stepped fully into the room.

Juliet supposed she should be grateful that he was at least more suitably dressed this morning, in a fitted super-fine coat of dark green, with a paler green waistcoat neatly buttoned beneath, a white cravat meticulously tied at his throat, and black Hessians worn over buff-coloured pantaloons. But that was all she could be grateful for.

'I meant, My Lord, that I do not recall giving you leave to just enter my bedchamber whenever you please!' Her eyes flashed her indignation at the liberty he had just taken.

'Not yet,' he acknowledged ruefully. 'I live in the hope that you will soon do so.'

Juliet watched somewhat incredulously as he bent to pick up her own teacup and sip the cooling liquid from the very same spot she had, only seconds ago, those beautiful whisky-coloured eyes deliberately meeting hers over the china cup's delicate rim.

He was still trying to seduce her, Juliet recognised with an uncomfortable fluttering sensation in her chest.

Sebastian St Claire really was too handsome for his own good. Or for any woman's good, either—including her own.

This would not do. It really would not do!

Sebastian recognised the signs of Juliet's impending temper. The glitter of her eyes. The bright spots of colour that appeared in her cheeks. The tilting of her stubborn chin. The tightening of her determined jaw.

He placed the cup unhurriedly back in its saucer. 'The other female guests are intending to stroll down to the village to look at the Norman church.' His derisive expression showed exactly what he thought of that plan. 'I thought perhaps you might prefer to go on a carriage ride with me?'

If anything, her jaw clenched even harder, until he could almost hear her teeth grinding together. 'Then you were mistaken!'

'You are looking pale this morning, my dear Juliet,' Sebastian observed soothingly. 'Hopefully a little fresh air will bring some of the colour back into your cheeks.'

She drew herself up to her full diminutive height. '*Lord St Claire—*'

'Yes…?' His expression was innocently enquiring.

This man was incorrigible, Juliet decided in total frustration. Absolutely impossible! 'I have *no* wish to go on a carriage ride—or indeed anything else—with you!'

He raised dark brows. 'You would rather that we spend the morning together here instead?'

Juliet blinked. By 'here' did he mean in her *bedchamber*? Or was he merely referring to Banford Park?

Whatever his meaning, Juliet was not agreeable to either suggestion. 'I have no desire to spend the morning in your company *at all*, My Lord.'

'Then it is your intention to depart today, as planned?'

'You must know that it is not.' She snapped her impatience, sure that he could not have helped overhearing her conversation with Dolly Bancroft the evening before. She'd certainly intended that he hear the remarks she'd meant for *him*!

'Must I?'

'My Lord—'

'Could you not call me Sebastian when we are alone? I assure you I already think of you as simply Juliet,' he murmured huskily.

'I repeat, I have *not* given you permission— What are you doing?' Juliet gasped as he took a step that brought him within touching distance, her eyes widening in alarm as she stared up at him.

Sebastian scowled as he once again saw that look of wariness in her face. The same emotion he had recognised in her yesterday evening. An emotion that had kept him awake for some time after he had retired to bed.

He knew that Juliet's husband had been a much admired and respected member of the House, and an invaluable advisor to the War Cabinet during England's years of war against Napoleon. He also knew the Earl of Crestwood had been a casual acquaintance of his eldest brother, Hawk. There had never, to Sebastian's knowledge, been even a whisper of scandal attached to the Earl's name.

Until after his death.

Even then it had been his wife's name that had been whispered by the closed ranks of the ton.

But if not Edward Boyd, then who could have put that look of fear into Juliet's eyes? Whoever or whatever it had been, Sebastian had no intention of adding to it— but he couldn't give up his pursuit of her now. 'Juliet, would you please do me the honour of accompanying me on a carriage ride this morning?' He gave her an encouraging smile.

Juliet was momentarily disconcerted by the sweetness of his smile. 'It is no more acceptable for the two of us to be alone in a carriage than it is for us to be alone here,' she declared.

'It is acceptable to me, Juliet,' he assured her. 'And to you, too, I hope?'

This man disturbed her. Disturbed, as well as confused her.

Two very good reasons why she should not allow herself to be persuaded by the beguiling boyishness of his smile! 'I think not, Lord St Claire.' She used his title deliberately.

Those whisky-coloured eyes looked directly into hers. 'You have such an intense interest in Norman churches?'

'I am not interested in them in the least,' she

admitted. 'And you do not appear to have any interest in your own good name,' she added waspishly. 'To pay marked attention to me once is to risk your reputation,' she explained at his raised dark brows. 'To do so twice may mean you lose it completely!'

His mouth quirked. 'I believe I am the only one who needs be concerned with that unlikely occurrence.'

'My Lord, you have far more to lose by this association than I—'

'Juliet, will you please stop arguing and just say yes to my suggestion of a carriage ride?' he interrupted.

Juliet was torn. On the one hand it would be nice to get away from the curious and censorious gaze of the other guests at Banford Park. But accepting St Claire's invitation would surely only expose them both to further speculation and gossip.

It would also put her in the position of being completely alone with him in his carriage....

'You have hesitated long enough, Juliet.' Sebastian decided to take matters into his own hands. 'I will collect my hat and gloves and meet you downstairs no longer than ten minutes hence.' He strode purposefully towards the door.

'Sebastian!'

A satisfied smile curved his lips at her use of his given name and he turned slowly to look at her.

She closed her eyes briefly. 'Could you...? Would it be to much to ask that you return to your own room in the same way that you arrived?' She frowned. 'It would not do for someone to see you leaving my bedchamber at this hour,' she explained ruefully.

Sebastian chuckled softly as he inclined his dark head in acknowledgement of her point. 'Ten minutes, Juliet. Or I will be forced to come looking for you.'

It was impossible for her to miss the threat behind his words. Just as it had been ultimately impossible for her to resist the beguiling nature of his smile. A smile that could charm the birds out of the trees if he so wished. A smile that had certainly charmed Juliet into behaving less than sensibly…

'…the Black Widow—'

'I wish you would not call her by that disgusting name!' Sebastian exclaimed as he and Gray stood talking together in the cavernous entrance hall of Banford Park whilst Sebastian waited for Juliet to join him. 'Address her as either Lady Boyd or the Countess of Crestwood.'

Gray grimaced. 'I noticed your marked interest yesterday evening, and was merely enquiring as to whether her presence here could possibly be the reason for our attendance at this house party?'

'Perhaps,' Sebastian said coolly. 'You have some objection to make?' he added challengingly.

'I would not dare to, old chap,' Gray retorted. 'You may like to give the impression that you live a life of idle pleasure, but I am well aware of how often you spar in the ring, and the many hours a week you spend honing your skill with the sword! If it's any consolation, Seb, I am in complete sympathy with your interest in the widow. I had forgotten how beautiful she was until I saw her again yesterday evening.'

Sebastian appreciated this observation even less than he had his friend's earlier remarks. 'I hope it is not your intention to practise your own charm upon her, Gray?'

Gray opened wide, innocent eyes. 'I make a point of never incurring the displeasure of a man who can fight and handle a sword better than I!'

The tension in Sebastian's shoulders relaxed slightly as he finally saw the teasing humour in the other man's gaze. 'Tell me, Gray, what do you know of Edward Boyd?'

'The husband?' His friend gave a shrug. 'Would your brother Hawk not be the best man to ask such a question?'

'Unfortunately, Hawk is not here.' Sebastian's eldest brother might give the impression that he was too aristocratically top-lofty to even notice lesser beings than himself—which included just about everyone!—but that indifference was a façade; Hawk's intelligence was formidable, and if he chose he could be the most astute of men. Certainly Hawk's opinion of Edward Boyd would be worth hearing.

'Most people seem to have held Crestwood in high esteem,' Gray observed with a slight frown. 'He was a hero at Trafalgar, don't you know?'

Of course Sebastian knew of the Earl of Crestwood's war record. He might have been still at school when the famous sea battle had occurred, but as a fifteen-year-old youth he had of course been very interested in it, and had read about the heroes of that battle.

His interest in the Earl's wife had come much later, when he had happened to see Juliet during a ball at which he'd been forced by Hawk into acting as escort to their young sister Arabella during her first Season.

Tiny, almost ethereal, the Countess had nevertheless possessed a presence, an otherworldly beauty, that had instantly captured Sebastian's interest.

He realised now that perhaps he should have paid more attention to Crestwood that night as he'd stood so arrogantly at Juliet's side. That he should have observed more closely the relationship that existed between the married couple….

'Our host is probably the chap you need to speak to if you want to know more about Crestwood,' Gray suggested.

'Bancroft?'

Gray nodded. 'Both members of the House of Lords. Both were advisers to the War Cabinet during the war against Napoleon. Bancroft is sure to know something of the other man.'

'Never mind that for now, Gray…' Sebastian's interest was swiftly distracted as he spotted Juliet, moving gracefully down the wide staircase to where he stood waiting.

A silk beribboned bonnet of the same peach colour as her high-waisted gown covered the darkness of Juliet's curls, and she carried a lacy parasol to keep the worst of the sun's rays from burning the pale delicacy of her complexion.

Everything about Juliet Boyd was delicate, Sebastian acknowledged with a sudden frown. From the top of her dark curls down to her tiny slippered feet.

Juliet's gaze became wary as she looked up and saw the fierce expression on Sebastian's face as she joined him. 'Am I interrupting…?' She voiced her uncertainty.

'Not in the least, Lady Boyd,' Sebastian's companion assured her warmly. It was a fashionably dressed dark-haired, grey-eyed gentleman that Juliet vaguely recalled as being seated some way down the dinner table from her yesterday evening. 'Lord Gideon Grayson,' he introduced himself smoothly as he gave a courtly bow.

Juliet curtseyed, at the same time raising her hand. 'I am pleased to meet you, Lord—'

'If it's all the same to you, Gray, the Countess and I are in something of a hurry,' Sebastian cut in, before the other man could take her hand. Instead he placed that gloved hand on his own arm and held it there by placing his hand firmly on top of it. 'Enjoy your morning, Gray,' he added mockingly.

With her fingers firmly tucked in the crook of his arm, Juliet had little choice but to follow as Sebastian strode arrogantly across the hallway and out through the front door to where one of the grooms stood waiting beside a gleaming black curricle drawn by two matching greys.

Juliet did not need to be told that the vehicle belonged to Sebastian St Claire; the rakish style of the carriage matched its owner perfectly!

'Were you not a little rude to Lord Grayson just now?' Juliet ventured, once Sebastian had aided her ascent into the carriage before dismissing the groom to step in beside her and take up the reins.

'Was I?' he said evasively, his expression unreadable beneath the brim of his hat as he flicked the greys into an elegant trot.

Juliet fell silent as she pretended an interest in the countryside that surrounded Banford Park. Pretended, because after that scene in the hall her thoughts were all inward!

She knew she should be used to the cuts and snubs of the ton after being the subject of them so recently. And she was. It was just that after his earlier contempt for such behaviour she had expected more of Sebastian St Claire. The fact that he had not even wanted to introduce her to a man who was obviously his friend showed Juliet how naïve had been that expectation.

No doubt it was all well and good for St Claire to accost her on the privacy of her balcony or in her bed-chamber. To whisk her away from curious eyes in his curricle. But to have him actually introduce her to one of his friends was obviously too much to ask.

For all Juliet knew she could be the subject of some sort of wager between St Claire and his friends. It was common practice, she believed, for gentlemen to make such wagers at their London clubs. In this case perhaps the first man to bed the Black Widow was to become the winner of this wager.

'Juliet…?'

Her eyes flashed with anger. 'I have changed my mind, My Lord,' she snapped, her back rigid. 'I wish for you to take me back to Banford Park immediately!'

Sebastian glanced down at her searchingly. Whatever thoughts had been going through her head the last few minutes they had not been pleasant ones—as the anger in those deep green eyes testified.

He shook his head. 'Not until you tell me what I have done to upset you.'

'I am not upset,' she denied.

'No?' Sebastian rasped, patently not amused.

She drew in a ragged breath. 'Would you please turn your curricle around and return me to Banford Park?'

'No.'

'No...?' she echoed uncertainly.

They were some distance from Banford Park now, but instead of continuing on the road as he had intended, Sebastian turned the greys down a rutted track, entering a grove of trees before pulling his horses to a halt.

Before Juliet could so much as voice a word of protest he had jumped lithely down from the curricle to come round and offer her his hand, so that she might join him on the ground.

She made no effort to do so, but instead raised her chin in challenge. 'I should warn you, Lord St Claire, that I have no intention of allowing you to seduce me!'

Sebastian found himself grinning at the fierceness of her expression. 'I assure you, my dear, that my preference is for the comfort of a bed, or perhaps even a well-upholstered sofa, when my thoughts turn to seduction!'

She blinked her surprise. 'Then why have you brought me here?'

'To take a stroll in the sunshine, perhaps? To breathe in the fresh, clean air? To appreciate the beauty that surrounds us?'

It *was* a pretty spot, Juliet acknowledged frowningly, with the dappled sun shining through the trees overhead upon wild flowers in bloom in pinks and yellows and purples.

Except Sebastian had been looking at Juliet and not the flowers or the trees when he'd made that last remark....

Warmth coloured her cheeks as he continued to look at her with unconcealed admiration. 'I can as easily appreciate all of those things from my balcony at Banford Park.'

The humour left his gaze. 'I believe we can talk more privately here, Juliet.'

Juliet didn't care for the sudden and probing intensity of that whisky-coloured gaze. 'Concerning what subject, sir?'

'If you join me I will tell you.' He held out his hand for a second time.

Juliet continued to eye him warily, at the same time impatiently dismissing her feelings of alarm. She was a woman of thirty years. Had been married and widowed. She ran the house, and the smaller estate she had moved to after Edward's death, with a competency that surprised even her. So why should a man younger than herself, whose reputation was that of a rake and an incorrigible flirt, give her reason to feel in the least uncertain of herself?

He should not!

'You really are behaving most childishly, My Lord,' she told him frostily, but she moved to place her gloved hand on his so that she might descend from the curricle.

Sebastian's face hardened as he ignored that hand and instead reached up to place both his hands about her waist, before lifting her aloft and swinging her out of the carriage.

For several seconds, as he lifted her, Juliet found their gazes on a level, and her body was perilously close to Sebastian's as she stared into the golden depths of his eyes and saw—

'I insist that you put me down *at once*, Lord St Claire,' she instructed him breathlessly.

'And if I choose not to do so?' His expression became one of amusement as he looked pointedly at the precariousness of her position as he held her aloft, several feet from the ground.

Her eyes flashed deeply green. 'You have been warned, My Lord!'

His amusement deepened. 'One kiss, Juliet,' he murmured throatily. 'One kiss and perhaps I will consider your request— Ow!' He yelped as Juliet's booted foot made painful contact with his knee, and he quickly lowered her to the ground before bending to grasp his injured joint. 'That was not kind, Juliet.' He scowled up at her.

She looked unrepentant. 'My only regret is that it was not many inches higher!'

Surprisingly, Sebastian found his amusement returning. 'I am thankful that it was not! You— Where are you going?' he demanded as she turned to begin walking away from him down the rutted track. 'Juliet…?' He began to hobble after her.

She spun sharply round. 'It is my intention to walk back to Banford Park if *you* will not return me there.'

'That really is not necessary—'

'I consider it very necessary, Lord St Claire,' she scorned. 'Against my better judgement I allowed myself to be persuaded into taking a carriage ride with you. My reserve has been completely borne out by your ungentlemanly behaviour towards me just now.' She put up her parasol against the sun's rays and turned and resumed her walk in the direction of Banford Park.

'Juliet?' Sebastian could only stand and watch in

frustration as she ignored him to continue her walk. Her face might be hidden by her raised parasol, but the ramrod-straightness of her back was more than enough to tell him of her anger.

Chapter Four

Juliet's temper had not abated in the slightest by the time she returned to Banford Park, some twenty minutes or so later. So it was perhaps fortunate that it was the Earl of Banford and not his Countess who chanced to greet her as she stepped inside the house; Juliet had not had the chance as yet to finish last night's conversation with Dolly Bancroft!

The Earl eyed her quizzically. 'You look slightly... flushed, Lady Boyd. Perhaps you would care to join me in my study for some morning refreshment?'

'I fear I am not good company at the moment, My Lord.' Juliet was feeling hot and bothered from her walk, and still flustered and out of sorts from this latest debacle with Sebastian St Claire.

He gave her an understanding smile. 'Has my wife been causing mischief again?'

'Oh, no— Well... Yes, actually,' Juliet acknowledged flatly when she saw the Earl's patent disbelief at her initial denial. 'But it is not all Dolly's fault,' she allowed fairly. 'I am sure Lord St Claire can be very persuasive when he chooses.' She was not altogether sure how much she could say to the Earl concerning her suspicions about his wife's friendship with St Claire.

'And have *you* found him to be so?' her host asked gently.

'Not in the least!' Juliet assured him vehemently.

Too vehemently? Perhaps. But after this morning Juliet intended being more on her guard than ever where Sebastian St Claire was concerned.

'Perhaps Lord St Claire has deceived Lady Bancroft into believing him to be more agreeable than he is?' she suggested tactfully.

'Do not look so concerned, my dear Lady Boyd.' William Bancroft said softly. 'I assure you that any friendship between my wife and St Claire has always been of a purely platonic nature.' He looked serious. 'I think that perhaps you should be made aware that, although he has certainly earned his reputation with the ladies, St Claire does not choose to "persuade" as often as the gossips care to imply that he does....'

Juliet felt the colour warm her cheeks. 'I must warn you, My Lord, that I really cannot even *think* of joining you for refreshment if you intend to continue discussing Lord St Claire with me.'

'As you wish, my dear.' The Earl stepped forward to place a hand lightly beneath her elbow. 'Tea for two, Groves,' he instructed the butler lightly, before guiding Juliet down the hallway to his study.

* * *

Much to Sebastian's chagrin, for once in his life he was completely at a loss to know what to do next where a woman was concerned.

He had allowed his desire for Juliet, when holding her aloft in his arms this morning, to overrule his awareness of that guardedness he sensed inside her, and had subsequently paid the price for that miscalculation when she'd walked off and left him. There had been no opportunity to see or speak to her since then.

Consequently, he sat broodingly at the dinner table that evening, watching Juliet down its length as she conversed easily and charmingly with Gray, sitting on one side of her, and the elderly and courtly Duke of Sussex on the other.

Sebastian's censorious glance towards his hostess for this arrangement was met by a pointed glance in her husband's direction, telling him that the Earl was the one responsible for the distance between Juliet and himself at the dinner table.

That Juliet had somehow succeeded in charming the Earl of Banford came as no surprise to Sebastian. Nor the fact that Gray and the Duke of Sussex seemed equally as enchanted by her company. What man could look at her—dressed this evening in a deep green silk gown, her hair an abundance of ebony curls, several of those curls temptingly loose against the long length of her creamy throat—and not be charmed?

Certainly not Sebastian. He found his hooded gaze shifting often in her direction as she chatted softly with her dining companions—whilst his own meal seemed to progress with excruciating slowness, and culminated in his imbibing far too much wine and not eating enough food.

If this continued he would be foxed before the meal even came to its painful end!

Even as Juliet responded to the polite dinner conversation of Lord Gideon Grayson, she was aware of St Claire's dark and brooding gaze fixed upon her whenever she chanced to glance up.

'Do not be too hard on him, Lady Boyd,' Lord Grayson drawled, after one such irritated glance. 'I assure you Sebastian is not usually so marked in his attentions,' he added dryly as Juliet looked at him enquiringly.

She frowned her annoyance. 'You are the second gentleman today to leap to his defence, sir!'

Gideon gave a rueful shrug. 'Sebastian is a capital fellow.'

'So I am informed,' she said, obviously unimpressed.

'But you still doubt it?'

Of course Juliet doubted it; so far in their acquaintance St Claire had tried—and failed—to seduce her at every opportunity that presented itself!

Lord Grayson raised his brows at her censorious expression. 'Has it not occurred to you that perhaps you should be thanking Sebastian rather than cutting him so cruelly?'

Her eyes widened. 'Thanking him for what, pray?'

'Has your time here not been a little easier today? Your fellow guests a little less…cool in their manner towards you?' he asked.

Juliet thought of the picnic lunch she had enjoyed

earlier today—a picnic lunch that her tormentor had been noticeably absent from! Surprisingly, several of the ladies had included her in their conversation as their party sat in the shade of one of the oaks beside the river that ran through the extensive grounds of Banford Park.

'I am sure you must be aware that Sebastian is considered something of a setter of fashion,' Lord Grayson continued lightly. 'If he has decided it is time to welcome you back into Society, then you may be assured the rest of the ton will quickly follow his example.'

'And I suppose you are telling me that Lord St Claire was demonstrating that "welcome" earlier today, when he did not even have the good manners to introduce us properly?' Juliet pointed out.

Lord Grayson looked at her for several seconds before answering. 'No, I cannot claim Sebastian had your own comfort in mind at that time…'

'Then—'

Lord Grayson looked rueful. 'I believe I have already said too much.' He lifted his wineglass and silently toasted her, before sipping some of the ruby-red liquid and turning to engage the young lady seated on his other side in conversation.

The Duke of Sussex took advantage of the younger man's distraction to begin conversing with Juliet on the deplorable state of the country since the war against Napoleon had come to an end. Something the Duke seemed to assume Juliet had some interest in—possibly because of her husband's involvement with the War Cabinet in the years before his death. Whatever the elderly man's reasoning, his comments did not require any input from Juliet except for an occasional polite nod or smile. Giving Juliet ample time in which to ponder Lord Grayson's last remarks to her.

The fact that he was a close friend of the irritating St Claire indicated to Juliet that his judgement lacked impartiality; as far as Juliet was concerned the arrogant and ridiculously self-assured Lord St Claire was the very *last* man in need of her gratitude or understanding—or indeed anyone else's!

Certainly Juliet felt no such softening of her regard as she watched him approach her after dinner, when the gentlemen rejoined the ladies in the drawing room. Juliet was not sure, but it seemed to her, by the reckless glitter in that whisky-coloured gaze and the slight flush to his cheeks, that His Lordship had imbibed far too much wine and port this evening to allow for even his usual questionable caution.

Indeed, that concern was borne out by the way he took a firm hold of her arm the moment he reached her side and urged, 'Walk out onto the terrace with me, Juliet.'

'I believe you would find it more beneficial to your current mood if you were to retire to your bedchamber, My Lord,' she insisted in low icy tones, but her outward demeanour was one of smiling graciousness as she sensed they were once again the subject of curious eyes.

He arched dark brows. 'Was that a proposition, Lady Boyd…?'

Juliet drew her breath in sharply. 'You must know it was not!' She gave him a warning glance from beneath lowered dark lashes.

'One can but live in hope,' he drawled, with a noticeable lack of concern.

The serene smile Juliet bestowed upon him was not matched by the angry glitter in her eyes. 'Release me at once, sir, and cease this licentious behaviour!' she hissed.

Sebastian frowned down at her. Juliet truly believed him to be foxed?

Admittedly Sebastian had been imbibing rather too freely during dinner, but he had put an end to that the moment he'd realised he felt a strong desire to stand up and walk the length of the room before grasping Gray by the throat and squeezing the life out of him—just because he, and not Sebastian, was the one sitting beside Juliet, and the recipient of one of her rare and beautiful smiles.

Strangling the life out of one of his best friends had not seemed to him to be a rational idea!

Sebastian felt no qualms, however, at the thought of using the fact that Juliet believed him to be foxed if it gave him the slightest advantage...

'Only if you will agree to help me to my bedchamber...?'

She looked disconcerted by the suggestion. 'You know that is not possible.'

He shrugged. 'Then I will remain here and endeavour to dazzle you with my wit and charm.'

'I assure you at this moment you do not possess either wit *or* charm!'

Sebastian grinned unabashedly at her vehemence. 'Implying that I might when I am *not* foxed...?'

'Implying that—' Juliet broke off to eye him in utter frustration. 'I really think it advisable if you retire to your room now, My Lord—before you do or say something you might later regret.'

'And what might that be?' He raised dark brows. 'Kissing your hand, perhaps?' He raised her gloved fingers towards his lips, but instead of the courtly kiss she was expecting, at the last moment Sebastian turned her hand and kissed the delicacy of her wrist, his fingers tightening about hers as she gasped and tried to pull sharply away. 'No, I feel no regret,' he murmured, after considering for a moment. 'Perhaps if I were to take you fully into my arms and—'

'I have reconsidered, Lord St Claire,' she cut him off in alarm. 'If you wish it I will see that you are safely delivered to the privacy of your bedchamber!'

He gave a seductive smile. 'Oh, I most certainly wish it, my dear Juliet.'

'Just remain here—endeavour to try not to get into any more mischief while I am gone!—and I will make your excuses to Lord and Lady Bancroft.'

'And your own, dear Juliet,' Sebastian advised softly.

Her mouth tightened. 'I will be but a few minutes.'

Could it really be so easy? Sebastian wondered, watching as Juliet gracefully crossed the room to talk quietly with their host and hostess. Of course she did believe him to be more than slightly the worse for drink, and so perhaps incapable of attempting her seduction once they were alone… A completely erroneous assumption— as the rapid hardening of Sebastian's thighs just at the thought of making love to Juliet testified only too well!

Not that he would seduce her before he had apologised for his behaviour this morning, of course. One should not even attempt to make love to a woman who was as displeased as Juliet still appeared to be.

Sebastian's gaze narrowed with displeasure as he watched his host stroll the length of the room to his side, whilst Juliet remained in conversation with Dolly Bancroft.

The Earl raised mocking brows. 'Lady Boyd seems to feel you may be indisposed, St Claire?'

'Lady Boyd is—' He broke off, his mouth tightening in frustration at the neat way Juliet had outmanoeuvred him.

'A very beautiful but equally mysterious young lady,' Lord Bancroft finished for him, not even attempting to hide his amusement at the other man's predicament.

Sebastian's gaze focused on his host. 'Mysterious…?'

The older man gave him an enigmatic smile. 'There are certain inconsistencies to the Countess that I find…questionable, shall we say?'

Sebastian's unhappiness with this conversation increased. 'Is it not impolite of you to discuss one of your guests in this way?'

'Do not attempt to tell me how to behave in my own home, St Claire!' The usual good humour had left Lord Bancroft's eyes, and his gaze had become steely. 'Considering your own continued interest in the Countess, you and I perhaps need to talk further,' he stated. 'Would ten o'clock in my study tomorrow morning suit you?'

Sebastian looked irritated. 'What is this all about, Bancroft?'

'Not here, St Claire.' The cordial smile returned to his host's lips, and the tension left his shoulders as he once again looked his usual amiable self. 'Dolly is about to propose a game of charades. I suggest you join us,' Lord Bancroft said lightly, before leaving to return to his wife's side.

Sebastian, as any man who valued his reputation as a gentleman of fashion, would as soon take a walk to the gallows as engage in a game of charades. Besides, he was too disturbed by Bancroft's strange behaviour just now to concentrate on such inanity.

Juliet, Sebastian noted, also remained as a spectator to the game rather than a participant. She had moved to stand near one of the sets of French doors that had been opened out onto the terrace to allow the warm evening air into the drawing room, completely ignoring Sebastian's existence as she gave every appearance of enjoying the fun as their fellow guests made complete cakes of themselves.

So intent was Juliet's attention on the party game that she did not even notice when Sebastian slipped out of the matching set of doors further down the drawing room and made his way silently across the terrace to where Juliet stood, chuckling at Gray's antics as she leant against one of the velvet drapes.

Totally oblivious of Sebastian standing directly behind her....

This second evening at Banford Park had definitely been easier to bear than the first, Juliet decided. She was enjoying watching the game of charades—not taking part, but certainly not feeling excluded, either.

Because, as Lord Grayson claimed, St Claire had set

the example he wished his peers to follow by making her socially acceptable once more?

Grateful as she was for a slight melting of the frost that had previously been shown to her, it was not quite within Juliet to allow that the outrageous Lord St Claire and his marked attentions towards her were indeed responsible for that change. Even if they were, he need not have been so persistent in his interest—especially as she had given him every indication that she wished him to cease all such attentions. Besides, there had been no one else but themselves present when he'd intruded onto her balcony yesterday evening. Or when he'd invaded the privacy of her bedchamber this morning.

Juliet became very still as she felt something touch the exposed nape of her neck. A fly, perhaps? Or possibly a bee…

'Do not turn around, Juliet,' Sebastian St Claire urged huskily, just as she would have done so.

Juliet stiffened. St Claire was standing directly behind her, in the shadow of the curtained doorway. Juliet's wide-eyed glance about the room showed that none of the other guests seemed in the least aware of his presence.

He was standing so close to her that Juliet could feel the heat of his body through the thin material of her gown. As she had yesterday evening, Juliet also smelled the sharp tang of male cologne and the cigar he must have smoked earlier with his port.

The fact that he was standing so close to her implied that the feather-light touch she had felt against her nape had very likely been St Claire's fingertips against her bare flesh…!

She flicked her fan open, bringing it up in front of her mouth so that their conversation would not be visible to the other guests. 'What do you think you are *doing*?' she whispered fiercely.

'Something I have been longing to do since Dolly interrupted us yesterday evening,' came St Claire's unapologetic reply. 'Did you know that your skin is as soft as velvet?' Once again those fingertips caressed the length of her nape.

Juliet was instantly aware of that quivering sensation once more as those fingers ran the length of her spine. Just as she had the previous evening, Juliet wondered whether it could be pleasure she was feeling. Certainly no one else had ever made her feel such a warmth and tingling in her body before. It was not an unpleasant feeling, and nor was she repulsed as she had always been whenever Edward had touched her.

On the contrary, that warm and tingling sensation was now spreading across her shoulders and down into her breasts…

'Has anyone ever likened your hair to the colour and texture of sable?' he murmured, and she couldn't suppress a tiny shiver as the warmth of his breath moved the curls at her nape.

It was strangely disturbing to have him standing behind her like this and for no one else in the drawing room to be aware of it. Again, this was not an unpleasant feeling— more of a deliciously wicked one that Juliet could enjoy without feeling any regret or embarrassment.

'Does your skin taste as good as it feels, I wonder…?' he whispered.

Juliet gasped, and her back arched involuntarily as she felt the softness of his chiselled lips against her nape, those quivers down her body increasing in urgency as she felt the gentle rasp of his tongue against the bareness of her flesh.

'Mmm, it tastes even better than it feels,' he murmured appreciatively as he alternately kissed and licked a heated path down the length of her spine. That path came to a halt as he reached the top of her gown. 'May I...?' he asked huskily.

Juliet was too hot, too confused by the strange clamouring of emotions she was feeling, to immediately comprehend his meaning. By the time she *did* understand what he was asking Sebastian had already unfastened most of the buttons down the back of her gown!

'I ask that you do not turn around, Juliet,' Sebastian reiterated as she once again made an attempt to do so, placing his hands firmly upon her shoulders to accompany this reminder as he held her in place. 'I wish for you to remain exactly as you are so that I might...explore.'

Juliet's gaze moved wildly about the drawing room, but no one was paying her—or consequently him, where he stood hidden by the drapes—any attention. They remained engrossed in their party game.

Having Sebastian touch her in this way was so sinfully wicked that Juliet could not possibly allow him to continue. Could she...? Yet with her gown unbuttoned down her back did she really have any choice but to remain standing exactly as she was?

Did she even *want* a choice?

Juliet could not deny that she felt a curiosity. A

wanting. An aching to know if the sensations she was feeling really were pleasure.

Juliet gasped again as she felt the heat of Sebastian's hands about her waist. Only the thin material of her silk chemise separated those hands from her bare flesh. That gasp became a tiny moan as his hands shifted beneath the loose material of her high-waisted gown to move caressingly upwards to just below the pertness of her breasts.

'Shh, sweet…' Sebastian murmured soothingly.

How could Juliet possibly remain silent when those hands touched her so intimately? When she could feel her nipples become engorged in anticipation of caresses yet to come?

She felt a warm flooding between her thighs as Sebastian continued to touch her just beneath her breasts. A hot dampness in her most secret place. A clenching spasm deep inside her as Sebastian's hands trailed a slow path from her breasts down to her waist and then back again.

'You must stop, Sebastian!' she protested agonisingly from behind her fan. Her knees seemed in danger of buckling beneath her.

His only reply was to tighten his hands about her waist as he held her more firmly in place and his lips explored the bareness of her shoulder, licking, gently sucking.

Juliet was in no doubt now—this *was* pleasure!

Unimaginable, indescribable pleasure.

It was a sensation unlike any Juliet had ever known before.

A sensation she wanted to continue….

* * *

Sebastian knew that he should stop. That he *must* stop soon or risk exposing them both to a scandal that the ton would never forgive or forget.

But finally being able to kiss Juliet, to touch her, to feel her pleasure in his caresses, to hear her little panting breaths and feel the response of her body, was feeding his own desire, so making it impossible for Sebastian to do anything other than continue the wild, illicit caresses.

Her skin smelt of spring flowers and tasted like silken honey as he continued to explore its smoothness with his lips, feeling the arch of Juliet's back as he ran his tongue down the ridges of her spine. Her bottom was pressed against him, and the hardness of his throbbing, aching arousal fitted perfectly against her.

That Juliet was completely naked beneath her chemise Sebastian had no doubt, and he allowed one of his hands to glide lower down over her stomach, to cup her between her parted legs. He was able to feel her dampness through the thin material that was the only barrier to his questing fingers.

A barrier Sebastian pushed impatiently aside, skilfully drawing the material of her chemise up to her waist.

Growling low in his throat, he was finally able to touch, to explore the soft and downy thatch where the hard bud of her arousal was hidden.

She was swollen.

So swollen.

And so responsive as Sebastian lightly stroked, above and below, never quite touching that engorged nubbin as his fingers became wet and slick.

'Please…!' Juliet's groan was so low and aching that Sebastian felt a leaping response between his own thighs. 'I want—Sebastian—I need—'

Sebastian knew what she wanted, what she needed, what she craved.

What he craved, too.

But not here.

How could either of them enjoy complete pleasure when they were standing here so publicly?

When anyone in the room might turn at any moment and see them together?

Juliet's slippered feet no longer touched the floor as Sebastian placed a strong arm about her waist, and she felt herself being lifted, carried backwards out of the room and into the dark shadows of the terrace before he lowered her to turn her in his arms. His mouth claimed hers hungrily.

The new, craving sensations in Juliet's body caused her to return the hunger of that kiss as she silently pleaded, begged for an end to the tormenting, unbearable ache between her thighs.

Her lips parted to the hard invasion of Sebastian's tongue, and those moist, rhythmic caresses once again pushed her to the brink of— Of what…?

Juliet didn't know.

But she wanted to know.

She *needed* to know!

'…was most enjoyable. But I am so warm after all the excitement that I simply must go outside and take some air.'

Juliet barely had time to register that she and Sebastian were about to have their privacy interrupted before he wrenched his mouth from hers to place silencing fingertips against her lips. He swiftly manoeuvred her backwards, even further into the shadows.

Only just in time, too, as the elderly Duchess and Duke of Sussex strolled out onto the terrace before crossing to stand at the balustrade.

Juliet looked up in the gloom at Sebastian face, to find the darkness of his gaze glittering down at her.

In laughter, or in triumph?

Chapter Five

'Personally, I fail to see what is so funny in the two of us nearly being found together in such a compromising situation.' Juliet stood in the middle of her bedchamber, frowning her consternation as Sebastian, having refastened her gown for her, stood before her, clutching his sides with laughter. 'Lord St Claire, you must desist!' She glared at him reprovingly when her previous admonition had no effect.

His laughter finally ceased, although his eyes continued to gleam with merriment as he looked at her, and a grin still curved those sculptured lips. 'I apologise. I simply found myself imagining how the Duke's jowls would wobble and the Duchess's mouth gape open like that of a fish if they had happened to turn and see us as we made good our escape!'

'That is most unkind, My Lord.' Although Juliet could not deny that their flight from the terrace *had* been in the nature of an escape.

The Duke and Duchess of Sussex had stood at the

balustrade for several minutes, talking softly together on the success of the evening, before the Duchess had linked her arm with her husband's and the two had begun to walk down the terrace.

Thankfully in the other direction from where Juliet and Sebastian had still been hiding in the shadows.

An occurrence which had caused Sebastian to take a firm clasp of Juliet's hand before pulling her down the steps into the garden, to stride around to the side of the house.

And all that time Juliet had clutched at the front of her unbuttoned gown in an effort to stop it sliding completely from her body, her mood one of horror as she imagined what a pretty sight she would look, with her gown about her ankles and wearing no more than her chemise and her stockings!

Luckily that had not happened, and the two of them had been able to find access to the house through one of the servant doors. They had then proceeded to sneak through the house and up the back staircase to Juliet's bedchamber. Much like two thieves in the night!

Juliet knew she had never behaved in such an undignified manner in the whole of her thirty years. And as for finding the situation *amusing*, as Sebastian St Claire so obviously did…!

'Can you not imagine it, my dear Juliet?' he prompted with an irrepressible smile. 'The Duke's jowls a-wobbling and the Duchess opening and shutting her mouth like a fish!' He went off into another bout of laughter.

Juliet could imagine it—she would just rather not. What had happened this evening—especially her own behaviour—was no laughing matter. 'Do you ever take anything seriously, My Lord?' she murmured critically.

He sobered immediately. 'Of course I do. Family. Honour. Loyalty to friends.'

Family. Honour. Loyalty to friends. They were indeed fine sentiments.

They did not signify where Juliet was concerned, however. She was neither friend nor family to Sebastian St Claire. As for honour—Juliet's own honour was in shreds!

'I think it better if you leave now.' She spoke softly, avoiding so much as looking at him as she rearranged her perfume bottles on the dressing table. 'This evening was—'

'I trust you are not going to say regrettable?' Sebastian cut in sternly.

Regrettable? Of *course* Juliet regretted it! Her only consolation was that it had not been the complete success Sebastian had hoped for. 'I was about to express my doubts that this evening's little adventure would be enough to win the wager for you!' she said scornfully.

'What wager?' He frowned down at her.

'Oh, come, My Lord.' Juliet gave a disdainful grimace. 'It is common knowledge that young gentlemen such as yourself enjoy certain wagers at their clubs. Escapades like curricle races to Brighton at midnight? Or the seduction of a certain woman…?'

Sebastian winced at the accusation. It was true that many such wagers took place in private—at least he had thought it was in private!—at the gentlemen's clubs. It was also true that a year or so ago Sebastian *had* entered into such a wager himself, concerning another Countess. Although he very much doubted that was the wager Juliet referred to…

'To my knowledge there is no such wager in existence where you are concerned,' he denied. 'And what do you mean by a man such as I…?' he grated.

Juliet gave him a pitying look. 'You are nothing but a rake, sir. A scoundrel. Indeed, a privileged fop, who meanders his way through life, imbibing too much alcohol, seducing women and laughing at anything or anyone who does not share those excesses!'

As set-downs went, this was certainly the harshest that Sebastian had ever received. In fact, it was the first of its kind that he had ever received!

He was a St Claire. The youngest brother of the Duke of Stourbridge. As such, he was untouchable—both in word and deed.

Except Juliet Boyd's opinion of him had touched him in a way he did not care to dwell upon. Perhaps because he suspected that essentially she had only spoken the truth…? He *had* made such wagers as those she had accused him. He *was* also a rake, and often behaved the scoundrel. And, as his two older brothers were so fond of telling him, his profligate lifestyle left much to be desired.

But he was the youngest son of a Duke, damn it, and had been left his own estate in Berkshire and a veritable fortune to support it and himself on the death of his parents more than eleven years ago. More wealth than even Sebastian could run through in a dozen lifetimes.

What choices did a third son have but the church—

for which he had no inclination!—or to live the life of a profligate?

Sebastian's intention, his interest in Juliet Boyd, had been no more than the light-hearted seduction of a woman who had so far proved elusive to all men but her husband. He had certainly not expected to have his very lifestyle brought into question by that lady.

He gave a stiff bow. 'Once again, let me assure you that I know of no such wager where you are concerned, Lady Boyd. I apologise if I have offended you with my unwanted attentions. I assure you that it will not happen again.' He turned abruptly to cross the room and open the door before stepping out into the hallway.

Juliet felt as if her chest were being squeezed, making breathing difficult and speech impossible, as she watched him leave her bedchamber. The grimness of his countenance had erased all evidence of his usual handsome good humour, making him instead every inch the aristocrat he was.

Juliet remained standing in the middle of the bed-chamber as the door closed behind him with a loud click of finality. At which time Juliet ceased even trying to maintain her dignity and instead collapsed weakly onto the bed, her shoulders shaking uncontrollably as tears fell hotly down her cheeks.

It really did not signify whether or not a wager concerning her seduction did or did not exist when her own behaviour this evening had been so shocking. Scandalous, even. The sort of behaviour that only a woman of loose morals could possibly have enjoyed. Women of breeding, of decency, did not—*should* not—

feel physical pleasure in the way that she had earlier, when Sebastian had caressed and touched her in such an intimate way.

'It would appear, Sebastian, that you have been scowling at my other guests in such a way as to cause them to completely lose their appetites!'

The darkness of Sebastian's scowl did not lessen in the slightest as he turned to look at Dolly as she entered the dining room to sit down beside him at the breakfast table. A deserted breakfast table apart from the two of them, he now noticed. Although he seemed to recall there *had* been several other people present when he'd entered the room ten minutes or so ago...

He grimaced. 'I doubt it will hurt some of them to miss a meal or two.'

'True,' Dolly acknowledged with an amused laugh.

Sebastian gave up even the pretence of eating his own breakfast and leant back in his chair. 'Dolly, I am thinking of taking my leave later this morning—'

'You cannot!' Dolly looked shocked at the suggestion. 'I really cannot allow you to even think of doing such a thing, Sebastian,' she continued lightly. 'You will quite put out the even number of my guests. Besides, we are to have a ball tomorrow evening, and I am sure you would not want to deny the daughters of the local gentry the opportunity to see and perhaps dance with the eligible Lord Sebastian St Claire!'

Sebastian did not return her teasing smile. 'I am sure they would be all the better for being denied it!'

'What is wrong, Sebastian?' Dolly looked at him in

genuine concern as he stared down grimly into his teacup. 'You do not seem at all your usual cheerful self this morning.' She gave him an encouraging smile.

'You mean, my usual privileged and foppish self? Given to excesses and licentious behaviour?' Sebastian didn't attempt to hide his displeasure concerning Juliet's opinion of his character.

Dolly looked taken aback. 'What on earth do you mean, Sebastian?'

He grimaced in self-disgust. 'The description is entirely fitting—do you not agree, Dolly?'

Sebastian had indulged in much deliberation over the last twelve hours. Since Juliet had told him exactly what sort of man she believed him to be. The sort of man he undoubtedly was, Sebastian had realised during those hours of reflection.

'Of course it is not—' Dolly broke off to consider him closely. 'Who has said such things—surely not Juliet?' she exclaimed. 'Have the two of you argued?'

Sebastian gave a hard, humourless laugh. 'I do not believe it can be called an argument when I merely listened as she told me exactly what sort of man she believes me to be.' His expression darkened. 'It did not paint a pretty picture.'

'No, I would not think it did, if it was the one you have just told to me,' Dolly conceded. 'What she thinks of you bothers you that much?' she asked shrewdly.

Sebastian's scowl turned blacker than ever. 'Only in as much as it appears to be true!'

Dolly shrugged. 'Easy enough to change if you wish it, surely?'

He snorted. 'And how would you suggest I go about doing *that*? Hawk is the Duke. Lucian is a war hero. And I very much doubt the church would suit me, or I it! No, it appears I'm stuck with being the profligate rake.'

'I believe Bancroft mentioned he is in need of another gamekeeper... No, perhaps not,' she said hastily, as Sebastian's gaze became steely at her levity.

Sebastian took advantage of Dolly's introduction of the Earl into the conversation. 'Bancroft expressed a wish to talk to me this morning. Do you have any idea what it can be about?'

Dolly shook her head. 'I am sure Bancroft will tell you that himself shortly.'

'In other words you have no intention of discussing it with me even if you do know?' Sebastian guessed wryly.

'I would rather not,' Dolly admitted. 'What did you do to Juliet to make her say such hurtful things to you? Dare I ask what had happened shortly before this... exchange?'

Sebastian shifted uncomfortably. 'No, Dolly, you may not.'

He had no intention of telling Dolly—or anyone else, for that matter—what had transpired between himself and Juliet prior to the verbal tongue-lashing he had received from her that had resulted in his present foul mood. He might be all of the things Lady Juliet Boyd had accused him of, but he was also a gentleman, and a gentleman did not discuss with a third party his relationship with a lady. Or the lack of it!

'However, I do not believe I am being indiscreet by confiding that she is of the opinion that my marked interest in her is due entirely to a wager amongst the gentlemen at my club.'

Dolly raised an eyebrow. 'Such wagers do exist, do they not?'

'To my knowledge, none that concern the Countess!' Sebastian glowered fiercely.

'Did you inform Juliet of that?'

'I did.' He gave a humourless smile at the memory. 'She chose not to believe me.'

'Hmm.' Dolly nodded thoughtfully. 'You know, Sebastian, I am not at all convinced that life can have been particularly pleasant when spent with a man of such high moral reputation as Admiral Lord Edward Boyd...'

'You think perhaps he was not so perfect in his private life?' It was something that Sebastian was also beginning to suspect....

'I offer it merely as an explanation for Juliet's condemnation of your own licentious behaviour,' his hostess said airily.

Sebastian's gaze narrowed. 'Dolly, I do not suppose that you and Boyd ever—'

'No, we most certainly did not!' She laughed huskily. 'My dear, he was far too much the paragon to form an alliance with one such as I. And I am sure his sort of perfection must have been very tiresome to live with on a daily basis.'

Sebastian made an impatient movement. 'Surely you are not suggesting that tiresomeness was enough to merit his being pushed down the stairs to his death?'

Dolly grimaced. 'I am merely saying that Juliet might be forgiven if she *did* want to be rid of such a man.

I believe that if Bancroft should ever become so pompous and self-important I might consider taking such action myself!'

Sebastian gave a throaty chuckle. 'If every dissatisfied wife in Society were to follow Juliet Boyd's example as a way of ridding herself of a disagreeable husband then I believe there would be only widows left—'

Sebastian broke off abruptly as he heard a shocked gasp behind him, turning sharply to see the edge of disappearing silken skirts as the eavesdropper on his conversation with Dolly made good her escape.

He stood up abruptly. 'Dolly, please tell me that was not she!' he groaned. But he knew by the consternation on his hostess's face that it had indeed been the Countess of Crestwood who had overheard their damning conversation....

Once dressed, Juliet had gone upstairs to check on Helena, who was thankfully much improved yet still in considerable discomfort, before proceeding down to the breakfast room. Her intention had been to seek out Sebastian and offer him an apology for some of the things she had said to him the previous evening. She had come to realise, through the long hours of a sleepless night, that it was herself she was angry with, not him.

She had heard the murmur of conversation as she'd approached the breakfast room, coming to a halt in the hallway when she heard Edward's name mentioned. She'd regretted that hesitation almost instantly, as she hadn't been able to help but overhear the rest of the conversation.

Sebastian St Claire believed her as guilty of Edward's death as surely as did every other member of the ton!

Hateful, *hateful* man. And to think it had been her intention to apologise to him this morning for her insulting remarks to him the previous evening! How much more hurtful had been his own comments just now than anything she had said to him.

'Juliet!'

She glanced back over her shoulder to see Sebastian pursuing her down the hallway, his expression grim as his much longer strides brought him ever closer, making a nonsense of Juliet's attempt to avoid him.

She came to a sudden halt in the hallway and turned to face him. 'Do you have more accusations you wish to make, Lord St Claire? Possibly to my face this time?' she challenged scathingly. 'Do you not think that overhearing you accuse me of killing my husband is enough insult for one morning?' Her hands were shaking so badly that she had to clasp them tightly behind her back.

Sebastian frowned. 'I do not believe myself guilty of having done that.'

'No?' Juliet's chin was raised in challenge, her eyes sparkling angrily. Anger was by far a better emotion than the tears that threatened but which she absolutely refused to shed.

'No,' he maintained harshly, those whisky-coloured eyes dark and stormy. 'I accept it was wrong of Dolly and I to repeat the—the speculation that has abounded since your husband's sudden death. But at no time did either of us claim to be expressing our own views on the subject.'

Juliet eyed him in a seething fury. 'Perhaps you would care to do so now?'

No, Sebastian did not believe that he would. Juliet's mood was such that anything he said to her now, especially concerning his opinion of the circumstances of her husband's death, was sure to be misconstrued by her. 'Perhaps the speculation would not be so rife if you ceased to maintain your own silence on the subject…'

'What would you like me to say, Lord St Claire?' she scorned. 'That it was *I* the servants believe they heard arguing with Edward only minutes before he fell to his death? That I hated my husband so much, wanted rid of him so much, I deliberately and wilfully pushed him down the stairs in the hopes that he would break his neck?'

No, Sebastian had no desire to hear Juliet say those things. He did not want to even think of this beautiful and delicate woman behaving in such a cold and calculating way. Nor to imagine what desperation she'd felt— what Edward Boyd's behaviour towards her could possibly have been—to have driven her to such lengths in order to be rid of him….

A nerve pulsed in his tightly clenched jaw. 'Are you telling me that is what happened?'

'Oh, no, My Lord.' Her laugh was hard and humourless. 'It is not for me to tell you anything. You must decide for yourself what you believe to be the truth.'

His mouth tightened. 'Is that not difficult to do when you steadfastly refuse to defend yourself?'

She gave him a pitying look. 'I am certainly not so naïve as to even attempt to proclaim my innocence to one who has so obviously already decided upon my guilt.'

Sebastian made an impatient move. 'Then you presume too much, madam.'

'Do I?' Juliet Boyd snapped. 'All evidence is to the contrary, My Lord.'

Sebastian had never experienced such frustration with another human being as he felt at that moment towards Juliet Boyd. Could she not see that her words and actions, her continued refusal to defend herself, only damned her as being the murderess the ton believed her to be? To others, if not to him.

Her eyes, those beautiful green eyes, viewed him coldly. 'Are you not relieved, My Lord, that I did not take your attentions to me more seriously?'

'My *attentions*, as you call them, were never intended to be taken seriously,' he bit out curtly.

'Of course they were not.' She gave him a disdainful glance. 'Everyone knows that Lord Sebastian St Claire does not take anything in life seriously!'

Once again she meant to insult him. And once again Sebastian realised he had no defence against those insults....

Dolly claimed that if he felt so inclined Sebastian had the means and the ability to change his way of life. That, third son or not, he did not *have* to live the life of idleness and pleasure he had so far enjoyed.

Until the last twelve hours Sebastian had never had reason to even question that life! Nor did he thank Juliet for being the reason he was questioning it now....

'If you will excuse me, Lady Boyd, I have a prior engagement.' He gave a less than elegant bow. 'Please accept my apologies for any insult, real or imagined, that you may have felt during the conversation you overheard earlier. I do assure you that no insult was intended by either Lady Bancroft or myself.' He turned sharply on his heel and took his leave.

Tears burnt Juliet's eyes as she watched him go. She knew that Sebastian St Claire's light-hearted pursuit of her was finally at an end. That she had rended his interest in her asunder with her criticism of him and the way he lived his life.

Chapter Six

'**Y**ou are here, too, Gray?' Sebastian did not even try to hide his surprise upon finding his friend already seated in the Earl of Banford's study when he duly presented himself there at the assigned hour of ten o'clock.

Nor did Sebastian attempt to conceal his irritation as he refused to take the seat the Earl offered, facing him across the width of his leather-topped desk; Sebastian had suffered through enough such interviews over the years with his brother Hawk, to know better than to meekly sit and accept the set-down he believed was coming. A set-down he deeply resented.

'I am perfectly comfortable standing, thank you,' he assured the older man, and he moved to stand with his back towards the window, hands clasped behind his back, the width of his shoulders blocking out most of the sunlight.

The Earl nodded. 'My wife tells me that you and Lady Boyd have argued…?'

'What the——?' Sebastian's scowl deepened as he stiffened resentfully. He had believed his earlier conversation with Dolly to be of a private nature, known only to the two of them. And in part to Juliet Boyd herself, of course… 'Dolly had no right to relate any of that conversation to you,' he said, outraged.

'I am afraid that she did.' The Earl's expression was sympathetic, but at the same time determined. 'You see, it is not in our interest that you argue with Lady Boyd.'

'"Our interest"?' Sebastian's brow darkened ominously as he looked at the earl and Gray. 'Would someone kindly tell me what on earth is going on?'

'Calm down, old chap,' Gray advised him.

'No, I do not believe I will,' Sebastian grated.

'At least hear what Bancroft has to say before you threaten to call him out,' Gray soothed.

The Earl rose to his feet, as if he too found the confinement of being seated irksome. 'Have you not wondered why it was, when two weeks ago you made your request to my wife that she invite the Countess here to stay, she had already done so?'

'Why should I?' Sebastian shrugged. 'The two ladies were friends once, were they not?'

'Perhaps,' the Earl acknowledged cautiously. 'But I am afraid in this instance that friendship did not signify. My wife issued the invitation to Lady Boyd at my behest.'

'You have lost me, I am afraid.' Sebastian's morning so far had not been in the least conducive to holding on to his temper, and the Earl's enigmatic conversation now was only succeeding in increasing his annoyance.

'I am sure you are aware of the…rumours surrounding the Earl of Crestwood's death?'

'Not you, too!' Sebastian strode forcefully, impatiently, into the middle of the book-lined room. 'You—' he looked pointedly at the Earl of Banford '—gave every indication that you'd befriended the Countess yesterday evening. And you—' his eyes glittered dangerously as he turned his attention on Gray '—flirt with the lady every time the two of you meet. Am I now to believe that you *both* think her capable of killing her own husband?'

'That is the whole point of this conversation, Sebastian.' Once again it was Gray who answered softly. 'The simple answer is we do not *know* what the lady is capable of.'

'Boyd has been dead these past eighteen months,' Sebastian said coldly. 'If by some chance Juliet did do away with him—' his gaze narrowed '—then I am sure she was justified.' That look of wariness, almost of apprehension, he had on several occasions seen in Juliet's eyes, certainly seemed to indicate that someone—and who else could it be but Crestwood?—had given her good reason to fear.

'Ah.'

'Hmm.'

Sebastian easily noted the glance that passed between the other two men in accompaniment to their unhelpful replies.

He could not ignore the uneasy feeling that was starting to settle in the pit of his stomach. The Earl claimed Dolly had invited Juliet here at *his* behest. And Gray, Sebastian now recalled, had made only a nominal complaint at being dragged along to a summer house party he would normally have refused to attend. Gray had also been the one chosen to sit next to Juliet at dinner yesterday evening in Sebastian's stead. Now he discovered that Gray and the Earl of Banford were far better acquainted than he had previously thought….

'Very well.' He seated himself in one of the winged armchairs beside the unlit fireplace before looking at the other the two men with grim determination. 'One or both of you had better tell me exactly what is going on, or you will leave me with no choice but to go to the Countess of Crestwood and inform her of this conversation.'

'You know, Grayson, I do believe you and Dolly may have been correct in your opinion of St Claire's intellect,' the Earl commented with approval.

'Seb's a capital chap,' the younger man answered blithely.

'Seb is fast becoming a blazingly angry one!' he warned them harshly.

'Very well.' The Earl looked him straight in the eye. 'I am happy to talk frankly, but before doing so I will require your word as a gentleman that once this conversation is over you will not discuss its details with a third party.'

Sebastian knew without the other man saying so that in this case the 'third party' he referred to was the Countess of Crestwood….

Up till now Sebastian had always found Dolly's husband to be an affable and charming man. A man it was difficult not to like, but with no more to him than that.

These last few minutes of conversation showed there was much more to the Earl of Banford, and to his own

friend Gray, than Sebastian had previously realised…
and he didn't like knowing that at all.

'…and so you see you have totally misjudged poor St
Claire, I am afraid, dear Juliet,' Dolly admonished gently
as the two women sat together in her private parlour.

Juliet had been reluctant to accept Dolly's invitation
to join her here when the other woman had come upon
her still standing in the hallway after Sebastian had so
abruptly taken his leave. After all, Dolly had been just as
guilty of discussing her as Sebastian had! To now hear
that he had actually been *dismissing* the idea of Juliet
being guilty of any involvement in Edward's death, rather
than accusing her, made her feel more than a little foolish.

For now it appeared she owed Sebastian not one
apology but two!

'After all the gossip and speculation this last year and
a half, it is a subject about which I am naturally a little
sensitive,' Juliet acknowledged stiffly.

'But of course, my dear.' Dolly gave her hand an
understanding pat. 'I can be a sympathetic ear if you
ever feel the need to talk privately….'

How Juliet longed to tell someone about her years as
Edward's wife. Longed to tell of those nights when he
had come to her bed and taken her with cold indifference to the pain he was inflicting. Of his cruelty in the
early months of their marriage, when she'd still thought
it worth pleading for his gentleness and understanding.
Pleas she had ceased to make after that single occasion
when Edward had shown her just how much *more* pain
and humiliation he could inflict when thwarted.

Oh, yes, Juliet longed to tell someone of those things, but knew that she never would....

'I thank you for the offer, Dolly.' She smiled, to take any offence from her refusal. 'But for the moment I would much rather discuss how I am to go about apologising to Lord St Claire for this latest misunderstanding.'

If Dolly was disappointed in Juliet's determination not to talk about the past, then she gave no indication of it as she instead laughed huskily. 'Oh, my dear, you must not be so eager to concede that you were in the wrong. Men are fond of believing themselves in the right of it, you know, and to eat a little humble pie on occasion does them no harm whatsoever.'

Despite her earlier tension, Juliet found herself laughing at Dolly's nonsense. 'But in this case Lord St Claire *was* in the right of it...'

'I did not say you have to punish him for ever, my dear.' Dolly gave her a conspiratorial smile. 'Just long enough for him to feel the cold chill of your displeasure. The ball I am giving tomorrow evening should be time enough to allow yourself to forgive him.'

Juliet raised dark brows. 'So I *am* to forgive him, then?'

'Of course.' Dolly gave a gracious inclination of her head. 'I have found with Bancroft that it is by far the best way. By the time I have finished forgiving him he is usually so befuddled he has quite forgotten that he was not actually to blame for our fall-out, and is just grateful that we are...friends again!'

Juliet felt colour warm her cheeks as she realised what sort of friendship the other woman was alluding to. 'You quite misunderstand my relationship with Lord St Claire—'

'It is still early days yet, Juliet,' Dolly pointed out.

She shook her head. 'I assure you I have no intention of ever becoming that sort of friend with Sebastian St Claire.'

Or any other man….

Sebastian's expression remained outwardly calm as the Earl talked. Which was not to say that he was not disturbed by the older man's conversation—only he had no intention of revealing his own thoughts at Bancroft's talk of agents of the Crown and treachery.

Bancroft, it appeared, had for some years been involved in such a network of agents, of which Gray— a man Sebastian had known since childhood—appeared to be a member! Dolly, too, if Sebastian understood the Earl correctly; all those years Dolly had been the mistress of one member of the aristocracy or another she had been reporting information back to Bancroft!

'So it appears Crestwood was either responsible himself for passing along privileged information, or it was someone else close to him in whom he confided,' Bancroft finished gravely.

Sebastian realised he had been guilty of allowing his thoughts to wander. But, hell, what man would *not* when confronted with such a fantastic tale? 'Let me see if I understand this clearly. You are saying that Crestwood, or someone close to him, for years passed along privileged information to the French? That such information was used to forestall several English efforts to defeat

Bonaparte, and also to aid the Corsican's escape from Elba two years ago?'

'I am saying exactly that,' the Earl confirmed.

Sebastian's brother Lucian had resigned his commission in the army when Bonaparte had finally surrendered, but he had returned to duty the following year, along with his fellow officers, in order to participate in the battle at Waterloo, following Napoleon's escape from Elba. Lucian had returned from that last battle a hard and embittered man, and most of his friends had not returned at all….

Sebastian raised an eyebrow. 'You also believe that this "someone close" to the earl was his wife? That if the heroic Crestwood did not do it, then it must therefore have been Juliet who was the traitor?'

Gray frowned. 'Crestwood was a hero and a gentleman, Seb. But he was not a man who had close friends as you and I do. In effect, there *was* no other person close to him except his countess. Now Crestwood is conveniently dead, and so unable to deny or admit these allegations.'

Sebastian stood up restlessly. 'You are claiming that Lady Boyd deliberately pushed Crestwood down the stairs to his death in order to cover up her duplicity?'

His friend nodded. 'It is reasonable to suppose that Crestwood finally discovered his wife's treachery, and that when he confronted her with it, she pushed him down the stairs to stop him from making her conduct public.'

'Is it not a simpler explanation that the man was foxed?'

'The man did not drink strong liquor of any kind.'

'Then perhaps he fell.'

'He stood the deck of his own ship for over twenty years—are you seriously expecting us, or anyone else, to believe that he lost his balance at the top of his own staircase?' Gray calmed with effort. 'Besides, several of the servants heard the sounds of an argument only minutes before the Earl's fall.'

Sebastian gave a disdainful snort. 'Servants have been known to say anything if they believe it might earn them a guinea or two!'

'No such bribery was offered,' the Earl assured him.

Still Sebastian could not countenance the idea that Juliet was guilty of deliberately murdering her husband, let alone of treason. Although the sacrifice Lucian and his friends had made during the war said he had to hear Bancroft out… 'The man was such a prig that he had no real friends, and such a paragon that he did not drink alcohol. Therefore it *must* be his wife who is the one guilty of treason? Of pushing Crestwood to his death so that he could not reveal her perfidy?' Sebastian shook his head. 'That seems to be rather a leap to have made on so little evidence, gentlemen.'

'There is more, St Claire.' The Earl's tone immediately drew Sebastian's attention. 'Lady Boyd's aunt, the sister of her mother, lived in France with her French husband—Pierre Jourdan. As a child, Juliet Chatterton spent many summers in France, with this aunt and uncle and her young female cousin.'

'Does that mean that *every* English man or woman who has connections with the French, however tenuous, is suspect? My own valet is French. Does that make me guilty of treason, too?'

'You are not taking this at all as I had hoped, St Claire.' The Earl looked most unhappy with Sebastian's response.

Possibly because Sebastian would much rather not think of Juliet in the role Bancroft and Gray had chosen to thrust her into!

She was full of defensive bristles, yes. But what woman would not be when she had come to Banford Park knowing she was entering the lions' den? That all of Society believed her as guilty of killing her husband as Bancroft and Gray so obviously did? But Sebastian had seen that air of vulnerability and fear that Juliet was normally at such pains to disguise.

Until now Sebastian had assumed that fear to have somehow been caused by Crestwood's treatment of her during their marriage, but logically it *could* likewise be apprehension at the thought of discovery…

Two weeks ago he had told Dolly that he did not care one way or the other whether or not Juliet had killed her husband, but his loyalty for Lucian said he should take Bancroft's suggestion of treason much more seriously.

'The Countess's young cousin arrived in England six years ago, after her parents were killed during a raid by French soldiers on their manor home,' Bancroft continued remorselessly. 'The girl was held prisoner by the French for a week before managing to escape and flee to England. We can only guess at what she must have suffered at the soldiers' hands.'

'Would those events not mean that Juliet Boyd has every reason to hate the French rather than aid them?' Sebastian pounced on this inconsistency in their argument.

'Alternatively, she may have been responsible for

betraying her relatives to the French because she knew of their sympathies towards the English,' Bancroft pointed out.

Sebastian felt a coldness slither down the length of his spine at the thought of the beautiful Juliet betraying her family and husband—his brother Lucian and his fellow soldiers, too—in the way Bancroft described. It could not be true. Could it?

'There is something else, St Claire,' the Earl added.

'Go on,' he rasped.

'Two weeks ago a missive to a known French agent was intercepted by one of my own agents. It read simply, "Active again. J."'

Active again. J.

And the missive had been sent two weeks ago.

The exact time Dolly had issued her invitation to Juliet to attend this summer house party....

'I have always believed, my dear Juliet, that if a woman decides to take a lover then she should at least ensure he is an accomplished one,' Dolly Bancroft advised archly.

Juliet's cheeks burned at the thought of the intimacies she had already allowed Sebastian St Claire. Intimacies Juliet had shared with no other man....

She shook her head. 'I assure you I have no intention of taking a lover.'

'Why would you not?' The other woman looked scandalised. 'You have been widowed these last eighteen months, Juliet; do not tell me you do not miss the pleasure of having a virile man in your bed?'

How could Juliet miss something she had never

known? Something she had only begun to guess at since Sebastian had touched and caressed her…?

Would this burning in her cheeks ever stop? 'I am not sure this is a—an altogether fitting conversation, Dolly.'

'I am sure it is not!' Her hostess laughed naughtily. 'But men, I am sure, discuss such things at their clubs all the time, so why should the ladies not do the same when alone together? I can claim with all honesty that Bancroft is a wonderful lover. Was Crestwood the same?'

'Dolly!' Juliet gasped weakly.

The other woman's gaze was shrewdly searching. 'I see by your reaction that he was not.' She gave a disgusted shake of her head. 'How disappointing for you. I am of the opinion that being proficient in the art of lovemaking is as important for a man to learn as running an estate or riding a horse.'

Juliet really was unused to such frank and intimate conversation. 'Crestwood ran his estate with precision, and he could ride a horse, as well as any man.'

'Then it was only as a lover that he failed to please?' Dolly nodded knowingly. 'One only has to look at St Claire to know how wonderful he would be as a lover. The width of his shoulders. His muscled chest and the flatness of his stomach. As for the pleasure promised by his powerful hips and thighs… My dear, I am sure he is virile enough to keep even the most demanding of women happy in his bed!'

All this talk of pleasure and virile men, and most especially of Sebastian St Claire's bed, was only increasing Juliet's discomfort. But in a way that made her breasts swell beneath her gown and their tips harden as she once again felt that strange warmth between her thighs she had known when Sebastian had touched and caressed her so intimately the evening before....

Sebastian's mouth thinned. 'I agree the truth needs to be established. But,' he added firmly, 'I refuse to condemn Lady Boyd on what amounts to superficial evidence.'

William Bancroft gave an inclination of his head. 'I am pleased to hear it.'

Sebastian's gaze narrowed suspiciously. 'You are?'

'But of course.' The older man resumed his seat behind the leather-topped desk. 'That is the very reason we are having this conversation.'

'Explain yourself, if you please.'

'Seb—'

'Do not concern yourself, Grayson,' the Earl interjected. 'St Claire is quite right to advise caution. To accuse someone of treason is a serious business. And while Lady Boyd—this French agent—remained inactive, indeed there was no need for haste. The fact that she—or he—is now back amongst us, prepared to take up their treasonous role once more, has changed things somewhat. I should, of course, have had this conversation with you some weeks ago, St Claire, when you first spoke to my wife concerning your interest in the Countess of Crestwood. I delayed doing so only because I felt it best to wait and see if the lady returned your interest.'

'She does not.'

'Oh, we believe that she does.' The earl smiled knowingly.

'Then you believe wrongly.' Sebastian glared coldly

at the older man. 'Lady Boyd has strongly resisted all my advances.'

'She is naturally cautious, I admit.' The older man nodded. 'But I have known the lady for some years, dined with her and Crestwood on a number of occasions, and as such I have had ample time in which to study her. She is a woman of reticence. Of reserve. So much so that she is polite to all but allows none close to her. You have managed to breach that reserve on several occasions in the last few days, I believe…?'

'Damn it, I refuse to discuss a lady in this way!'

'You do not need to do so, St Claire. Dolly is talking with Lady Boyd even as we speak. I have no doubt that she will ably ascertain whether or not the lady has developed a…*tendre* for you.'

'You go too far, sir!' Sebastian could never remember feeling so angry with anyone before.

'I go as far as I need!' the Earl assured him evenly. 'If Lady Boyd is guilty of all we suspect, then I consider my actions as necessary as a soldier's in battle when confronted with the enemy.'

'*If* she is guilty!' Sebastian repeated pointedly. 'Until you have positive proof of that I, for one, will not condemn the lady.'

'I was hoping that you might feel that way….'

He eyed the older man suspiciously, even as a nerve pulsed in his tightly clenched jaw. 'Exactly what are you suggesting…?'

William Bancroft eyed him speculatively. 'Why, that you find some way to go about either proving or disproving the lady's innocence, of course.'

'*Some way?* What way do you have in mind, exactly?' Sebastian wanted to know.

The other man shrugged. 'A man and a woman are apt to discuss many things once the bedding is over.'

Sebastian stared at the other man as if he had gone completely insane. Bancroft *must* be insane if he really thought that Sebastian could play Juliet so false. Was this Dolly's idea of what Sebastian should do in order to change his life from one of idleness and pleasure?

Family. Honour. Loyalty to friends…

Those were the things Sebastian had last night informed Juliet Boyd he took seriously. To behave in the way William Bancroft described—to bed Juliet, make love to her, with the sole intention of discovering her innocence or guilt in treason and murder—would be to behave completely without honour.

But if the Countess of Crestwood really *was* as guilty as Bancroft seemed to think, then did not Sebastian also owe it to Lucian, to all his brother's friends, so many of whom had fallen at Waterloo, to apprehend someone who might have been instrumental in aiding Bonaparte's escape from Elba and so precipitated that bloody battle?

Which left loyalty to friends…

The Earl gave a weary sigh. 'I am well aware of what we ask of you, St Claire, and appreciate that you will need some time to think on it.'

'Why do you not merely question the lady and be done with it?' Sebastian, despite that loyalty he felt towards Lucian, was still loath to agree to such a nefarious and ungentlemanly plan.

'As I have already explained, while Agent J was

inactive there was no haste to do anything but keep a silent watch. Now that Agent J *is* active again we stand a chance of locating and ultimately arresting a whole network of French agents. Besides, at this moment in time we do not have enough evidence to either question the Countess in connection with treason and murder or indeed clear her name of all such charges.'

He was asking Sebastian to find and then produce that evidence….

His gaze narrowed on the two men. 'And if I had not succeeded in finding favour with the Countess? Who was to take my place in her bed then? You, Gray?' He looked accusingly at the other man, knowing by the way Gray moved uncomfortably in his chair that his surmise was a correct one. 'You are both mad, I think!'

'Your own brother returned from Waterloo, Seb. Mine did not.' Gray's face was pale and tense.

Sebastian's fingers involuntarily clenched into purposeful bunches of five. What would Hawk do in such a situation? What would Lucian do if offered the chance of avenging some of the friends he'd lost at Waterloo?

'And if I refuse?' He eyed the Earl warily.

'Then be assured I will take your place, Seb,' Gray told him bluntly. 'I feel no reservation, no hesitation in attempting to woo and win the Countess's confidence. I will bed her, too, if it will give us the answers we require.'

Gray to flatter and charm Juliet? *Gray* to seduce her? To bed her? Never!

'I feel no hesitation, either, in giving you both my answer,' Sebastian said stiffly.

Gray sat forward anxiously. 'Seb, I ask that you do not act in haste—'

'You no longer have any part in this conversation, Gray,' he told his friend. 'The two of us will talk together at some later date about the role you have played in this farce.' A later date when Sebastian was not so angry he felt like striking Gray rather than talking to him, his steely tone warned! He turned back to Lord Bancroft. 'I will endeavour to engage the Countess's interest further,' he accepted, feeling utter distaste for such deceit. 'But only on the understanding that I do this for Juliet Boyd's own sake, and not your own,' he added firmly. 'When I have assured you of her innocence, I will then expect you to apologise both to her and to me.'

If Sebastian succeeded in assuring these two men of Juliet's innocence….

Chapter Seven

'You look perfectly lovely this evening, Juliet.' Helena beamed at her approvingly as Juliet stood in front of the cheval mirror, studying her reflection.

Her cousin, restless from being confined to her room for two days now, had this evening insisted that she was recovered sufficiently from her fall to come downstairs and help Juliet prepare for dinner. Juliet knew she should have insisted that Helena rest her ankle further, but she had nevertheless appreciated her cousin's help in dressing and arranging her hair. She wanted to look her best this evening.

Following her candid conversation earlier today with Dolly Bancroft, she had decided to give Sebastian St Claire the opportunity in which to make his apologies to her, at least. The rest of Dolly's advice she was less sure about!

Unfortunately there had been no opportunity to see or speak with Lord St Claire after talking to Dolly. He had gone out riding late this morning, and had not returned until much later in the afternoon. So this evening would be the first available opportunity Juliet would have to see him again. And for him to see her.

Dolly had advised that Juliet take Sebastian as her lover. The question was, did Juliet *wish* to take a lover? Not if, as she had always thought, all men were as brutish as Crestwood had been! Dolly's description of her own relationship with William Bancroft seemed to imply that they were not, but still Juliet felt uneasy—

She was getting far ahead of herself!

After their two fallings out there was absolutely no reason to presume that Sebastian still wished to become her lover....

Sebastian paid little attention to his fellow guests as they gathered in the drawing room before dinner, his mood not improved since that morning, despite riding for an hour across the countryside in order that he might pay an unexpected call upon Lucian and his bride of less than one month at their own Hampshire estate.

The recently married couple had welcomed him most warmly; it had been Sebastian's own distraction that had prevented him from enjoying the visit. Within a few minutes of his arrival Sebastian had known that he should not have gone there. Lucian was so obviously happy with his bride, and Sebastian's word to Bancroft prevented him from discussing with his brother any of the conversation of this morning in any case.

There was no one, it seemed—not Lucian, not Gray, not Dolly—with whom Sebastian could talk about the web of intrigue in which he now found himself entangled.

The fact that Juliet Boyd looked breathtaking and innocently lovely as she entered the drawing room at that moment did not improve Sebastian's temper. To such an extent that he realised he was actually scowling across the room at her as she fell into conversation with the Duchess of Essex.

Juliet's gown this evening was of cream satin and lace that complemented perfectly the pearly translucence of her skin, its low neckline revealing the full swell of her breasts. The darkness of her hair was arranged artfully in tiny curls about the beauty of her face and nape, the green of her eyes made all the deeper by a fringe of thick dark lashes and her mouth a full and sensuous pout.

Sebastian stiffened as she turned and seemed deliberately to meet his gaze, leaving him with no other choice but to make an abrupt bow of acknowledgement before turning immediately away again, his hands clenching tightly at his sides.

This was going to be so much harder than he had imagined if he could not even bring himself to relax when Juliet was only in the same room as himself. How on earth would he get close enough to her to ascertain her innocence if he did not get a firmer grip on his emotions? After all, he was ultimately doing this with the intention of proving her innocence to those who seemed all too ready to believe in her guilt.

'Good evening, Lord St Claire.'

For the first time in their acquaintance Juliet Boyd had approached *him*! Yesterday Sebastian would have rejoiced in that fact. Today he could not rid himself of the weight of duplicity pressing down upon him so heavily.

'Can it be that you are still angry with me, My Lord…?'

Juliet felt nervous, and not a little foolish, as she attempted to flirt with Sebastian. She had watched other women do it for years, of course, but it was a different matter entirely to behave in such a fashion herself. There had been little occasion for her to do so during her one and only Season, and Edward would have dealt with her most severely if he had so much as suspected her of flirtation during their marriage.

But if she and Lord St Claire did not talk to each other, how was he to be persuaded into making his apologies to her?

He looked so very handsome this evening, too, in a tailored black superfine, snowy white linen beneath a waistcoat of the palest silver, white pantaloons fitted quite shamefully to the long muscled length of his hips and thighs, and polished black Hessians.

Ordinarily Juliet knew she would not have noticed how perfectly a man's clothes were tailored to him. That she did so now where Sebastian was concerned was due, she had no doubt, to the candidness of Dolly Bancroft's conversation that morning.

Juliet felt warm just looking at him as she recalled that conversation. She was totally aware of the width of his shoulders and muscled chest. The flatness of his stomach. The promised power of his thighs…

Oh, dear Lord!

Juliet flicked her fan open and wafted it up and down in front of her face in an effort to cool her burning cheeks.

His gaze was narrowed as he looked down at her. 'I

believe it is *you* who were angry with *me*, ma'am,' he pointed out rather curtly.

Juliet tried to remember how, over the years, she had seen other women behave in the presence of such an attractive man as he.

A glance from beneath lowered lashes, perhaps?

No, that had only made him scowl all the more!

A mysterious little smile that hinted at invitation?

No, that had only made him narrow his gaze on her questioningly!

Perhaps she should just be herself, after all? Sebastian had seemed to find that attractive enough yesterday evening, when he'd made love to her so illicitly.

Juliet snapped her fan closed and gave up every pretence of flirtation. 'We both know I have good reason to be angry with you, Lord St Claire.'

'Then I wonder you have troubled yourself to seek me out,' he retorted.

Her smile was brittle. 'I did not "seek you out", as you call it, Lord St Claire. I was merely passing this way in order to talk to Lord Grayson, and it would have been rude of me not to have acknowledged you at least. If you will excuse me…? My Lord!' she exclaimed sharply as Sebastian reached out and grasped her wrist, so that she could not escape without drawing attention to the two of them. 'You are hurting my wrist, sir!' Her eyes flashed up at him warningly.

Sebastian would have liked to do more than hurt Juliet Boyd's wrist—he wanted to wring her damned neck! First she threw him completely off balance by approaching him. Then she seemed almost to have been flirting with him, before transforming into her usual waspish self. This woman was such a tangle of contradictions she had Sebastian tied up in knots!

He gave a hard smile. 'Take my advice, Juliet, and stay well away from Lord Grayson.'

'I *beg* your pardon?'

She looked so outraged. So indignant. So hurt… Yes, this woman was a mass of contradictions that promised to drive Sebastian quietly out of his mind!

His grip on her wrist gentled and he pulled her slowly towards him, watching as her eyes opened wider and wider as he pulled her ever closer. Until she stood so near to him their bodies almost touched. Until he could see the quick rise and fall of her breasts. The trembling of her slightly parted lips. Feel the softness of her breath against his throat.

God, he wanted to crush Juliet's lips beneath his own. Just as he longed to rip the gown from her body before making love to her until she screamed out in pleasure. Until she screamed out her innocence!

The image of making love to her formed so vividly in his mind that Sebastian felt his thighs hardening. Throbbing. Aching…

His jaw clenched. 'You are playing a dangerous game, my lady!'

Juliet blinked her confusion. 'Game, My Lord? I have no idea what—'

'I am sorry to interrupt, but it is time to go into dinner.'

Juliet turned blankly to look at Dolly Bancroft, where she stood beside them, smiling. The Duke of Essex stood to one side, waiting to escort their hostess in to dinner, but otherwise the drawing room had emptied of the other twenty or so guests.

Leaving Sebastian once again to escort Juliet into dinner….

Something she was sure neither of them desired after this latest heated exchange.

Far from feeling remorse at the wrong he had done her this morning, Sebastian seemed almost angry with her. Coldly, remorselessly so. And Juliet had seen far too much coldness and remorselessness during her marriage to Crestwood to tolerate any more of it.

'How kind of you to wait for me, Your Grace.' She stepped away from Sebastian to place her hand upon the Duke of Essex's arm, thereby allowing him to escort her into dinner. The Duke was far too much the gentleman to point out that she had taken Dolly Bancroft's place.

Sebastian's eyes blazed deeply golden as he turned from watching Juliet's departure on the arm of the Duke of Essex. 'Do not!' he grated, as Dolly Bancroft would have spoken as he offered her his arm. He had no intention of discussing her husband's conversation of this morning with her. Or indeed anything else!

'Did I not initially try to persuade you from your interest in Juliet?' Dolly nevertheless attempted.

'*Before* you saw that my interest could be to your husband's advantage?' Sebastian scorned. 'Perhaps one day I may be able to forgive you for this, Dolly—but it is certainly not going to be today!'

'Life cannot always be a game, Sebastian.' She sounded wistful.

Sebastian looked down at her bleakly. 'When all of

this is over I think it best if you and I do not meet again for some time.'

The hurt she felt was reflected in the deep blue of her eyes, but the inclination of her head was as gracious as always. 'As you wish.'

What Sebastian wished was that he had never seen Juliet Boyd. Never desired to bed her. Never come to Banford Park in pursuit of her. More than anything else he wished he could just leave here today, now, and forget he had ever been told of the suspicions harboured against her.

But Sebastian's sense of fair play, his honour, his loyalty, said that he could do none of those things. That, no matter how Juliet might one day despise him for his actions, he owed it to her to see that she was given every opportunity to prove herself innocent of Bancroft's accusations.

Or not...

'Are you feeling unwell, Juliet...?' Helena hovered behind her as she sat in front of the mirror. Juliet had dismissed her cousin once she had helped her out of her gown, wishing to be alone when she removed the pins from her hair, but Helena's glance at her reflection showed Juliet's face to be exceedingly pale, the green of her eyes the only colour, and there was a frown of tension upon her brow.

Altogether it had not been a successful evening. Yet another unpleasant exchange with Sebastian St Claire had occurred. Followed by a lengthy dinner when Juliet had found herself seated between two gentlemen who wished only to converse on fox hunting and their hounds. She had then been persuaded into partnering Lord Grayson in a game of whist, all the time aware of Sebastian as he sat at the next table, partner to the beautiful Lady Butler. Juliet's distraction at the other woman's obviously flirtatious manner had been such that she and Grayson had lost miserably. Juliet had been relieved when she could at last excuse herself and retire to her bedchamber.

The greatest disappointment, of course, had been the way Sebastian had seemed too preoccupied to notice her. For the first time in her life Juliet had deliberately set out to see if she could attract the attention of a certain man, and the man had shown her nothing but indifference!

'I have a slight headache, that is all,' she assured her cousin ruefully. 'But I am perfectly capable of taking down my own hair. It would please me if you would go back upstairs and rest your ankle.' She smiled encouragingly, knowing that she wished only to be alone to lick the wounds to her pride.

She maintained that smile until Helena turned and left the bedchamber, only relaxing into dejection once she knew herself to be completely alone.

What Juliet would have really liked to do was go out onto her balcony and breathe in some of the warm summer air. But she was loath to do so after the last time she had done just that. It would be too humiliating if by chance Sebastian happened to find her there once again. If he were to assume that she was deliberately trying to attract his attention.

Not that it was particularly likely; if Sebastian had already retired to any bedchamber then it was probably Lady Butler's!

Sebastian was sprawled atop the bedcovers in a state of disarray, drinking brandy copiously, when he heard the first scream.

It had not been easy to turn down Lady Butler's obvious invitation to retire with her to her bedchamber, without causing offence, but somehow Sebastian had managed it. As he had also managed to procure a decanter of brandy and a glass from a footman, before mounting the staircase two steps at a time and then striding to his bedchamber to close the door firmly behind him.

Watching Gray's solicitations to Juliet Boyd for two hours had induced a need in Sebastian not to see or speak to anyone else this evening. He had thrown open the doors out onto his balcony before undressing down to his pantaloons, his intention to lie down upon his bed and get roaring drunk before hopefully falling into an unconscious stupor.

The fear and desperation he heard in Juliet's scream wiped all thought of sleep from Sebastian's mind, and he slammed his glass down on the bedside table before jumping to his bare feet.

It did not even occur to him to use the door out into the hallway. He rushed out onto his balcony to vault over the top of the ridiculous barrier before throwing open the door to Juliet's room, fearful of what or who he might find there.

The bedchamber was lit by a single candle placed on the dressing table, its reflection in the mirror behind adding more light to the room.

The bedchamber showed only one occupant.

Juliet.

She lay alone in the centre of the bed, her fingers tightly clutching the bedclothes to her chest as she tossed and turned her head on the pillow.

Her eyes were firmly closed.

Sebastian stood very still beside the bed as he looked down at her. That Juliet was still sleeping, probably completely unaware that she had cried out, was obvious.

Her hair was a midnight curtain on the pillow beneath her. Her shoulders were bare, except for the thin straps of a white silk nightgown, and the revealed swell of her breasts was full and creamy.

Sebastian felt the fierceness of his expression soften as he took in how beautiful she looked. How fragile. How utterly—

'No!' Juliet suddenly cried out again, her eyes still closed but her features contorted. 'Do not! Please do not!' She sat up abruptly in the bed, her eyes wide and fearful as she stared straight ahead. 'Please!' she groaned achingly once again, before burying her face in her hands and beginning to sob.

Her distress was unbearable. Certainly more than Sebastian could bear anyway!

He quickly sat down on the side of the bed to reach out and draw her into his arms. 'You are safe, Juliet,' he assured her fiercely. 'There is no one here who shall harm you.' His arms tightened about her and he held her cradled against his chest.

Juliet froze as she became aware of bare flesh beneath her cheek.

Arms like steel bands were about her, holding her so tightly she could not break free.

Crestwood!

He was here. In her bedchamber. And if he was here it could mean only one thing!

She could not bear it. Not again. Never again could she lie unmoving, silent, while he—

No, Crestwood was *not* here!

He could not be here.

Crestwood was dead….

Then who was holding her so tightly?

The skin Juliet felt beneath her breast was smooth and deeply muscled, rather than pale and lined, with no sign of that flabbiness of flesh she had become used to in a man thirty years her senior, and the softness of hair that covered this chest and stomach was dark rather than coarsely grey.

Juliet raised her gaze almost fearfully to the firmness of jaw, and above chiselled lips, a long aquiline nose, high cheekbones, eyes the colour of honey, and dark hair shot through with gold in rumpled disarray onto the broadness of those wide shoulders.

'Lord St Claire!' she gasped in recognition, even as she attempted to pull away from him. His arms tightened to prevent her. 'You must release me, My Lord!' She breathed unevenly.

'Why must I?' His voice sounded dark and mesmerising in the silence of the bedchamber.

'Because—because—you should not be here, Sebastian,' Juliet whispered shakily. 'Why did you come?' She pulled back slightly to look into the brooding darkness of his face.

Such a handsome face. So sinfully, magnificently handsome…

Sebastian's breath caught in his throat as he looked into the deep green of Juliet's eyes. 'You do not remember, do you?'

Her throat moved convulsively as she swallowed. 'Remember what, My Lord?'

'You called me Sebastian just now,' he reminded her huskily. 'And I am here because you cried out loudly in your sleep and I heard you.' His eyes narrowed as he saw the sudden wariness in her expression before her gaze dropped away from his. 'Who did this to you, Juliet? Who has hurt you enough that you are plagued by nightmares that make you cry out even in sleep?'

Her face had been pale before, but now it grew even paler. 'I do not know what you mean, My Lord—'

'Do not lie to me, Juliet,' he warned harshly, his hands grasping the tops of her arms as she would have pulled away from him. 'Did Crestwood do this to you? Did he frighten you in some way? Is that why you—?' He broke off, his jaw tight.

She raised startled eyes. 'Why I what, Sebastian?'

She was so beautiful, so utterly desirable as Sebastian held her soft lushness in his arms, that he did not want to think of anything else—to see or feel anything but Juliet. At this moment she was all that mattered.

Juliet knew Sebastian was going to kiss her the moment she saw the hunger in his gaze as it dropped to the softness of her lips. Knew it. And craved it…

She had no memory of calling out in her sleep or of what she had said. But she could imagine what it might have been. She had been dreaming of Crestwood. Of how so often he had hurt her. How there had never been anyone there, ever, to stop him from hurting her.

Not so tonight. Tonight Sebastian St Claire was here. In her bedchamber. Not Lady Butler's, as Juliet had imagined. And Juliet *wanted* him to hold her. To kiss her. To caress her. To block out and destroy for ever all those painful memories of Crestwood that so tormented and disturbed her.

'Juliet…?' St Claire groaned as she raised her lips willingly to his.

Such a strong and sensuous mouth as it claimed hers. His shoulders were hard and muscled beneath Juliet's fingers as she clung to him. He felt so firm and smooth, and the muscles rippled beneath the warmth of his skin. Those muscles told her that no one would get past him, that if she wished it he would protect her.

Even from a ghost…

Her eyes closed and her lips parted willingly beneath the gentle sweep of his tongue. That tongue flicked lightly over her inner lip and the small ridge of her teeth before exploring further as it moved teasingly against hers.

Sebastian felt the leap of his body and the hardening of his thighs as Juliet's tongue began a sensuous duel with his. Moving enticingly forward, before retreating, tempting him deeper still. Her warm curves pressed against him were driving him wild with desire, and he could hold back no longer as he thrust fully inside her mouth, to possess her with his tongue.

It was not enough. It would never be enough with this particular woman. Sebastian wanted all of her. Wanted every part of her to be his!

Even as his mouth continued to claim hers, he slipped the thin ribbon straps from her shoulders and down her arms, moving slightly to let the material fall down to her waist before he pulled her back against him, crushing her bared breasts against his chest. Such softness. Such warm, tempting softness. A softness Sebastian had so longed to touch, to kiss.

He moved one of his hands to cup beneath one of those gentle slopes, testing the weight of her breast against his palm, able to feel if not see the pout of her nipple. Knowing even as he ran the pad of his thumb against that pouting softness and felt it harden that he had to have it in his mouth so that he might pleasure her with his tongue.

Juliet felt bereft when Sebastian pulled his mouth from hers to look down at her with eyes of dark honey-gold that seemed to be asking her a question.

'Do not stop, Sebastian,' she pleaded huskily. 'Please, do not stop!'

Whatever question had been in his eyes, she appeared to have answered it, and his gaze continued to hold hers as he lowered his head to place his caressing lips against the gentle curve between her neck and shoulder. Those lips were feather light as they moved lower. And then lower still.

Juliet gasped, her nails digging into his shoulders as she realised his destination. 'Sebastian…?'

'Let me, Juliet.' He raised his head to take one of her hands in his and kiss the palm, before placing it down on the bed beside her and then doing the same with its twin. 'I promise I will not hurt you.' His eyes looked intently into hers. 'I will never hurt you. Do you believe me?'

She moistened her lips with the tip of her tongue, her eyes wide and apprehensive as she reached to clutch and pull the material of her nightgown up over the bareness of her breasts. 'What—what are you going to do?'

'Nothing you will not enjoy, I promise.' He made no effort to touch her, to use physical coercion of any kind. 'Do you trust me not to hurt you, Juliet?'

Did she trust him? If she said no would he stop now? If she said no at some later point would he still stop?

Sebastian could read the thoughts racing through Juliet's mind. Could read them—and wanted to do physical harm to the man who had caused such apprehension inside her. Sebastian was convinced now that it had to have been Crestwood. Even Bancroft, suspicious and accusing, had agreed there had been no other man in Juliet's life this last twelve years but her husband.

Damn Bancroft! Now was not the time to think of either the man or any of the things he had said to Sebastian this morning.

His hands moved up to gently frame either side of Juliet's face.

'Tonight is for you, Juliet. Only for you.'

Much as it might kill him, Sebastian meant to give this woman pleasure—as much pleasure as she could take—whilst taking nothing for himself but the knowledge of that pleasure. Whatever will-power it took, whatever he suffered later, Sebastian was determined to replace that look of fear on Juliet's face, in the dark green depths of her eyes, with one of joy.

'Juliet…?' he prompted gruffly.

Juliet remained unmoving, not even breathing as she looked at him. Her gaze was seeking. Probing. Searching, no doubt, for any sign in his expression that said he lied. Sebastian's gaze remained fixed and steady on hers.

'Yes,' she finally breathed. 'Yes, Sebastian, I will trust you.' She allowed the material of her nightgown to fall softly down to her waist.

Chapter Eight

Sebastian moved back slightly, so that he might drink his fill of her. The candle-light added a glow to skin as smooth and white as unmarked snow, and the long length of her ebony hair cascaded silkily over her shoulders, down the length of her slender back and waist.

Her breasts were perfect. Not too large and not too small, but a perfect pouting swell, the nipples a deep rose-pink, the tips full and still aroused from his earlier caresses.

'Do not be afraid, Juliet, I am only going to kiss your breasts,' he assured her gently, when he saw the tension in her face and the sudden rigidity of her shoulders.

Juliet swallowed hard, not sure what he meant—until he lay across her thighs and she felt the warmth of his lips and mouth close about the tip of her breast. She gasped slightly as heat coursed through her body the moment she felt the rasp of his tongue against the sensitive nipple.

Her back curved instinctively as she arched into that caress, her eyes wide as she looked down at him. His eyelids were closed as he drew her more fully into his mouth, the slight drawing sending strange, pleasurable sensations through her body to centre between her thighs.

Juliet's arms moved up—one to curve about Sebastian's shoulders, the other to cradle the back of his head, her fingers entwining in the silky thickness of his hair as she held him to her.

His hand moved to cup and hold her other breast, the pad of his thumb moving caressingly across its tip. Juliet watched as the nipple swelled and hardened beneath his ministrations.

Until now her body had always been a mystery to her, something that Crestwood had taken whenever he pleased but which Juliet had tried not to even acknowledge existed in between those times. She had believed that her breasts were only there to suckle the child she had never had, but now, as her body trembled and warmed, as a low groan escaped her throat, she became aware of how sensuous, how pleasurable it was to have a man touch her in this way.

She made a protesting movement when Sebastian released that hardened tip, that movement turning to a moan of pleasure as he turned the attentions of his mouth and tongue to her other breast.

Juliet had no idea what was happening to her as the warmth increased between her thighs and she felt herself swelling there, aching as Sebastian continued to kiss and stroke her breasts, teeth gently biting as he rolled her other nipple between thumb and finger, squeezing slightly, never painfully, just enough to increase the intensity of her pleasure.

He was such a big man, so strong and muscled, and

yet he made love to her with a gentleness that totally belied that strength. That gentleness encouraged Juliet to start touching him tentatively in return.

Sebastian groaned low in his throat as he felt Juliet's hands moving, caressing, as she sought out the muscled contours of his back and chest. His thighs, already hard with arousal, tightened and throbbed as he drew her deeper into his mouth, laving that hardened tip even as he increased the pressure of his caresses on its twin.

She fell back against the pillows and Sebastian followed, only relinquishing her breast to kiss the flatness of her stomach, the erotic dip of her navel. Juliet gasped, but didn't protest as Sebastian dipped his tongue into that hollow, filling it as he longed to fill all of her.

Her nightgown was still draped across her hips and thighs, hindering any further exploration. 'May I?' he asked, and he moved up on his knees to look at her, taking the silent blinking of her eyes as a yes before he pulled back the bedclothes. Slowly he peeled her gown down over her hips and thighs, revealing the triangle of black curls between her legs. 'No.' Sebastian stilled her hand as she would have covered herself. 'You are very beautiful, Juliet. All of you,' he assured her huskily, as he bent to place a kiss on those silky curls. She smelled deliciously of spring flowers and woman.

Juliet was too shocked to speak, to protest any further as Sebastian threw her gown onto the floor beside the bed, leaving her completely uncovered. She kept her gaze fixed on his face rather than look down at her own nakedness.

His hair fell silkily onto his shoulders, his chest and the flatness of his stomach as naked as Juliet now was.

His eyes were dark as he looked down at her, his gaze moving slowly, caressingly across her breasts to the gentle curve of her own stomach, and then lower still, that gaze becoming hungry as it stilled on the darkness of the curls between her thighs.

Juliet felt very hot there, strangely damp, was sure that her curls were wet, too. She moved as if to stop him as he gently parted her legs. 'No—'

'Yes, Juliet,' Sebastian encouraged throatily, and he moved to kneel between her parted legs, holding her gaze with his as one of his hands moved to cup between her thighs just as he had the night before. Except tonight two of his fingers parted her silky curls to touch her more intimately.

Juliet's eyes widened as those two fingers squeezed slightly together, trapping something there and causing a fresh rush of heated wetness between her legs. 'What—?' she gasped.

'It is the centre of your pleasure, Juliet,' Sebastian reassured her, his gaze holding hers captive as his fingers began to stroke her. First softly and then gradually more firmly.

Again and again those fingers stroked, until Juliet felt so hot, such a burning ache, she wasn't sure if she wanted him to stop or continue. Her fingers dug into the mattress beside her as the pressure inside her built and grew to such a degree that she felt she might explode within.

'I am going to kiss you now,' Sebastian murmured.

But instead of moving upwards Sebastian moved down, towards her parted thighs. His fingers released her and his lips took their place, drawing her place of pleasure into his mouth as he rasped his tongue rhythmically against her.

Juliet had never known such intimacy existed. Part of her wanted to protest, but another part of her was eager to know this intimacy. And every other one too....

Again and again Sebastian stroked his tongue across the hard button nestled between Juliet's curls. Then he moved his fingers back to continue that caress and went lower still, his tongue lightly tracing her swollen folds before plunging moistly inside her.

The instinctive arching of her hips allowed him to plunge deeper still, in the same rhythm as his fingers continued to caress that hard button above. The dampness between her thighs increased, flooding her, and Sebastian sensed she was poised on the edge of release.

His mouth returned to that pulsing bud even as his fingers circled her swollen sheath, feeling her contract about his fingers as they entered her one slow inch at a time.

Juliet could feel the pleasure building, growing inside her. A hot ache she could not describe would soon break free and leave her shattered and broken in its wake.

'Sebastian—I cannot! I—' Her protest died in her throat as he moved up to claim her mouth fiercely with his, even as his fingers continued to move into and then out of her, his thumb caressing that tiny nub above with the same slow and sensuous rhythm.

His tongue plunged into her mouth at the same time as his fingers claimed her below, this dual assault on her senses driving her into a frenzy of need as her hips moved up to meet those thrusts.

The release, when it came, was like nothing Juliet had ever dreamed of—beginning between her thighs in a hot burst, before spreading outwards to claim every part of her as she inwardly convulsed in a continuous outpouring of unimagined pleasure until she finally lay spent beneath him.

No one had ever told Juliet—she had never dreamt—would never have guessed… She had never known that such pleasure as this existed!

It was beyond description. Beyond anything she could have imagined.

Sebastian broke the kiss as he gently slid his fingers from inside her, cradling Juliet in his arms, resting his head against her temple as her body continued to quiver and spasm in little aftershocks of pleasure.

Her release had been so beautiful, so complete, that the unfulfilled ache of Sebastian's own body did not signify. All that mattered at this moment was Juliet. He wanted only to give her pleasure, to feel her pleasure. His own arousal was unimportant.

Finally she stirred slightly in his arms. 'You did not— You have not—'

'Neither will I.' Sebastian moved up on his elbow to look down searchingly into her flushed and beautiful face. 'Have you never known that pleasure before?'

The blush in her cheeks deepened. 'Never,' she breathed huskily.

What sort of man had Crestwood been? Sebastian wondered angrily. What sort of man could even *look* at Juliet and not want to give her pleasure time and time again?

'Have you never discovered these pleasures for yourself, Juliet?' he asked, with caution for her obvious shyness with intimacy. 'Are you not familiar with your own body?' he added as she looked confused.

'I have arms, legs—and—other parts of my body, like any other woman.' She still looked puzzled.

'But when bathing or dressing have you never… explored your own body? Touched your intimate places? Learnt of the pleasure they might give you?' Sebastian persisted.

Juliet looked shocked by the suggestion. 'Of course I have not!'

Sebastian gave a slight shake of his head. Juliet was thirty years old, had been married for over ten of those years; it was unbelievable to think that he was the first to ever give her pleasure.

'Give me your hand…' He held his own hand out to her, palm upwards.

'Why?' She eyed him suspiciously.

'Please?'

She moved her hand up reluctantly and placed it in his, gasping as she realised his intent when he took it and guided it down between her thighs. 'Sebastian…!'

'I only want to show you, Juliet, nothing more,' he encouraged huskily as she would have wrenched her hand away. 'Just feel. Touch…'

Juliet had never done anything so shameless. Had never even thought of—

She was not just damp between her legs, but wet. So very wet. The folds of her sheath still felt swollen and sensitive. It was such a strange…

She gave a start as Sebastian guided her fingers to that nub hidden amongst her curls. It felt hard still, and the caress of her fingers caused another quake of pleasure inside her.

She looked up at him in wonder. 'Are my breasts still as sensitive too…?'

'Feel,' he said gruffly, once again leaning on his elbow as Juliet raised her hands to cup her breasts, before running a fingertip lightly across one nipple.

Again her thighs contracted hotly. 'I had no idea…' she gasped.

Sebastian smiled wickedly. 'Tonight is for you, Juliet. Only for you.'

Her hands fell back to her sides, her eyes deep, dark pools of green as she stared back at him. 'I still do not understand why you have not taken your own pleasure.'

His smile was gentle as he smoothed a dark curl from the dampness of her brow. 'The only thing I require tonight is pleasuring you,' he assured her.

Juliet really did not understand. What she had just felt, experienced when Sebastian made love to her, was unlike anything she could ever have imagined. But she knew well enough a man's need for release. And Sebastian had not attained the release that was all Crestwood, it seemed, had ever wanted or taken from her.

Juliet could see by the long length of arousal so clearly outlined beneath Sebastian's pantaloons that he wanted to take that from her, too. She swallowed hard. 'I do not mind if you wish to—to take your own release now.'

A frown darkened his brow. 'Is that what Crestwood

did to you? Took his own pleasure while giving you nothing in return?'

Her gaze slid away from his. 'Is that not what all men do?'

'Did I?' he pointed out.

She moistened dry lips. 'No, but—I know that you want to.' She glanced down at that telling bulge in his pantaloons, before looking up at him with a quick frown.

Sebastian shook his head. 'What I want and what I do are two entirely different things. I told you, Juliet, tonight is for you.' He reached down to pull the bedcovers up and over the two of them. 'Sleep now,' he murmured. 'And when you wake I intend giving you pleasure all over again.'

'A woman can—can do that twice in one night?' she gasped.

He smiled at her surprise. 'If the man knows what he is doing, as many times as she wants or needs.'

'Is that not a little unfair, when a man can only do it the once?'

She really was an innocent, Sebastian realised with dawning wonder. 'Some men can find release several times in one night,' he revealed.

Her eyes widened. 'Can you?'

'With the right woman, yes.' He stroked light fingers down one of her burning cheeks. 'I suspect that with you I might manage to make love all night long without becoming tired or satiated.'

'And yet just now you did not?'

The ache in Sebastian's thighs was becoming more painful by the second with all this talk of his own release. 'Do you know how to give a man pleasure in the way I did you?'

She moistened dry lips. 'There is a—a way to do that?'

Once again Sebastian decided that if Crestwood were alive then he would have no choice but to kill him!

Not that Crestwood was unique in his complete disregard for his wife's pleasure during lovemaking. There would not be as many married women of the ton ready to take a lover if their husbands were satisfying them in their marriage bed!

But Sebastian's father, the late Duke of Stourbridge, had been at great pains to impress upon all three of his sons that when a man took a woman to bed, be she liaison or wife, she was deserving of receiving *all* of his attention—to her pleasure, as well as his own. A man did not selfishly take his pleasure without giving it in return.

Juliet's innocence concerning intimacy, her lack of knowledge of lovemaking, were entirely due, Sebastian now realised, to the fact that her husband had been one of those selfish men who simply took his own pleasure from the woman spread beneath him—from Juliet!—whilst withholding that same pleasure from her.

Yet, at the same time as he wanted to kill Crestwood, Sebastian also knew that he wanted to thank him—for in effect Crestwood's lack of care and attention to Juliet's needs made Sebastian her first real lover. The thought of introducing her, initiating her, into all the pleasures to be had between a man and a woman, was more erotic than anything Sebastian had ever known.

'There is a way.' He nodded. 'But not tonight, Juliet. Tonight, and all of tomorrow too, are only for you.'

'We cannot just spend the day in my bedchamber, Sebastian!' She looked scandalised at the thought.

'Then we shall have to see how inventive we can be at finding other places and opportunities for your pleasure, shall we not?' Sebastian settled down on the pillows and gathered Juliet to his side, so that she rested her head upon his shoulder, before he turned to blow out the candle.

'No!' Juliet cried sharply as she realised his intent. 'I prefer to always leave one candle alight in my bedchamber,' she explained shakily, when Sebastian looked a question at her.

'Why?'

Why? Because Crestwood had always blown out the candle as soon as he entered her bedchamber with the intention of taking his pleasure! Because in the dark she had not seen, only felt, what he was doing to her! Because at night even now, in the dark of her bedchamber, she would still lie waiting, dreading Crestwood's climbing into her bed and painfully taking her...

'The moon is bright tonight, Juliet. Will that not suffice?' Sebastian asked.

'I wish the candle to remain alight,' she repeated stubbornly, avoiding that searching whisky-coloured gaze as he continued to look down at her.

'Juliet, would you care to talk about—?'

'No!' Again she spoke sharply, trembling slightly just at the thought of reliving any of her marriage after experiencing something so wonderful as Sebastian's lovemaking. 'I wish to sleep now, Sebastian. Only to sleep.' She closed her eyes, effectively shutting him out.

Sebastian lay awake long after he knew by the even tenor of her breathing that Juliet was asleep.

She was a woman of almost one and thirty, and must have known of all the gossip and speculation she would have to face in agreeing to come here to Banford Park. Yet she had met that controversy with all the grace and confidence of the countess she undoubtedly was. But here, in the privacy of her bedchamber, she became the young and naïve eighteen-year-old girl she must have been when Crestwood had married her, twelve years ago.

There were many more ways, Sebastian realised, for a man to abuse a woman than with his fists....

'You wish us to go boating on the lake?' Juliet was wide-eyed as she repeated Sebastian's suggestion as to what they might do for the rest of the morning. The rest of the morning because it was now almost noon...

Juliet had been slightly disorientated when she'd awoken early that morning to find Sebastian St Claire in bed beside her. Even more disconcerting had been the memory of waking in the night and finding herself once more aroused by the feel Sebastian's lips and hands upon her body as he made love to her for a second time. As she found pleasure and release for a second time!

Sebastian had not apologised to her for his conversation with Dolly, after all, but last night he had done so much more for her than that. Last night, for the very first time, Juliet had known and appreciated fully what it was to be a woman. To enjoy intimacy with a man.

Sebastian had been lying on his stomach beside her, still sleeping, when she'd awoken later, and Juliet had indulged herself for a few minutes by just looking at him. That dark hair shot through with gold had been tousled on the pillow, lashes of the same colour resting against high cheekbones. His was a strong face rather than hard, his features chiselled but not unrelenting, the mocking curve of his mouth softened in sleep. The bareness of his shoulders were firm and muscled, his back long and sensual, almost begging to be touched. A temptation Juliet had not been able to resist as she ran her fingertips lightly over that golden flesh.

Yesterday, after talking with Dolly Bancroft, Juliet had wondered how it would feel to take a lover. Now she knew. It was truly wonderful. Liberating, in fact. As Juliet had quickly discovered when her caresses had become bolder still.

Sebastian's lids had risen over eyes the colour of warm honey, and the smile he'd given her had been slow and seductive. 'Again…?'

'Again…' Juliet had groaned happily, past all pretence where Sebastian was concerned; he knew her body far better than she did, so how could she possibly feel any lingering shyness with him?

They had spent another enjoyable hour in bed together before Juliet had reminded Sebastian that her maid would be arriving shortly to bring her breakfast and then help her to dress. Muttering about only having to undress her again once he returned, Sebastian had kissed her briefly on the lips before climbing smilingly out of bed and crossing the room, to depart out onto the balcony to his own bedchamber.

Only just in time as Helena had entered, after the

briefest of knocks, with Juliet's breakfast tray. Obviously her cousin had not for a moment expected that Juliet might not be alone in her bedchamber!

Spending the night in bed with Sebastian St Claire, having been introduced by him to the wonders of sensual pleasure, becoming his lover, was not something Juliet felt able to confide in her cousin as yet. It was something to be savoured inside herself for now. A secret for Juliet alone to enjoy.

Just as she had enjoyed Sebastian's return to her bedchamber only minutes after Helena had departed, when, as he had said he would, Sebastian had proceeded to undress her once again, before undressing himself!

Now, an hour later, Sebastian was suggesting they escape from the company of the other guests by going for that row on the lake he had proposed once before.

Sebastian nodded. 'The house is being readied for the ball this evening. I cannot abide all the fuss and bother that precedes such events,' he admitted ruefully as he continued pulling his black Hessians on over black pantaloons. He was already wearing his pale blue waistcoat over snowy white linen and a perfectly tied cravat. His dark blue superfine was lying across the bedroom chair, where he had thrown it an hour or so ago, after returning to the bedchamber to climb back into bed with Juliet.

He had very much enjoyed making love to Juliet these last twelve hours, and had found pleasure in that look of surprise that entered her eyes, and her little gasps, as her release claimed her. As if she still did not quite believe what was happening to her.

Juliet laughed softly as she restyled her hair in front of the mirror. 'All men are the same, it seems.'

Sebastian straightened swiftly. 'I sincerely hope you no longer believe that to be true.'

Juliet glanced at his reflection in the mirror, her face paling slightly as she looked away from the intensity of his gaze. 'I meant only in regard to fuss and bother, of course.'

'Of course.' Sebastian inclined his head as he stood up to cross the room and stand behind her.

Juliet was looking very lovely, in a rose-pink gown that perfectly complemented the darkness of her hair and the pearly lustre of her skin. There was also an added glow about her this morning: her eyes were deeply green, there was a blush to her cheeks, and her lips were slightly swollen from the intensity of the numerous kisses they had shared.

'I meant no offence, Sebastian.' Her gaze was slightly anxious as she looked up at him in the mirror.

'I am not about to beat you even if you did,' he snapped, as he easily guessed the reason for her anxiety. 'Not all men are like your husband, Juliet!' he rasped.

She stiffened, that becoming blush quickly fading from her cheeks. 'I do not recall ever saying that my husband beat me!'

Sebastian met her gaze challengingly. 'Did he?'

She turned away. 'It is far too lovely a morning to discuss Crestwood.'

'You never wish to discuss him, Juliet. Why is that?'

She stood up abruptly to move away from him, her back towards him as she collected her gloves.

'My husband has nothing to do with our own… liaison.'

'Liaison?' Sebastian repeated harshly. 'Is that what I am to you?'

'Of course.' She was once again the proud and slightly distant Countess of Crestwood—rather than Juliet, the woman Sebastian had made love to so thoroughly the night before and then again this morning. 'What else could we ever be to each other?' she added with cool dismissal. 'No doubt we will enjoy each other's company for the time we are here. Then you will return to your life and I will return to mine.'

Sebastian looked at her searchingly for several long seconds, knowing by the firm set of Juliet's mouth and slightly raised chin that she would not be moved on the subject of Crestwood.

Damn the man, anyway, for not appreciating such a woman as Juliet when he'd had her!

Sebastian gave a rueful shake of his head. 'I do believe you are trying to bring about an argument between us, Juliet,' he chided.

'You are entitled to your opinion,' she accepted haughtily.

Once again Sebastian felt the inclination to put Juliet over his knee and spank her—but in such a way that she would enjoy the punishment. No doubt Juliet would be as surprised by that as she had been by all their lovemaking!

'I am ready to leave, if you are?' In truth, Juliet did not at all wish to argue with Sebastian. She much preferred it when he was making love to her.

He straightened to give her a courtly bow. 'I am completely at your service, ma'am.' The teasing glitter in those whisky-coloured eyes told her which service he referred to.

Juliet felt the colour warm her cheeks. 'You are incorrigible, Sebastian!'

'So I have oft been told!' He chuckled softly, before opening the door for Juliet to precede him from the bedchamber.

Juliet kept her gaze lowered as she swept past him and out into the hallway, relieved that there was no one about to see the two of them leaving her bedchamber together.

Sebastian's words had reminded her all too forcibly that he was considered a charming libertine by the rest of the ton. The ladies in particular.

The recollection confirmed Juliet's claim earlier that their own relationship was nothing more than a diversion for Sebastian St Claire in a long career of such diversions. It would be extremely foolish on her part to allow herself to feel any more towards him than a curiosity to learn more of the physical pleasure he had already shown her.

Extremely foolish…

Chapter Nine

'There you are, St Claire!'

Sebastian stiffened as he and Juliet reached the bottom of the wide staircase to turn and see their host approaching them from the direction of his study.

'And Lady Boyd, also.' William Bancroft beamed at Juliet warmly as she rose from her curtsey. 'I hope you do not mind if I take Lord St Claire from you for a few minutes, my dear? There is something of import I wish to discuss with him. And I do believe my wife has been looking for you.'

Sebastian refused to release his hold upon Juliet's elbow when he felt her attempt to move away. Instead he kept his steely gaze fixed on the Earl as he answered the other man. 'Can it not wait until later, Bancroft? I was about to show Lady Boyd the delights of boating on the lake.'

Lord Bancroft met the challenge of Sebastian's gaze. 'A pastime not to be rushed, to be sure. Perhaps, as it is so close to luncheon, *you* could wait until later?'

Sebastian's mouth tightened. 'I—'

'But of course we can wait,' Juliet assured the older man, very much aware of Sebastian's tension as he stood so close beside her. 'Lady Bancroft is looking for me, you said…?'

The Earl smiled easily. 'Something to do with the flowers for this evening, I believe.'

'Of course.' Juliet smiled warmly. 'We can easily arrange our outing for another time, Lord St Claire.' She lowered her own gaze as saw Sebastian's eyes blaze with displeasure as she extricated herself from his grasp. 'I will leave you two gentlemen to talk.' She excused herself, before moving away with the intention of going in search of their hostess.

Perhaps this interruption to spending yet more time alone with Sebastian was for the best, Juliet consoled herself as she made her way to the ballroom. Last night had been a revelation to her, but nevertheless it would not do to become dependent upon such intimacy.

It would not do at all….

'I am in no mood for your schemes and manipulations this morning, Bancroft.' Sebastian made no effort to keep the distaste from his tone as he closely watched Juliet's departure from his side. She had taken the cancellation of their outing far too easily for his liking.

The older man dropped his pose of congenial host. 'No schemes or manipulations this time, St Claire, but facts,' he announced curtly.

'Facts!' Sebastian exclaimed as he gave the other man his full attention. 'What do you have this time,

Bancroft? A novel printed in French has been found in Juliet's bedroom, and you believe it may be her code book? That is how it works, is it not? Code books? Secret messages? Or perhaps you have discovered something else you believe brands her as guilty of the crimes you related to me yesterday—?'

'If you will calm down, St Claire, and come with me to my study, then I will show you what we have found.' The earl cut across his tirade.

'*We?*'

'Lord Grayson is awaiting us in my study.'

Sebastian fixed the other man with a steely glare. 'Did I not tell you both to leave this to me? Was that not our agreement?'

Bancroft shrugged. 'Events have overtaken us, I am afraid.'

As he had the day before, Sebastian felt that cold shiver of apprehension down the length of his spine. He had made love to Juliet last night, not once but many times, and the predominant emotion he had sensed in her was vulnerability. There had been wonder at the pleasures he had introduced her to, but also vulnerability at allowing him so close to her, especially in a physical way. She was innocent of the accusations against her. He was sure of it.

So what did Bancroft have on Juliet that made a nonsense of Sebastian's own estimation of her character?

'You are very quiet this afternoon, My Lord.' Juliet eyed Sebastian teasingly as he sat opposite her, capably handling the oars of the small boat they had commandeered for their delayed row on the huge lake in the gardens of Banford Park. 'Perhaps you would rather we had not come boating, after all?'

He frowned darkly. 'Was I not the one to seek you out after luncheon and suggest we resume our plans?'

Yes, he had. But Sebastian's mood since they had strolled outside and procured one of the row-boats had been taciturn, to say the least. 'Did Lord Bancroft have bad news to relate this morning?' she enquired.

Some would call it that, Sebastian acknowledged grimly. Bancroft and Gray did, at least. Sebastian chose to remain unconvinced.

Apparently the papers on top of Bancroft's desk were not in the same order in which he had left them. And the contents of the drawers, the other man believed, had been gone through. The top drawer, although it showed no signs of having been broken into, was nevertheless unlocked, and Bancroft swore that he always locked that particular drawer whenever he left his study.

Someone—and Bancroft and Gray obviously believed it to be Juliet—had rifled through the papers on and in the Earl's desk some time since the three of them had talked together there yesterday morning, which was the last time Bancroft had been in his study.

Sebastian was more inclined to believe the Earl had simply forgotten to lock the drawer, and that one of the maids had disturbed the papers whilst dusting.

He had certainly left the Earl, and Gray, in no doubt that *he* would need a lot more evidence than that with which to accuse Juliet!

Sebastian forced himself to relax now as he smiled

across at her. 'It was merely a trivial estate matter he wished to discuss with me,' he dismissed easily.

Juliet looked so beautiful this afternoon. She was still wearing the high-waisted and short-sleeved rose-coloured gown that suited her dark hair so perfectly. She also wore white gloves, and tilted a rose-coloured parasol above her head, to keep the heat of the sun's rays from burning the pale magnolia of her skin. The revealing swell of her breasts above the low neckline of her gown was enough to make Sebastian's thighs harden in arousal.

'Shall we go onto the island, do you think?' he suggested gruffly.

Juliet felt her cheeks warm as she heard that huskiness in Sebastian's tone. Avoiding looking at the seductive honey of his eyes, she instead turned to look at the island in the middle of the lake. It was rather a large island, with a grove of tall fir trees at its centre. A grove of fir trees that would no doubt shield them from all but the most curious of eyes. A grove of fir trees into which, whilst it was perfectly proper for them to be boating on the lake together, it would be considered totally improper for them to be seen disappearing!

'The ladies are all writing letters or gossiping together in the drawing room this afternoon, and the gentlemen have decided to ride into the village,' Sebastian remarked softly.

Juliet's cheeks felt decidedly hot as she realised he had read her thoughts. 'In that case, I believe I might like to explore the island…'

'It is not the island that I wish you to explore, Juliet,'

he murmured as he rowed in the direction of the island's mooring.

She gave him a look of rebuke. 'You should not tease me, Sebastian.'

'But you look so lovely when you blush!' He moved to tie the small boat to the moorings, before climbing out onto the small wooden quay and turning to hold out his hand to her.

Juliet was well aware of what she was agreeing to if she took the hand Sebastian offered and went with him into the privacy of the trees. She was both aware and elated at the thought of yet more pleasure as Sebastian kissed and caressed her. In fact, her body had begun to tingle just at the thought of the pleasures he had already shown her.

'Nevertheless…' She reached up and placed her hand in his before standing. 'It is still unkind of you to mock me in this way.'

'I would never do that, Juliet,' Sebastian assured her seriously, and he placed her gloved hand firmly in the crook of his arm before turning to march towards the woods.

'Are you in hurry, My Lord?' Juliet gasped, as she almost had to run to keep pace with his much longer strides.

Sebastian arched dark brows as he slowed his pace. 'Now it is you who is mocking me, My Lady.'

'I would never do that, Sebastian,' she said teasingly, repeating his own remark.

Sebastian returned her smile and determinedly shook off the last remaining feelings of distaste from his conversation before luncheon with Bancroft and Gray. It was a beautiful day. The sun was shining down upon them warmly. The birds were singing gaily in the trees above. And he had Juliet at his side. Juliet, whose beautiful lushness was begging to be made love to.

It was only when they reached the privacy of the grove of fir trees that Sebastian realised he had come ill prepared for what he now had in mind. Ideally he should have thought to bring a blanket with him, that he could spread upon the ground before laying a naked Juliet down upon it. But no one had ever accused him of being slow when it came to improvisation!

He began to shrug out of his perfectly tailored jacket. His valet would no doubt have a fit when Sebastian returned it to him later today, covered in grass stains, but Laurent's sensibilities were the least of Sebastian's concerns at the moment.

'It will be ruined.' Juliet hesitated about accepting Sebastian's invitation to sit down as he spread the jacket on the grass at her feet.

Sebastian lowered himself elegantly onto the garment before holding his hand up to her invitingly. 'We will only talk, if that is what you would prefer…' he offered, when she still hesitated to join him.

Juliet had no idea what she wanted to do. Well…she *did* know—it was only that even the idea of it now seemed perfectly shameless out here in broad daylight!

Not that she was in the least shy of Sebastian seeing her nakedness any more. After the intimacies they'd already shared how could she possibly be? It was just that it seemed so much more scandalous here in the sunshine, where anyone might chance upon them.

Oh, Juliet knew that the majority of the other house guests were engaged in the activities Sebastian had already described, but what if one or several of them decided that boating on the lake seemed a good idea, too? There would be the most horrendous scandal if she and Sebastian were caught in such a compromising position.

And the Black Widow feared the idea of yet more scandal, did she?

'What shall we talk about?' she asked, as she took Sebastian's hand before lowering herself gracefully down beside him. Shameless. She had become shameless in the matter of hours that had passed since Sebastian had come to her bedchamber the night before.

He shrugged broad shoulders beneath the full sleeves of his white shirt. 'Your childhood, perhaps? Was it happy?'

'Very.' She gave a wistful sigh as she arranged the skirt of her gown decorously about her legs. 'My parents were everything that is good and kind.'

'Mine also.' He nodded. 'I was sixteen when they both died in a carriage accident,' he added, which surprised even himself. He never talked to anyone of the loss he had felt when his beloved parents had died.

'My own parents had also both died by the time I was eighteen.'

Sebastian at once looked concerned. 'I had not realised…' He reached out to clasp both her tightly clenched hands in his. 'You still miss them?'

'Always. You?'

'Always,' Sebastian echoed sincerely. Not that Hawk had not been a capital guardian to him, and Lucian a fine example for any fellow to emulate—and his young sister Arabella was someone for them all to love and spoil. But his parents' marriage had been a love-match. The sort of love that had encompassed all four of their children, too, once they were born. The only consolation any of those four children had had after the accident, almost twelve years ago, had been that their twenty-five-year marriage had been a happy one to the very end.

Sebastian rarely spoke of their deaths to anyone. Of how, at the tender age of sixteen, their loss had devastated him. That he had now revealed as much to Juliet was more than a little unsettling for a man who preferred that people see him only as a charming libertine.

'Your marriage was less happy than your childhood?' he probed delicately.

Juliet instantly stiffened. 'I would rather not speak of that.'

'Was Crestwood such a monster, then?' Sebastian pressed.

'I have said I will not speak of it.' Her eyes were dark at she looked up at him reproachfully.

'No, you said you would not speak of your marriage, not of Crestwood.' Sebastian realised he was angry. So much so that he was deliberately baiting Juliet. Hurting her. And he had no idea why.

Because Juliet's gentleness, her own loss, had encouraged him to speak of his parents, perhaps?

No, the more likely cause was Bancroft's renewed accusations of her this morning!

'The two are irrevocably connected,' Juliet answered him woodenly.

'You did not love Crestwood?'

'I did not love him,' she admitted.

'Perhaps you even hated him?'

Her eyes glittered brightly green. 'Hate is a destructive emotion for the person who feels it.'

Which did not answer Sebastian's question! 'Juliet, I already know from your surprised response to our lovemaking last night and this morning that your marriage was not a happy one—'

'Sebastian, if you continue with this present conversation then you will leave me with no choice but to ask you to return me to the house forthwith!'

Juliet's tension was a palpable thing.

Damn Bancroft. Damn Gray. Damn Dolly, too. To hell with all of them for their distrust of a woman who seemed, to Sebastian, to have already suffered enough unhappiness in her life.

'I apologise, Juliet.' He spoke stiffly. 'I had no right to probe into the privacy of your marriage.'

Now Juliet was the one to feel guilt. Against everything she had hitherto believed, Sebastian had become her lover. As such, it was only natural that he should feel curiosity about her marriage to Crestwood. Especially as she had demonstrated only too clearly her complete inexperience of the type of lovemaking Sebastian had already shown her!

She drew in a deep breath. 'It is I who should apologise, Sebastian. If anyone has the right to ask these things then it must be you. It is only—my marriage was an arranged one. My parents believed, I am sure, that they were making a good choice for me. After all, Crestwood was an earl. A war hero and an admiral.' She gave a weary sigh. 'He was also thirty years my senior. Set in his ways. His beliefs.'

The first two had not been an insurmountable hindrance to their marriage being a happy one. The third, however—his belief that a wife was but another chattel, to be used as Crestwood wished—most certainly had!

Sebastian reached out gently to touch the pale curve of her cheek. 'One of those beliefs being that he did not approve of a woman enjoying the marriage bed?' As so many men of their class did not, Sebastian acknowledged ruefully; a mistress was for pleasure, a wife to provide necessary heirs. Which was the reason so many of the female married members of the ton took a lover for themselves once an heir had been secured.

Juliet's eyes widened. 'This is not a fitting conversation—nor a—a comfortable one, Sebastian!'

No, it was not, Sebastian realised. Neither was it conducive to the seduction which he had intended this afternoon!

'Of course you are perfectly correct, my dear Juliet,' he drawled, and he lay back upon his coat to look up at her. 'Discussing a woman's husband while intending to make love to her yourself is definitely bad form!' He pulled her gently down to lie beside him, before turning on his side so that he could look down into her face. The sun shone down on the dark ebony of her curls, adding a sparkle to her deep green eyes and a golden hue to the paleness of her cheeks. 'You really are the most beautiful women that I ever beheld,' he murmured appreciatively.

Her perfect bow of a mouth curved into a wistful

smile. 'You have no further need to spout flowery compliments in order to win me over, Sebastian, when I am so obviously already won.'

'Are you?' he murmured throatily. 'Are you really won, Juliet? Or do I need to make greater efforts in order to capture you completely?'

He was suddenly very close. So close that Juliet could feel the lean length of his warm body pressed against her side. Feel the warmth of his breath against her cheek. See the darker brown flecks in the honeygold of his eyes as he gazed down at her so heatedly.

She moistened suddenly dry lips. 'Greater efforts, My Lord?' she echoed uncertainly.

'There is more, Juliet,' he revealed. 'So very, very much more,' he promised, as he lowered his head and his lips claimed hers.

Juliet's lips parted automatically beneath Sebastian's to deepen the kiss, even as her arms moved up to allow her fingers to become entangled in the dark thickness of his hair. She returned his kiss hungrily, fiercely. As if even a few hours of abstinence from their lovemaking had been too long.

It *had* been too long. Far, far too long without the feel of Sebastian's lips and hands upon her body. Sensations no longer denied her as Sebastian quickly unbuttoned her gown to peel it from her and throw it carelessly to one side before turning back to her. His eyes darkened as he gazed down at the full orbs of her breasts, so clearly visible to him through the sheer material of her chemise.

Juliet watched him as he cupped, encircled both those

breasts with his hands, before lowering his head to flick the moist tip of his tongue across the already aroused nipples. Not just her nipples were aroused, Juliet acknowledged with a groan, as Sebastian moved one of his hands to stroke his fingers over that hardened nub between her thighs.

Sebastian was constantly overwhelmed, stunned by how Juliet responded so easily, so totally without inhibition, to his every slightest touch. He had never known another woman as responsive as Juliet. Never had a woman opened to him so readily that he could already feel how wet she was beneath those dark curls.

'Sebastian…'

She was shaking beneath him, trembling like an aspen at his ministrations…

'Sebastian…'

His eyes were dark and slightly unfocused as he raised his head at her second, more insistent calling of his name. 'Yes, Juliet?'

Her smile was almost shy. 'You said you would show me today how I might…touch *you*…?'

Sebastian's heart stopped beating as he sat up to look down at her. Only to resume pounding again seconds later, but quicker, more erratically than it had been before, as the full import of her words took flight in his mind.

Juliet looked the siren as she gazed steadily up at him with those cat-like green eyes. Several of her curls had fallen down wantonly onto the bareness of her shoulders. The dampened material of her chemise clung to the twin orbs of her breasts, and the nipples were revealed perfectly as they jutted forward temptingly.

Even as the darkness of Sebastian's gaze returned to the flushed beauty of Juliet's face the tiny tip of her pink tongue flicked moistly across those full and sensuous lips that she was now suggesting she pleasure him with.

A siren.

And a temptress.

Did Sebastian have enough control at this moment to tutor her in the delicate art of pleasuring him? Could he hold long enough, if she were to touch him so intimately, not to give in and release like a callow boy at the first touch of her lips, and in doing so probably frighten her half to death?

No—those were not the questions he should be asking himself! The question was, could Sebastian live for another moment *without* the feel of those lips and tongue around his increasingly aroused flesh?

No, he could not!

'May I?' Juliet prompted softly as she reached for the buttons on his pantaloons.

'Yes.' Sebastian's voice was as strained as the pulsating hardness that stretched the material tautly across his thighs as he lay back upon his jacket.

'You will be…patient with my lack of finesse?' she murmured as she slowly unfastened those eight buttons with fingers that shook slightly.

In truth, it was Juliet's innocence about such intimacy, her naïveté concerning all physical pleasure, that increased Sebastian's own arousal and made his thighs throb so painfully.

His gaze became riveted on her face as she slowly folded back the material at his waist to expose him fully to her wide-eyed gaze. He groaned achingly as she once again flicked her tongue across her bottom lip, his hands clenching at his sides as he imagined how it would feel to have that hot, wet rasp moving across his heated flesh.

He dropped his head weakly back on his jacket as he felt Juliet's fingers run inquisitively over the ever increasing tautness of his flesh. If he should look down and see those tiny fingers touching him, caressing him, then Sebastian knew he really would be unable to prevent himself from climaxing. So instead he lay back, to stare up at the blue of the sky as he gritted his teeth and suffered the torture of her caressing hands.

Dear God, he needed to— He wanted to— He had to—

'Hallooo, on the island!'

Juliet drew back in shock as the calling voice acted on her in the same chilling way as having a bucket of cold water thrown over her would have done.

Despite what Sebastian had said earlier, concerning their fellow guests being busy with their own pursuits, someone was approaching the island!

Someone who at any moment was going to catch Sebastian and Juliet in a very compromising position indeed....

Chapter Ten

❦

'What the hell do you want, Gray?' Sebastian glared at the other man as the two of them stood together on the island's small wooden quay, where Gray's boat was now also tied.

Sebastian was still without his jacket, but he had at least straightened and refastened his clothing before leaving the grove of trees, in order that he might confront the other man whilst giving Juliet the necessary time to adjust her own appearance. The evidence of Sebastian's arousal, still straining against his pantaloons as proof of their interrupted activity, was another matter entirely, however!

Grayson frowned darkly. 'To save you from making a catastrophic error in judgement, perhaps?' he clipped disapprovingly.

'Explain yourself,' Sebastian barked.

'Your own and the Countess's non-appearance most of this morning has already been cause for speculation by several of the other guests.' Gray grimaced. 'The fact that the two of you disappeared together immediately after lunch has also been remarked upon.'

'So?'

The other man sighed. 'Seb, you are only supposed to charm the truth out of the woman—not make yourself a subject for idle gossip.'

'Indeed?' Sebastian rasped. 'I was given the impression when the three of us spoke together yesterday that my methods were to be my own.'

Gray shot a concerned glance towards the grove of trees before turning back to Sebastian. 'Seb, do you not see that the Countess is the worst possible woman for you to fall in love with?' he muttered in concern.

'I am not falling in love with her, damn it!' Dark eyes glittered dangerously at the mere suggestion that Sebastian's emotions were becoming engaged. The Countess, like all his previous women, was a diversion—nothing more. She meant no more to him than any of the other numerous women he had made love to over the years.

Gray's gaze became searching. 'I believed this to be a good plan when Bancroft first suggested it, but now— now I fear for you, Seb.'

'I have no idea why you should do so.'

'Because I know you, Seb. I am well aware of the St Claire sense of honour and pride. And beneath the façade of charming rake you choose to present to the rest of the ton, it burns as strongly inside you as it does inside your siblings.'

'You do not know me as well as you think you do, Gray—otherwise you would never have colluded with Bancroft in suggesting I play Lady Boyd false,' he stated. 'Do not concern yourself. You will have your proof of the lady's innocence before I am done,' he added scornfully as the other man paled. 'And, once you do, I suggest that you take yourself out of my sight for the foreseeable future!'

Gray winced. 'Seb—'

'Why did you come here, Gray?' Sebastian cut in. 'What was so urgent that you felt the need to interrupt my efforts to charm Lady Boyd?' Although, in truth, Sebastian was unsure as to who had been seducing whom, when it was *his* loins that still throbbed and ached from the need for release…

The other man looked at him searchingly for several long seconds before sighing deeply. 'I cannot tell you how much I regret that this business appears to have damaged our friendship.'

'No doubt I will overcome my distaste for your company at some future date, Gray,' Sebastian said wearily. 'For now, I think it best if we just concentrate on the matter in hand—do you not agree?' The challenge in his gaze left the other man with no other option.

Gray gave a reluctant nod. 'I came in search of you because another guest has arrived, and has been persuaded to stay overnight at least—so that he might attend the ball this evening. I thought, as he is related to you, that you might wish to be amongst the first to greet him.'

Sebastian gave him a scathing glance. 'You also thought it a good excuse to try and save me from myself, did you not?' A member of Sebastian's own family was the last thing he needed to add to a situation that was already fraught with tension!

'I told you, I am concerned for you—'

'And I have assured you there is no reason for your concern. Lady Boyd means no more to me than any of the other women I have seduced and bedded these last ten years,' Sebastian growled.

Juliet, her appearance now returned to some semblance of order, was about to leave the protection of the trees and join the two men on the quay when she heard Sebastian's last remark.

His last painful remark!

Oh, it wasn't painful because she had thought Sebastian genuinely cared for her—neither of them had admitted to feeling any emotion for the other apart from insidious desire—it was the fact that he was talking with another man of the intimacy of their relationship that upset her so. Quite clearly Sebastian was not a gentleman if he felt no hesitation in discussing her in this way with one of his friends. Nor was he a man it would be wise for Juliet to continue being alone with.

Sebastian might have seduced her, but as yet he had not succeeded in bedding her—and, after the conversation Juliet had just overheard, neither *would* he!

'Your Grace.' Sebastian gave Lord Darius Wynter, Duke of Carlyne, a distracted bow as the two men greeted each other a short time later in the Bancrofts' drawing room, where many of the other guests had also gathered for tea.

'St Claire.' The older man bowed, the sunshine streaming in through the windows behind them turning his hair to gold and picking out the shadows and hollows of an arrogantly handsome face dominated by hard blue eyes.

Despite Gray's earlier claim, Sebastian considered the kinship between himself and Wynter to be of a tenuous nature, to say the least; the man was a half-uncle-by-marriage to Lucian's new wife, or some such. The other man was some years older than Sebastian—nearer his brother Hawk's age of two and thirty—although the two of them had met frequently over the years at their clubs, or across the gaming tables. Wynter had been something of a rake and a gambler until inheriting the Dukedom from his older brother some months ago.

Sebastian's distraction was for an entirely different reason than the arrival of Darius Wynter. And that reason was seated with several other ladies at the other end of the long drawing room.

Juliet was seemingly deeply engrossed in conversation with the Duchess of Essex when Sebastian glanced at her. She had been coolly withdrawn the whole of the time while Sebastian had rowed them back to the side of the lake before he'd stepped ashore to help her alight from the boat. Her nod had been one of gracious dismissal, and she'd raised her parasol before turning to walk unhurriedly back to the house.

Admittedly it had been a little awkward to have Gray interrupt them, but that in no way explained Juliet's coolness towards him now—after all, Sebastian was the one who had been caught with his pants down…literally! No, there had to be some other reason why Juliet was avoiding his company…

Could she have overheard his conversation with Gray? Was she now aware of Bancroft and Gray's suspicions about her? Worse, did she know that Sebastian had been asked to establish or disprove her innocence?

'I trust your family are all well?'

Sebastian brought his attention back to the new Duke of Carlyne with effort. 'As far as I am aware, Your Grace.'

'I believe Darius or Wynter will do.' The other man gave a grin that took years off his age and made him look more like the unprincipled rogue he had been considered for so many years. 'I am afraid I am still not thought to be quite respectable in the eyes of the ton,' he added dryly, and he gave a hard glance at their fellow guests. The ladies, old as well as young, were flushed in the face, their gazes over-bright, as they obviously gossiped about him behind their raised fans.

Sebastian relaxed slightly as he remembered that his lack of approval by the ton had been the reason he had always rather liked the older man. 'Hawk assures me that inheriting the title of Duke allows for a certain blindness where a man's earlier indiscretions are concerned,' he said.

'Does he indeed?' Wynter drawled, his eyes glittering deeply blue. 'So far I have not found that to be the case, I am afraid.' He raised his quizzing glass to glance about the room. 'Can that possibly be the lovely Countess of Crestwood I see, conversing with the Duchess of Essex…?'

Sebastian did not at all care for the calculating look that had appeared in the other man's shrewd blue eyes. 'I believe she still mourns the loss of her husband,' he bit out stiffly.

'That dry old stick Crestwood? Oh, I think not, St

Claire.' The Duke tapped him lightly on the arm with his quizzing glass before allowing it to drop down against his muscled thigh. 'If you will excuse me…' He didn't wait for Sebastian's reply before turning to stroll the length of the room.

Sebastian's mouth tightened as Juliet turned and greeted the Duke with a smile as he bowed before her.

Juliet had been aware of Sebastian's conversation with the Duke of Carlyne from the moment she had entered the drawing room a few short minutes ago, having retired briefly to her bedchamber in order to tidy her appearance before joining the other guests for tea. She was still hurt at hearing Sebastian discuss her with Lord Grayson in that ungentlemanly way, but one thing Juliet was decided upon: hurt or not, she had no intention of hiding or cowering in her bedchamber for the rest of her stay here.

What would be the point of that when she knew Sebastian was more than capable of invading her privacy there if he felt so inclined?

She allowed the wickedly handsome Duke of Carlyne to take her hand and raise it to his lips, her cheeks warming as she found herself the focus of knowing blue eyes. 'I had not realised you were to be a guest here too, Your Grace,' she said, delicately but firmly removing her hand from his grasp.

Those blue eyes gleamed with amusement as he allowed his own hand to drop back to his side. 'Only overnight, I am afraid, Lady Boyd. I merely called to conduct some business with the Earl of Bancroft, and now find myself in the midst of a summer house party.'

He did not look displeased by the fact as he flicked out the tails of his blue superfine before making himself comfortable beside her on the sofa. The black band about his arm was evidence of the recent death of his eldest brother. 'I understand there is to be a small ball this evening?'

From the number of guests Lady Bancroft had informed Juliet had been invited, the grandeur of the decorations in ballroom she had seen earlier, and the mountain of food apparently being prepared downstairs in the kitchen, Juliet did not think it was going to be a *small* ball at all. But the Duke of Carlyne's older brother had been dead only a few months, so perhaps Dolly had decided to downplay the size of the event slightly, in order to secure the social feather in her cap that would be the appearance of the Duke of Carlyne at her ball this evening?

According to the gossips, Carlyne had been as socially elusive as Juliet since inheriting the title a few months ago. Much to the chagrin of all the marriage-minded mamas!

'Perhaps you would do me the honour of reserving the first waltz for me?'

Juliet's eyes widened warily on Darius Wynter. Wildly handsome, an acknowledged rake and a gambler, he was yet another man that Crestwood had not included in his close circle of acquaintances. As such, he was not a man Juliet knew at all well.

He chuckled as he saw her obvious uncertainty. 'I assure you that my attentions are purely innocent, Lady Crestwood.'

'Indeed?' she said coolly.

He nodded. 'But imagine how seeing the two of us together will set the tongues a-wagging, dear lady!'

The Black Widow and the Notorious Rake?

That would certainly be a cause for gossip. It would also, Juliet decided shrewdly, show Sebastian that he was not the only man here who found her attractive enough to pursue. Or beddable. Yes, perhaps Lord Darius Wynter was exactly the man Juliet needed to flirt with in order to show Sebastian St Claire that she did not at all care for his conversing about her with other men!

'You will have no teeth left at all if you continue gnashing them together in that way, Sebastian!' Dolly Bancroft murmured, coming to stand beside him as he stood on the edge of the dance floor, watching the other guests twirling about the room in a waltz.

Watching Juliet dancing a waltz with Darius Wynter, of all men!

Sebastian's jaw clamped tightly as he glanced down at his hostess. 'Are you concerned that I may have lost the Countess's interest?'

Dolly arched blond brows. 'Surely more to the point, are *you*…?'

Sebastian had no idea what he felt at this moment. He had found no opportunity during tea this afternoon to speak privately with Juliet, and then she'd retired to her bedchamber with the obvious intention of resting before she had to change for the ball this evening. Excusing himself minutes later, with the intention of joining her, Sebastian had found the doors to Juliet's bedchamber—both the one in the hallway and those on the balcony—locked to bar his entrance. Neither had Juliet responded to his knock on either door.

As if that were not bad enough, he had been slightly late arriving downstairs—only to find Juliet already dancing the first set with Gray. To be followed by Bancroft. Then the Duke of Essex. Now, worst of all, she was dancing the waltz—a dance still considered one of the most risqué by many of the ton—with that rake Wynter!

In Sebastian's opinion the other man was holding Juliet far too closely, and his conversation was causing a becoming blush in her cheeks. What was he saying to her? It was all Sebastian could do to prevent his teeth grinding together again!

Juliet's gown of ivory silk, with only that string of pearls once more adorning the darkness of her hair, gave her the appearance of a beautiful swan set amongst a gaggle of overdressed peacocks; the other ladies were all dressed in the brighter colours so much the fashion at the moment, with outrageously large feathers in their hair.

'They make a becoming couple, do you not agree?' Dolly jibed slyly as she easily followed the direction of Sebastian's brooding gaze.

'No, I do not agree!' He glowered down at her. 'If you will excuse me, Lady Bancroft?' He bowed briefly, before turning on his heel and striding from the room in search of some stronger refreshment than was currently being served.

Allowing himself to over-imbibe alcohol was probably not a good idea, Sebastian appreciated, but at the moment it was certainly an appealing one!

* * *

'Has St Claire done something to offend you?'

Juliet stumbled slightly in the dance and looked up to give the Duke of Carlyne a startled glance. 'I am at a loss to understand, Your Grace,' she said.

He easily corrected her stumble before he continuing to twirl Juliet about the room, his grin rakishly teasing. 'I believe that you and St Claire were out boating on the lake together when I arrived this afternoon?'

'Yes…'

'Alone?'

Juliet bristled. 'There was nothing improper in it, Your Grace,' she defended—not quite truthfully. Her behaviour in the privacy of the grove of fir trees had been completely improper!

'Perhaps that is the reason for your annoyance?' the Duke drawled mockingly.

Juliet felt the colour warm her cheeks. 'Your Grace?'

Darius Wynter chuckled softly. 'A handsome rake alone with a beautiful woman, and St Claire did not even *try* to seduce you? How disappointing for you!'

Sebastian had not needed to 'try' to seduce her, Juliet acknowledged with self-disgust—she had already been seduced willingly several times!

She gave a reproving shake of her head. 'You are talking nonsense, Your Grace.'

'Am I?'

Juliet gave him an irritated glance. 'I am a widow of almost one and thirty, Your Grace, and I have no interest in having a young man such as Lord St Claire attempt to seduce me.'

'No?'

'No!'

'Then perhaps you can explain why is it that you have been aware of St Claire's every move this past hour?'

Juliet stumbled again, allowing the Duke no opportunity to cover the stumble this time. She came to an abrupt halt in the middle of the dance floor. Much as she was still angry with Sebastian for his behaviour this afternoon, much as she might wish to ignore his very presence, Juliet knew that she had indeed been aware of his every move for the last hour—just as the Duke had said…

How could she *not* be aware of Sebastian when he looked so magnificently handsome in his black evening clothes and snowy white linen, with the bright candle-light bringing out those golden streaks in the darkness of his hair?

'You are drawing attention to us, Lady Boyd,' Darius Wynter pointed out, with a distinct lack of concern.

'I have a headache, Your Grace. Perhaps some air will be beneficial. If you will excuse me…?' She attempted to extricate herself from his arms, but failed as he refused to release her. Instead he took a firm hold of her elbow in order to walk with her towards the French doors opened out onto the terrace. 'Release me, sir.' Her eyes flashed up at him in warning as she realised it was the Duke's intention to accompany her outside.

'I fear I have offended you.' There was genuine regret in his tone as he did as she asked.

'I cannot think why you might imagine I should be offended at having been accused of allowing Lord St Claire to seduce me!' Juliet said haughtily.

'I believe my intimation was that you were offended because you had *not* been seduced!' The Duke looked down at her and raised an imperious eyebrow. 'Perhaps you would benefit from a change of companion?'

Her mouth firmed. 'Yourself, perhaps?'

'I fear you would be more disappointed than ever, dear lady,' he drawled ruefully.

'In what way, Your Grace?'

He shrugged. 'My recent experiences with women have soured my regard towards relationships somewhat.'

Juliet's eyes widened at the bitterness she detected in his tone. As Lord Darius Wynter this man had certainly earned his reputation as a rake and a gambler. As the Duke of Carlyne he was still an unknown quantity.

She arched dark brows. 'One experience in particular…?'

He gave a weary sigh. 'Perhaps. But how amusing,' he murmured as he glanced briefly over Juliet's left shoulder. He grinned wickedly and turned back to her. 'I do believe St Claire is about to attempt to save you from what he perceives as my lecherous advances!' he confided with a certain glee.

'What?' Juliet turned just in time to see a thunderous-faced Sebastian bearing down on them, a look of grim determination in his eyes.

'This is our set, I believe, Lady Boyd.' Sebastian didn't wait for Juliet's agreement or refusal, but took her hand in his before accompanying her onto the dance floor and leaving her with no choice but to follow his lead. 'You are making an exhibition of yourself, madam,' he bit out stiffly as they came together for the first time.

Her eyes widened indignantly. 'How dare you?'

Sebastian continued to hold her gaze with his as they parted, before once more coming together again. 'Wynter is not a man on whom feminine wiles should be practised. Not unless a woman wishes to find herself flat on her back and naked in his bed!'

Juliet gasped at his deliberate crudity. 'You are insulting, sir!'

'I mean to be.' Sebastian was so angry with her he was beyond caring whether or not any of the other couples dancing could overhear their argument.

Not only had Juliet completely ignored him since they'd left the privacy of the island earlier today, but he had returned to the ballroom—after helping himself to a fortifying glass of brandy from the decanter in Bancroft's library—just in time to see Juliet being escorted from the dance floor by Darius Wynter, the intimacy of their conversation evident for all to see.

'You have led me to believe that you value your reputation,' Sebastian continued furiously as they came together for a third time. 'But perhaps you now consider the possibility of ensnaring a duke as your second husband worth the risk of losing that reputation entirely?'

'Sebastian!' Her eyes were full of reproach as she looked up at him, and her fingers trembled slightly against his.

Sebastian remained unmoved as he returned her gaze. 'You will go to Lady Bancroft once this dance has ended and make the excuse of a headache before retiring to your bedchamber. I will join you there shortly.'

'You will join—? I most certainly will *not* excuse

myself!' Juliet gasped indignantly before they were forced to part once again. 'How dare you speak to me in this way?' she hissed, as it became their turn to move together down the centre of the other dancing couples.

'How dare I?' He gave a cynical laugh. 'I am your lover, madam, not some irritating youth you can just discard when a bigger catch arrives to take your fancy.'

Juliet really did have a painful pounding at her temples as she looked about her, to see if any of the other couples were actually listening to this conversation. If they were, then they were too polite to show it. Which did not mean they had not overheard every word spoken!

Sebastian really thought— He truly believed—

'For your information, *Lord St Claire*,' Juliet told him fiercely beneath her breath, 'the Duke of Carlyne spent the majority of his time quizzing me about my relationship with *you*!'

He gave a hard smile of satisfaction. 'Indeed?'

'Indeed,' Juliet snapped. 'I had just finished assuring him that the two of us do not *have* a relationship when you dragged me away in what I can only describe as a proprietorial manner!'

Perhaps because—to Sebastian's surprise—he *felt* proprietorial where Juliet Boyd was concerned!

She was *his*, damn it, and the sooner she realised that the better he would like it. The sooner he claimed her completely the better it would be for both of them!

'Make your excuses, Juliet,' he advised softly as the music came to an end and signalled the finish of their dance together. 'Or I will make them for you,' he warned, and he kept his hand firmly beneath her elbow to guide her to the side of the brightly lit ballroom.

He could clearly see the sparkle of anger in Juliet's eyes as she glared up at him. And something else... There was another emotion besides anger in that green sparkle and the flush to her cheeks. Could it possibly be excitement...?

'I think that would be most unwise, Sebastian.' She gave a slow shake of her head as she continued to look up at him with those glittering eyes. 'If the Duke's questions are any indication, then people are already speculating that there is a relationship between the two of us.'

'I do not care for other people's speculation. Do you?' Sebastian frowned down at her broodingly.

Her chin rose challengingly. 'What *I* do not care for, My Lord, is hearing myself discussed between you and another gentlemen as meaning no more to you than any of the other women you have bedded these last ten years!'

Ah....

Chapter Eleven

Sebastian grimaced. 'I meant you no insult, Juliet—'

'I assure you, My Lord, insult was *definitely* taken.' Her tone was brittle, her gaze hard and unyielding.

Sebastian knew from the frostiness of her manner that Juliet was not going to make this in the least easy for him. He also knew that his cutting response earlier to Gray's concerns that he might be falling in love with her had been a purely defensive one.

Sebastian was not—absolutely *was not*—falling in love with Juliet Boyd!

Admittedly, he had wanted her for a long time now, but since coming here, and since having that talk with Bancroft yesterday morning, Sebastian's main concern had become that of Juliet being accused of treason and murder unjustly. But he would have felt the same way about anyone who was not being given the opportunity to defend themselves. It was that St Claire honour and pride coming into effect once again, along with his innate sense of fair play. Gray had annoyed him intensely earlier today by suggesting that there was any more to his feelings for Juliet than that.

Just as Sebastian had perhaps annoyed—hurt?—Juliet by making such a cavalier remark in her hearing…?

'Let us go upstairs, Juliet.' His voice had lowered. 'And I will endeavour to show you how sorry I am for speaking of you so inelegantly.'

She arched dark brows. 'By bedding me, My Lord?'

Sebastian drew in a sharp breath. 'Juliet—'

'In future, sir, you will address me as either Lady Boyd or the Countess of Crestwood,' she informed him coldly.

He winced at that coldness. 'I would much rather *un*dress you….'

Her eyes glittered furiously at his levity. 'I realise now how foolish it was of me to have allowed someone such as you to take liberties with me!'

'Someone such as me?' Sebastian echoed. 'What exactly does that mean?'

Juliet was only too happy to elaborate further. 'You are obviously a young man who cares only for indulging his own wants and needs—'

'Was that what I was doing last night? And again this morning?' He scowled darkly. 'Forgive me, madam, if I have quite a different memory of those occasions!'

Two bright spots of colour appeared in the paleness of her cheeks. 'Believe me, Lord St Claire, when I tell you there will be no other such incidents for you to either discuss or laugh about with your equally rakish friends!'

Sebastian straightened at this insult to his honour. 'I have *not* laughed—'

'Then perhaps that comes later?' she suggested disdainfully as she looked down her haughty nose at him. 'Or perhaps you have won your wager, after all?'

'For the last time—*there is no wager*!' Sebastian bit out between clenched teeth, his hands equally clenched at his sides. 'I am a gentleman, madam. The son and brother of gentlemen. We do not discuss the women we are involved with. Neither do we laugh about them with our friends.'

'Really?' Juliet scorned, far too angry now to even try to check her temper. 'Then I must have been the exception to your rules. Or perhaps you just assumed, as the rest of the ton refer to me as the Black Widow and think me responsible for killing my husband, that those rules of gentlemanly behaviour do not apply to me?'

She was absolutely mortified at the thought of Sebastian discussing the intimacy of their relationship with another man. So much so that it was all she could do not to slap him across his arrogantly handsome face!

She had trusted this man. Foolishly, perhaps. But nevertheless she had trusted him. With her honour. With her friendship. With her vulnerability. With her inexperience of physical pleasure….

Because of those things Sebastian St Claire now knew her nature more thoroughly, her body more intimately, than any other man ever had. Or would!

Juliet set her shoulders stiffly. 'It would be foolish of me to attempt to deny that you have hurt me with your lack of concern for my—my vulnerability, Lord St Claire.' Her voice was husky as she fought back the threatening tears. 'But you may be assured it has been a lesson well learned. And not one to be repeated, either.' She turned away blindly.

Sebastian had been rendered speechless by Juliet's tirade, by her inference that he had treated her with less respect than other women because he considered her reputation to be already lost.

But that speechlessness left him as abruptly as Juliet was now attempting to leave him. 'We have not finished talking yet, My Lady,' he said grimly as he grasped her arm in a vice-like grip to pull her along beside him as he strode forcefully across the ballroom.

'People are staring, Sebastian!' Juliet hissed, as she almost had to run to keep pace with him.

His smiled humourlessly. 'Let them.'

'Lord St Claire?'

Sebastian came to a sudden halt in the cavernous hallway to turn sharply, his expression darkening thunderously, and watch the Duke of Carlyne stroll forward to stand pointedly, challengingly, between Sebastian and the staircase. 'What do you want, Wynter?' he demanded impatiently.

The Duke bowed politely to Juliet, before turning back to the younger man, his smile one of lazy unconcern. 'I believe the Countess is promised to me for the next set....'

'The Countess,' Sebastian grated harshly, 'is promised to *me* for the rest of the night!' He met the challenge in the other man's gaze.

The Duke appeared completely unruffled by Sebastian's obvious anger. 'Is that not for the Countess to decide?'

'Would you kindly get out of my way?' Sebastian ordered. 'Otherwise I will be forced to rearrange certain of your much-admired features.' He barely heard Juliet's gasp of dismay as he continued, 'This is none of your concern, Wynter.'

Instead of answering him, the Duke turned to Juliet. 'Lady Boyd…?'

Juliet chewed on her bottom lip as she worried about which course she should take. If she asked the Duke of Carlyne to take her back to the ballroom, then she knew that Sebastian, in his present mood, was quite capable of carrying out his threat of physical violence against the other man. If she did not ask for the Duke's aid then she would have no choice but to accompany Sebastian up the stairs.

She didn't want to do either of those things….

To accompany the Duke back into the ballroom when all of the ton had seen her leave with Sebastian—no, seen Sebastian all but drag her from the room!—would make her the object of further curiosity. To disappear up the stairs with Sebastian, no doubt to her bedchamber, was unthinkable….

She moistened the dryness of her lips. She spoke quietly. 'I believe, Your Grace, that what I would like most of all is some refreshment.'

'Indeed.' Those blue eyes had darkened in sympathy for her plight. 'St Claire?' His voice became steely as he glanced at the hold Sebastian still had upon Juliet's arm.

Juliet chanced a glance at Sebastian's face, not at all reassured by the stubborn set of his features. His eyes were so dark as he stared at the other man it was almost impossible to distinguish the pupil from the iris. His cheekbones were starkly visible against the hard contours of his cheeks and his mouth had thinned. His clenched jaw was thrust forward aggressively, and a nerve pulsed rapidly in his throat.

Juliet hoped Sebastian would restrain himself from attempting physical violence against the Duke of Carlyne. She knew from past memories of the other man before he had inherited his dukedom that he was more than capable of returning any blows he might receive. In fact, he might relish them!

'My Lord.' She turned to Sebastian, her gaze beseeching. 'You must release me.'

That nerve in his jaw pulsed more rapidly as he continued to look at the other man rather than at Juliet. 'Must I?'

'Yes—'

'Ah, there you are, St Claire!' A completely unruffled Dolly Bancroft left the ballroom and came smilingly towards them. 'Have you forgotten we are promised for this set?'

Juliet was not fooled for a moment by the other woman's apparent lack of concern. She was sure that Dolly could not be unaware of the tension that existed between Sebastian and the Duke of Carlyne. No one could be anywhere near them and *not* be aware of it!

Sebastian spared their hostess a scathing glance. 'Interfering again, Dolly?'

'Not at all.' She gave him a reproving frown. 'I am simply avoiding having fisticuffs at my ball. Bancroft would be most displeased to have blood spilled on one of his beautiful Aubusson carpets!'

Sebastian was torn as to how to proceed. What he wanted to do was continue up the stairs, dragging Juliet with him if necessary, and have this out with her once and for all. To tell her everything—Bancroft's suspicions of her traitorous behaviour during the war against the French, her involvement in Crestwood's death, that damning letter signed simply 'J'—and demand that she proclaim her innocence in all of those matters.

Yet by doing so he would lose Juliet's good will for ever.

For, whether she was innocent or guilty, she would hate him for his part in the conspiracy against her—regardless of how unwilling he had been to undertake it in the first place....

Damn, damn, *damn*!

'Very well, Dolly. You and I shall dance.' He released Juliet so suddenly that she stumbled slightly, although she was cautious enough, after a glance at Sebastian's tautly set features, not to accept the arm that the Duke of Carlyne immediately offered her.

Until these last few days Sebastian was aware he had been known for his amiable temperament. His lazy good humour. His charm and ease in any given situation, and especially with women of all ages.

Until these last few days....

Sebastian had been in a rage of emotion of one kind or another ever since his arrival at Banford Park. Desire for Juliet. Fury towards any other man who even looked at her. Even now he knew he would not be responsible for his actions if Darius Wynter so much as laid an unnecessary finger upon her...

Juliet gave Dolly a grateful glance, relieved that the other woman's intervention had prevented the two men from actually fighting each other. 'Shall we, Your

Grace?' She avoided looking at Sebastian again as she placed her hand on the Duke's arm and allowed him to escort her to the refreshment room.

But Juliet would have been deceiving herself if she had not admitted to being aware of that narrowed golden gaze of his as it followed every step of her departure....

Juliet had never felt so emotionally drained as she did three hours later, as she made her way wearily up the wide staircase to her bedchamber.

There had been no more scenes involving Sebastian St Claire and the Duke of Carlyne, thank goodness. Mainly because, following dancing a set with Dolly Bancroft, Sebastian had disappeared from the ballroom completely. And had not returned.

The evening had dragged by so slowly after his departure that Juliet had dearly wished she might follow his example. But propriety had dictated she could not. To be seen retiring to her bedchamber so soon after Sebastian had left the ballroom would only have led to further speculation about the two of them.

And so she had remained in the ballroom, dancing every set with one or another of the Bancrofts' male guests. The last set of the evening, danced only few minutes ago, had once again been reserved by the Duke of Carlyne.

Juliet found him to be a strange, unpredictable man. In the company of others—and especially in front of Sebastian!—he gave every appearance of being the rakish flirt he was reputed to be. But when talking to Juliet he proved to be a man of impeccable manners and high intellect, that flirtatiousness nowhere in evidence.

All of which succeeded in proving to Juliet that she did not understand men at all!

Before their marriage Crestwood had appeared to be a serious and honourable man her poor deceived parents had so approved of. Once Juliet had become his wife—in the privacy of their bedchamber most especially—Crestwood had become a monster.

She had found Sebastian St Claire to be the opposite: concerned only for her pleasure and comfort in the bed-chamber, but totally unpredictable outside of it.

The Duke of Carlyne was another man of contradictions. A man who had obviously once been hurt by love himself somewhere in his disreputable past, and who still suffered from that disillusionment.

Juliet dearly hoped that Helena would not be waiting in her bedchamber in expectation of helping her to undress and prepare for bed. She knew that her cousin would demand a minute-by-minute account of the ball, and its guests, before allowing Juliet to retire.

It was a habit the two women had fallen into over the years—due mainly to Helena's social inability to attend such grand occasions herself, but partly to a young woman's interest in all things to do with the ton. But tonight Juliet was just too weary, too disheartened by the events of the day, to have the patience to describe such tedious inanity.

So it was with a heavy heart that Juliet opened the door of her bedchamber and found the room brightly lit by several candles, rather than just the one on her night-stand—an indication that Helena did indeed wait for her.

Not just several candles, Juliet realised with a frown

as she stepped reluctantly inside the bedchamber. Dozens of them. On every conceivable surface. So many that the room was as well lit as a bright summer's day.

What on earth…?

'Close the door, Juliet.'

Her shocked gaze moved to the bed, her brows rising, her eyes widening incredulously as she saw Sebastian St Claire lying in the bed, the covers about his waist revealing that his chest was completely bare.

Sebastian sat up against the downy pillows, his heart plummeting as he saw Juliet's initial shock replaced by outrage. She did indeed close the door—no, slam it!—before turning back to glare at him with blazing green eyes.

'How dare you?' she demanded indignantly. 'After our conversation earlier this evening, I cannot believe you have the temerity, the sheer *nerve*, to assume I would welcome your presence in my bedchamber ever again!'

Now was not the time, Sebastian appreciated ruefully, to tell Juliet how beautiful she looked when she was angry. Even if it happened to be the truth. The darkness of her hair was in slight disarray from her hours of dancing. Her eyes glittered like twin emeralds. Her cheeks were flushed. Her lips full and pouting. The fullness of her breasts quickly rose and fell above the low neckline of her gown as she breathed agitatedly.

Juliet wasn't just beautiful in her anger—she was magnificent!

And, far from assuming anything where she was concerned, Sebastian knew exactly the risk he had taken by waiting for her in her bedchamber in this way. A long and tedious wait it had been, too. Hours and hours of it.

All spent with the added apprehension that Juliet might not be alone when she did eventually retire for the night—that the arrogantly handsome and no doubt completely willing Duke of Carlyne might have persuaded her into allowing him to accompany her....

Not that Sebastian believed Juliet made a habit of bringing men to her bedchamber. He knew she did not. But she had been angry enough with him earlier, disgusted enough with him over the overheard remark to Gray, that she might just have considered the idea of bringing Darius Wynter to her bed as a suitable punishment for Sebastian's behaviour.

That she was alone after all gave Sebastian some hope, at least, that Juliet might eventually be persuaded into forgiving him. 'One of the things you said earlier was that I have taken advantage of your vulnerability,' he reminded her huskily. 'I am here now to make you a present of my own vulnerability.'

Juliet frowned fiercely. 'I have no idea what you are talking about—' She broke off abruptly as Sebastian threw back the bedcovers and rose slowly to his feet.

He was completely naked!

'Sebastian…!'

Juliet's protest did not come out as strongly as she would have wished. How could it when she was almost overwhelmed by his physical beauty? Tall, and leanly muscled, he had not an ounce of superfluous flesh upon his body! His hair fell onto the broadness of his shoulders in dark waves shot through with gold. The muscled contours of his chest were covered in silky hair that thickened about his nipples, then thinned out over the flatness of his stomach before thickening again about his—

Juliet's shocked gaze moved back to fix determinedly on the beauty of Sebastian's face. 'I see no vulnerability, Lord St Claire, only a naked man!' A naked man who, as she had already observed, was magnificently aroused!

He held his arms out from his body. 'Considering all the mores and inhibitions of our society, is that not the best vulnerability one person may offer another?'

Juliet's gaze became uncertain and she looked at him searchingly. What did he mean?

Sebastian's expression softened as he saw her confusion. 'I am giving you leave to do with me as you will, Juliet. To touch me. Caress me. Arouse me,' he said gruffly. 'Do exactly as you wish with me, Juliet. I will not speak, or touch you in return, unless you bid me do so. Neither will I attempt to stop you in anything you wish to do to me. Earlier this evening you accused me of boasting to my friends of bedding you.' His mouth compressed in memory of that conversation. 'I am now offering you the opportunity of bedding me. Or not,' he added evenly. 'It is your choice, Juliet. For you to decide. For you to claim the victory of bedding me, taking me for your own pleasure before discarding me, if that is what you choose.'

Sebastian had thought long and hard as he waited for Juliet to return to her bedchamber, before finally realising that the only thing he had to offer as proof of his genuine regard for her was exactly what he was now offering her. Would she take it? Would she take *him*? Or would she simply dismiss him from her bedchamber and completely ignore him for the rest of her stay here? Either way, Sebastian's offer had ensured that the victory would be Juliet's alone.

Juliet's thoughts were a complete contradiction. The wisest thing to do would be to tell him to leave her bed-chamber now. To just go and never approach or address her ever again. The alternative was to accept his offer of doing with him as she would. Of taking him for her own pleasure….

There was no denying she was filled with a trembling anticipation at the thought of having Sebastian St Claire completely at her mercy. Of caressing each and every hard plane of his beautifully sculptured body. Of indulging her earlier curiosity until she was satisfied. Of this time caressing that hardness with no interruptions. To taste him as she had so longed to do this afternoon….

Sebastian had to be insane or drunk—or both—to make her such an offer!

Surely a woman could not seduce a man against his will?

Yet he had not said it would be against his will. In fact, his words had implied the opposite. He had invited her to touch him, caress him, arouse him, take him for her own pleasure, and in return he would neither speak nor touch her unless she asked him to do so. He was giving her free will to explore his body exactly as she chose.

Sebastian wasn't insane—*she* was!

For her to treat him merely as an object for her own sexual gratification would surely make her behaviour no better than Crestwood's had been towards her all the years of their marriage.

'I did not say that I would not enjoy it, Juliet,' Sebastian remarked softly, as if he could easily read the thoughts racing so rapidly through her mind. The initial glow of anticipation in her eyes. Then the self-doubt. Quickly followed by the realisation that he really was offering her free will to do with him as she chose. Before her pained frown told him that her thoughts had in all probability turned to Crestwood's treatment of her during their marriage. 'I assure you, Juliet, whatever you do to me I will enjoy it,' he encouraged, and he took a step towards her.

'Would you break the agreement already, Sebastian, by moving when I did not bid you do so?' She held up a defensive hand to ward him off. 'You—' She broke off as the door to the bedchamber suddenly opened behind Sebastian and she saw her cousin Helena standing there.

'I am so sorry I was not here when you retired—'

Juliet stared wide-eyed across the room at the shocked Helena as she stood transfixed in the doorway, her gaze riveted on the lean length of St Claire's naked back, hips and thighs!

This was shocking. Worse than shocking. It was, without a doubt, the most embarrassing moment of Juliet's entire life.

'Get out!' Sebastian instructed harshly, without turning round.

'I—Yes. I will leave you now and come back in the morning, Juliet.' An obviously flustered Helena shot her an apologetic grimace, before backing out of the room and closing the door hastily behind her.

Juliet closed her eyes, willing all of this to be a dream. A nightmare from which she would soon awaken and—

No. When she opened her lids, Sebastian still stood naked in the middle of her bedchamber. Naked and rampantly aroused.

Juliet felt the return of some of that anger she had experienced towards him earlier. How dared Sebastian invade her bedchamber in this way? How dared he make wild erotic suggestions about her taking her revenge upon him by seducing him? How dared he make a show of himself like this in front of her young and impressionable cousin? Something Juliet would no doubt have to explain fully on the morrow!

More importantly, how dared Sebastian order Helena to leave Juliet's bedchamber in that arrogant fashion?

Juliet's mouth firmed and she snapped. 'I do not remember giving you permission to talk!'

Sebastian relaxed slightly as he realised Juliet's reprimand meant she was accepting his offer of seduction after all.

Only to tense again as the glitter in Juliet's eyes promised retribution of some kind for his high-handed behaviour just now in ordering her maid from the room. That sensuous gaze held his for long, timeless seconds, before moving deliberately down to watch the response of Sebastian's hard arousal as she slowly, delicately, began to peel one of her gloves down her arm, to pull it from her fingers one by one....

Sebastian groaned low in his throat as he realised his torture had just begun....

Chapter Twelve

He had been wrong, Sebastian very quickly realised; torture did not even begin to describe the torment he was very shortly to suffer at Juliet's hands. And lips. And tongue!

She placed her gloves carefully down on the dressing table and moved to stand behind him, her fingers as soft and fleeting as the touch of butterfly wings as they became familiar with the hard tension of Sebastian's shoulders, before moving caressingly down the length of his spine. His buttocks tensed. Waiting for a caress that never came, as Juliet ceased touching him altogether.

Sebastian couldn't see her as she stood behind him, could only hear the rustle of her gown as she moved. Doing what? Sebastian cursed the promise he had made as seconds, minutes passed, without his having any idea what Juliet was about. Was she just standing there, looking at him? Was that to be his punishment?

'Dear God…' he groaned as suddenly he felt the firmness of naked hard-tipped breasts against the curve of his spine, the brush of her loosened hair against his sensitised flesh, before warm lips and a moist tongue began to seek out the muscled contours of his back.

Once again those caresses stopped suddenly.

Because he had broken his promise not to speak?

Juliet was standing so close to him that Sebastian could feel the warmth of her breath against his back. So close, but no longer touching him.

Fine beads of moisture appeared on Sebastian's forehead as he forced himself not to speak again, knowing that he could not if he wanted Juliet to continue to touch him, to caress him. If he wanted to know release from the hell of arousal that the last twenty-four hours of making love to this woman without taking her had induced so achingly.

Sebastian stiffened, his arousal throbbing, pulsing, as the softness of Juliet's breath moved lightly, hotly against his parted thighs and told him that she was on her knees behind him.

Dear God, what was she going to do next?

It was all he could do not to cry out as her hands moved delicately along the length of his thigh before moving forward to curve hotly about his arousal.

His back arched involuntarily even as he gritted his teeth in order not to move against that disembodied hand. Slowly it stroked the length of his aching shaft, from base to tip, the soft pad of her thumb briefly pausing to seek out the beads of moisture released from the intensity of his arousal.

Sebastian had never experienced, never *seen*, anything as erotic as Juliet making love to him in this way. He knew that if she didn't soon stop those caresses he was going to climax before they had even begun!

'Juliet…!' he pleaded.

'Yes, My Lord?' Juliet replied huskily.

'I so desperately need to kiss you!' Sebastian gasped hoarsely, and he turned to pull her to her feet and take her in his arms before fiercely claiming her mouth with his.

He kissed her hungrily, deeply, the thrust of his tongue into the hot cavern of her mouth telling her of his need. Of his desperation to be inside her.

Juliet returned the hunger of Sebastian's kiss, her arms up about his shoulders. Her fingers became entangled in the silky thickness of his hair, those fingers tightening to pull his head back and break their kiss as one of his hands moved to cup the thrust of her breast. 'Not yet, Sebastian. I have not finished my own…explorations yet,' she reproved, and she took his hand to sit him on the side of the bed.

'What—?' Sebastian's question ended in another tortured groan as Juliet knelt before him, her hand moving about his throbbing arousal before she bent her head and began to pleasure him in the way she had so longed to do this afternoon, totally emboldened, made wanton, by the licence Sebastian had given her to do with him as she wanted.

Juliet's actions were instinctive rather than knowledgeable, but she knew her caresses pleased Sebastian when she felt his arousal pulsing beneath her hand as she ran her tongue lightly across the head of that shaft, cupping him lower down as she explored the length of that hardness from base to tip. He was so big, so swollen with need as she continued to tease and taste him with her tongue.

Sebastian believed he might truly go insane as he looked down at Juliet pleasuring him, the darkness of her loosened hair silky across his thighs. 'Juliet!' he gasped as she finally took him into her mouth. That heated moisture was almost his undoing. 'No more, Juliet!' he entreated weakly as he threaded his fingers into the long length of her hair and pulled her away. 'I will not be able to hold if you continue to do that,' he explained painfully, when she looked up at him with sultry green eyes.

She moistened her lips with the tip of that wicked tongue. 'But have you not told me that a man may make love all night with the right woman?'

He swallowed hard. 'Yes, I did say that—'

'Are you saying I am *not* that woman, Sebastian?' She sat back on her heels to look up at him challengingly, her bare breasts full and pouting, the nipples hard and thrusting.

'Of course you are—'

'And did you not say I may do with you as I will?' She arched dark brows.

Yes, Sebastian had said that. But twenty-four hours of making love to this woman and taking no release for himself meant that his control was already at breaking point. 'I need to be inside you—'

'And you will be,' she assured him as she stood up.

Sebastian's breath caught in his throat as he looked at her slender nakedness: silken legs, that tantalising thatch of dark curls between her thighs, her hips gently curvaceous, her waist slender below the fullness of those beautiful breasts. Her lips were full and swollen from the force of the kisses they had shared, her green eyes dark and enticing as she moved, so that Sebastian lay beneath her on the bed. Now she could straddle the hardness of his thighs.

'Just not yet,' she added naughtily.

Sebastian lay unmoving as her hands moved to press his own hands on the pillows either side of his head. Her breasts were jutting forward just beyond the reach of his mouth as she began to move against his thighs without quite taking the throbbing length of him inside her. And all the time those green eyes gazed seductively into his, tormenting him almost beyond his endurance.

He had created a monster, Sebastian acknowledged wildly to himself, as he realised that Juliet intended driving him quietly but most assuredly out of his mind!

Juliet was punishing herself as much as Sebastian. She longed, ached to have his lips about her breast as she took him deep inside her.

'I *need*, Juliet,' he whispered hoarsely.

'What do you need, Sebastian?'

'For God's sake, woman—*take me*!'

She held his gaze as she slowly lowered herself towards him. Her breasts were no longer just beyond his reach—an advantage Sebastian took full advantage of as he latched on thankfully, his lids closing as he drew the hardened nipple into his mouth to suckle hungrily.

Juliet felt a new rush of hot moisture between her thighs and knew that it was time—that she couldn't wait any longer, either. She had to have Sebastian inside her, filling her. Except, for all her earlier daring, Juliet wasn't quite sure how to go about achieving that….

Luckily she was saved having to admit that as Sebastian, obviously goaded beyond endurance, turned suddenly on the bed, taking Juliet with him, so that she now lay beneath him. He parted her thighs and entered her in one long, slow thrust before resting there, his weight on his elbows, as he allowed her to become accustomed to having the thick length of him inside her.

'Do not move!' Sebastian pleaded gruffly, resting the dampness of his forehead against Juliet's. Just being inside her threatened to shatter all his earlier control. She was so hot and moist, her inner spasms telling him that she, too, was on the point of release.

Sebastian held Juliet's gaze with his as he rolled onto his side, taking Juliet with him, so that they lay side by side. One of his hands moved in between their joined bodies in search of the centre of her pleasure. One caress of his fingers against that swollen aching flesh and Juliet's body shattered into fierce release, the whole of her body shaking with the force of it.

It was too much—far, far too much for Sebastian to withstand after Juliet's earlier teasing, and as her inner convulsions pulsed hotly around him he knew his own release could no longer be held at bay. He surged up and over her to thrust fiercely, wildly inside her, continuing those thrusts long after he knew himself drained, and the aftershocks of their pleasure continued remorselessly, endlessly, until Sebastian collapsed weakly against her.

He couldn't breathe. Couldn't move. He just wanted

to stay buried deep inside Juliet, connected to her, a part of her.

Except he couldn't do that. He knew his weight alone was enough to crush her.

Sebastian moved to gently disengage himself. 'Stay there,' he murmured, before getting up and crossing the room to where a jug of water and a bowl stood on the washstand. The water was only luke-warm, but it was better than nothing, Sebastian decided as he dampened a cloth and returned to Juliet's side.

Her eyes opened wide in alarm as he gently drew back the bedclothes she had pulled over her nakedness. 'What are you doing?'

'Gently, Juliet,' Sebastian soothed, much as he might a young filly in his care. 'I will not hurt you.' He wiped her with the damp cloth, easing whatever soreness she might be feeling at the same time as he cleansed her.

She gasped, her cheeks flushing brightly red. 'I am not sure you should be doing that!'

'I am,' Sebastian insisted. 'Let me care for you, love,' he insisted, and he parted her thighs to continue that gentle cleansing.

He still hungered! He had just made love with this woman, had climaxed until he felt as if he had nothing left inside him to give, and yet Sebastian could once again feel the stirrings of his body as he looked down at Juliet's loveliness.

He pulled the bedclothes back over her before moving away from the bed to replace the bowl and cloth on the washstand, his thoughts racing as he tried to make sense of his burning hunger to take her for a second time. How could he possibly want her again so quickly?

What was it about Juliet alone that brought him to his knees with aching want? That made him want to take her again and again, until only exhaustion prevented him from continuing? What made her so different to any other woman Sebastian had ever known…?

Juliet lay silently in the bed as she watched Sebastian move restlessly about the bedchamber, his gaze studiously avoiding meeting hers. For which Juliet felt grateful; she was achingly, painfully embarrassed by his gentle ministrations to her comfort.

She had absolutely no idea what thoughts were behind his harshly hewn face as he collected up his clothes, but her own were thoughts of turmoil and confusion.

She felt pleasure and wonder at the joy she had once again experienced as Sebastian made love to her. And surprise, because Sebastian had not hurt her—not once. Not even when he had been buried so deeply inside her Juliet had felt as if he touched the very centre of her being.

She felt hatred towards Crestwood, because he *had* hurt her, time and time again, and she knew now that he need not have done so. A little patience and kindness on his part, and Juliet knew those painful years of being his wife need never have been. Sebastian St Claire, a man she had known only a matter of days, had shown her the kindness, the consideration and care, that her husband had not. *Would* not…

'I should go,' Sebastian said abruptly as he sat down to pull his pantaloons over his nakedness. 'It would not do for your maid to return and find me still here.'

'No,' Juliet agreed huskily—painfully.

Helena had taken one look Sebastian's nakedness earlier and said she would not return until morning. Sebastian was leaving now because he wanted to—not because propriety dictated he must.

Because Juliet had been a disappointment to him? Because he had found little pleasure in her inexperienced caresses?

Tears of humiliation burned her eyes. Tears Juliet hoped would not fall until after Sebastian had departed her bedchamber!

Sebastian stood up to pull his shirt over his head, his hair a dark tumble of mahogany and gold. 'We will talk in the morning.' He carried the rest of his clothes and his boots as he moved to the door out onto the balcony.

Somehow Juliet doubted very much that she and Sebastian *would* talk in the morning. Or indeed at any other time. He had taken what he had come here for, and now, hard as it was for Juliet to accept, his interest in her, in the chase, was over.

'Of course,' she agreed evenly.

Sebastian paused in the open doorway, his gaze narrowing on the paleness of her face. 'Juliet…?'

She roused herself with effort. 'Yes?'

He frowned darkly. 'It *is* for the best if I leave now. It really would not do for your maid to return, either tonight or in the morning, and find me still here.'

Her gaze did not meet his as she nodded. 'I have already said that I understand, Sebastian.'

Then Juliet understood a damn sight more than Sebastian did—because he had no idea what had happened tonight! Between the two of them or inside himself. And until he did know Sebastian felt it wiser to put some distance between himself and Juliet….

'I do not wish to talk about it, Helena,' Juliet told her cousin stiffly, when she entered the bedchamber the following morning.

Helena looked disappointed as she crossed the room, hardly limping at all now, to where Juliet sat listlessly in the chair beside the window. 'But—'

'I said no, Helena.' Juliet stood up, her face as pale as the nightgown and robe she had quickly pulled on after Sebastian's hasty departure the night before. 'There are some things that are…too private to be discussed even with you, dear Helena. Sebastian St Claire is one of those.' Her frown was pained as she remembered the way he had left, immediately after the two of them had made love together.

Because he, like Crestwood, had ultimately found her a disappointment in bed…?

'So that is the handsome Lord Sebastian St Claire the other maids have been twittering about the last few days…' her cousin murmured speculatively as she moved about the room, collecting up Juliet's clothes from where she had discarded them so carelessly the evening before. 'They say he is the brother of a duke.'

Juliet frowned at Helena's persistence. 'I really cannot talk about this now, Helena!' Her voice broke emotionally.

Although she doubted there were any more tears left inside her. She had cried so long and so hard the previous night, after Sebastian had left, that her throat now ached and her eyes were red and swollen.

What could have possessed her to accept the challenge that Sebastian had thrown down when he'd invited her to do with him as she would? What madness had driven her to tease and torment him in that utterly shameless way? To behave with a wantonness that had so obviously shocked Sebastian he had left her as soon as was politely possible!

'Being the wife of just a lord would not be as grand as being a countess, of course, but—'

'It is not my intention to marry the man, Helena!' Juliet interrupted sharply.

Her young cousin gave her a teasing look. 'I seem to recall, before coming here, it was not your intention to take a lover, either.'

Juliet closed her eyes as she drew in a deep breath in an effort to control the roil of emotions coursing through her. There was no longer any doubt about it. Last night Sebastian St Claire had become her lover in the fullest sense of the word. Even thinking of the wonder of the pleasures he had introduced her to made Juliet feel weak at the knees.

As for how intimately she had touched and kissed him in return…

How could Juliet ever look at him again and not remember her wanton behaviour? How would she ever be able to face him again and not remember the disgust he had felt afterwards…?

'I am not in the mood for your speculations or innuendos this morning, Gray,' Sebastian warned the other man harshly, when he strolled into the breakfast room to find Sebastian sprawled in a chair, scowling into the bottom of his empty teacup.

He had been sitting there for some time, completely alone—apart from the footman who occasionally came in to ask if he could serve Sebastian breakfast. Considering even the tea Sebastian had drunk was still churning uncomfortably inside him, he had refused all offers—even the idea of adding food to that discomfort made him feel ill.

Gray, completely unperturbed by Sebastian's surliness, poured himself some tea before moving to occupy the chair directly opposite Sebastian's at the table. 'Am I permitted to observe that you look like hell?' he murmured dryly.

Sebastian felt like hell, too, after making love with Juliet for half the night and then lying awake and restless in his own bed for the remainder of it! 'No, you are not,' he bit out curtly, well aware that, although his valet had assured him that his appearance was as impeccable as usual, there was nothing to be done to hide the dark circles beneath Sebastian's eyes or the pallor of his skin. 'And if you have nothing better to do this morning than irritate me, Gray, then might I suggest you go away and find something?'

His friend raised dark brows. 'Am I irritating you…?'

'Intensely.'

Gray gave an unconcerned smile. 'I have some business in London that requires my attention this morning; I wondered if you would care to accompany me?'

His mouth twisted. 'And would this *business* have anything to do with the Countess of Crestwood?'

Gray gave him a reproving glance. 'I assure you, my movements and thoughts do not revolve solely around the activities of the Countess of Crestwood.'

Sebastian's scowl deepened. His own movements and thoughts did not revolve solely around the activities of the Countess of Crestwood, either—but enough so that he found the idea of leaving Banford Park for some hours, possibly overnight, deeply appealing.

Last night had been a revelation. Of what, Sebastian was still not sure. That he had lain sleepless in his bed, continuing to desire Juliet long after leaving her bed-chamber, was in no doubt. That it had taken every ounce of his will-power not to return and make love to her again was also in no doubt. Why she, of all women, should have such a profound effect on him was what continued to mystify him.

Something else had happened last night to disturb him. But while Sebastian's thoughts were so centred on Juliet he could not recall what that something was. Or why it was. Perhaps time away from Banford Park, away from Juliet, would help him to remember....

Chapter Thirteen

"You have decided not to leave this morning after all, Your Grace?' Juliet's expression was politely interested as, after making his bow, Darius Wynter lowered his elegant length onto the seat beside Juliet's own where she sat on the terrace, watching the other guests participate in a riotous game of cricket.

The Duke shrugged. 'I am in no hurry to leave now that I have completed my business with Bancroft. Are you desirous of another boating trip on the lake, my lady?'

Juliet gave a rueful shake of her head. 'I fear my interest in boating has waned, Your Grace.'

As her interest in Sebastian St Claire had waned....

Or perhaps a better way of putting it was that Sebastian was no longer at Banford Park for her to be interested in!

Juliet had lingered in her bedchamber this morning, long after Helena had helped her dress and style her hair, delaying the moment when she would have to face him again; she still blushed to the roots of her hair to remember her wanton behaviour of the night before!

It had been yet another blow to Juliet's shaky self-esteem, once she had finally come downstairs, to be informed by an obviously ruffled Dolly Bancroft that two of her guests—Lord Gideon Grayson and Lord Sebastian St Claire—had decided to ride to London this morning. Dolly had added waspishly that she had no idea when they would return. Her tone had implied *if*…

Having thought long and hard through a disturbed and sleepless night, Juliet had come to the decision to make her excuses to her hostess and depart for home herself this morning. Helena's ankle had made an excellent recovery, so there was nothing standing in her way. She certainly had not expected that Sebastian would already have made his own departure from Banford Park, without so much as a word of farewell!

'I see,' the Duke murmured softly, that blue gaze narrowing on her shrewdly. 'I take it that boating with someone else does not hold the same…appeal as it did with St Claire?'

'It no longer holds appeal with or without Lord St Claire,' she said coolly.

Darius Wynter steepled his fingers together before turning that piercing blue gaze onto the other guests, as they rampaged about the grass with an enthusiasm that would no doubt rival that of the children they had left at home in the nursery. 'Country pursuits such as these have never particularly interested me,' he said, with obvious distaste for the antics of their fellow guests.

'Or me,' she acknowledged ruefully.

'Even so, the constraints of the widowed state can be a tiresome business, can they not?'

Juliet instantly remembered that this man's wife had died the previous year. Although rumour had it amongst the ton he had not suffered too badly at the loss....

'Very tiresome where no love existed, yes,' she admitted.

That blue gaze became even sharper. 'As so often it did not.'

Juliet turned away. 'I would not advise involving oneself in another relationship that might prove just as disastrous, either,' she said bleakly.

'I assure you I have no intention of doing so,' the Duke said firmly.

'Nor I,' Juliet said.

'St Claire left for town earlier this morning, I believe...?'

Juliet's spine stiffened defensively before she answered. 'Lady Bancroft mentioned those were his plans, yes.'

Blond brows rose over those incredibly blue eyes. 'He did not tell you so himself?'

'I can think of no reason why he should have done so, Your Grace.' Juliet gave a lightly dismissive laugh—utterly unconvincing.

'No?'

Had Juliet's budding relationship with Sebastian been as obvious to the Bancrofts' other guests as it had to the Duke of Carlyne? Following Sebastian's arrogant behaviour the evening before, when he had all but dragged Juliet from the ballroom, then the answer was most probably yes. The fact that he had now left so unexpectedly for London only added to Juliet's public humiliation.

Sebastian's invitation for her to do with him what she would had resulted in Juliet behaving in a quite shameless and wanton way. A wantonness that had so obviously disgusted Sebastian he had decided to go back to town this morning.

She stood up gracefully. 'If you feel so inclined, I am sure that the…constraints of our widowed state do not prevent us from strolling in the garden together, Your Grace.'

The Duke smiled up at her, those blue eyes crinkling at the corners as he stood up, too, a tall and elegant figure in brown superfine, gold brocade waistcoat, white linen, beige pantaloons and brown black-topped Hessians. 'I would be more than happy to walk with you for a while before taking my leave.' He offered her his arm.

Sebastian felt a cold rage such as he had never known before when he stepped out onto the terrace at Banford Park and saw a happy and smiling Juliet, strolling about the garden arm-in-arm with Darius Wynter.

He and Gray had been halfway to London before the other man had admitted that he was, after all, going to London at Bancroft's behest—that he would be bringing back information from other agents because the older man could not go to London to collect it himself when he had a houseful of guests.

No matter what Sebastian's private reservations might be concerning the continuation of any sort of relationship with Juliet, this disclosure had made him realise that he could not, after all, desert her in this way, when he had made a promise to himself several days ago not to abandon her to Bancroft's suspicions.

Sebastian had instigated his meeting Juliet at Banford Park with the intention of indulging in a light-hearted flirtation with her. Followed by a short-lived seduction. He had flirted. He had seduced. He had been seduced in return.

As with his other affairs, that should have been an end to it.

Instead, Bancroft and Gray's continuing suspicions concerning Juliet dictated it could not end here. Honour—that damned St Claire honour, taught to him on his father's knee!—dictated that Sebastian could not simply just walk away and leave Juliet to deal with those suspicions on her own.

Gray's negative response to Sebastian's sudden decision to return to Banford Park had been predictable, if irritating. The other man had reminded Sebastian that the Countess was a widow, several years older than himself and, worst of all, a woman of questionable character where the death of her husband was concerned. Sebastian's response to those insults might have been less easy for Gray to predict, but no doubt the bruise upon his jaw would fade in time!

To then return and find a happy and contented Juliet, strolling about the garden in the company of that rake Wynter, looking cool and oh-so-beautiful in a gown of pale green muslin, carrying a matching parasol, made a nonsense of Sebastian's earlier concern for her.

'I would not advise another scene like yesterday evening, St Claire.'

Sebastian turned narrowed and glittering eyes upon his host as the Earl moved to stand at his side. 'I have already received quite enough advice from my so-called friends this morning, thank you, Bancroft!'

The older man gave an unperturbed grimace. 'I do not believe that you and I have ever considered ourselves as friends, St Claire.'

Nor were they ever likely to do so once this fortnight came to an end. Just as Sebastian believed his friendship with Dolly had been damaged beyond repair. As for Gray…! That friendship might never recover, either.

'Neither are Wynter's attentions to Lady Boyd anything for you to be concerned about,' Lord Bancroft assured him.

Sebastian turned sharply to the older man. 'Explain yourself!' he demanded.

'I am not in the habit of explaining myself to anyone!' the older man rasped back.

Sebastian looked at Wynter as he once again caused Juliet to laugh huskily at one of his softly spoken remarks. 'He is another of your spies?' he said, outraged.

'Hardly,' Bancroft drawled dryly. 'I merely wished to reassure you that Wynter is no more interested in a relationship with the Countess than I am!'

'Am I supposed to feel grateful for your assurances?' he said sarcastically.

The older man gave a weary shrug. 'Do with them what you will.'

What Sebastian wanted was for this whole charade

to be over and done with! 'Are you expecting the papers Gray is to collect today to bring you any closer to learning the identity of the person or persons who have spied for the French?' he asked Bancroft.

The other man seemed unperturbed by Sebastian's knowledge of Gray's purpose for going to London. 'Perhaps. But my investigation here continues.'

The very reason Sebastian had returned so hastily. 'And has it provided you with anything new?'

'I have…further information, yes,' the older man allowed grudgingly.

Sebastian's eyes sharpened. 'Did something else happen last night?'

Bancroft raised grey brows. 'Why do you ask?'

Sebastian winced inwardly at the lack of discretion he was about to reveal. 'If it did, then I believe you should know that Lady Boyd was with me.'

'I do not believe you can account for *all* her movements last night, St Claire,' Bancroft said pointedly. 'Nevertheless, I agree that she did not leave her bedchamber after retiring,' he allowed.

It was not too difficult for Sebastian to guess how the other man might know of Juliet's movements the night before. And the thought of some faceless person—one of the servants, perhaps?—spying on Juliet in this way was totally repugnant to him. 'Then perhaps you would care to enlighten me as to this "further information"?'

'And perhaps I would not.' The older man easily met the challenge in Sebastian's gaze.

Sebastian scowled darkly. 'This whole business

seems a lesson in futility when we are no longer at war with France!'

William Bancroft frowned. 'Perhaps you would like to tell that to the families of the many people who died as a result of the information passed to the French by this agent J?'

Sebastian's jaw clenched. 'I simply do not believe that Juliet could ever be involved in such deceit!'

'Then find me evidence to support your claim,' the Earl advised harshly. 'Prove to me beyond a shadow of a doubt that the Countess is innocent, and I will gladly call off my men.'

'Your *spies*, you mean!' Sebastian corrected.

The Earl frowned again. 'As Grayson has already pointed out, would you still feel this way if it had been Lucian who had perished at Waterloo?'

Sebastian knew that he would not. It was because Gray's own brother had been killed there that he allowed his friend even the grudging benefit of the doubt.

'What a pleasant surprise to see you so unexpectedly returned, St Claire.' The unmistakable voice of the Duke of Carlyne sounded behind Sebastian. 'And so quickly, too!' he mocked.

Sebastian schooled his features into an expression of boredom before turning to face the older man, glad of that composure when he saw Juliet standing beside the Duke, her gloved hand still resting upon his arm. 'Wynter,' he greeted him tersely. 'Lady Boyd.' He gave her a stiffly formal bow.

Juliet had been stunned when, as she and the Duke strolled back to the house, she had recognised Sebastian standing on the terrace talking with the Earl of Banford, knowing he could not possibly have ridden to London and back again so quickly. Which begged the question: why had Sebastian returned without reaching London, as he had originally planned?

'Lord St Claire.' Juliet curtseyed, her lashes lowered as she refused to meet the intensity of his searching golden gaze. Sebastian had departed Banford Park this morning without so much as a single word of goodbye. Such behaviour after their night together was unforgivable. 'If you will both excuse us…?' She smiled at the Earl of Banford. 'His Grace has suggested taking me boating on the lake,' she added, with a pleading glance at the Duke for having changed her mind without consulting him. He gave a silent, but gracious acknowledgement with his head in reply to her plea.

Her chin lifted determinedly, green eyes sparkling with challenge as she turned back to Sebastian and saw the blaze of scorn that darkened his face. After leaving her so suddenly the night before, and his abrupt departure this morning, how dared Sebastian look at her in that contemptuous way? How *dared* he!

'Did you not see enough of the wildlife on the island yesterday?' he asked insultingly.

Juliet felt the bloom of heat in her cheeks even as she continued to meet his derisive gaze. 'Admittedly, our little excursion yesterday was…informative. But I am sure that another visit to the island today in the company of His Grace will prove to be as much if not more so.' Her eyes glittered in triumph.

Sebastian was left in no doubt, during this conversation of *double entendres*, as to Juliet's anger towards him. Indeed, she had every reason to be angry, he acknowledged painfully, after his behaviour in leaving her last night. But was she really angry enough with him to allow the Duke of Carlyne to row her over to the island and then seduce her?

Sebastian had a sinking feeling that she just might be…

'I am sorry if you found my own…knowledge to be so limited.' Sebastian's mouth thinned as Juliet's gaze continued to battle silently with his own. 'Perhaps I should accompany the two of you this morning, so that I, too, might learn from His Grace's experience?'

Juliet had never felt so much like striking someone as she did Sebastian at that moment. His whole demeanour was intolerable. Inexcusable. Totally unacceptable when he had made it more than obvious by his behaviour last night, and again this morning, that she was no longer of interest to him now that he had finally succeeded in bedding her!

It was also totally ridiculous to even suggest that Sebastian might learn anything from the Duke of Carlyne on the subject of 'experience' when their own lovemaking the night before had proved so exquisite Juliet still trembled at the knees just thinking about it.

'I very much doubt that the row-boat is big enough to accommodate three people, My Lord,' she told him sweetly. 'And, even if it were, you have already explored the island once—so rendering it of no further interest to you.'

Sebastian's jaw clenched. 'In *your* opinion.'

'In my *considered* opinion, yes,' Juliet corrected him,

with a gracious inclination of her head. 'We really should go now, Your Grace.' She turned to the Duke. 'Otherwise we will have no time for our excursion before luncheon.'

Those wicked blue eyes laughed down at her appreciatively. 'Your wish is my command, dear lady.'

Juliet gave Sebastian a challenging glare as she answered the Duke. 'You are everything that is accommodating, Your Grace.'

'Where ladies are concerned I find it wiser to be so,' he drawled dryly, before turning to the other two men. 'No doubt we will see you later, St Claire, Bancroft.'

Juliet would most definitely see him later, Sebastian decided furiously as he found himself left with no choice but to stand on the terrace and watch her as she accompanied the reputedly fickle but equally seductive Duke of Carlyne down to the lake....

'Did you find Wynter's *experience* as *informative* as you had hoped it would be?'

Juliet came to a stunned halt in the doorway of her bed-chamber as she saw Sebastian's elegant figure once again sprawled on top of her bed, his head resting against the raised pillows as he looked across at her with narrowed eyes. Thankfully, he was fully dressed this time!

As it happened, boating with the Duke of Carlyne had proved a more pleasant experience than Juliet could ever have imagined as once again, away from the curious gaze of the other members of the ton, he had proved himself to be a pleasant and intelligent companion, with no hint at flirtation. He had also been polite enough not to mention Juliet's decision to accept his invitation, after all. Or the reason for it….

Sebastian's arrogance in invading her bedchamber once again was intolerable. 'I found His Grace most knowledgeable, yes,' she returned coolly as she strolled into the room and closed the door behind her. 'I do not recall giving you leave to come and go in my bedchamber whenever you please, Sebastian,' she added firmly.

'No?' Sebastian drawled as he sat up to swing his legs over, so that his booted feet now rested on the floor. 'I had believed last night gave me that right.'

'Considering the haste with which you left my bedchamber once you had succeeded in what you came for, I cannot imagine why you should do so!' She raised scornful brows.

Sebastian bit back his angry retort. 'I warn you not to push me any further today, Juliet.'

'Do not attempt to threaten me, Sebastian,' she returned frostily, those green eyes glittering like twin emeralds between thick dark lashes, and her cheeks flushed with temper.

She had never looked more beautiful, Sebastian acknowledged heavily. If they were to make love now he had no doubt that Juliet would be utterly magnificent. But their earlier conversation, and the challenging look in Juliet's eyes before she disappeared to the lake with Darius Wynter, warned Sebastian it would be a grave mistake on his part to even attempt to make love with her in her present mood. A mood his own cavalier behaviour the night before had no doubt created.

He drew in a controlling breath as he forced himself to relax. 'Juliet—'

'Would you please leave, Sebastian?' she cut in impatiently. 'I wish only to forget what transpired between us last night.'

'I doubt very much that you are any more able to forget it than I am!' Sebastian rasped harshly.

Her chin rose. 'You think too much of yourself, My Lord. I assure you that the attentions of a man such as Duke of Carlyne are more than adequate to banish any thoughts of our own time together completely from my memory!'

Sebastian became very still, breathing deeply, his hands clenched at his sides as he fought to control the urge he once again had to either kiss Juliet into stunned silence or put her over his knee and spank her little bottom until it was warm. But he knew that to do either was guaranteed to alienate her even further. If that were possible…

He sighed, making a monumental effort to relax. 'Juliet, I apologise if any of my actions have offended you—'

'Neither you nor your actions have offended me, Lord St Claire,' she said waspishly. 'Obviously I have little experience in such matters, but I believe it is the way of the ton to—to enjoy a flirtation at gatherings such as these, before both parties move on to other amusements?' She gave a dismissive trill of laughter. 'Heaven forbid that you should find me any less sophisticated than the women you usually consort with!'

A nerve pulsed in Sebastian's jaw. 'I do not believe I have ever given you reason to believe I regard you in that casual way—'

'And I do not believe you gave regard to me at all

when you deserted my bedchamber so abruptly last night or left Banford Park so suddenly this morning!' Her eyes flashed furiously.

'I have come back.'

'And am I supposed to feel grateful for that?' she snapped.

'You might have waited a day or so, at least, before taking Carlyne into your bed in my place!' he retorted jealously.

'The Duke will not be here in a day or so.'

'So you thought to take your chance with him today, while there was still time? Now that you find yourself sexually liberated, who is to be next, I wonder? Bancroft, perhaps? Or Grayson? Or perhaps you might like to try your newly found experience with the Duke of Essex? I doubt a man of his years has been capable of satisfying his wife in bed for some years now, but it may be different with a woman so much younger than himself.'

'You are *despicable*!' Juliet cried, and she slapped Sebastian hard against one rigid cheek. She gasped, her eyes wide with distress, as she realised what she had done. 'Please leave, Sebastian,' she choked as she raised her hands to the heat of her own cheeks. 'Leave now, before we succeed in hurting each other any more than we already have.'

Sebastian closed his eyes briefly, the stinging slap to his cheek having succeeded in bringing his emotions back under his control, at least. He raised his lids to look at Juliet. 'We should not be hurting each other at all,' he admitted wearily.

'And yet we are doing so.'

'And yet we are doing so,' Sebastian acknowledged heavily. 'I should not have left you so abruptly last night.'

'You should not.'

'Or again this morning.'

'No.'

Sebastian sighed. 'I can only apologise again, Juliet.'

She gave a stiff inclination of her head. 'Your apology is accepted.'

He nodded. 'It would go some way to cooling my anger if you would assure me that you have not been foolish enough to succumb to Carlyne's brand of seduction?'

'Foolish, My Lord?' Juliet echoed sharply.

Sebastian grimaced as he easily heard the return of indignation to her tone. 'Perhaps I chose my words badly…'

'Perhaps?' The scorn was evident in Juliet's eyes. 'Tell me, My Lord, why should it be any more foolish of me to allow the wealthy and eligible Duke of Carlyne to seduce me than Lord Sebastian St Claire? I seem to recall that you told me yourself that a duke is much more of a social catch than a lord? I believe that must apply to a lover as much as a husband!'

Yes, he had said that, Sebastian recalled with disgust. He had said and done a lot of things, hurtful things, to this woman that he now wished undone and unsaid….

It was one of the reasons he had lain awake most of the previous night, trying to find the answer to those questions, only to be left with another question he had no answer to: why was it that Juliet brought out such possessiveness in him as Sebastian had never encountered before? Or felt comfortable with…

'Is Wynter now your lover?' he pressed.

Juliet raised dark brows. 'I believe His Grace is in his bedchamber even now, preparing to leave Banford Park.'

'You did not answer my question!'

'Neither will I!' Juliet told him impatiently. 'It really is past time you to left my bedchamber, Lord St Claire,' she insisted.

Sebastian's mouth thinned at her formality. 'Juliet—'

'Now,' she ordered. 'I am currently undecided as to whether or not I intend remaining at Banford Park or taking my leave. But you may be assured that if I *do* decide to stay then I will be asking Dolly Bancroft to move me to another bedchamber as soon as is possible!'

'Perhaps the Duke of Carlyne might be persuaded into staying after all if you were to move into the bed-chamber next to his?' Sebastian jeered.

Colour brightened her cheeks. 'Perhaps he might!'

Sebastian once more drew in a controlling breath before slowly releasing it again. 'We appear to be having our first lovers' quarrel, Juliet.'

'You are quite wrong, My Lord,' Juliet assured him coolly.

He raised dark brows. 'How so?'

She gave a brief nod. 'This is our last quarrel, not our first.'

Sebastian scowled. 'You are ending our relationship?'

Juliet gave a weary sigh. 'I believe you have done that quite effectively already. You came to Banford Park, bent on seduction. You have more than succeeded.' Beyond Juliet's wildest dreams! 'Let that be an end to it.'

'And if I do not wish for it to end?'

'If that should be the case—'

'It is.'

Juliet grimaced. 'Then I am sorry. It is over,' she added with finality. Whatever madness had possessed her, whatever attraction Sebastian still held for her, Juliet knew that if she were to retain anything of her pride then it must cease. Now.

'You—'

'I am late again, Juliet…'

Juliet turned to see her obviously embarrassed cousin once again standing in the open doorway of her bedchamber. 'Please come in, Helena,' she said. 'Lord St Claire was just leaving.' She turned to him and raised a challenging eyebrow.

Sebastian was filled with frustration as he returned that gaze, knowing by the determination in Juliet's expression that if he left now she would do everything in her power to make sure they were never alone together like this ever again. Neither could he continue this conversation in front of her maid.

'Come back later.' He dismissed the younger woman without so much as a glance.

'I do not think so, My Lord,' Juliet was the one to answer him firmly.

His mouth thinned. 'We need to finish this conversation *now*, Juliet.'

'It is finished, Sebastian.' Her voice was husky. Final.

Sebastian looked at her searchingly, knowing by the calmness of Juliet's gaze and the proud tilt to her chin that she was not referring only to their conversation. That she *really* meant this to be an end their relationship….

Chapter Fourteen

Sebastian's eyes narrowed to chilling slits as he turned to Juliet's maid. 'I believe I told you to leave,' he said to the unattractive stick of a girl. Only to see her wide pale blue gaze turn to Juliet. '*I* am the one who has instructed you to go,' Sebastian ordered harshly.

'Fortunately, My Lord, *you* do not have the authority to say yea or nay to any member of my household.' Juliet's tone was positively starchy. 'Therefore, *you* are the one who will leave my bedchamber. Before I need to ask Helena to summon Lord Bancroft so that he might have you forcefully removed.'

He was behaving more like his arrogant brother Hawk than himself, Sebastian thought with disgust—and he was seriously annoying Juliet into the bargain. When all he wanted to do was talk to her. No, he would be lying if he claimed that was *all* he wished to do with her! Just being in the same room with her was enough for Sebastian to want to make love with her again. Something, in her present mood, she would obviously welcome as warmly as a dip in the ice-cold water of the lake!

He forced the tension from his shoulders. 'Perhaps if I were to politely request that you dismiss your maid?'

'It would not make the slightest difference to the outcome when it is Helena I wish to stay and you to leave,' Juliet insisted.

Sebastian scowled at her stubbornness. 'Then might I have your promise, at least, that you will not think of leaving Banford Park until we have had the opportunity to speak again?'

'I will give no such undertaking.' Juliet snapped her impatience with his persistence. Why could Sebastian not just leave? Could he not see that there was nothing left for them to say to each other? That for him to be here at all was only causing her discomfort? 'My decision to stay or to go will be set against my own needs and not those of Lord Sebastian St Claire!'

A nerve pulsed in his jaw. 'You—'

'It really is not acceptable for you to continue to bully Jul—My Lady in this way,' interjected Helena, obviously completely forgetting the role of maid she had chosen to play.

Dark brows rose above an expression of incredulous disdain as Sebastian slowly turned to look at Helena. Juliet very much doubted that, as the son and brother of a duke, he usually deigned to notice household staff at all. Or had ever been spoken to by one of them like that! That Helena had done so would have been laughable under any other circumstances.

As it was, there was nothing about this present situation that Juliet could find in the least amusing. 'I am sure Lord St Claire was about to take his leave…' She frowned her irritation as Sebastian made no move to go, but instead continued to glower at Helena. 'Sebastian?' she prompted sharply.

He drew his attention back to her with an effort, that scowl still darkening his brow as he spoke. 'If that is your wish. But I should not make too hasty a departure if I were you, Lady Boyd,' he added. 'The Duke of Carlyne might be leaving later today, but Lord Grayson has informed me that he fully expects to return this evening, once he has dealt with the necessary business matters that so urgently required his attention in London.'

Juliet eyed him warily. 'Lord Grayson's movements are of little interest to me, I assure you.'

'How so, when he is another of your admirers?' Sebastian taunted her.

Juliet could see exactly where he was going with this conversation, and the thought of spending even one more night at Banford Park was becoming less and less appealing to her. 'Whether he is or he is not, Lord St Claire, I have now definitely decided that this evening shall be my last at Banford Park,' she informed him.

'Is that not a little…precipitate on your part, Lady Boyd?' he jeered.

'I find the company here not at all to my liking,' she said coolly.

Sebastian eyed her ominously for several long seconds before giving a token bow. 'Until later, then, Lady Boyd.' He completely ignored the existence of her maid as he strode forcefully from the room.

'Oh, Juliet, I do most sincerely apologise!' Helena instantly turned to give Juliet a rueful grimace. 'I did not realise until it was too late that, as your maid, I should not have spoken to Lord St Claire in that familiar way!'

'Do not give it another thought, dear Helena,' Juliet said tiredly as she moved to sit before her dressing table. After all, Helena was not really a maid, and her only purpose in speaking as she had had been to defend Juliet.

Helena winced. 'It was only that I could not stand silently by while he bullied you like that. It reminded me too much of how Crestwood always treated you.' She frowned.

Juliet could not imagine two men more unalike than her husband and Sebastian St Claire! She had found Sebastian to be full of laughter where Crestwood had been dour. Sebastian warm where Crestwood had been cold. Sebastian a considerate and satisfying lover, whereas Crestwood—

Juliet broke free of those disturbing thoughts. Crestwood was dead. Dead, dead, *dead*! As dead as her relationship with Sebastian now was… 'As I have every intention of leaving in the morning, Helena, Lord St Claire's behaviour does not signify,' she said dully.

Helena moved to stand behind Juliet and began tidying her hair. 'I would not allow a man such as Lord St Claire to force *me* into leaving if I did not wish to go.'

Juliet gave a rueful smile. 'I assure you it *is* now my dearest wish to leave here as soon as is politely possible!'

Her cousin looked wistful. 'He did not seem at all as charming as the other maids claim him to be.'

Juliet eyed her cousin teasingly. 'Perhaps you preferred what you saw of him last night?'

Helena cheeks coloured warmly as she met that teasing gaze in the mirror. 'Was he as formidable a lover as his body promised?' she asked eagerly.

'Formidable indeed,' Juliet murmured with a self-conscious laugh.

Her cousin chuckled softly. 'Then perhaps the handsome lord might succeed in persuading you into staying on here after all?'

Juliet sobered. 'I am afraid not, dear Helena. My mind is quite made up. Is your ankle fully recovered?' When her cousin nodded in the affirmative, she continued, 'Then I will inform Lady Bancroft later tonight of our departure tomorrow, and you must prepare to leave first thing in the morning.'

And once returned to Shropshire, Juliet hoped that she would be able to put all thoughts of Sebastian St Claire completely from her mind.

If her memory would allow her that luxury....

'Laurent...'

'Milord?' his valet answered distractedly.

Sebastian watched their reflection broodingly in the cheval mirror later that evening, as his dapper little valet flicked imaginary pieces of lint from Sebastian's exquisitely tailored black evening jacket. Laurent had been with him for almost five years now, and Sebastian had always found the other man to be as quiet as he was efficient, with no inclination to gossip as Sebastian's previous valet had been wont to do. Not altogether a helpful circumstance in his present situation!

'Laurent...' he started again.

'*Oui*, milord?' The older man stopped fussing over Sebastian's appearance long enough to look up at him with quizzical brown eyes.

Sebastian turned away from his reflection in the mirror and straightened the lacy cuffs of his shirt so that they showed just beneath his jacket. 'Your accommodation here is...comfortable?'

Laurent looked shocked that his employer should even ask such a question. 'Yes, milord.'

He nodded, avoiding the older man's gaze. 'Is there much gossip below stairs?'

The older man grimaced. 'There is always gossip below stairs, milord.'

'Of course,' Sebastian allowed dryly, still unable to meet the other man's puzzled gaze. 'Such as...?'

Laurent's brows disappeared beneath the grey fringe brushed so meticulously across his receding hairline. 'Milord...?'

'Oh, for goodness' sake, man!' Sebastian gave up all attempt at casual uninterest in their conversation. 'I wish to know what is being said below stairs concerning the guests!'

His valet looked stunned. 'Milord, a good servant would not *dream* of discussing—'

'Poppycock!' Sebastian dismissed. Sebastian was fully aware that valets and maids—household staff in general—usually knew *exactly* what was going on in the lives of their employers. Especially in their bedrooms!

'Now, get on with it and tell me some of the gossip, before I decide to send you to my estate in Berkshire for a month to deal with my wardrobe there!'

Laurent looked suitably dismayed at the idea of being banished to the wilds of Berkshire. 'Well, milord, Lady Butler—having attempted and failed to attract a certain gentleman…'

'If you mean me, man, then say so!' Sebastian said, suddenly amused.

'Yes, milord.' Laurent looked uncomfortable. 'Failing to engender your interest, she has now turned her attention to Lord Montag—'

'I have absolutely no interest in knowing who Lady Butler is currently attempting to seduce into her bed,' Sebastian interrupted.

His valet gave him a searching glance. 'Perhaps if you were to tell me which of the guests you *are* interested in…?'

Sebastian sighed, hating this conversation, but knowing it was necessary for him to act quickly now that Juliet had informed him she had every intention of leaving here on the morrow. 'I wish to know if there has been any gossip concerning the Countess of Crestwood.'

His valet's brows rose even higher. 'The lady in the bedchamber next to this one, milord?'

Sebastian grimaced. 'Exactly.'

'Gossip about the Countess and whom, milord?'

'Me, of course!' he said.

'*You*, milord?' Laurent looked suitably—genuinely—surprised.

Sebastian's eyes narrowed. 'Her maid has not…

gossiped with the other servants concerning my... interest in her mistress?'

'Miss Jourdan is the epitome of discretion, milord. As am I,' Laurent added stiffly, making Sebastian aware that this topic of conversation was as painful for the other man as it was for him. 'Perhaps Miss Jourdan's reticence is because she is unaware of the existence of such an...interest?'

Somehow Sebastian doubted that very much, considering that he had been completely naked the previous evening when Miss Jourdan had entered her mistress's bedchamber! 'I assure you, Miss Jourdan's silence on the subject is much more likely to be because she does not like or approve of me,' he drawled ruefully.

'Surely you are mistaken, milord?' Laurent looked shocked at the mere idea that a lowly lady's maid should approve or disapprove of anything his lordly employer did. 'Perhaps you have mistaken shyness for disapproval?'

'Perhaps,' Sebastian allowed—although he somehow doubted that very much after the girl's outspokenness earlier!

His valet nodded. 'In our own conversations I have found Miss Jourdan to be very quiet and unassuming.'

Sebastian nodded. 'No doubt the two of you have enjoyed talking together of your mutual homes in France?'

'Not really, milord.' The older man shook his head regretfully. 'I left France many years ago, as you know, and Miss Jourdan, although she enjoys listening to and talking with the other members of the household staff, hardly talks of herself at all.'

'No?'

'Nor her employer,' his valet assured him firmly.

Sebastian smiled grimly. 'Meaning my secret is safe in the hands of yourself and Miss Jourdan?'

'What secret, milord?' Laurent responded discreetly.

'Indeed!' Sebastian gave a chuckle. 'Thank you, Laurent, you have been most helpful.'

'You are welcome, milord.' The valet hesitated, and Sebastian looked a question at him. 'I have just recalled, milord, something that Miss Jourdan said which was rather curious.'

'And what was that?' Sebastian asked.

'Once she said "my cousin" instead of "My Lady"—I considered it a slip of the tongue at the time, but as you have shown such an interest in the maid I thought I should mention it.'

'Very good, Laurent,' Sebastian said thoughtfully.

The valet took this as the dismissal that it was, and collected up the clothes Sebastian had worn that day before quietly leaving the bedchamber.

Sebastian stayed in his bedchamber for some time after Laurent had gone, a dark frown marring his brow. Time was quickly running out to either disprove Juliet's guilt or claim her innocence.

Which meant that Sebastian needed to follow up every piece of evidence, however small. He should speak to Bancroft right away....

'As we are both in disgrace with Dolly, it is perhaps politic that the two of us engage in conversation together!'

Juliet had been doing her utmost to ignore Sebastian's presence in the drawing room as she chatted with some of the other guests gathered before dinner and he engaged in a lengthy conversation with their host. Although that did not mean she was not completely aware of his imposing and handsome presence across the room in tailored dark evening wear and snowy white linen.

'My Lord?' Turning to look at him, seeing the candle-light highlighting the gold amongst the darkness of his hair, his face arrogantly handsome, was enough to make Juliet's mouth go dry, her cheeks become flushed and her body suffuse with heat. He, on the other hand, looked as self-confident and amused as usual. Almost as if their disagreement earlier today had not happened, damn him!

He gave that lazily seductive smile. 'Now I have informed Dolly that I intend leaving tomorrow, she has accused me of attempting to ruin her house party.'

Her eyes widened. 'You too are leaving…?'

He shrugged. 'I see little point in staying on here once you have left.'

Juliet felt a jolt in the region of her heart. Although why she should be in the least concerned at Sebastian's claim that the timing of his departure was due solely to her, she had no idea. Especially as she had every intention of not even thinking of him again once she left here tomorrow!

She gave him an irritated frown. 'I am sure there are plenty of other ladies present who would welcome the attentions of the handsome and eligible Lord Sebastian St Claire.' She would also guess that the departure of both of them on the morrow would engender even more unwelcome gossip!

He shrugged those broad shoulders. 'But none he has any interest in showing attention to.'

'Really, Sebastian,' she huffed, 'can you not see that any further attempt on your part to charm me is a complete waste of your time and energy—not to mention my own?'

His mouth tightened. 'Perhaps you are so dismissive of our relationship because you and Wynter have made an assignation to meet elsewhere?'

'The Duke and I—!' Juliet gasped at the directness of Sebastian's attack, her face paling. 'You are being ridiculous, Sebastian,' she breathed raggedly.

'Am I?'

'Most assuredly,' Juliet told him firmly. 'The Duke was only being kind to me today.'

'Wynter is not known for his kindness!'

Her eyes flashed deeply green. 'And you are?'

As it happened, Sebastian was indeed known for his agreeable temperament and his lazy charm. It just seemed to desert him every time he came anywhere near Juliet! Why that should be—when Sebastian wished only to be with her, to kiss her, to hold her, to make love with her—was still a mystery to him.

'I would like to think so, yes,' he bit out.

'We are not good for each other, Sebastian.'

'On the contrary, Juliet, we are very good together,' he murmured.

She shook her head. 'That was not the impression you gave me last night, when you left my bedchamber so abruptly.'

Sebastian stared at her blankly. What? 'Juliet, I did

not leave you last night because of any disappointment on my part in our lovemaking!' On the contrary, he had left because their lovemaking had been so unlike, so much more than, anything Sebastian had ever experienced before!

Her stance was defensive. 'No?'

'Of course not!' he insisted. 'Was that what today was about?' His eyes narrowed. 'Did you encourage Carlyne's attentions earlier as a means of punishing me because I did not stay with you last night?' If she had, then the punishment had worked; Sebastian's emotions towards Juliet today had been fluctuating between frustration, desire and sheer bloody anger!

She drew herself up proudly. 'You think far too much of yourself, sir.'

'Juliet—'

'If you will excuse me, Lady Boyd, there is a matter I urgently need to discuss with Lord St Claire…?'

Sebastian turned his furious gaze upon his host at his untimely interruption. 'Can it not wait, Bancroft?'

'I am afraid not.' The older man held his gaze steadily. 'Lord Grayson has returned from London, and there are some things we need to discuss with you urgently in my study before we all dine. If you will excuse us, Lady Boyd?' His smile was apologetic as he bowed to Juliet.

She gave a gracious inclination of her head. 'I believe my own conversation with Lord St Claire was at an end.'

Sebastian did not care for the finality in Juliet's tone. And their conversation was far from over! 'I will join you shortly, Bancroft,' he told the other man, even as he reached out and took a firm clasp of Juliet's arm to prevent her moving away.

Even that light touch was enough to make Sebastian completely aware of the silkiness of her skin. To remind him of how he had caressed and kissed every inch of her the night before. And the instant hardening of his thighs was enough to tell him how much he longed to do so again....

Sebastian almost groaned out loud at the need, the hunger he felt, to put his lips against her skin and feel the heat of her blood pulsing beneath.

Dear God, his desire for this woman was going to drive him out of his mind!

Lord Bancroft looked at him for several seconds from beneath hooded lids, and obviously saw the implacability in Sebastian's expression. 'Very well. I will expect you to join me shortly, St Claire,' he capitulated. 'My dear.' He bowed briefly to Juliet.

Juliet waited only as long as it took their host to walk to his wife's side before turning back to Sebastian and attempting to release her arm from his grasp. She looked about her uncomfortably, sure that they must be the cynosure of all eyes. These elite members of the ton were, as usual, studiously looking the other way—at the same time no doubt totally aware of the intensity of the exchange between the Countess of Crestwood and Lord St Claire!

'Sebastian, you must cease drawing attention to us in this way!'

His mouth tightened as he refused to release her. 'Why must I?'

'Because I do not like it.' Her frown was pained. 'I

hate having everyone look at me in this way. For them to think—to know… Sebastian, it would be far wiser for you to attend Lord Bancroft in his study,' she pleaded.

'Lord Bancroft can go to the devil!' Sebastian rasped as he stared down at her intently. 'Juliet, I need to talk to you,' he begged. 'There are things I need to tell you. To say to you—'

'Can they not wait?'

He turned to glance briefly in William Bancroft's direction before muttering, 'No, I do not believe they can.'

Juliet shook her head, even as she looked up searchingly into his heartbreakingly handsome face. 'I do not know what you want from me, Sebastian… Another night like last night, perhaps?' she choked. 'I cannot do it, Sebastian. I thought last night that I could. That, like some of the other ladies present, I could take a lover and enjoy the encounter before returning to my quiet life in Shropshire with no regrets.' She gave another shake of her head. 'But I cannot. I do not condemn or judge those who do. It is simply not the way I wish to conduct my own life.'

Sebastian could see by her determined expression that Juliet meant what she said. And he knew by the firmness of her tone that she wanted no more to do with him or their so far turbulent relationship.

He had wanted this woman, desired her, from the first moment he had noticed her at some otherwise totally forgettable ball a long time ago. That desire had increased to the point of madness during these last few days of closer acquaintance. The thought of simply letting her leave him tomorrow morning and go back to Shropshire was totally unacceptable to him.

Only the resolve in her face told Sebastian that she did not intend giving him any choice in the matter....

His hand moved reluctantly, caressingly, down the length of her arm as he finally, slowly, released her. 'We will talk again before you leave.'

'I do not think that wise, Sebastian.'

'To hell with what is wise!' He scowled down at her darkly. 'Juliet, we have been unwise any number of times in the last few days.' His voice softened as he saw the alarm that suddenly appeared in her eyes. 'What possible harm can it do if it happens one last time?'

The harm, Juliet knew, was that it *would* be for the last time....

During this conversation—a conversation that had battered and then stripped away all Juliet's defences as she tried to hold Sebastian at arm's length and failed!— she had realised something so profound, so disturbing, that she could barely think at all.

She was in love with Sebastian St Claire!

Not lightly. Not in the way of some young girl's infatuation with a handsome and charming man who had flattered and beguiled her. But totally, irrevocably, completely in love with him....

Chapter Fifteen

'Juliet…?'

Juliet's mouth had become dry, her breathing shallow and laboured, as she tried to deal with her momentous discovery. She was in love with Sebastian St Claire. Utterly. Futilely!

'Juliet!' Sebastian pressed sharply when she seemed totally lost to him, her face pale, her gaze dark and guarded as she finally looked up at him. 'Tell me what is wrong!' His eyes moved searchingly over the delicate loveliness of her face.

'Wrong?' She gave a broken laugh and seemed to collect herself with effort. 'What could possibly be wrong, Sebastian? I have been seduced. You have allowed me to seduce you in return. Now we are to part ways. Is that not the usual outcome of relationships formed at parties such as these?'

Sebastian had never before attended one of these summer house parties—had always in the past considered them the height of boredom. But, from the little he had observed of the behaviour of their fellow guests, no doubt Juliet was right in her surmise....

His mouth firmed. 'We do not have to part. Instead of returning alone to our respective homes when we leave here tomorrow we could both go to London—'

'I have responsibilities in Shropshire that are in need of my attention.'

'Then I could accompany you to Shropshire.' Until he spoke the words Sebastian had had no idea that he wished to accompany Juliet to her home in Shropshire! But, having made the suggestion, he now fully appreciated the benefits of such a plan. The members of the ton who returned to London for the Little Season would not start arriving back in town for several weeks yet. Weeks he could spend in Shropshire with Juliet....

Her eyes were wide. 'I think not, Sebastian.'

'Why not?' He reached out to take one of her gloved hands in his, and stroked the soft pad of his thumb against the warmth of her skin through the lace. 'We could continue to explore and enjoy this passion we have discovered we feel for each other.'

Juliet's knees felt weak at the thought of spending hours, days, weeks alone with Sebastian in the privacy of her estate in Shropshire, the two of them indulging fully in the physical delights she had so recently discovered in his arms....

But that weakness was quickly followed by thoughts of her recently realised love for this man. Of the increase in pain she would suffer when the time came for them to finally part from each other. As they inevitably would.

Her smile did not reach her eyes when she looked

up at Sebastian once more. 'Pleasurable as these days may have been, I assure you my own desire for you is completely spent,' she lied, and removed her hand from his before stepping away. 'Please do not attempt to speak to me on this subject again,' she added, as Sebastian would have done so. 'This has been a…pleasant interlude, and I thank you for it, but now you must return to your own life and I to mine.' She gave him a cool nod before turning away to cross the room to where several ladies stood in conversation. Juliet's smile was polite as, completely contrary to her reception a few short days ago by the other guests at Banford Park, she was warmly welcomed into their circle.

Sebastian ignored William Bancroft as the other man indicated he should now follow him to his study, and instead watched Juliet as she walked away from him. He knew himself well and truly dismissed, and was unsure who he was most angry with. Himself for allowing himself to become embroiled in a situation that was surely going to blow up in his face, or Bancroft and Gray for embroiling him in it in the first place!

He was still consumed with that anger when he left the drawing room and finally joined Bancroft and Gray in the Earl's study. He thrust the door open without first knocking, glaring at the two men seated there as they turned to look at him. 'This had better be good, Bancroft,' he barked. 'I assure you I am in no mood for more of your theatrics!'

'No theatrics, St Claire, but irrefutable proof of guilt. Helped by the information you gave me earlier today,' the Earl announced as he rose to his feet behind the desk, his expression grave. 'If you would please join us, so that we might talk in private…?'

Sebastian's heart felt heavy in his chest as he slowly entered the room and closed the door softly behind him.

Juliet, having been quietly and discreetly summoned to Lord Bancroft's study as soon as the lengthy dinner came to an end, had absolutely no idea what she was doing there. Or why Sebastian and Lord Grayson were also present—Lord Grayson standing in front of the curtained window, Sebastian standing behind the chair in which she sat, his expression grimly unapproachable despite that almost protective stance.

She looked quizzically at Lord Bancroft as he stood in front of her before the unlit fireplace. 'Perhaps you would care to tell me why I have been brought here?'

The prolonged dinner had been something of a trial for Juliet to get through, as she'd tried to engage in polite conversation with the two men seated either side of her, all the time aware of Sebastian's broodingly silent figure seated on the opposite side of the table. The tension she could now feel emanating from the three gentlemen present was doing little to ease that sense of disquiet.

William Bancroft gave a grimace. 'It is rather a—a delicate matter we wish to discuss with you.'

'Yes?'

'Very delicate.' Her host looked distinctly uncomfortable now.

Juliet turned to glance sharply up at Sebastian, where he stood with one hand resting on the back of her chair, but she could still read nothing from the remoteness of his expression. Surely he had not discussed the intimacy of their relationship with these two gentlemen? And even if he had, of what possible interest could it be to either of them?

Sebastian's mouth tightened grimly as he saw the look of confusion on Juliet's face. 'Perhaps you should tell Juliet the good news first, hmm, Bancroft?' he suggested. 'Or perhaps *I* should.' He stepped away from Juliet's chair to move so that he was standing beside her. 'The good news, Juliet—contrary to what Bancroft and Grayson initially believed—' he swept the two men a contemptuous glance '—is that you are no longer suspected of being a spy for the French!'

She gasped, her face paling, those green eyes deep pools of bewilderment. 'I—What *are* you talking about?'

'Perhaps you should allow *me* to explain matters to the Countess, St Claire.' Bancroft shot him a reproving frown.

Sebastian remained totally unmoved by that disapproval, and continued to look down piercingly at Juliet. 'You were invited to Banford Park for one purpose, Juliet, and one purpose only,' he revealed. 'So that Bancroft and his fellow agents of the Crown might ascertain the necessary evidence that would convict you of both treason against your country and the murder of your husband!'

'That is enough, St Claire!' the older man warned coldly.

'Not nearly enough,' Sebastian countered furiously. He was in the grip of a totally impotent fury because Juliet, once made aware of how Sebastian had been privy to the suspicions against her almost since his arrival here, but had done nothing to prevent them, would never forgive him. As she should not.

It did not signify that he had told Bancroft and Gray he believed they were wrong to accuse Juliet. That he had insisted there had to be some other explanation for the evidence the two men had gathered against her. That even if she had killed her husband he believed she would have had good reason for doing so—a reason that had nothing to do with treason.

Ultimately, despite the deepening of his intimate relationship with Juliet, Sebastian had done nothing to stop or hinder Bancroft's investigations. In his own eyes Sebastian's silence damned him completely. In Juliet's he would become nothing but a cheat and a liar.

Juliet's bewilderment with this situation had only worsened at Sebastian's furious outburst. 'I— The suspicion of my having somehow been involved in Crestwood's death is nothing new,' she exclaimed. 'But why should anyone think me guilty of *treason*?'

'Because that is why Crestwood died,' Sebastian explained. 'For a number of years he had been giving information to the French concerning the movement of English troops and ensuing battles. Including the necessary information that resulted in Bonaparte escaping from his confinement on Elba.'

'*Edward* had?' Juliet gasped. 'You are mistaken.' She shook her head in disbelief. 'Edward was totally loyal to the Crown. Always. He would *never* have done the things you are accusing him of.'

'Not knowingly, no,' Sebastian agreed.

'What do you mean?' Juliet asked.

He drew in a deep breath. 'It is now known that the information was…gathered…encouraged from Crestwood during and after times of intimacy.'

Juliet felt the colour drain from her cheeks at the memory of her own times with Crestwood during and after intimacy. They had never spoken. Not before. Not during. Not after.

She swallowed down the nausea that had risen in her throat at just thinking of those nights when Crestwood had come to her bedchamber and invaded her body, taking his own pleasure before leaving again, without so much as a word—kind or otherwise—having been spoken between them.

Sebastian St Claire, more than any other man on this earth, knew of her complete inexperience with physical intimacy, let alone the seduction of any man. Including her husband!

What part had Sebastian played in Lord Bancroft's investigations? Could it be that he had deliberately set out to seduce her in the hopes of ascertaining such evidence as was needed to—?

'It was your cousin Helena.'

'*What?*' she cried, a hand brought up to her throat in utter shock.

'The French spy was your cousin. Helena Jourdan.' Lord Bancroft was the one to speak gently after giving Sebastian another censorious glance. 'She was also responsible for killing your husband when he finally realised and confronted her with what she had done.'

Juliet was so pale Sebastian was concerned she might actually faint. 'You are mistaken, sir,' she insisted shakily. 'Helena's parents were killed by the French six years ago. She herself was held captive for over a week before she managed to escape and find passage to England and safety at Falcon Manor. She—'

'Your cousin was confronted earlier this evening and has admitted to being guilty of all the charges made against her.' Lord Bancroft looked down at her sympathetically.

Juliet stood up abruptly, two wings of colour appearing in the pallor of her cheeks. 'Then she is doing so in some mistaken belief that she is protecting me. Because she believes you think me the one guilty of these crimes. Helena would *never* do the things you are accusing her of. Her own parents—my aunt and uncle—were killed by Napoleon's army.'

'Juliet, Helena was the one responsible for bringing those soldiers to the farm of your aunt and uncle, after she gave them information concerning her parents' sympathies towards the English cause.'

Sebastian hated with a passion what they were doing to Juliet. Hated it, but could do nothing to change it. Could do nothing to change the accusation he could see in Juliet's eyes as she turned on him angrily.

'Helena would never have done such a thing! She hates Bonaparte and everything he stands for; anyway, she was only sixteen at the time.'

Bancroft interrupted her outburst. 'Her lover was the French captain in charge of the soldiers the day her parents were killed and the farm ransacked.'

Sebastian sank down wearily into the chair placed in front of the desk, relieved that Bancroft had taken over the conversation, knowing he could not bear to cause Juliet any more hurt himself. To completely devastate the life she had so carefully constructed for herself since Crestwood's death.

Juliet became very still as she looked from William Bancroft to Lord Grayson, and then finally to Sebastian. 'And you, sir? You have implied that these other two gentlemen are agents of the Crown. What part did you play in this charade? Or needn't I ask?' she added contemptuously.

A nerve pulsed in his tightly clenched jaw. 'Juliet—'

'You have St Claire to thank for clearing your name,' Bancroft interjected.

'Indeed?' Juliet's contemptuous gaze did not waver from Sebastian's, and he could only guess at the thoughts, the memories, that were going through her mind. Sebastian's relentless, single-minded pursuit of her almost from the moment of his arrival. How he had seduced her…

'Certainly,' Bancroft continued, ignoring the knife-edged tension between Sebastian and Juliet. 'It was he who brought to my attention earlier today the fact that your maid was in fact not your maid at all, but your French cousin, Helena Jourdan. That being so, she could easily have carried out the earlier misdeeds, as well as the search of my study yesterday—'

'Your study was broken into yesterday?' Juliet interrupted.

The Earl nodded. 'The drawer to the desk had been unlocked and my private papers were disturbed. That, along with St Claire learning your maid's identity, and the information Grayson brought back with him from town, was enough for me to question your cousin earlier and so ascertain the truth.'

'I see.' Juliet turned back to Sebastian. 'No doubt your name will be mentioned favourably in Lord Bancroft's report of this affair?'

The strength of Juliet's anger was the same as his brother Hawk's, Sebastian realised with an inward groan: one tenth of it on the surface, and ninety per cent of it hidden beneath an icy contempt! The contempt she obviously now felt for him and his involvement in this investigation....

Her shoulders firmed determinedly. 'I wish to talk to Helena.'

'I doubt that would be a good idea,' Lord Bancroft said quietly.

'Oh, but I insist, Lord Bancroft, since you have accused my cousin of such heinous crimes.' Juliet stood firm, sure that there must have been some mistake—that Helena could not possibly be guilty of any of the things these men were accusing her of.

Or Crestwood. Her husband had been many things, but a traitor to his king and country had not been one of them. He— Her thoughts came to a sickening halt as she suddenly remembered something Lord Bancroft had said earlier.

'You implied that Crestwood passed along information during and following intimacy?' she whispered, her face once again deathly pale. 'Are you saying—? Are you implying—?'

'Juliet, your cousin has admitted that she and your

husband were lovers almost from the time she entered your household six years ago,' Sebastian told her gently.

'*No!*' She shut her eyes in horror. 'That cannot be. Helena would never— Crestwood was not a sensual man. He was cold. Unfeeling. Totally lacking in all warmth.'

Lord Bancroft looked uncomfortable. 'Crestwood *was* a sensual man—but perhaps not in the way you imagined. For years before your marriage Crestwood, whilst he was in the navy, was attracted to very young, immature females.' His gaze did not quite meet Juliet's. 'Young girls completely lacking in—in the fullness of a womanly figure, shall we say. It did not take your cousin long to discover these preferences, and once she realised his weakness she exploited it to the full.'

Juliet stared at the Earl blankly as she tried to comprehend what he meant. Then she realised what her own figure had been like twelve years ago, when Crestwood had married her; she'd still retained the slimness of her girlhood, before the passing of the years had given her more alluring womanly curves...exactly the sort of womanly curves that Lord Bancroft claimed would not have been at all attractive to Crestwood.

Oh, dear God...!

'These preferences were apparently not seen or recognised whilst Crestwood was away at sea,' Lord Bancroft continued evenly. 'But once he left the navy and took up his seat in the House, became adviser to the government, such things were not acceptable. Hence his late marriage, apparently, to a woman much younger than himself.'

To Juliet. At eighteen years of age. With a figure that

had barely begun to blossom and with no knowledge at all of physical relationships—let alone those as unnatural as Lord Bancroft described!

Juliet felt ill, sick, as she relived every horror of her marriage to the Earl of Crestwood.

'Lady Boyd, I am so sorry—'

'Do not!' Juliet flinched as Lord Grayson would have reached out and taken her trembling hands in his. At that moment she could not bear to be touched. She felt unclean, sullied by the things Lord Bancroft had told her of the man who had been her husband for so many years.

Crestwood had been a man of perversion. A— Juliet could not even think the word, let alone say it. 'I wish to talk to my cousin now,' she told Lord Bancroft flatly.

If Sebastian had not already had reason to admire this woman, then he most certainly did so now, as she stood so erect in the centre of the room, looking at the three men with a proud bearing that refused to be bowed by any of the horrors she had been told.

Juliet Boyd was without a doubt the woman most deserving of being regarded as a lady that Sebastian had ever met.

A lady now totally out of his reach....

'Have you come to gloat?' Juliet snapped miserably, turning to face Sebastian as he stepped from her balcony into her bedchamber.

'Never that.' He gave a weary shake of his head, his expression grim. 'Juliet—'

'Do *not* touch me,' she bit out icily, as Sebastian would have reached out and taken her into his arms.

Juliet could not bear for him to touch her. Could not bear for anyone to touch her. She knew that if anyone did so the brittle shell she had erected about her emotions these last two hours would surely shatter and break, leaving her completely exposed to the pain she was trying so hard to keep from totally overwhelming her.

The pain of having Helena admit—no, proudly claim!—to being guilty of all the charges Lord Bancroft had made against her in the face of overwhelming evidence against her.

The Helena that Juliet had spoken to an hour ago had been a stranger to her—no longer the child she had once played with, nor the friend and confidante of these last six years.

Helena had betrayed her parents, England and Juliet. All without remorse, as far as Juliet could tell.

God knew all of that was difficult enough to bear— and would still have been impossible to believe if Helena had not so defiantly admitted her actions. But for all those things were so horrendous, so numbing, Juliet suffered from a disillusionment even worse than that....

A pain worse than anything she had ever suffered before. Worse than the hell of her marriage to Crestwood. Worse even than Helena's betrayal.

Sebastian's deceit and duplicity these last few days were beyond bearing. To know that he had flirted with her, charmed her, made love to her—all in an effort to discover whether or not she was guilty of heinous crimes. That was more humiliating than anything else Juliet had suffered, either at Crestwood's or Helena's hands.

To know that she had fallen in love with him while

he had only been playing a game in the hope of possibly entrapping her…!

She drew in a deeply controlling breath. 'I wish for you to leave, Lord St Claire.'

His worst fears had been realised, Sebastian thought in despair as he heard and saw the utter contempt in Juliet's voice and expresion as she looked up at him. 'Juliet, please let me explain—'

'There is nothing left to explain.' Her tone was icy. 'Impossible as it still seems, my cousin has admitted to me that she is guilty of all Lord Bancroft accuses her of.' Her voice wavered emotionally. 'There is nothing more to be said. Either on that subject or any other,' she added more firmly. 'My only wish now is to leave here and return to the privacy of my estate in Shropshire.'

Sebastian grimaced. 'Your cousin's confession does at least clear you of any involvement in your husband's death. It means that you will be able to return to Society—'

'I do not *wish* to return to Society!' Her eyes flashed deeply green. 'Helena is my cousin. She has been my constant companion and confidante these last six years. To now discover that she had a hand in her own parents' deaths, as well as that of Crestwood, is beyond endurance!' Her breasts quickly rose and fell as she breathed agitatedly. 'I almost wish I *had* been the one to kill Crestwood rather than Helena—if only so that it would banish the hurt and betrayal I now feel so deeply!'

Sebastian did not need to hear Juliet say that she felt the same hurt and betrayal where he was concerned. It was there in her gaze as she looked at him, in the twist of her lips. 'Juliet, you have to believe me when I say I never believed you guilty of any of Bancroft's accusations.'

'I no longer choose to listen to, let alone believe anything you have to say to me, Lord St Claire!' she declared. 'I am leaving here at first light tomorrow. The two of us will not meet again.'

'Juliet—'

'We will *never* meet again, Sebastian,' she repeated with finality.

A finality that Sebastian knew Juliet meant with every fibre of her being....

Chapter Sixteen

Two months later. The Countess of Crestwood's house, Berkeley Square, London.

Juliet looked up from her embroidery as the elderly butler at her home in London stood hesitantly in the doorway to the family parlour. 'What is it, Haydon?' she prompted, when she saw how uncomfortable he looked.

'I— You have a visitor, My Lady.'

'A visitor, Haydon?' Juliet asked warily.

The butler nodded stiffly. 'A Lord St Claire.'

Juliet swallowed hard. Sebastian! It could be no other. Was she ready to see him yet? That she would have to see him before returning to Shropshire she had already accepted. But did it have to be this morning? Could it not wait until Juliet felt more able to face, deal with, such a confrontation?

'I am afraid the gentleman is refusing to leave until he has spoken with you, My Lady.' Haydon looked even more uncomfortable at relating this information.

Apparently it could *not* wait…

'In fact—' the butler gave a pained wince '—Lord St Claire—'

'Has stated that it is his intention to sit in your hallway until such time as you will agree to see me!' Sebastian finished as he strolled into the parlour to hand his hat and cane to the butler before turning to hold the door open and quirk an imperious brow to indicate the other man should leave. Now.

Such was Sebastian's forceful arrogance that Haydon did so without a single murmur of protest, Juliet noted with a sinking feeling as she carefully laid her embroidery aside.

'Ah,' Sebastian drawled in satisfaction as he shut the door firmly behind the other man. 'It is something of a relief to know that the St Claire air of authority is still fully functional!'

Juliet stared at Sebastian as she slowly rose to her feet. Although how she managed to do either of those things was beyond her when her heart had ceased to beat. When every part of her was alive and sensitised to every part of him!

Her memories of Sebastian these last two months—those vivid memories Juliet had known she would not be able to put from her mind, haunting as they had been—had not done him justice.

The darkness of his hair shot through with gold was longer than she remembered, and slightly tousled, as if he had been running agitated fingers through it before coming here this morning.

Those whisky-coloured eyes—Juliet would never be

able to look at a whisky decanter again without thinking of Sebastian—gazed boldly into hers, as if daring her to deny him.

His mouth—that wickedly sensual mouth that knew and had kissed every inch of her body—was curved into a humourless smile.

As for the muscled strength of his body...

No, Juliet's memories of Sebastian were nowhere near as disturbing as the flesh-and-blood man himself!

She collected herself with effort as she challenged him, 'Have you ever had reason to doubt your authority?'

'Many times during these last two months,' Sebastian admitted.

Two months since Sebastian had last set eyes upon Juliet. Nine weeks, two days, and almost three hours, to be precise, since he had stood aside and watched her coach departing down the driveway of Banford Park.

And not a waking moment of that time had passed without his having thought of her. Wondering if she was well. If she ever thought of him as he thought of her.

If she still hated him...

Sebastian crossed the room in two long strides so that he now stood directly in front of her. She looked so delicately beautiful, in a gown of the palest lemon that perfectly complemented the darkness of her hair and the magnolia of her complexion, the short puff sleeves leaving her arms, throat and the tops of her breasts bare. It was a delicacy that was completely at odds with the angry glitter burning in the depths of those deep green eyes.

'I have missed you, Juliet,' Sebastian told her huskily.

Juliet's heart stalled for a second time before

resuming its beat again, harder and faster. She would not—could not allow herself to be seduced by him again.

Except…

Now that Sebastian stood closer to her, Juliet could see subtle changes in his appearance. Fine lines fanned out from those gloriously golden-brown eyes. There were deep grooves etched beside the firmness of his mouth, and his face looked thinner too—harder, and much less inclined to smile.

'Are you unwell, Sebastian?' she asked, with a concern she couldn't hide.

Sebastian's mouth thinned. 'Other than the fact that I cannot eat, sleep, or make merry as I used to, I believe I am perfectly well.'

Juliet did not know what to make of Sebastian's last statement. Was he implying that *she* was in any way responsible for his insomnia and lack of appetite, either for food or the carnal delights he had once so enjoyed to excess? Or had it been the events of the summer, that insight into the sometimes dark and painful reality of life, that had effected these changes in him? Until she knew the answer to that question, Juliet had no idea what to do or say to him next. Or whether she *should* do or say anything at all, in fact!

'So much so,' Sebastian continued dryly, 'that out of a complete lack of anything else to do with my time I have opened the stables at my estate in Berkshire for stud and training.' He gave an almost embarrassed shrug as Juliet's eyes widened. 'Even my worst enemy would assure you that I have always been a fine judge of prime horseflesh. A stud seemed a logical choice when I looked for something to do with both my time and my money.'

Juliet regarded him quizzically. 'I thought your time and money were to be fully occupied in the pursuit of pleasure?'

He frowned. 'As I said, I no longer have an interest in such things.' Sebastian couldn't even look at a woman nowadays without Juliet's face taking that woman's place. And neither gambling nor drinking managed to banish her from his thoughts, either.

'Really?' Juliet looked far from convinced by his claim.

Sebastian sighed. 'Juliet, will you at least allow me to ask your forgiveness for what occurred during the summer?'

Juliet bristled into unapproachable stiffness at his mention of the summer. 'Exactly *what* are you asking forgiveness for, Sebastian?' she said coldly. 'My name has been totally vindicated by my cousin's admission of guilt and her subsequent arrest. Lord Bancroft has seen to it these last two months that I am welcomed back by the ton, if I wish it.' She raised an eyebrow. 'I see nothing there to ask forgiveness for.'

Sebastian wasn't fooled for a moment by the logic of Juliet's words—knew by the brittleness of her tone that she was still grieving over the disillusionment she had suffered concerning her friendship and love for her cousin, that none of the things Juliet had mentioned could ever make up for the loss and betrayal she still felt.

He shook his head. 'I deeply regret that I was in any way to blame for causing you hurt—'

'You think altogether too much of yourself, Sebastian!' Juliet snapped. 'You deliberately set out to seduce me, and in that you succeeded. Admittedly, your reasons for doing so were reprehensible—'

'My reason for doing so was because I had desired you from the moment I saw you, when I accompanied my sister Arabella to the Chessinghams' ball two years previously!'

Juliet eyed him uncertainly. 'What?'

Sebastian began to pace the room. 'I doubt you will choose to believe me—why should you?—but my wanting to see you again this summer, to meet and be introduced to you at the Bancrofts' house party, was strictly to do with pleasure. I went to Dolly in all innocence and asked her to issue an invitation to you.'

'*You* asked Dolly to invite me?' Juliet echoed sharply, still totally befuddled by Sebastian's claim that he had seen and desired her even before they had been introduced at Bancroft Park, when she had still been married to Crestwood….

He nodded. 'She assured me that she had already invited you, at the same time leaving me completely unaware that she had issued that invitation at her husband's request.' His mouth compressed. 'I had no idea of Bancroft's reasons for inviting you until after we had met and I had already begun my pursuit of you. If I *had* known—' He broke off in obvious frustration.

'If you *had* known…?' Juliet prompted softly.

Sebastian scowled darkly. 'I would not have allowed it. As it was, I was put in the invidious position of having to continue to woo you myself or standing back and allowing Grayson to do so.'

'Lord Grayson?' Juliet exclaimed. 'But I had absolutely no interest in being pursued by *him*—' Juliet broke off, realising too late what she had just admitted! She quickly changed the subject. 'Why should I believe any of your claims?'

'Why?' Sebastian became very still. 'Because I do not lie, Juliet. I have *never* lied to you. Except perhaps by omission,' he allowed grimly. 'But that will never happen again, either—no matter what the cost to myself. Ask me anything, Juliet, and on my honour as a St Claire I swear I will tell you the truth.'

'Anything?' she asked doubtfully.

'Anything.'

'Very well.' Juliet drew in a deep breath. 'On your honour as a St Claire, are you lying to me now?'

He met her gaze steadily and clearly. 'I am not.'

'Very well.' She nodded. 'Were you and Dolly Bancroft ever lovers?'

'No.'

'Sebastian—'

'I swear it is the truth, Juliet,' he growled. 'She was kind to me when I first came to London at seventeen. Nothing more than that. Ever.'

'Why was the thought of Lord Grayson seducing me so unacceptable to you?' Was it the same reason Sebastian had not introduced her to Lord Grayson that day? The same reason he had scowled down the dinner table at her on the evening she was seated next to Lord Grayson?

'Not unacceptable, Juliet, but completely abhorrent,' Sebastian rasped. 'And it is not just Grayson; I dislike it when *any* other man dares to come near you!'

Her brows rose. 'Including the Duke of Carlyne?'

'Especially the Duke of Carlyne!' he muttered. 'Arrogant son of a—!' He broke off, a tinge of colour in his lean cheeks.

Juliet almost smiled at his vehemence. 'I believe you misjudge him, Sebastian. Personally, I find him a most attentive and charming companion.'

Sebastian breathed deeply. 'I really do not care to hear your favourable opinion of other gentlemen.'

'Why not?'

His jaw was clenched. 'For the reason I have already stated.'

Juliet swallowed hard. 'Sebastian, why did you leave my bedchamber so—so abruptly that night after I had…'

'Made love to me?' he finished gently.

She winced. 'You said once it was not because I had disappointed you.'

'You did not,' he insisted forcefully. 'It was my own emotions, my response to you, that I so distrusted that night, that I did not fully understand.'

Juliet looked at him searchingly. 'Do you understand them now?'

'Oh, yes,' he admitted.

'Will you tell me?'

'When you have finished asking your other questions,' he promised.

Her questions? Oh, yes—her questions. 'How did you know I had come to London at this time?'

Sebastian's gaze avoided hers. 'I have been aware of your every move since we parted at Banford Park.'

Her eyes widened incredulously. 'You have had me followed?'

'Not I,' he assured her hastily as Juliet's eyes glittered her displeasure. 'Bancroft is the one who has had you watched. But only for your own protection. In case any of your cousin's associates should decide to pay you a visit. Bancroft owed you that, at least, after the erroneous suspicions he had harboured against you,' Sebastian told her.

Juliet swallowed hard. 'So Lord Bancroft was the one to inform you of my—my visit to London?'

Sebastian nodded stiffly. 'It was the least he could do, in the circumstances.'

'Why were you even interested?' Juliet frowned, not altogether happy with the idea of being watched. What if Sebastian had been informed as to where she had been yesterday morning? 'It has been two months since we last met, Sebastian.'

Sebastian was well aware of exactly how long it had been since he'd last seen Juliet! 'I wanted to give you time to get over the well-deserved anger you felt towards me. To find myself an occupation, so that when I did come to you, you would see that I have at least tried to change from your description of me as being "nothing more than a rake and a wastrel".'

'Why?'

Sebastian had made his promise to answer her truthfully, and he would keep to it, but this was much harder than he could ever have imagined it being. Just seeing Juliet again, being with her, was more painful than he could ever have imagined.

'Sebastian, *why*?'

He drew in a harsh breath. 'For the same reason I left your bedchamber so abruptly that night.'

'Which is?'

'Because I am in love with you! Because I love you, damn it. Every part of you. From your head to your toes. Oh, God, Juliet, I love everything about you!' he groaned huskily. 'Your innocence. Your vulnerability. Your pride. Your courage. Juliet, I have spent the last two months longing, aching to see you again, to be with you again. To tell you how I feel about you.'

Juliet began to tremble even as she felt the wall she had kept so securely about her own emotions begin to crumble and fall.

Sebastian gave a self-deprecatory shake of his head at Juliet's silence. 'It was not my intention to fall in love with any woman. I did not even recognise the emotion for what it was until it was too late and you had gone from my life. That night I waited in your room for you, and you made love to me so—' He stopped and breathed raggedly before continuing, 'I left your bedchamber that night because I did not understand my own emotions. Had no idea what was happening to me. I only knew that I had to leave, be apart from you, in order to try to collect my thoughts and feelings.'

Juliet moistened the dryness of her lips with the tip of her tongue. 'And have you now collected your thoughts and feelings?'

'It appears they have collected me,' he said ruefully. 'Juliet, I promise you I have changed in the two months we have been apart. I have found a purpose for my life at my estate in Berkshire. Will you not—could you not give me another chance to prove myself to you?' He reached out to grasp both her hands in his. 'I swear on my honour that I had no part in Bancroft's machinations. Damn it, I only wanted to protect you.'

'I know.'

'And in trying to do so I— What did you say?' Sebastian stared at her incredulously.

She nodded. 'I have had the same two months in which to think, Sebastian. In which to remember. I was naturally upset that last evening at Banford Park. So shocked by what Helena had done that I did not listen properly to what else was being said. But I have realised, from the things you said that night, that you meant me no harm.'

'I would never do anything to harm a hair upon your head,' he vowed.

'I know, my dear.' Juliet squeezed his hands.

'Then you will let me woo you?' he prompted anxiously. 'I do not care how long it takes—weeks, months, even years. I warn you now that it is my intention to woo you until I have worn you down into agreeing to be my wife.'

'You wish to *marry* me?' Juliet gasped breathlessly.

Sebastian frowned fiercely. 'What else have I been telling you? Juliet!' he exclaimed, as he realised she had believed him to be suggesting they simply resume their affair. 'I would *never* dishonour you, what I feel for you, by offering you anything less than marriage!'

'But you have not…'

'I have not what?' he asked.

'Offered me marriage,' Juliet said a little shyly.

Sebastian grimaced. 'But I have not yet wooed and won you.'

'Oh, Sebastian!' Juliet sighed. 'I believe that you won me the moment you first kissed me!'

He stood back to look at her uncertainly, searchingly. 'Juliet, are you sure…?'

She laughed softly, a warm bubble of happiness building inside her and longing to break free. 'Your behaviour in setting out to seduce me at Banford Park was totally reprehensible.'

'I will spend the rest of my life apologising for that if you will only marry me!'

'*Totally* reprehensible,' Juliet repeated huskily. 'But it was also wonderful, Sebastian. Exciting. So pleasurable that even now it makes me tremble to think of it. Oh, Sebastian, I had never known such wonders before as when you kissed and touched me!' She looked dazed just at the memory. 'I did not know that physical love could be so—so beautiful.' She suddenly frowned. 'Crestwood—'

'We will never talk of him, Juliet, if it makes you unhappy,' Sebastian said firmly.

'It does not.' And, strangely, it no longer did.

Juliet had come to realise these last two months, whilst alone in Shropshire, that Crestwood had been a man she could never have understood. Nor pleased. She had always believed the unhappiness of their marriage in the bedroom must have been because of a fault within her. That *she* was the one who was somehow lacking. Helena's revelations of her own twisted relationship with Crestwood had finally proved that to be untrue, and released her from her feelings of guilt and shame.

As Juliet's response to Sebastian's lovemaking had shown her how deep was her own sensuality…

'I will talk of him this once, Sebastian, and then never again.' She removed her hands from his to move away and stare sightlessly out of the window as she began to talk. 'I can say it now—he was a brute of a man. Hard. Implacable. Totally lacking in warmth of any kind.' She swallowed hard. 'He showed absolutely no mercy, no tenderness, when he took my virginity on our wedding night. Or any of the nights he came to me during our years of marriage.' She gripped her hands tightly together. 'I think it was made worse because he—he would always snuff out the candle when he came into my bedchamber, and in the darkness I was never sure where he was or when he would take me.'

'So that is the reason you did not want me to blow out the candle that first night!' Sebastian breathed.

She shuddered at the thought of those other, painful memories. 'On one of the occasions Crestwood came to me I tried to talk to him, to explain that if he would only be a little kinder—' She shook her head. 'He beat me so badly that night I could barely stand afterwards.'

'*Juliet!*' he choked.

'It is all right, Sebastian.' She turned to reassure him shakily. 'Oh, my dear…!' She quickly crossed the room to smooth the devastation from Sebastian's expression. 'It really is all right,' she soothed again. 'Until I met you I had not known what it was to find joy with a lover. To laugh and talk, and just enjoy lovemaking.' She shook her head sadly. 'It is true I did not kill Crestwood—but I wanted to. On several occasions I certainly wanted to!'

'He deserved to die!' Sebastian rumbled, his eyes glittering darkly. 'If he were not already dead, I would take great pleasure in killing him myself!'

Juliet regarded him warmly. 'That would not do at all, Sebastian.'

A nerve pulsed in the rigidity of his jaw. 'I would have enjoyed making him suffer as he made you suffer all those years!'

Juliet's smile widened. 'But then the father of my baby, the man I love to distraction, would be in prison rather than free to be with the two of us, would he not?'

'Yes, but— *Baby?*' Sebastian echoed sharply, his gaze avidly searching the pale oval of Juliet's face as she gazed up at him. 'Juliet—'

'I am with child, Sebastian!' she announced happily, her face lighting up with joy. 'I came to town yesterday in order that I might have a physician confirm my suspicions.' Tears of joy glistened in her eyes. 'I have been trying to find the courage since yesterday in which to come to you and tell you…! Oh, Sebastian! My darling, wonderful Sebastian, in seven months' time we are going to have a son or a daughter. You are going to be a father!'

Sebastian felt as if someone had dealt him a severe blow to the chest. He couldn't breathe. Couldn't speak. Could only look down at Juliet in wonder.

He became very still. 'Juliet, did you just call me…? Did you just say that you loved the father of your baby to distraction?'

She beamed up at him. 'I did. I do. I love you, Sebastian. To distraction.' She laughed gaily at his dumbfounded expression.

That Juliet carried his child was a shock. A wonderful one, to be sure. But that she loved him too…!

Sebastian swept her up into his arms and began kissing her as if he never wanted to stop.

Which he did not. He was hungry for Juliet. The taste, the feel of her after two months of not seeing her. Being with her. Of wondering whether or not she still hated him, doing all that he could in order to show her that he had changed.

They were both trembling with longing when Sebastian finally broke the kiss to rest his forehead against hers. 'Have you ever made love on a sofa, Juliet?'

She gave a husky laugh. 'The only occasions on which I have ever *made love* have been with you,' she murmured softly, her expression quizzical as Sebastian released her to collect the chair from in front of the bureau. 'What are you doing?'

'Making sure that we cannot be interrupted,' he explained, as he propped the chair beneath the door handle before returning to her side. 'I hope you do not mind, my darling Juliet, but I intend to make love to you until you scream!' He swept her up into his arms and carried her over to the sofa.

Juliet did not mind at all….

'Why are you smiling?' Juliet was completely naked, as was Sebastian, as they lay in each other's arms upon the sofa much, much later.

His grin widened. 'I am going to have such fun informing my haughty brother Hawk that not only is his reprehensible youngest brother about to take himself a wife, as soon as can possibly be arranged, but that he is also to be a father!'

Fun…

It was something that Sebastian had brought into Juliet's life.

Along with love. And laughter. And the simple joy of being alive.

And of loving and being loved in return….

Epilogue

'How on earth did the Duchess manage to organise such a wonderful wedding supper for us in just a few days?' Juliet said wonderingly, as she and Sebastian began the first dance of the evening in the crowded ballroom at St Claire House.

'Jane is a mystery to us all,' Sebastian agreed admiringly.

All of the ton were there, many of them having travelled from their country estates in order to attend the October nuptials of Lord Sebastian St Claire, youngest brother of the Duke of Stourbridge, and Lady Juliet Boyd, Countess of Crestwood. They had been married earlier that afternoon at St George's Church in Hanover Square, and were now at St Claire House in Mayfair.

Juliet would be eternally grateful for the warm welcome shown to her by both the Duke and Duchess of Stourbridge. Lord Lucien St Claire and his wife had also been extremely kind to her. As had their sister,

Lady Arabella. So much so that Juliet felt as if she had a family again.

Most especially, she had Sebastian for her husband. The man she loved. The man she had no doubt she would always love, and who would always love her. And in just under seven months' time they would welcome their child into that love.

'I wish everyone could be as happy as we are, Sebastian!' She smiled up at him glowingly as they danced together, completely oblivious of everyone else in the room.

'They could not possibly be,' Sebastian assured her gruffly as he gazed down lovingly at the woman who was now his wife. Lady Juliet St Claire. How absolutely, perfectly right that sounded.

'I am so pleased that you were able to forgive the Bancrofts and Lord Grayson enough to invite them to our wedding,' Juliet approved.

Sebastian was not sure that he had completely forgiven any them for their earlier mistrust of Juliet. Or if he ever would. But it had been Juliet's wish that the three be invited today, and Sebastian loved her so deeply that he was unable to deny her anything that she wished for.

God knew Sebastian had had enough cause to regret those invitations earlier today, when Bancroft had taken him aside to confide that Helena Jourdan had somehow escaped imprisonment and her whereabouts at this moment were unknown…!

Something Sebastian had no intention of Juliet learning today, of all days. This was their wedding day. The beginning of the rest of their lives together.

'I am less inclined to forgive the Duke of Carlyne's obvious pleasure in seeing you again when he arrived earlier.' He frowned as he saw his sister, Arabella, being escorted onto the dance floor by that very same duke.

Juliet gave a trill of laughter at his jealous grumble. 'I am sure he enjoyed annoying you more than seeing me again.'

Sebastian's arms tightened about her still slender waist. 'Now that others are dancing, do you think anyone would notice if we were to slip away and find a secluded and private place where we might make love?' he asked huskily.

Juliet smiled. 'Oh, I think that the disappearance of the bride and groom might be cause for comment!'

He arched quizzical brows. 'Would you mind very much if it were?'

'Not in the slightest!' she admitted happily.

Sebastian grinned down at her. 'You have become shameless, wife.'

Juliet arched a teasing brow. 'Are you complaining, husband?'

'Never!'

Juliet laughed again as Sebastian took a firm hold of her hand to lead her from the ballroom in search of 'a secluded and private place' so that they might make love.

She had no doubt that everything between herself and Sebastian, for the rest of their lives together, would be about love....

* * * * *

Lady Arabella's
Scandalous Marriage

CAROLE MORTIMER

For my readers, for helping to make writing
The St. Claires such a wonderful
and rewarding experience for me.

Chapter One

'How I have come to hate weddings!' Lady Arabella St Claire muttered inelegantly as her partner in the waltz—a dance still considered slightly risqué by the older members of the ton—swept her assuredly amongst the two hundred or so other wedding guests milling about the candlelit ballroom of St Claire House in London.

'Could that be because in the past year you have been three times the sister of the groom rather than being the bride?' drawled Darius Wynter, the Duke of Carlyne.

Arabella looked up sharply, intending to give him a set-down for the mockery she detected in his cynically bored tone. That was her intention, but instead Arabella found her attention caught and held by the hard and perfect male beauty of his face—a face Arabella had once described to one of her sisters-in-law as being that of an angel. Or a devil...

Six or seven inches taller than her own five feet and

eight inches in stockinged feet, Darius Wynter had stylishly overlong golden hair, which gleamed in the candlelight, and his eyes were of dark cobalt-blue, edged by long lashes of that same gold. His nose was long and aristocratic, his cheekbones hard, and he possessed perfect sculptured lips above a square and determined jaw.

The stark black of his jacket over snowy-white linen emphasised rather than hid the width of his shoulders, his muscled chest and taut abdomen, and the lean elegance of his hips and thighs was defined by tailored black pantaloons.

Yes, Darius Wynter, Duke of Carlyne, was certainly elegance personified—and he was also the most compellingly handsome man Arabella had met since her coming out the previous year.

Until a few short months ago he had been Lord Darius Wynter, a man well known for his numerous exploits in the bedroom and at the gaming tables. A wild and reckless reputation that had only been added to when he'd married the heiress Sophie Belling a year ago, only to be suddenly widowed one short month later, when his bride was thrown from her horse while out hunting and killed.

As expected, the majority of the ton—marriage-minded mamas especially!—had forgiven Darius Wynter all his previous sins when he'd inherited the title of the Duke of Carlyne on the death of his elder brother seven months ago.

Arabella had been drawn to his decadent good-looks the first time she'd seen him at a ball some eighteen months ago. An attraction, despite the many social occasions at which they had both been present, that Darius

Wynter had unfortunately never given any inclination of returning.

Her top lip curled now with haughty disdain. 'I am sure you did not mean your remark to be so insulting, Your Grace.'

Darius gazed down into the beautiful face of Lady Arabella St Claire. With three brothers older than herself, one of them Hawk, Duke of Stourbridge, Darius knew that this young lady had been petted and spoilt for most if not all of her almost twenty years.

Nevertheless, her beauty was dazzling: a riot of honey-gold curls framed her heart-shaped face, her eyes were the colour of melted chocolate, and she had a tiny up-tilted nose, full and sensuously pouting lips, and a pointedly determined chin. The pale cream gown she wore revealed a spill of creamy breasts above a narrow waist and rounded hips, and her tiny feet were covered in cream satin slippers.

Yes, Lady Arabella St Claire was without doubt a very beautiful and highly desirable young lady. But as the young and so far unattached sister of the Duke of Stourbridge, wealthy in her own right following the death of her father eleven years ago, this haughtily condescending young lady had been hotly pursued by every eligible buck during the past two Seasons. Darius, whilst still only the lowly Lord Wynter, had even made an offer for her himself the previous year. An offer that had been summarily dismissed by this wilful baggage, he recalled grimly.

'Are you so sure?' Darius taunted.

Those deep brown eyes narrowed slightly. 'I am but nineteen years of age, Your Grace, hardly old-maid material yet!'

Darius rather liked the angry flush that had entered her cheeks. It made her eyes appear darker, the fullness of her lips redder. Lips that it would no doubt be a pleasure to kiss and explore, he noted. 'Nevertheless, you have been out for two Seasons now, with no hint of a betrothal being announced.'

Those expressive dark eyes flashed her displeasure. 'Is it your opinion, then, that all young ladies are so giddy and empty-headed that their only aim in life must be to snare themselves a suitable husband?'

He raised enquiring blond brows. 'By *suitable* I presume you mean wealthy, as well as titled?'

Her pointed chin rose challengingly. 'It is the enlightened year of eighteen hundred and seventeen, Your Grace, a time when not all women feel that they need a husband—*any* husband—by which to justify their very existence!'

'Then it is not your intention to marry?' he asked curiously.

'Not for some years, no,' she answered stubbornly.

'A pity.'

Her brows drew together. 'I beg your pardon?'

Darius shrugged broad shoulders. 'At nineteen a woman's body is still firm and ripe—' He broke off as Arabella gave a shocked gasp and attempted to pull away from him, yet Darius easily prevented her withdrawal by tightening his arm about the narrowness of her waist and his fingers about her tiny gloved fingers.

Her eyes glittered up at him angrily when she found herself forced to continue dancing, the softness of her thighs pressed against his much harder ones. 'Release me at once, sir!'

Darius grinned down at her unrepentantly. 'I am merely endeavouring to show you what you are missing by spurning the idea of marriage whilst you are still young enough to enjoy it.'

Arabella had not grown up with three older brothers without learning at least some of the mechanics of a man's body. And at the moment she could feel *exactly* what she would be missing as the hard press of Darius Wynter's thighs became a shocking torment against hers. A shockingly sensual torment…

Her legs felt weakened by the intimacy. Her breasts were swelling against her gown, her palms becoming slightly damp inside her gloves, and her cheeks were burning as she glanced about them self-consciously.

Luckily there was such a crush of people attending the celebration of her brother Sebastian's wedding to his darling Juliet that no one—not one of her brothers or their wives, nor indeed her many aunts and uncles and numerous cousins—seemed to have noticed the Duke's over-familiarity with Arabella.

Arabella's eyes gleamed as she turned back to face him. 'Surely it is not necessary for a woman to marry in order for her to enjoy such…intimacies?' She looked up at him challengingly, hoping to shock him.

The Duke narrowed his eyes. 'Perhaps you have already done so?' he retorted.

Of course Arabella had not. She might not as yet have found any man interesting enough to even think of marrying him, but for her to go to her husband on their wedding night as anything but pure and untouched would cause the most tremendous scandal. Besides which, her three over-protective older brothers would never allow it.

However, she considered this taunting mockery from a contemporary of her eldest brother Hawk intolerable. At one-and-thirty years of age, he should know better! 'Perhaps…' she echoed enigmatically.

Those sculptured lips curved into a hard smile. 'Why is it I find that so very hard to believe, Lady Arabella?'

She drew in a sharp, indignant breath. 'Are you calling me a liar, Your Grace?'

'I believe I am, yes,' Darius murmured.

Arabella St Claire really was a wayward little baggage, he acknowledged with admiration as he continued to twirl her about the magnificent candlelit ballroom. A wilful baggage with a complete disregard for the fact that she was playing with fire by behaving in this flirtatious way with a man she had refused to marry so condescendingly the previous year.

She held herself very erect, her challenging stance pushing up the full swell of those creamy breasts so that Darius now felt their warmth against his chest.

'I do not tell lies, Your Grace.'

He quirked a brow over lazily sensual blue eyes. 'Prove it.'

Her eyes opened wide at the challenge. 'I *beg* your pardon?'

They might have been the only two people in the room as Darius regarded her from between narrowed lids. The air between them was charged with expectation as he noted the loss of colour to her cheeks and the shocked uncertainty that now shone in those previously rebellious brown eyes. 'I am merely inviting you to prove your claim, Arabella,' he repeated softly.

'I— But— How am I to do that, Your Grace?'

His mouth repressed a smile. 'Surely there is only one way in which a woman might prove her…experience in the matter of physical intimacy?'

Arabella stared up at Darius Wynter in disbelief. He could not seriously mean for her to—? He did not expect her to—?

Yes, he *did*!

His intent was blatantly plain for Arabella to read in that single raised brow. In the deep blue of his eyes. In the cynical half-smile on those perfect lips.

Darius Wynter, Duke of Carlyne, was openly challenging her to indulge in physical intimacy with him!

Arabella's heart fluttered wildly in her chest at the mere thought of the muscled strength of this man's hard, naked body pressed against her own; those wide shoulders, the firmness of his chest and stomach, his powerful thighs and the naked glory of his—

'I assure you, sir, that the infamous Darius Wynter is the very last man I would ever contemplate becoming intimate with,' Arabella bit out with deliberate insult.

He looked down his aristocratic nose at her. 'Is that so?' he responded icily.

She nodded. 'You are undoubtedly the rake everyone believes you to be. A rake and a scoundrel. A man who married for money before being suspiciously widowed only a month later.'

'*Suspiciously?*' His voice was deceptively, dangerously soft.

'Conveniently, then,' Arabella substituted recklessly. 'As you were then able to keep your heiress's money without the bother of the heiress. In other words, sir, you are a man no decent woman should ever align herself with, as wife or mistress, regardless of your newfound wealth and respectability as the Duke of Carlyne!'

Arabella was instantly aware of her serious error in judgement in insulting this particular man as those dark blue eyes narrowed dangerously in a face gone hard with displeasure. His mouth was a thin, uncompromising line above a clenched and unrelenting jaw. That very stillness was in itself a warning of the coldness and depth of his anger.

Arabella swallowed hard. 'Perhaps I have said too much—'

'Only perhaps?' Darius grated menacingly.

She *had* said too much. Far too much, and most assuredly to the wrong man. That the Duke had challenged her into being so indiscreet Arabella had no doubts. That she should not have taken up that challenge was also beyond doubt. As was the retribution promised in the hard blue of his eyes…

'I believe we should retire somewhere a little less…crowded so that we might continue this conversation in private,' Darius growled, his fingers firmly gripping Arabella's elbow as he left the dance floor to pull her along at his side through the crush of people.

'We cannot be seen leaving the ballroom together,' Arabella hissed self-consciously, hoping that at any moment one or other of her brothers would arrive and demand to know what they were about.

Darius did not so much as falter in his departure as he glanced down at her with cold, remorseless blue eyes. 'I believed you to be unconcerned by such impropriety in this enlightened year of eighteen hundred and seventeen!'

Arabella felt her cheeks warm as he neatly turned her earlier bravado back on her, to good effect. 'I assure you *I* am completely unconcerned, Your Grace, but my brothers may perhaps be less...guarded in voicing their opinions.'

His mouth twisted derisively. 'Sebastian and his bride disappeared some minutes ago, and Hawk and Lucian also seem to be similarly engaged with the charms of their own wives.'

Another hurried glance about the ballroom did indeed show an obvious lack of the presence of Arabella's brothers. How typical! Since her coming out last Season her brothers had made her life almost impossible with their over-protectiveness, and now, when Arabella would actually have welcomed their high-handed interference, they had all disappeared to goodness knew where to dally with their wives. Even Aunt Hammond, her chaperon during these past two Seasons, appeared blind to Arabella's unwilling departure from the ballroom as she stood across the room engrossed in conversation with several of their relatives.

'As I said,' Darius drawled with dry satisfaction, 'I think it better by far that we retire somewhere less crowded in order to continue our present...conversation.'

Arabella had no doubt from the determined tone of his voice that conversation was the last thing the arrogant Duke of Carlyne wished to continue....

Darius strode from the ballroom, pulling Arabella through yet another crush of people where they stood chattering and laughing in the cavernous hallway, although he was not unaware of the expression in her beautiful brown eyes as he looked for a room where he could be alone with this insultingly outspoken young madam. Those eyes of hers, Darius knew, could sparkle with laughter as easily as they now snapped with anger.

So far the former had never happened in his presence....

Whenever he and Arabella St Claire had chanced to meet this past year and a half it had always been at one function of the ton or another. Occasions when this feisty little miss had treated the disreputable Lord Darius Wynter with all the haughty disdain of which a St Claire was capable—if she deigned to acknowledge him at all. Which usually she had not.

The tenuous accuracy of Arabella's recently voiced insults proved that although she had appeared to be completely unaware of him personally, she had obviously not been above listening to the scandalous gossip that so often circulated about him amongst the ton!

It was time—past time—for Darius to demonstrate to her that as the Duke of Carlyne he would no longer tolerate such dismissive behaviour from her or anyone else!

The noise and heat of the wedding party faded, and Darius kept his hand tightly about her elbow as he strode forcefully down a corridor towards the back of the house.

'What is in here?' He indicated a door to the left of the hallway with his free hand.

'It is a linen closet, I believe. Lord Wyn— Your Grace,' she corrected herself hurriedly as she stumbled along beside him, 'this really is most improper—'

'Here?' Darius ignored her protests, his expression grim as he indicated a door to the right.

'Hawk's study. But we cannot go in there!' she protested agitatedly.

Darius thrust the door open before pulling her into the darkened room behind him. 'Now.' He took both her hands in one of his and lifted them over her head as he pushed her back against the closed door and pressed the length of his body against hers. 'Shall we put to the test your claim that I am the very last man you would ever contemplate being intimate with?' His eyes glittered down at her as he slowly lowered his head with the intention of capturing her pouting lips with his own.

Arabella couldn't speak. Couldn't breathe. Her struggles to release her hands from Darius's steely restraint were only causing her body to become pressed more intimately against his. Causing her to feel more closely the hard warmth of his chest and thighs even as those cynical lips claimed hers.

Despite her earlier attempt at sophisticated bravado, Arabella had never even been kissed before. Her own lack of any deep interest, along with the threat of her brothers' wrath raining down on the head of any man who dared take such liberties with their young sister, had been enough, it seemed, to warn off any of the young bucks she had met so far.

Not so in the case of Darius Wynter who, at one and thirty, was most certainly not a young buck. Nor, as the illustrious Duke of Carlyne, was he in awe of any of her brothers.

A mouth that had appeared hard and sculptured was instead softly intimate as Darius kissed Arabella with a thoroughness that made her body tremble and shake even as it burned. Her breasts somehow felt fuller as they pressed against the restraining material of her gown, and there was a heat between her thighs that

Arabella had never experienced before. A flowering that caused her to shift her hips in restless need. What she needed exactly, she was unsure. She only knew that she wanted something more than he had so far given her.

Darius raised his head to look down into the flushed and beautiful face reflected in the moonlight that shone so brightly through the window directly across the room. He noted the feverish glitter of Arabella's eyes as she looked up at him. The warmth in her cheeks. The fullness of her lips. The uneven rise and fall of the creamy breasts that spilled so temptingly over the low neckline of her gown.

The burn of Darius's gaze returned to the pout of her mouth. 'Open your lips for me,' he encouraged gruffly.

Arabella frowned. 'Certainly not!'

She was such a little vixen in her condemnation of him. So critical of his reputation. The same reputation that, along with his lack of wealth, had no doubt caused this haughty young lady to refuse his offer for her the previous year.

Darius's grip tightened as he held her hands pressed to the door above her head, his eyes glinting down in promised retribution for all of her earlier slights. 'Open your mouth, Arabella,' he rasped. 'Show me how a real woman kisses,' he added, with challenging scorn for her earlier effort.

He was instantly rewarded by the light of battle that caused Arabella's eyes to shine more brightly in the moonlight as she glared up at him. 'If you will but release my hands, Your Grace?' she snapped angrily.

He gave a hard smile. 'I have no intention of releasing you only to have you use your little claws on me.'

Arabella was furious. More angry than she could ever remember being in her life before. Which, considering how often in the past her brothers had caused her to lose all patience with them, was impressive indeed.

She narrowed her eyes at him. 'Perhaps you might *enjoy* the way I use my little claws on you…'

'Perhaps.' Darius Wynter gave a soft appreciative laugh and slowly released her hands before taking a step back. 'I am waiting, Arabella,' he drawled seconds later, when she made no attempt to make good on her threat.

Arabella's mouth firmed determinedly. She could do this. She could do anything she wished if she set her mind to it.

Even seduce Darius Wynter…

How hard could it really be? The man was, after all, an acknowledged and indiscriminate rake.

Arabella gave a knowing smile as she closed the distance between them, her gaze holding his as her hands moved up to caress lightly across his shoulders before touching the silky softness of that golden hair where it rested on the collar of his jacket. Her fingers became entangled in that silkiness as she pulled his head down to hers so that she might be the one to instigate the kiss. As instructed, she parted her lips this time, immediately aware of the deeper intimacy of their kiss. Of the way her pulse quickened and her body suffused with a new heat as she felt the hot rasp of Darius's tongue against her parted lips, that tongue retreating slightly, only to repeat the heated caress seconds later. Beckoning. Enticing. Encouraging Arabella to do the same to him, perhaps?

How Arabella wished at that moment that she knew more about the intimacies that took place between a man and a woman. How she wanted to bring this arrogant man to his knees in the heat of his desire for her. Longed to have him beg and plead for her capitulation as he became lost to that need.

His need for her, Arabella St Claire, and for no other woman...

She allowed her instincts to take over as she pressed her body against Darius's to run her tongue lightly over his parted lips, at once feeling the leap of the pulse in his throat. A second, deeper penetration of her tongue elicited a low and throaty groan.

Emboldened, empowered by this evidence of Darius's pleasure in the caress, Arabella stroked her tongue into his mouth. Again. Then again. And each time she felt the intriguing pulsing of the firm length of Darius's thighs as they pressed into the welcoming well of her own heat.

What had started out as a game to Darius, a punishment for both that past slight in refusing his offer for her and Arabella's scorn earlier this evening, was a game no longer. His arousal was hard and throbbing inside his pantaloons, and he was consumed by the overwhelming need to carry this interlude to its natural conclusion.

Darius satisfied himself momentarily by using his own tongue to duel for dominance. Finally winning that battle, he returned those delicate strokes of hers with penetrating thrusts.

Yet it was not enough—in light of the many months that Darius had desired this particular young woman perhaps it never would be—and he groaned his frustration with the clothes between them that prevented him from touching every inch of Arabella's firm and ripe body.

Still kissing her, he manoeuvred her away from the door and guided her towards the huge desk that stood in front of the window.

The top of the desk was completely clear of the clutter that littered Darius's own desk in Carlyne House, Belgravia—which of course it would be, this room being the fastidious Hawk St Claire's own private domain!—and Arabella stiffened in surprise as she felt the backs of her thighs came into contact with that sturdy piece of furniture. At least Darius hoped it was sturdy enough for what he had in mind.

This young woman had accused him of being a rake and a scoundrel—amongst other things—and Darius did not intend to disappoint her. His fingers deftly unfastened the buttons on the back of her gown.

Arabella had absolutely no idea how it was that only seconds later she came to be sitting atop her brother's desk, with her dress down about her waist and only the sheer material of her camisole to cover the firm thrust of her breasts.

Although the *how* ceased to matter as Darius gently pushed her gown up and her legs apart to stand between them, his eyes gleaming in the darkness. He slowly lowered his head to run his tongue expertly over the exact spot where the swollen tip of one of Arabella's breasts showed dark against the creamy material.

Arabella gave a breathy gasp as that caress caused

pleasure to course through her body, tingling down her arms, the length of her spine, before centring as an ache between her heated thighs.

'You like that?' Darius murmured with satisfaction as he slowly repeated the caress against her other breast.

Of *course* Arabella liked that! What woman would not enjoy such heady pleasure as these caresses aroused in her?

For all her earlier claims, Arabella had certainly never experienced such intimacy. Had never really known what transpired between a man and woman when they were alone together. Her mother had died when she was but eight years of age. And her Aunt Hammond, a widow for some years, had never discussed such matters with her. As for her three older brothers—Hawk, Lucian and Sebastian all considered Arabella to be still too young to even *think* about such things, let alone indulge in them. And Arabella, her outward demeanour deliberately one of a sophisticated young lady about town, was far too embarrassed by her ignorance on the subject to have questioned any of her sisters-in-law.

Which explained why Arabella had reached the age of almost twenty years without knowing of the sheer pleasure, the beauty of physical intimacy…

This time she was prepared for Darius's kiss, but so lost was she in the heat of that kiss that she offered no objection as he slipped the straps of her camisole down her arms and bared her breasts completely for him to cup and caress.

Arabella had never known, never guessed that such pleasure as this existed. Her back arched as she pressed herself against the caress of Darius's fingers. Light touches that made the rosy tips of her breasts swell to such an aching sensitivity that it sent an echoing surge of pulsing pleasure between her thighs.

Darius broke the kiss to seek out and taste the hollows of her throat, his lips warm, tongue moist, teeth lightly nipping at her sensitised flesh as he moved lower still.

'You are so very beautiful here,' Darius murmured throatily, his breath a warm caress against her bared breasts before he slowly drew one of those pouting tips into his mouth.

Arabella gasped and writhed in pleasure, her fingers becoming entangled in the silky hair at his nape as she held him tightly to her. She felt so hot. So needy. So very needy…

She trembled with that need as Darius pulled back slightly to look at her, and her cheeks were burning as she looked down and saw that her nipple was twice its normal size and much darker in colour than when she sometimes looked at herself in the mirror after bathing.

Her breasts seemed altogether larger, as if they had swollen beneath the caress of Darius's hands and lips. But Darius had said her breasts were beautiful, so perhaps that was supposed to happen?

'May I…?' Arabella now longed to touch Darius as intimately as he had just touched her, and her hands were moving hesitantly to the buttons on the front of his waistcoat as she waited for his reply.

Darius nodded briefly in the darkness and as he straightened, eyes glittering darkly. 'That seems only fair,' he invited huskily.

At that moment, aroused as he was, Darius could have denied Arabella nothing. He drew in his breath on a sharp hiss as she peeled his waistcoat and tailored jacket down his arms to allow them to drop to the carpeted floor, before unbuttoning his shirt down to the middle of his chest, and he felt the first touch of the slender warmth of her exploring hands upon his bared and heated flesh.

Darius gritted his teeth, his jaw clenching as her hands trailed in a soft caress over his chest before she found the hardened nubs nestled amongst the mat of golden hair that lightly covered them.

She looked so beautiful in the moonlight, her bared breasts a proud thrust, her waist so slender, Darius thought he might span it with his two hands. It was all he could do to restrain himself from the urge he had to lay her across the length of the desk before moving between her parted thighs and burying the throbbing ache of his arousal inside her.

'Kiss me, Arabella!' he encouraged hoarsely.

He almost became undone completely when he felt the first moist lap of her little pink tongue against his nipple. As it was Darius had to clench his hands into fists at his sides as he fought to stop from spilling himself like some callow youth.

Instead he reached up and entangled his fingers in Arabella's golden curls to press her mouth harder to his sensitive flesh, drawing in a harsh breath as she copied the caress he had so recently given her.

'I am sure that you must have been mistaken, Lord Redwood,' Hawk St Claire, Duke of Stourbridge remarked pleasantly as he pushed open the study door.

'My sister the Lady Arabella has absolutely no reason to enter the privacy of my study—' The Duke broke off his disclaimer as the candelabra he carried in his hand to light the way clearly revealed that his sister had *every* reason to have entered the privacy of his study….

Chapter Two

'Perhaps you would care to give me your explanation as to *exactly* what Lord Redwood and I interrupted earlier?' Hawk, Duke of Stourbridge, Arabella's beloved eldest brother, was icily calm as he faced her across her bedchamber, but Arabella wasn't fooled.

She did not think she would ever forget the look of horror on her brother's face when, accompanied by Lord Redwood, he had walked into his study to find her and the Duke of Carlyne in a state of undress atop his leather-topped desk!

She gave an embarrassed groan just *thinking* of how her wilful determination to disprove Darius Wynter's mockery of her claim to experience had led to what was now undoubtedly her complete disgrace.

That Hawk, whom Arabella so looked up to and wanted to think well of her, should have found her in such a compromising situation was unbearable. That Lord Redwood, a member of the government and a man who had campaigned against and spoken in the

House on the subject of immorality within Society, should also have been witness to both Arabella and Hawk's shame was beyond enduring….

Regret was an emotion that Darius seemed patently incapable of feeling. He had certainly displayed no indication of it when Hawk had turned to hurriedly usher Lord Redwood from the study. Instead Darius had simply moved away from Arabella to calmly refasten the buttons on his shirt and straighten his cravat, before once again donning his waistcoat and jacket and neatly arranging his snowy white linen at the cuff. A single sweep of one elegant hand through his hair had tousled those golden locks back into their normally rakish style.

And all the time he was doing those things Arabella had been hurriedly straightening her own clothing, her fingers shaking and her face deathly pale as she realised the enormity of her indiscretion. As she considered what the repercussions of her impetuous actions might be…

Immediate banishment to the Stourbridge ducal estate in Gloucestershire would, Arabella felt sure, be the least of those punishments!

Now, she moistened her lips before answering. 'What explanation did Darius—er—the Duke of Carlyne give when the two of you spoke together just now?'

To Arabella's further dismay Hawk had returned alone to his study only minutes after that embarrassing interruption, his disposition stiffly disapproving as he sent her up to her bedchamber so that he and Darius might converse privately together. Until Arabella knew what had been said during that conversation she had no idea what answer to give her brother.

Hawk strode further into the bedchamber, tall and austerely handsome, his eyes a cold, forbidding glitter. 'He offered no explanation at all,' her brother answered testily.

She frowned. 'But he must have said *something*!'

Hawk gave a terse inclination of his head. 'He *offered* marriage.'

Arabella's eyes widened incredulously. Darius had offered for her?

It was the last thing, positively the last thing Arabella had been expecting when she considered Darius's cold and distant behaviour in those minutes after they had been discovered together.

'An offer you will, of course, refuse,' Hawk added autocratically, his top lip curled back with distaste.

Arabella stiffened with resentment at her brother's arrogance. She had already suffered the indignity of being mocked by Darius this evening. Then being made love to by Darius and, once discovered, sent to her bedchamber by Hawk as if she were a naughty child. And now it seemed she was also to suffer being told what to do by her arrogant eldest brother.

In truth, Arabella was not sure that she even *liked* Darius Wynter, let alone wished to marry him. She found his good-looks compelling. His physical attributes exciting. Was intrigued by his reputation. Had been infuriated earlier by his taunting as to her knowledge of physical intimacy. But *like* him? No, Arabella's feelings towards Darius could never be described by an emotion so…so lukewarm as liking!

Even so, her rebellious nature was such that she did not appreciate Hawk telling her what she would or would not do in regard to Darius's offer of marriage…

She held herself proudly. 'Surely that is for me to decide, Hawk, not you?'

Her eldest brother eyed her disapprovingly. 'The man is totally unsuitable.'

'His rank is every bit as prestigious as your own!' Arabella found herself defending the very man she had minutes ago been so angry with.

'His rank, perhaps, but not the man,' Hawk bit out contemptuously. 'Arabella, I cannot tell you how strongly I would disapprove of a match between you and Carlyne.'

She raised her chin in stubborn defiance of that disapproval. 'I am sorry you feel that way.'

Hawk's eyes narrowed. 'It is your intention to accept Carlyne's offer, then?'

'I have not decided,' she answered coolly. 'I will give you my answer once I have given Darius his.'

Her brother straightened, looking every inch the aristocratic Duke of Stourbridge. 'He has asked to speak to you in my study before he leaves.'

Arabella gave a haughty inclination of her head. 'In that case I really must not keep him waiting any longer.' She swept regally from the bedchamber and down the stairs.

Before her courage failed her!

'Your brother has graciously granted us five minutes alone together in which we might discuss this evening's events,' Darius said dryly when Arabella rejoined him in the now candlelit study.

Hawk St Claire was so damned toplofty. He obviously believed himself to be far superior to Darius in every way. He had seemed not to care a jot for the fact that Darius was himself now a duke, and therefore the other man's social equal, as he'd coldly informed him exactly what he thought of him for daring to dally with his sister.

Until Darius's offer of marriage—his second in regard to Lady Arabella St Claire—had robbed the other man completely of speech!

'So I understand.' Arabella looked at him with the same haughty disdain as her eldest brother had only minutes ago.

Even so, Darius could not help but admire the rebellious glitter in her eyes and the defiant tilt to her chin as she looked down the length of that haughty little nose at him. Not too many women he knew would be half so sure of themselves after being so recently discovered in a compromising situation with a scandalously notorious rake like him.

That Darius had ceased to publicly live up to that reputation since taking on the mantle of the Duke of Carlyne appeared to have gone unnoticed by the majority of the ton; it was a case of once a rake always a rake, it seemed. Not that this reputation was in the least a hindrance to Darius's eligibility. As Arabella's youngest brother Sebastian had once informed him, inheriting a dukedom tended to bring on a bout of amnesia amongst the ton concerning a man's previous indiscretions.

Which brought Darius back full circle to the purpose of this five-minutes conversation with the young lady standing before him...

His mouth compressed. 'I doubt we will need the whole of the allotted five minutes for me to make a formal offer for you and for you to refuse it.' Darius studied her from beneath hooded lids as he clinically admired her undoubted beauty: those deep brown eyes, that pert little nose, the perfect bow of her lips. Lips that had only minutes ago responded to his with a passion that had far exceeded any of Darius's expectations.

He was acquainted well enough with the three St Claire brothers to know that Arabella's earlier claims to physical experience were a complete fabrication. Her brothers would never have tolerated even a hint of licentious behaviour in their young sister. But it had been her defiance that at the time Darius had been unable to resist challenging.

He had never had any serious intention of making love to Arabella, only to exact a little revenge for her dismissal of his offer eighteen months ago. That revenge had neatly rebounded on him when she had responded to his kisses and caresses with a passion that had just been waiting, it seemed, to respond to a lover's touch…

His specific touch?

Somehow Darius doubted that very much. Since their first meeting Arabella had made her contemptuous opinion of him more than obvious.

'Marriage is not something I either seek or want,' he drawled now. 'Nevertheless, I am aware of the obligation I have to make such an offer. An offer that you, having already assured me that I am a man no decent woman would ever align herself with, need only refuse to bring an end to it.'

Arabella felt a shiver down the length of her spine as she heard the steely edge to Darius's tone as he repeated her earlier insult to him. An insult he had obviously taken exception to….

Enough to have deliberately made love to her a short time ago? No doubt. But it did not alter the fact that she had responded to him in such a wild and abandoned way.

Darius's arrogant certainty that Arabella would refuse his offer rankled in the same way as Hawk's cold assertion that she would refuse it had done earlier. 'Well?' she demanded haughtily.

Those deep blue eyes narrowed. 'Well, what?'

Arabella gave him a pert smile. 'I am waiting for you to make such an offer.'

Blond brows rose mockingly. 'I believe I just did.'

'No, you did not.' Arabella shook her head. 'You have explained that it is an offer you feel socially pressured into making. You have also said that I will refuse such an offer. You have yet to actually *make* me that offer.'

Darius gave an impatient grimace. 'You want your pound of flesh? Is that it?'

Her eyes flashed in temper. 'I merely want my offer!'

'Very well.' He took a deep breath. 'Lady Arabella, would you do me the honour of becoming my wife?' He made no effort to hide the sarcasm behind his proposal, or the cynical twist to his mouth.

It fired Arabella's temper anew. Darius Wynter was one of the most *arrogant* men she had ever met. He was just so absolutely sure of himself. Of Arabella's refusal to even consider his proposal. Of his ability to escape any lasting repercussions concerning their lovemaking— leaving *her* to bear the brunt of them with regard to her immediate family.

All her life, it seemed, Arabella had been surrounded

by arrogantly forceful men. Her father, Alexander. Her three older brothers. To tie herself to a husband who possessed that same arrogance would surely be the height of folly.

Or perhaps it would be the height of good sense?

Arabella had enjoyed her two Seasons, but only once during that time had she even come close to finding a man who held her interest beyond their initial meeting. And that man had been Darius Wynter himself…

His Grace was absolutely nothing like the young men who had flattered and flirted with her these past two Seasons, all proclaiming undying love for her until Arabella had become sickened by their attentions.

Darius, making no effort to hide his arrogance or his cynicism, had neither flattered nor flirted with her. Much to her regret…

Arabella's pulse fluttered anew just looking at him: that golden hair, those dark and unfathomable blue eyes, his arrogant slash of a nose above sculptured lips and jaw. And his perfectly tailored clothes covered what she had discovered such a short time ago was a surprisingly hard and muscled body.

No, Arabella was positive she would never find herself bored in the company of Darius Wynter…

'You are taking a deuced long time to refuse me!' he eventually growled in his impatience with her silence.

Arabella couldn't help giving a taunting, confident smile. 'I am still considering your offer, sir.'

He scowled darkly. 'What is there to consider?'

Arabella could no longer stand looking at the desk which had been the scene of her disgrace, instead strolling over to stand in front of the window to look out across the moonlit garden. 'Well, for one thing, by accepting your offer I would become a duchess.'

'The despised Darius Wynter's duchess, do not forget,' he reminded her harshly.

She gave a haughty inclination of her head as she turned to face him. 'There *is* that to consider, of course.'

His mouth twisted. 'And have you also forgotten that I was so "conveniently" rid of one wife but one short year ago?'

Arabella *had* forgotten!

'You must also be aware that none of the ton has a good word to say about me,' Darius said, pressing his advantage.

Arabella frowned slightly. 'My brother Lucian speaks very highly of you….'

Darius's mouth tightened. 'We are friends. Of a sort.'

She nodded. 'And I know that his wife, Grace, has taken several people to task for daring to criticise you within her hearing.'

His mouth quirked. 'We are related, after all.'

'Only tenuously.' Arabella dismissed the connection of him being Grace's half-uncle by marriage, or some such nonsense. 'My new sister-in-law, Juliet, was also most insistent that you be a guest at her wedding today.'

Darius's expression softened slightly as he thought of the gracious and beautiful Juliet Boyd, now Lady Juliet St Claire. 'Only because it was jealousy of my own friendship with the lady that was instrumental in bringing your brother up to scratch.'

Arabella's eyes widened. 'You had a—a romantic interest in *Juliet*?'

'Not in the least.' Darius gave a firm shake of his head. 'Sebastian *thought* I had a romantic interest in her,' he corrected. 'She and I were both aware at all times that that was not at all the case.'

'Why not?'

He raised surprised blond brows. 'I beg your pardon?'

'*Why* were you not attracted to Juliet?'

'I simply was not.' He snapped his impatience with the subject. 'Contrary to popular belief, I do not set out to seduce every beautiful woman I meet.'

Arabella frowned once more. 'I had not realised you were present at the Bancrofts' house party when Sebastian and Juliet met this past summer.'

Darius gave her an irritated glare. 'I see no reason why you should have been informed.'

Arabella's cheeks burned at the obvious derision in his tone. 'Were you there when the French spy was apprehended?'

It took great effort on Darius's part to keep his outward appearance coolly neutral. 'What French spy?'

Arabella shook her head. 'I have no idea. Sebastian and Juliet deny any knowledge of it. But rumour has it that the man was masquerading as someone's servant before the arrest?'

Rumour, as usual, was wrong. Darius knew with certainty that the French spy in question had been a woman...

'The incident must have happened after I had left,' he said. 'Now, could we get back to our own conversation? Our allotted five minutes was over long ago, and at any moment Hawk is likely to join us and demand to know our decision.' Darius would use any means at his disposal—even reminding her of his marriage offer—

to deter Arabella from showing any further interest in that French spy!

'*My* decision,' Arabella corrected haughtily. 'After all, *I* am the one who will decide whether or not we are to be betrothed,' she explained at Darius's questioning glance.

Darius studied her through narrowed lids, easily noting the glitter of challenge in those deep brown eyes, the high colour in her cheeks, the determined set of her mouth and that stubbornly angled chin.

All things that told him Arabella was seriously considering accepting his offer....

An offer she had felt no compunction in refusing the previous year. *Before* he became a rich widower. *Before* he inherited the title of Duke of Carlyne.

Darius's expression hardened. 'And have *you* now decided?'

She drew in a ragged breath. 'I...I believe I need more time in which to consider the matter.'

'How much more time?' Darius rasped harshly.

Arabella shrugged slender shoulders. 'These things cannot be rushed, Your Grace. After all, we are talking of the rest of my life, are we not?'

'And mine,' he grated between clenched teeth.

She eyed him knowingly. 'Perhaps you should have considered that before making love to me earlier?'

'Perhaps I should,' Darius said tersely. He had never met a young lady more deserving of having her backside paddled than Lady Arabella St Claire did at this moment. In hindsight, that was probably what Darius should have administered earlier this evening in response to her challenge, rather than making love to her!

She looked down her tiny nose at him. 'I suggest,

Your Grace, that in view of the lateness of the hour I consider your offer overnight and you call on me again tomorrow morning so that I might give you my answer.'

His mouth thinned. 'Whilst you are…*considering* my offer, might I also suggest you *consider* that any marriage between us would necessarily be of the fullest kind.'

Arabella gave him a frowning glance, colour warming her cheeks as the mockery in his eyes and the twist to his hard mouth told her exactly what he meant by that comment.

Was she seriously considering Darius's marriage proposal? Or was she merely toying with him?

Just as he had toyed with her earlier when he'd made love to her with such deliberation?

For that alone Darius Wynter deserved to suffer at least the overnight torment of uncertainty as to whether or not Arabella would accept him.

She could not deny that becoming a duchess—even the Duchess of the infamous Duke of Carlyne—would be a wonderful matrimonial feather in her bonnet. She was also sure that Darius Wynter was too complex a man ever to bore her. In their marriage bed or out of it.

She gave a gracious inclination of her head. 'That sounds perfectly reasonable in the circumstances.'

His eyes narrowed to icy slits. 'You understand that I would expect my duchess to be amenable to the idea of producing Carlyne heirs?'

'That is the normal consequence of a full marriage, is it not?'

In truth, Arabella could not imagine having a marriage *without* children in it. Having grown up with three older siblings, and with one young nephew already to love and adore, Arabella looked forward to one day having children of her own to pet and spoil and love.

Darius Wynter's children?

If Arabella were honest with herself—and she usually was—then she would have to acknowledge that she had been completely aware of this man from the moment they'd met. It had been impossible not to notice him as he'd done the rounds of the salons and balls. Arabella also knew herself, along with several of the other young ladies out that year, to have become slightly infatuated with the dangerously handsome Lord Wynter.

All of them had certainly heaved a sigh of disappointment when he'd announced his betrothal to the heiress Miss Sophie Belling later that year, before marrying her in a private ceremony in the north of England only weeks later.

To now have him offer for Arabella, for whatever reason, filled her with edgy excitement more than anything else!

Darius had no idea what Arabella was thinking as she stared at him so intently. He could only hope that she was working out how unsuitable this marriage would be for both of them.

Aware that he would have to marry again one day, if only to provide the necessary heir, Darius also knew that now was not the right time for him to even be thinking of matrimony. Not when he had learnt earlier this evening that the French spy Arabella had just alluded to was once again at large…

His mouth tightened. 'Might I also suggest, Arabella, that you consider the fact that in marrying me you would be tying yourself to a man you do not love, and who does not love you.'

Those brown eyes narrowed. 'Is that not what dalliances outside of marriage are for?'

A red tide of anger passed in front of Darius's eyes at the thought of Arabella taking a lover outside of their marriage.

Damn it, there was *not* going to be a marriage between them! Not if Darius could prevent it.

'Your brothers have all married for love,' he pointed out.

Her expression softened. 'So they have.' Her mouth firmed. 'They have obviously all been more fortunate than I.'

'You are but nineteen, Arabella—'

'Almost twenty,' she reminded him swiftly. 'Although I fail to see what my age has to do with anything.'

'It has to do with the fact that you may yet meet a man for whom you can feel love,' Darius bit out.

Her mouth quirked. 'Take care, Your Grace, you are allowing your own reluctance to take me as your wife more than obvious!'

Was he? If that were the case, then Darius was a better actor than he had ever given himself credit for being! In truth, he had only repeated his offer for Arabella at all because Hawk St Claire's haughty disdain had infuriated him.

But what man in his right mind, given the opportunity, would *not* want to take the beautiful and accomplished, the self-willed and haughty, the emotional and wildly passionate Arabella St Claire as his wife? To spend his days crossing verbal swords with her and his nights revelling in all the wild passion of which Darius now knew she was capable?

No man, in his right mind or otherwise, would even consider passing up the opportunity of marrying such a woman as the magnificent Lady Arabella St Claire!

Unless he was Darius Wynter. A man with whom it had already been proved it was dangerous for any woman to become involved. Especially now…

'Probably because I *am* reluctant,' he drawled scornfully.

'What a pity.' Arabella eyed him mockingly. 'When I am seriously thinking of accepting your offer!'

Darius's jaw tightened. 'Only because you are a contrary little baggage!'

She gave a trill of laughter. 'Do not expect that to change if I *should* decide to marry you.'

He scowled his displeasure. 'Arabella—'

'I believe we have talked on this subject long enough for one evening, Your Grace.' She affected a bored yawn as she crossed to the door. 'As I have said, I will inform you as to my decision in the morning.'

Darius could only stand and stare after Arabella in intense frustration as she left the room.

Would she have the audacity to inform him on the morrow that she had decided to *accept* his marriage proposal?

He realised with a heavy sigh that he was in for a long, sleepless night.…

Chapter Three

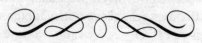

'I really wish you would reconsider your decision.' Jane, Duchess of Stourbridge, Arabella's sister-in-law, paced agitatedly up and down the nursery as Arabella sat in a chair in the bay window, attempting to soothe the young and teething Alexander, Marquis of Mulberry, as he moved fretfully on her shoulder. 'You may be assured that I have informed Hawk most strongly how wrong he is to allow you to align yourself to a man such as Darius Wynter!'

Arabella had confirmed to Hawk her intention of accepting Darius's offer as they had sat at the breakfast table together earlier this morning. An announcement her eldest brother had listened to in disapproving silence before proceeding to repeat all the reasons he considered the match unsuitable.

She almost never argued with Hawk, and had not enjoyed arguing with him this morning, either. But neither would her pride—that arrogant St Claire pride—

allow her to back down in the face of his icy disapproval.

In truth, once she'd learnt of Darius's offer, there had really been very little doubt as to her accepting it….

'I assure you that Hawk has left me in no doubt as to *his* doubts concerning the marriage, dear Jane.' Arabella shot the older woman a rueful smile. 'But the decision ultimately lies with me, does it not?'

'Well… Yes! But—' Jane gave a shake of her red curls. 'Can it be that you are in love with Carlyne, Arabella?'

'Certainly not!' Her expression was one of incredulous indignation.

'Then why think of marrying him?' Jane frowned her consternation.

Arabella gave a dismissive shrug. 'I have to marry someone, Jane, so why not the Duke of Carlyne?'

'Admittedly he is wickedly handsome…'

'My dear Jane!' She arched teasing brows. 'Are you supposed to notice such things when you are so happily married to Hawk?'

'This is not a teasing matter, Arabella.' Jane's expression was reproving. 'And being happily married, to Hawk or otherwise, does not render a woman blind to the fact that Darius Wynter *is* devilishly handsome.'

'He is rather,' Arabella acknowledged thoughtfully, a smile of satisfaction playing about her lips as she considered his golden hair, deep blue eyes, his wickedly sensual mouth and his hard and muscled body.

Jane eyed her uncertainly. 'Even if the two of you have…have anticipated the wedding vows, it does not mean you have to marry the man.'

Arabella smiled wickedly. 'My dear Jane, I believe

the Duke and I had barely begun to "anticipate the wedding vows" when Hawk and Lord Redwood interrupted us yesterday evening!'

'In that case why consider tying yourself to him for a lifetime?'

Indeed. It was a question Arabella had already asked herself many times. Yesterday evening. During the long, sleepless night she had endured. And again this morning, before she'd informed Hawk of her decision.

She had finally come to the conclusion that there was no single answer to that question. Although it could perhaps best be summed up by the fact that, after two Seasons spent being flattered and fawned over by all manner of eligible men, Arabella knew that Darius was the only man that she had found to be in the least exciting or intriguing. And dangerous…

'Not all women can expect to find a marriage of love, as you, Grace and Juliet have done with my brothers,' she answered Jane evasively.

Arabella knew she could not explain to anyone the strange satisfaction she felt in her decision to marry Darius—or the feeling of fluttering excitement she felt at the thought of becoming his wife. Of sharing his home and his bed.

Most especially his bed!

Far from repulsing her, as Darius had so obviously hoped that it might, the promise of sharing his bed on a regular basis filled Arabella with a delicious anticipation that made her tremble just to think of it.

Although it would not do to allow Darius himself to know of the eagerness of her feelings in that regard…

* * *

'There are several matters that need to be settled before I feel able to give you an answer to your offer of marriage.'

Darius looked between narrowed lids at the young and haughty miss before him as she stood up to receive him in the drawing room of St Claire House at precisely eleven o'clock. Arabella had offered him no word of greeting, instead simply proceeded to continue their conversation from the evening before as if there had been no break in their discussion.

Wearing a gown of the deepest gold, a colour that seemed reflected in her eyes, and with her golden curls arranged artfully at her crown with several tantalising wisps at her nape and temples, Lady Arabella St Claire was this morning in possession of an air of self-sufficiency and confidence that Darius found less than reassuring.

'Good morning to you, too, Arabella,' Darius said pointedly as he gave her a sweeping elegant bow.

Irritation creased her creamy brow, and she gave no curtsy in response to that formality. 'I had believed our present situation to have put us beyond the need for such inanities, Darius.'

'Had you?' He strolled further into the room, its cream-and-gold décor a perfect foil for Arabella's appearance, of which this self-possessed young lady was no doubt fully aware. 'Exactly what situation would that be?' His voice had hardened perceptively.

Irritation coloured her cheeks. 'Do not attempt to play games with me, Darius.'

His gaze was icy. 'I have no intention of attempting to play games with you, Arabella, considering what happened the last time I rose—quite literally—to your challenge.'

The colour deepened in her cheeks. 'There is no need for—for such indelicacy!'

'No?' He looked at her coldly. 'What would you rather I be?' He deliberately broke social etiquette by sitting down in one of the gold brocade armchairs whilst she still stood, leaning his elbows on the arms of that chair to steeple his fingers together in front of him as he looked up at her. 'The besotted lover, perhaps? We both know I am far from being that,' he said scathingly. 'The man resigned to his fate? But I am *not* resigned, Arabella,' he assured her, with a tightening of his jaw. 'Far from it!'

Faced once again with the flesh-and-blood man—a rakishly sophisticated man, far beyond her experience— Arabella could only wonder at her own temerity in daring to challenge him.

Once again he was dressed all in black, with snowy white linen and black Hessians, the sombre and perfectly tailored clothing giving him the appearance of that blond-haired devil Arabella had once considered him to be—still did.

'Might I remind you, Darius, that you were not forced into offering for me?'

He gave a hard, mocking smile. 'I thought it worth it just to see the look of outrage on Stourbridge's face.'

Her eyes widened. 'You *expected* me to refuse?'

He gave a dismissive shrug. 'Of course.'

'You would rather bring disgrace down upon both our heads than marry me?' Arabella said slowly, her anger rising.

Darius shrugged. 'I am no stranger to disgrace, Arabella. On the contrary, in the past I have considered it my duty to provide such scandalous diversions as I can, for the ton's entertainment.' He looked bored. 'On the basis that if they are gossiping and speculating about *my* behaviour then they are at least leaving some poor innocent alone.'

'*I* am an innocent, Your Grace—and if our actions yesterday evening are made public then I very much doubt the gossiping tongues of the ton will leave *me* alone!'

Darius shook his head. 'You are far from innocent, Arabella.'

Her eyes flashed. 'You still doubt my virtue?'

'Not in the least,' he said. 'I was referring to the fact that you are hardly the epitome of a young and innocent miss,' he pointed out. 'Neither did I say I would not marry you, if your decision is to accept. I merely stated that I am not resigned to such a fate.'

Arabella felt a shiver of apprehension down the length of her spine at the cold anger she read so easily in the harshness of Darius's expression.

Yet her own anger increased each time Darius voiced his reluctance to marry her!

What choice did she have?

Marriage to Darius, or eventual marriage to one of those young bucks of the ton with whom Arabella already knew she could never find any real happiness? A life of mediocrity, of boredom, when all the time she was aware that she could instead have had the exciting Darius Wynter, Duke of Carlyne, as her husband?

A man whose very presence in a room both thrilled and excited her.

A man who made love to her with a finesse and skill that left her hot and aching.

A man she had gazed at longingly from afar for far too long already…

Besides, his very reluctance to marry her was an insult. A challenge no St Claire would refuse….

She straightened determinedly. 'Then it is a pity I have decided to accept your offer, is it not?'

Darius's eyes narrowed speculatively on the young woman who faced him so defiantly across the drawing-room. The beautiful and feisty Arabella St Claire, a young woman that at any other time Darius would have enjoyed taking for his wife. No, would have revelled in taking as his wife. Most especially the 'taking' part!

But now was not the time for Darius to publicly tie himself down with emotional entanglement. To announce to the world at large that he had aligned himself to a young, and consequently vulnerable, wife.

Although he had no doubts that Arabella would dispute that she was in the least vulnerable!

'Why?' he bit out harshly.

She raised those haughty brows. 'I am sorry, I do not understand?'

His gaze narrowed. 'Did I inadvertently deliver some unintended insult to you in the past that you now feel I should be made to suffer? Some slight upon your person for which you feel I need to make suitable reparation?'

Her mouth twisted. 'Your obvious joy in my acceptance of your offer is overwhelming, Darius.'

He gave a hard grin at her sarcasm. 'It is difficult to feel joy when one feels one has a loaded gun placed against one's temple.'

Her cheeks flushed angrily. 'How flattering!'

He gave a mocking inclination of his head. 'Strange, when I intended to insult.'

Arabella was completely aware of what this man had intended. 'No one is forcing you to do anything, Darius. No matter what my own decision is, you have only to inform Hawk that you have changed your mind and now refuse to marry me.'

Darius gave a humourless laugh. 'And so allow him the pleasure of pulling the trigger?'

Arabella gave an inelegant snort. 'I assure you that Hawk has no more desire to see you become a member of his family than you have to become one.'

Darius did not doubt it. He had known for a long time—eighteen months, at least—that Hawk St Claire held him in complete contempt.

'Lucian is not so disapproving, however,' Arabella added slowly.

'Lucian?' Darius echoed slowly. 'Lucian has spoken on my behalf?'

'I believe he talked with Hawk after breakfast.' She nodded.

Darius didn't much like the sound of that. He didn't like the sound of it at all! So much so that he made a note to himself to talk to Lucian at the earliest opportunity. Damn it, if Lucian had dared to break the promise he had made to Darius seven months ago…

He had no doubt that Arabella would make an admirable duchess. That as both the daughter and the sister of a duke she was more than capable of fulfilling that role with grace and confidence.

Any duchess but Darius's!

He had made certain decisions concerning his life eight years ago. Decisions totally private to himself and a few chosen others. Immune, or simply uncaring of the danger those decisions represented to himself, he was nevertheless aware that they could become a threat to anyone with whom he became intimately involved. Most especially, it seemed, to any woman he became betrothed to or married!

Darius stood up impatiently, his eyes narrowing shrewdly at the way Arabella immediately took a deliberate and nervous step back from him. His mouth tightened as he mercilessly went for the attack. 'Am I right in thinking that a wealthy duke is a more attractive marriage prospect than a penniless lord?'

Arabella eyed him warily. 'Any woman who did not think so would be very foolish indeed,' she replied honestly.

'How unfortunate, then, that you are not a foolish woman,' Darius rasped bitterly.

Arabella gave a puzzled shake of her head. 'I fail to understand what—'

'Do not play the innocent with me, Arabella,' he growled.

'I am not—'

'I advise you to be absolutely certain that you are completely happy with your decision.'

'I have said that I am…'

'You have taken into account, I hope, that—as you have said—my previous wife "conveniently" died within a month of the marriage and left me all the richer for it?' he reminded her grimly.

Arabella felt all the colour drain from her cheeks.

Of course she had not forgotten that this man's first wife had died in a hunting accident a year ago, only weeks after becoming Darius Wynter's wife. Nor was she unaware of the suspicions that had been voiced amongst the ton about the suddenness of the other woman's death.

Suspicions that she had voiced to Darius herself, only the previous evening!

But she was sure he had only brought that up to try and make her change her mind about accepting his offer! She eyed him closely. 'I have no idea as to your first wife's family circumstances, but I have no doubt that my own brothers, Lucian included, would deal with you most severely were anything…untoward ever to happen to me,' Arabella told him firmly.

Once again Darius could not help but admire her. Whether Arabella believed those rumours concerning his wife's untimely death or not, she obviously had no intention of being deterred from marrying him herself. 'In other words you are hoping that the threat of your brothers' retribution will ensure that it does not?'

'Exactly.' She nodded coolly.

Darius gave a rueful shake of his head. 'I fail to see of what possible comfort that retribution could be to you if you were already dead.'

She gave a blithe smile. 'I assure you, knowing that Hawk, Lucian and Sebastian would instantly consign you to the devil is of tremendous comfort to me!'

Darius's mouth thinned. 'And if I were to admit to you right now that I *was* indeed responsible for my first wife's early demise?'

Arabella drew in a sharp breath and looked at him

searchingly. 'Why would you do such a thing?' she finally murmured.

Darius shifted impatiently. 'Possibly because it is the truth?'

She frowned. 'I believe you are trying to frighten me into refusing you!'

'Am I succeeding?' He scowled darkly.

'No,' she answered pertly. 'Now, if you have quite finished voicing your reservations concerning our marriage—'

'I do not recall voicing *any* of my reservations as yet,' Darius rasped harshly. 'The main one being, of course, that I have no use for a wife. Not now. Or in the foreseeable future.'

She blinked. 'Yesterday evening you mentioned the necessity for heirs.'

His mouth compressed. 'Which I would be just as capable of fathering in ten—twenty years as I am now. Arabella, have you seriously considered what it will mean to become my wife?' he continued impatiently. 'I am a man most of the ton still believe beyond the pale. A man who has only attained a tenuous respectability because of a title which should never have become mine.' His expression darkened. 'That would not have become mine if my brother had not died so suddenly and his legitimate heir, my nephew Simon, had not already been slain at Waterloo.'

Yes, of course Arabella had considered all of those things during the long hours of a sleepless night. But ultimately they had all been rendered insignificant against her own inexplicable desire to become this man's wife.

Inexplicable because Arabella refused to search her heart too deeply in order to find the answers to that particular puzzle…

'In that case, marriage to a St Claire can only but add to your newfound but shaky respectability!'

Darius could see from the firm tilt of those highly kissable lips and the stubborn light in those deep brown eyes that Arabella would not be swayed from her decision, that she was wilfully determined to become his wife whether he desired it or not.

And he most certainly did not.

But not for any of the reasons he had so far stated…

He admired Arabella St Claire. Desired her. He would not have offered for her eighteen months ago if he had not—an offer she had not hesitated to refuse when he was penniless and lacked a dukedom, he reminded himself testily.

He crossed the room in two long strides to reach out and grasp the tops of her arms, totally impervious to her sudden look of alarm. 'I advise you to be sure of exactly what you would be doing by marrying me, Arabella,' he growled.

Her throat moved convulsively as she swallowed nervously. 'What do you mean?'

'I am a man used to doing as I please. Going where I please, when I please, as I please. A circumstance I would see no reason to change simply because I have a wife.'

Arabella's eyes widened. 'You are telling me before we are even wed that you intend to continue your relationships outside of our marriage? That you perhaps already have a mistress you intend to continue to visit?'

Darius almost laughed at the ludicrousness of those questions.

Ludicrous because there had been no women in his life, mistresses or otherwise, for some time now. His brief foray into marriage had shown Darius how unwise it was for him to have an intimate relationship with any woman. How detrimental that very intimacy could be to her health...

He looked down at Arabella. She was so very young. So beautiful. So utterly and completely desirable...

Darius suddenly realised how he could dissuade the stubbornly determined Arabella from going ahead with their betrothal and marriage. He had only to ruthlessly demonstrate how unsuitable a candidate he was as a prospective husband to send her running back to the safe and welcoming arms of her three over-protective brothers.

Yes, Darius knew exactly how to go about achieving that end. But he also knew that having done so he would be giving up any chance of renewing his addresses to her in the future, however far ahead he was looking. That, believing herself rejected by Darius, Arabella was contrary enough to accept the next suitor who made an offer for her and in doing so making it impossible for Darius to ever claim her.

No, as inconvenient and risky as it was for Darius to marry Arabella now, for him not to do so would certainly mean losing her for ever. A possibility that he found was even more unacceptable to him than this forced betrothal, than knowing that she only wanted to marry him now because he was the wealthy Duke of Carlyne...

'I do not expect to need a mistress once we are married, Arabella.' He finally answered her previous question. 'I would expect you to cater to my physical needs. Whatever those might be.'

Arabella felt a shiver of apprehension down the length of her spine as she looked up into the hard implacability of his face. His mouth was a thin, uncompromising line. His eyes as hard and glittering as the sapphires in the necklace left to her by her mother.

It was the face of a man who would brook no challenge to his indomitable will. Least of all from a wife he felt had been foisted on him by the dictates of Society rather than one he had chosen for himself.

Any woman not born a St Claire would have been daunted by the risk that he represented at that moment. Yet it only made Arabella all the more determined to penetrate his arrogant façade. To poke and prod at that mockery and cynicism until she reached the man beneath that apparently impenetrable shield.

Perhaps if she had not had the cynically remote Hawk and Lucian as her brothers, or the softer but just as arrogant Sebastian, then Arabella may have believed that outer shell to be all there was to Darius Wynter. But, as their petted and spoilt younger sister, Arabella had come to know her brothers' natures well, and she knew all of them to be capable of deep and tumultuous emotions. To be men who were all deeply and irrevocably in love with their wives....

Was she hoping, once they married, that Darius would similarly fall in love with her?

Arabella stifled a disbelieving gasp at even the suggestion of such a hope. Did that mean she had feelings for Darius she hadn't even dared to suspect existed?

Darius raised a brow as he saw Arabella's reaction to his suggestion that she alone would satisfy his physical needs. 'My physical needs are really not as debauched as the ton would have you believe.' He eyed her teasingly. 'I can at least assure you that there will be no whips or chains involved!'

'Whips or chains?' she gasped breathlessly, her face paling.

It was a response that reminded Darius more than any other, despite her claims to the contrary yesterday evening, just how innocent she really was when it came to physical intimacy. 'I am sure you will very quickly learn to satisfy all my *very normal* sexual appetites, Arabella.'

Once again her throat moved convulsively as she swallowed before raising her chin proudly. 'As, no doubt, *you* will learn to satisfy mine?'

She was a vixen. A little hellcat. Verbally spitting and clawing despite her obvious unease at discussing such an intimate subject with him. 'That part of marriage I am already looking forward to with the greatest of pleasure,' Darius assured her throatily.

A challenge entered the deep brown depths of her eyes. 'I would prefer us to have a lengthy betrothal in order that we might become better acquainted with each other on a social level before—'

'No.'

She eyed him uncertainly. 'No?'

Darius looked down at her between hooded lids. 'No,' he repeated firmly. 'If we are to marry at all, then it must be immediately.'

'I— But— Why?' Arabella didn't even attempt to hide her bewilderment.

She had been envisaging spending the winter
months as Darius's betrothed. With perhaps the
wedding planned for next spring or summer. Six,
possibly nine months when the two of them could
spend time together, tormenting and challenging each
other if they must, before contemplating the complete
intimacy of marriage.

The implacability of Darius's expression told her
that such an arrangement was totally unacceptable to
him. 'Take it or leave it, Arabella,' he stated uncom-
promisingly. 'You will either marry me by special licence next week or we will not marry at all.'

Next week? Was he *insane*?

Arabella pulled out of Darius's grasp to move away
from him. 'I cannot possibly organise a wedding by next
week!'

'I fail to see why not.' Darius appeared unmoved by
her obvious shock. 'Obtaining a special licence should
pose no problem. All of your family and the majority
of the ton have already gathered in town in order to attend your brother's nuptials yesterday. Hawk's duchess
has proved she is capable of being hostess to a wedding
supper at short notice. As I see it, a week is more than
time enough for you to obtain a suitable wedding gown.'

As *he* saw it, perhaps. As *Arabella* saw it the idea of
marrying this man as early as next week was unacceptable. Terrifyingly soon, in fact.

'Why the rush, Darius?' She made her tone deliberately light. 'I realise that this situation has been thrust
upon us by—by certain actions that took place between
us yesterday evening, but we both know that there is no
real reason for such a hasty wedding to take place.' Her

cheeks burned at the memory of the intimacies the two of them had shared the previous evening.

Darius felt a sharp stab of sympathy for Arabella's obvious bewilderment as to his insistence on a short betrothal and a hasty wedding. Reminding him that for all Arabella was a St Claire, and as such in possession of the same arrogant self-confidence as her three older brothers, she was nevertheless still only nineteen years of age. A very young and innocent nineteen years, despite her previous claim otherwise.

He wished that he could grant Arabella the lengthy betrothal she so obviously desired—months during which the little minx had no doubt intended to tempt and bedevil him!—but the truth was, once their betrothal was publicly announced, Darius simply dared not leave her for any length of time without his full protection.

He dared not.

'Next week, Arabella. Or there will be no wedding.'

Arabella looked up at him searchingly, knowing by the grimness of Darius's expression—the stern set of his mouth and the coldness of his blue eyes—that he was unshakeable in his decision that she would marry him next week and be damned, or the two of them would not marry at all.

She drew in a deep breath. 'Very well, Darius.' She gave a tiny inclination of her head. 'I will inform Hawk that we have decided to marry as early as possible next week.'

'*I* will be the one to inform your brother as to our intentions, Arabella,' Darius cut in decisively, a cynical curl to his top lip. 'As is my right as your future husband.' He quirked one arrogant brow.

Arabella bit back the argument that had been hovering upon her lips, wisely deciding that prudence was probably the better course at this point in time. There would be plenty of opportunity after they were married for her to show Darius that she had no intention of being a conventional meek or obedient wife....

Chapter Four

'It is still not too late to change your mind, Arabella, if you have a single doubt as to the wisdom of marrying Carlyne.'

Arabella turned to look across her bedchamber as Hawk, her tall and imposing brother, stood in the doorway dressed in his own wedding finery of snowy white linen beneath a tailored claret-coloured jacket of the very finest velvet, black pantaloons and shiny black Hessians.

The rest of the family had already departed for St George's Church in Hanover Square, but as the eldest of her brothers Hawk was to ride with Arabella in the bridal carriage, and then accompany her down the aisle before handing her into the care of her husband-to-be.

Into Darius Wynter's care.

Arabella swallowed down her feelings of nervousness as she presented her brother with a widely confident smile. 'I have no doubts at all, Hawk.'

This past week had been a busy one of hectic arrangements. Arabella had never been left alone for a moment as the dressmaker was visited, the ivory silk chosen for her gown and fittings arranged, flowers obtained, and the menu for the wedding breakfast decided upon in consultation with Jane.

There had been little or no time for second or third thoughts, and with everything there had been to arrange or decide upon, Arabella had seen very little of Darius himself. Despite that, Arabella was more convinced than ever that her choice of husband was the correct one. For her.

Arabella knew herself well enough to realise that she could never be happy with a weak man, a man she could bend to her will by artifice or design. And Darius would never be such a man.

Despite their lack of opportunity to spend time together, Arabella had nevertheless had the chance to witness for herself what she viewed as the strengths of Darius's character. His arrogance was more than a match for any of her brothers whenever they chanced to meet. He had been charm itself on meeting Jane and being faced with her obvious uncertainties as to his suitability as a husband for Arabella.

Most surprising had been Darius's consideration and gentleness with his brother's widow, the Dowager Duchess of Carlyne, when she had arrived in London three days ago for the wedding and the betrothed couple had been invited to dine with her that evening.

Arabella had reassured herself that any man capable of showing such kindness as Darius had to Margaret Wynter, even a man who preferred the ton to think of him as a rake and a cynic, could not possibly be all bad.

Hawk's austere expression softened slightly as he

stepped further into the bedchamber. 'You look so much like Mama today.' He gazed down at her admiringly in the ivory silk gown, her golden curls enhanced by a matching bonnet, her bouquet a simple arrangement of deep yellow roses from the St Claire hot-house.

'Really?' Arabella glowed; she had been aged only eight when her mother and father were killed in a carriage accident, and over the years her memories of her warm and beautiful mother had become hazy at best.

'Very much so,' Hawk assured her gruffly as he reached out to take both her hands in his own. 'How I wish our parents could be here to see how beautiful you look on your wedding day.'

Arabella squeezed his hands. 'Perhaps they can.'

'Perhaps,' Hawk allowed gently.

She gave her brother a searching glance. 'I *am* going to be happy, Hawk.'

'So Lucian never fails to assure me.' His eyes narrowed. 'Even so, I am sure I have made no secret of the fact that Carlyne is not the man I ever envisaged as a husband for you.'

'No.' Arabella smiled slightly as she thought of the battle of wills that had ensued between Darius and Hawk on the few occasions the two men had met during this past week. Battles which Darius had—surprisingly—invariably won…

Her brother gave a rueful shake of his head. 'Perhaps if I had known of your preference for him then I would not have been so hasty in refusing him when he last offered for you.'

Arabella's eyed widened incredulously. 'Darius has offered for me *before*?'

'During your first Season,' Hawk acknowledged heavily, releasing her hands to cross the bedchamber and stand with his back towards her as he stared out of the window into the busy street below.

'I— But— Why did you not tell me?' Arabella frowned in disbelief as she stared at the implacability of Hawk's stiffly erect back and shoulders.

Darius had offered for her the previous year?

Before he had made a similar offer for Sophie Belling and been accepted, obviously.

Hawk turned, the sternness of his features twisted into a grimace. 'I did not tell you because I was not— am still not—convinced as Lucien appears to be as to Carlyne's suitability as a husband for you.'

'So you refused his first offer for me without even consulting me?' Arabella accused.

'I did.' Hawk looked haughtily unrepentant. 'And I would have done so again this time if the—the circumstances had not been as they were. If you had not informed me it was your sincere wish to marry him.' His expression was grim. 'The fact that Carlyne offered for Sophie Belling too last summer, and then married her after approaching me in regard to you such a short time before, only confirmed to me that his reasons for offering for you then were of a mercenary nature rather than because his emotions were truly engaged.'

Arabella knew she couldn't refute that claim. She doubted that Darius could, either. But for Hawk to have refused Darius's offer without even asking her opinion was beyond belief.

Although it went some way to explaining Darius's remark a week ago that a wealthy duke was obviously a more attractive marriage prospect than a penniless lord. He obviously believed Arabella's only reason for accepting him now was because he *was* now a wealthy duke!

Would she have accepted if she had known of Darius's offer a year ago?

At the time he had been known as a rake and a gambler. A man who, with little personal wealth left at his disposal, was deeply in debt. A man whose only means of alleviating that debt had appeared to be in the taking of a wealthy woman to wife.

Hawk was Arabella's guardian, charged with her welfare, and she knew that he had been perfectly justified in refusing him on her behalf when Darius had offered for her last summer.

But as the young woman who had compared every man she had met these past two Seasons with the devilish good-looks and magnetic charisma of Lord Darius Wynter—and found them all wanting!— Arabella could not help but feel resentful at Hawk's highhandedness. She might not be in love with Darius, or he with her, but Arabella had absolutely no doubt that she would have accepted him the previous summer.

Much as she hated Darius to think badly of her, Arabella knew she would be wise to make sure Darius didn't discover that she had not known until today of his previous offer for her, and to keep to herself her reasons for marrying him. The battle of wills that existed between them would be lost before it had even begun in earnest if Darius were ever to guess that Arabella was entering into their marriage with an eagerness for her husband's kisses and caresses that would be shocking if the anticipation did not feel so deliciously exciting…

'You are looking very lovely today,' Darius remarked dryly to his wife of two hours.

Hours during which he had smiled and been polite to both Arabella's family—all those St Claire aunts and uncles and cousins—and numerous members of the ton, who ordinarily would have returned to their country estates this late in the year, but had instead stayed on in town to attend two fashionable St Claire weddings.

No doubt gossip and speculation about the second of the two weddings would sustain many a conversation on a cold winter's evening before the ton returned to London *en masse* in the spring—with the added and erroneous assumption that the heir to the Carlyne dukedom would be born an indecently short time after the wedding!

'Thank you.' Arabella had no intention of returning the compliment by telling Darius how breathtakingly handsome *he* looked, in his snowy-white linen and austere black jacket and thigh-hugging black pantaloons, with his hair gleaming deeply gold in the reflection of the hundreds of candles illuminating the ballroom at St Claire House.

Seeing Darius in church earlier, as he'd stood at the altar waiting for her to join him, had literally robbed Arabella of her breath. So much so that for a few brief moments she had been unable to move as the organ began to play. Only the recently acquired knowledge of Darius's previous offer for her, one that had been made *willingly*, had prompted her into moving forward on silk-slippered feet.

Apart from her three brothers, Darius now stood head and shoulders above their wedding guests. Even if he had not, the deep gold of his hair and the handsomeness of his features would have distinguished him from every other man in the room.

Or perhaps that was only Arabella's biased opinion?

'When can we decently take our leave, do you think?' Darius looked bored by the whole proceeding.

Arabella arched blond brows. 'Decently?' she prodded.

Darius shrugged broad shoulders. 'Or indecently?'

'I would have thought, having been through this once before, that you would have more knowledge of the correct etiquette than I? Or perhaps your previous marriage was of such short duration that you have simply forgotten?' she taunted.

His eyes narrowed. 'Have a care, Arabella,' he warned her softly.

'Or what, Your Grace?'

'Or I might give myself the pleasure, once we are alone, of placing you over my knee and administering suitable punishment,' Darius murmured huskily, and was instantly rewarded by the flush that appeared in Arabella's cheeks.

Of anger? Or *anticipation*?

This past week had shown Darius that his new bride possessed all the courage he had imagined and more, as she had steadfastly refused to be daunted by any of the underlying displeasure of the ton in her choice of husband. Just as she had withstood all the gossip and speculation that had circulated around town after their wedding was announced. She had also, without fuss or ado, aided her sister-in-law Jane with the arrangements of that wedding. Best of all, she had been gracious and compassionate to Margaret, his brother's widow, a lady that Darius himself held in high regard, when they had dined with her.

In fact, Darius could not fault Arabella's behaviour towards everything and everyone this past week. Everyone but himself, that was…

Whenever the two of them had chanced to be alone—which, admittedly, had not been often—Arabella had tended to be either sharply critical or coolly dismissive, giving him little idea as to how she really felt about him. But Darius had every intention of rectifying the coolness of her manner towards him later this evening, once they were finally alone together at Carlyne House.

In fact, the anticipation of at last being alone with her was only adding to Darius's frustration with the social expectations it was so necessary to fulfil at one's own wedding. He physically ached to finish what the two of them had started in Hawk St Claire's study a week ago. Especially when he considered it had been that intimacy which had forced him into having to offer Arabella marriage!

His promised conversation with Lucian St Claire, once he'd finally managed to get the other man alone, had assured him of the other man's silence. Lucian had confirmed that he had not in any way broken the promise he had given to Darius six months ago. Nor would he.

Arabella looked down her provocative little nose at him. 'Am I to assume from that remark that I should expect to be beaten on a regular basis in our marriage, Your Grace?'

'You can expect to receive *something* on a regular basis in our marriage, Arabella,' he warned harshly. 'Especially if you intend to continue addressing me as "Your Grace" in that patronising manner.'

Her cheeks coloured prettily. 'I am not sure that I altogether approve of a man who would threaten to beat his wife.'

Darius raised blond brows. 'I do not believe I have ever asked for your approval, Arabella.'

No, he never had, Arabella acknowledged with a frown. In fact, she could never remember Darius, either as the disreputable Lord Wynter or the more respectable Duke of Carlyne, ever asking for, or indeed needing, anyone's approval. Least of all her own.

Arabella grudgingly admitted that it was this very arrogance, the feeling of dangerous uncertainty whenever she was in Darius's company, that made him so fascinatingly attractive to her....

'Nor,' Darius continued softly as he moved to stand in front of her, and so effectively shut the two of them off from their guests' curiosity, 'did I, in fact, threaten to beat you in the manner you describe. I assure you, Arabella, that I would endeavour to ensure that you thoroughly enjoy any...punishment that I choose to administer to you.'

Arabella felt colour blaze in her cheeks at the bluntness of his conversation. 'Perhaps the women you are used to associating with enjoy such—such rough treatment, Darius, but I assure you that I do not.'

'I hope you will come to appreciate at least a little

sport in our marriage bed, Arabella.' His eyes gleamed down at her mockingly. 'I assure you, there is nothing quite like it for rousing the blood.'

Arabella felt herself becoming flustered. Had she, after all, taken on more of a challenge in becoming Darius's wife than she was capable of dealing with?

Darius had been married before, and had indulged in a prodigious number of affairs with ladies both in the ton and out of it. In comparison to those women Arabella knew herself to be very young and inexperienced. Perhaps too much so to sustain the interest of a man as experienced as Darius undoubtedly was?

It was a little late for her to be having second thoughts now, when the wedding had already taken place and she would shortly be retiring for the night with her husband to Carlyne House!

She looked searchingly into his face. 'I believe, sir, that you are deliberately trying to alarm me…'

His mouth quirked. 'Am I?'

'Yes.' Arabella felt more and more confident of the fact as she saw the humour deepen in his vivid blue eyes. 'It is very cruel of you to tease me in this way, Darius.'

He raised a wicked brow. 'Perhaps in the same way it was cruel of *you* to tease *me* this past week?'

Her eyes widened. 'I was not aware of indulging in any such teasing.'

She was so very young, Darius realised ruefully. And so completely unaware, it seemed, of the physical provocation of the creamy swell of her breasts and the way her hips swayed so seductively beneath the soft material of her gown when she walked. Of the perfume that he had begun to associate only with her—a soft and enticing floral, womanly scent that he knew belonged uniquely to Arabella.

Of how the soft gold of her curls enticed him to release those tresses from their pins and allow them to tumble down the length of her slender spine.

Of how the soft fullness of her mouth just begged to be kissed.

In fact, it was all he could do now not to totally scandalise their wedding guests by taking his wife in his arms and kissing her in a thorough manner that was guaranteed to shock the avidly watching ton and no doubt confirm all their suspicions!

'I assure you, I have been well and truly teased by you,' he confirmed abruptly. 'Although I have high hopes of that situation changing very shortly—'

'I am sorry to interrupt, Carlyne.' William Bancroft, Earl of Banford and an active member of the House, had approached them unobserved. 'I wonder if I might steal your husband away for just a few moments, Your Grace?' He smiled warmly at Arabella.

Arabella instantly found herself blushing at being addressed by her new title for the first time, but at the same time recognised that she would appreciate a few minutes' respite from Darius's overwhelming presence. 'Of course, Lord Bancroft.' She smiled graciously at the other man in an effort to make up for the fact that Darius looked intensely annoyed at the interruption.

Which was less than gracious of him, considering that the Earl and Countess of Banford had been on Darius's guest list rather than Arabella's own.

It was a fact that Arabella had found curious to say

the least, and she had wondered if it was not *Lady* Bancroft, a woman reputed to have been mistress to several high-ranking male members of the ton before her marriage to the Earl three years ago, with whom Darius was better acquainted…

'Can this really not wait, Bancroft?' Darius felt no qualms about voicing his displeasure. 'It is, after all, my wedding day.'

'I require only two minutes of your time, I assure you,' the older man placated him lightly.

'I really should circulate amongst our other guests anyway, Darius.' Arabella looked up at him reproachfully.

'We will shortly be leaving, Arabella.' Darius said. 'Before anyone else feels themselves urgently in need of my company.' He scowled darkly at the other man.

Arabella shot the Earl a reassuring smile before taking her leave, but that smile was replaced by a frown as she could not help but overhear Darius's muttered words to the other man.

'What the hell can be so urgent, Bancroft,' he rasped impatiently, 'that you feel the need to bring it to my attention during my wedding celebrations?'

'I thought, before you left town, that you should be apprised of how events are developing concerning a certain matter,' the older man answered softly.

Arabella had moved too far across the ballroom by this time to be able to hear what Darius said in reply. But that did not stop her from wondering to what 'events' Lord Bancroft was referring. Or in what way they had 'developed'.

Although the conversation *did* imply that it was the deeply respected Earl of Banford, after all, with whom

Darius was acquainted, and not the other man's beautiful wife...

It was an indication to Arabella that there was still much she did not know about the man to whom she was now well and truly married....

'Did you and Lord Bancroft manage to settle your differences earlier?' Arabella asked Darius lightly.

They were travelling together in the Carlyne ducal carriage some half an hour later, having just departed St Claire House to the cheers and well wishes of both their families and friends after Arabella threw her bouquet into a group of young unmarried ladies.

The curtains were drawn across the windows, but a lighted lamp prevented the inside of the carriage from being in complete darkness. The reflection given off by the flickering light threw Darius's face into darkly satanic relief as he scowled across at her. 'I do not remember either of us stating that any such differences existed.'

'No, of course you did not,' Arabella accepted with a frown. 'But you did not seem very pleased at his interruption.'

'I believe my irritation with his intrusion to have been completely merited, considering this is our wedding day.'

Darius rose suddenly to cross the carriage and sit beside Arabella on the cushioned seat, the hard length of his muscled thigh pressed intimately against her much softer one.

Very intimately. Far too intimately for comfort. For Arabella's comfort, anyway. Enough to once again make her feel flustered and a little unsure of herself. A little? Arabella was a *lot* unsure of herself!

She moistened dry lips. 'I admit it will be a relief to reach Carlyne House and remove all this wedding finery…' Arabella's words trailed off into embarrassed awkwardness as she realised that she had unwittingly broached the very subject she had been trying to avoid. 'I meant, of course—'

'I know exactly what you meant, Arabella,' Darius drawled, deliberately moving closer to her as he turned in the seat to look at her before raising a hand and touching the flushed heat of her cheek. 'As your husband, I assure you I consider it my duty to aid you in removing your wedding finery at the earliest opportunity.'

'I had not thought you to be a man to whom duty meant very much.' Her eyes gleamed challengingly.

For all her youth and inexperience his little wife had the tongue of a viper!

A tongue Darius was sure could be put to much better use than deliberately insulting him…

'Usually only in regard to entertaining the ton,' he reminded her. 'But I am willing to make an exception when it comes to the comfort of my wife.'

Darius held that snapping brown gaze as his hand moved to deliberately pull on the ribbon that untied the bow of Arabella's bonnet, before removing it completely to reveal those enticing golden curls, long fingers moving confidently as he systematically removed the pins that held those curls in place.

'I— What are you doing…?' Arabella raised a hand in half-hearted protest as her hair began to fall wildly about her shoulders.

Darius smiled. 'I believe it is called making love to one's wife.'

The creaminess of Arabella's throat moved convulsively as she swallowed nervously. 'Can you not wait until we reach Carlyne House and the privacy of our bedchamber?'

'Why should I?' Darius retorted. 'You are mine now, Arabella. To do with as I wish, when I wish—remember?'

Arabella felt a shiver of—of what...? Was it apprehension? Or excitement?

This past week, despite all the rush and bustle of the wedding arrangements, Arabella had still found herself thinking of her wedding night whenever there was the slightest lull in those arrangements. Thinking of it. Anticipating it. Longing for it. For the touch of Darius's lips and hands upon her once again. In the certain knowledge that this time he would not stop at touching but would take their lovemaking to its fullest conclusion.

Yet now that the time had come Arabella found herself both shy and not a little apprehensive!

To their obvious embarrassment—and Arabella's own, if the truth be told—she had spoken with all of her sisters-in-law this past week concerning what her role should be in the bedchamber.

Jane had advised that lovemaking was a mutual giving and receiving of physical pleasure.

Grace had said that it was perhaps best if Arabella allowed her husband to take all the initiative until they knew each other's likes and dislikes.

Juliet's slightly flustered opinion, when Arabella had questioned her shortly after her arrival this morning, was that husbands were sometimes appreciative of the woman taking the initiative.

Advice which had left Arabella more confused than ever as to what Darius might expect of her in the marriage bed.

So far there had certainly been no mention at all of what Darius might expect of her as they travelled in the coach to Carlyne House!

'Better,' he murmured appreciatively now, as he ran his fingers through the heavy thickness of her hair so that it cascaded loosely over her shoulders and down the length of her spine. 'Whenever we are alone, Arabella, I would prefer that you wear your hair just so.'

She touched her loosened curls self-consciously. 'I— What would the servants think?'

He raised blond brows. 'I do not pay them to think, Arabella.'

'Yes, but—' Her words ceased as Darius's hands cupped either side of her face, the soft pads of his thumbs a light and evocative caress against the softness of her lips. 'Darius…?'

Darius was fully aware of Arabella's uncertainty, knew she had no idea how sexually provocative she looked at this moment, with her golden curls wild about her shoulders, eyes dark and uncertain beneath lowered lashes, and her parted moist lips in a full and inviting pout.

He had begun this flirtation with his wife as a means of diverting her from questioning him any further as to his earlier conversation with Bancroft, but now Darius found that his gaze was fixed upon the invitation of Arabella's parted lips, and ruefully he recognised that his only desire now was to taste them.

Arabella felt small and slightly fragile as he curved his arms about her waist and crushed her breasts against his chest, pulling her hard against him before lowering his head to capture those pouting lips with his own.

She tasted of wine and peaches, which Darius now recalled were the only two things Arabella had consumed at their wedding feast. The wine perhaps to allay some of her nervousness? The peaches because they were light and exotic? Whatever the reason for Arabella's choice, they were a heady combination to Darius's senses. Intoxicating, as well as inviting.

As Arabella herself was intoxicating and inviting.

It seemed to Arabella at that moment as if no time had elapsed at all since Darius had made love to her in Hawk's study a week ago. The desire she had known then was once again bursting into flames as he kissed her with a thoroughness that took her breath away and made her body burn.

All of her sisters-in-laws' contradictory advice fled as Arabella returned the heat of those devouring kisses, pressing against Darius to make even closer contact as her arms entwined about his neck and her fingers became entangled in the thick silkiness of the hair at his nape.

His lips were firm and commanding against her own, teeth gently biting, tongue tasting as it explored the shape of her lips before slipping into the heated cavern of her mouth.

Arabella gasped slightly when she felt Darius's hand curve around one of her breasts as he continued to kiss her. His thumb caressed unerringly over its sensitive tip as it pressed against the soft material of her gown, sending rivulets of desire coursing down between her thighs, readying her, she felt sure, for even deeper intimacies.

It was—

There was a sudden shifting, a lurching of the ducal coach, and it tilted precariously to one side, tossing Darius back against the door, his arm still about Arabella's waist. Her eyes went wide with shock and fear as Darius pulled her down on top of him to land on the floor of the coach in a tangle of arms and legs. The lamp swayed precariously for several long seconds before it too fell to the floor beside them, extinguishing the candle inside and plunging them into complete darkness.

Arabella began to scream.

Chapter Five

'Calm down, Arabella! Arabella, I order you to stop that noise instantly and allow me to think!' Darius said firmly.

His words had no effect on her obvious hysteria. Not that he could exactly blame her for her distress, when they were blanketed in darkness inside the tilting carriage with a cacophony of noise outside made up of men shouting, dogs barking, and horses whinnying in a horrible manner that seemed to imply at least one of them had been injured in the crash.

For a crash it had most certainly been. Whether they had collided with another vehicle or not, the precarious tilt of the Carlyne carriage proclaimed that the vehicle had somehow either been damaged or had lost a wheel and was now lurched dangerously to one side.

The door above them on the other side of the carriage was suddenly wrenched open and one of the grooms, his grey wig askew, peered down at them in the darkness. 'Your Grace?' he gasped as he gazed in upon the tangle of legs, arms and bodies. 'Are you injured?'

'I myself am not,' Darius answered grimly as he attempted to sit up and found Arabella's arms so tightly clutched about his neck he could barely move. 'Are *you* hurt, Arabella?' he asked with concern, and he released her clinging fingers and held her slightly away from him so that he might inspect her for obvious injury.

'I do not—do not know.' Her voice was faint and slightly shaky. 'Please get me out of here, Darius.' Her eyes glittered wildly in the darkness as she reached up and clung to him once again. 'Please!'

Darius had become accustomed to her stoicism this past week, her bewitching and tempting air of self-sufficiency that challenged him into wanting to tame her. In his bed, if not out of it. To see her reduced to such trembling distress by a simple carriage accident seemed totally out of character.

Until, that was, he suddenly recalled that the ninth Duke of Stourbridge and his duchess, Arabella's parents, had both been killed in a carriage accident eleven years ago….

Darius's face was like stone as he turned to look up at the groom. 'I am going to lift my wife so that you can remove her to safety.' He wasted no time in suiting his actions to his words as he placed his hands about Arabella's waist and lifted her up, allowing the other man to pull her outside into the darkened night. Darius quickly followed by placing his hands either side of the open doorway and levering himself up and out of the badly listing carriage.

Another of the grooms had managed to quieten the horses by the time Darius lowered himself down onto the cobbled road beside a now quietly sobbing Arabella.

He moved to place his arms protectively about her as he turned to take in the scene of the accident.

There was no other carriage in sight, but one of their nearside back wheels had come completely adrift and lay some distance away. The terrible screeching noise Darius had heard earlier had obviously been that of the axle of the carriage as it was dragged along the cobbles for several feet before the groom had managed to bring the horses to a halt.

Luckily they had not been travelling at any speed when the wheel had parted company with the carriage, which accounted for the lack of any serious injury. Even so, Darius's face was stern as he turned his attention back to his distraught young wife. 'You really must calm yourself, Arabella.' He frowned as he realised how harsh his voice sounded. 'It is all over now and there is no harm done,' he added in a much gentler tone.

Arabella was shaking so badly, her teeth chattering together so loudly, that for a moment she didn't hear Darius, let alone comprehend what he had just said to her. Even once she did understand his reassurances she could not stop the trembling of her body or the shaking of her hands as she still clung to—and no doubt ruined—the lapels of his jacket. 'I thought—I believed we were about to—to—' She broke off with a telling shudder.

'I understand, Arabella.'

Looking up into Darius's face, Arabella saw that he did indeed understand the reason for the depth of her distress. Understood it, perhaps, but the harshness of his expression implied that he also found her hysteria less than becoming in his wife. In his duchess. His rigidly controlled demeanour was so like Hawk's would have been in the same circumstances that Arabella instantly calmed, straightening her back and shoulders and releasing Darius's jacket before turning to look at the carriage.

'The grooms and horses also escaped injury?'

'Yes. But at a guess more by luck than judgement.' Darius nodded, his eyes narrowed as he looked again at the precariously tilted carriage.

'What do you mean?' Arabella frowned her confusion as she turned back to him.

Darius forced his anger over the accident to the back of his emotions, to be dealt with at a later date rather than expressing it here and now in front of Arabella. 'I was merely questioning the care that was taken in preparing the carriage for our use today,' he explained.

Her breath drew in sharply. 'I am sure that none of your grooms would have been negligent, Darius. After all, they were travelling on the coach too.'

'Of course.' Darius forced a tight smile. 'It was just an accident, as you say. One that unfortunately seems to have left us a little distance from arriving outside Carlyne House,' he added ruefully, realising they still had a quarter of a mile or so to travel before they reached his—their—London home.

'I doubt that a walk will do either of us any lasting harm.' Arabella tucked her hand into the crook of his arm with the obvious intention of beginning that walk immediately.

The dignity of her expression prevented Darius from pointing out how much in disarray was her appearance, with her hair loose and falling wildly down the length of her spine, and her gown less than pristine. It had several dirty smudges down its front and a slight tear in the material along one side. In that moment, dishevelled and still slightly unnerved by the accident, Arabella still managed to look every inch a duchess.

His duchess.

'At least you now have a valid reason for the dishevelled state of your hair,' he teased lightly as they began to walk along the street with every appearance of simply being out for an afternoon stroll.

Arabella had visited Carlyne House several times this past week, to be introduced to all of the household staff, as well as become acquainted with one of the houses that would become her home once she and Darius were married.

Having decided that the spring, when hopefully the weather would be more clement, was a much nicer time to honeymoon on the Continent, Arabella and Darius had instead made arrangements to travel to Winton Hall on the day following the wedding. They would spend several weeks there before travelling into Gloucestershire in December, to spend the Christmas season with Arabella's family.

Arabella's cheeks warmed slightly as she recalled the reason her hair was tumbled loosely about her shoulders and down her spine. That soft thrumming resumed in her body as she recalled the ardour of Darius's kisses. Her heart started pounding as she wondered how much further he would have gone in his lovemaking if the accident had not brought such an abrupt end to their intimacy.

Then the warmth in her cheeks became due to embarrassment as Arabella recalled, and deeply regretted, her behaviour following the accident. That she had the excuse of her parents' death in a carriage accident to explain her hysteria did not make it any less undignified.

She drew in a sharp breath. 'I can only apologise for behaving like a—a ninny just now, Darius. It was inexcusable of me to take on so. I should not have screamed or clung to you in the way I did.'

'I assure you I found your behaviour highly diverting,' he said.

'Diverting?' she echoed sharply.

'Why, yes.' The humour that curved Darius's mouth was also reflected in his eyes. 'It is not every day that one sees the Lady Arabella St Claire appearing less than composed.'

'You forget, Darius, that I am now Arabella Wynter, Duchess of Carlyne!' she reminded him tartly, stung by his amusement at her expense.

He snorted. 'That is even more reason to marvel at your recent loss of control.'

'I am pleased to have provided you with some amusement!' she huffed.

'Are you?'

'No!' Arabella glared up at him in the moonlight.

'Perhaps that is as well—as I am actually far from amused.' His expression turned suddenly grim once more, his eyes taking on the cold sheen of ice.

A frown creased the creaminess of her brow as she looked up at him searchingly. 'You are angry with me, Darius?'

With her usual intelligence Arabella had managed to pierce straight to the heart of Darius's mood! It *was* anger he felt. Cold. Steely. Implacable. Remorseless anger. But he was not angry with *her*.

What had just happened only proved to Darius that he should never have persuaded himself into believing the best course of action to keep Arabella safe was for him to marry her. In his defence, it had been done in the mistaken belief that once their intimate interlude in Hawk's study had become public knowledge—as it invariably would have done, thanks to Lord Redwood— it would be far safer for her if they married and then shortly thereafter removed themselves from London and became ensconced in the privacy and safety of Winton Hall.

Darius had certainly not expected the first attempt at an 'accident' to occur before they had even had a chance to leave London.

It was too much of a coincidence, too soon after his earlier conversation with William Bancroft, for Darius to believe that the wheel coming loose from his carriage was truly the accident it gave every appearance of being.

He knew he had made enemies this past eight years. Dozens of people, traitors to their country, who had every reason to want to cause him harm. Now that Arabella had become his wife, those same people might wish to cause her harm too.

One person in particular, perhaps…

But Arabella must be kept in ignorance of that, at least for now—she was still not recovered from her shock after the accident, and Darius had no intention of alarming her further with tales of possible mortal danger. He would have to tell her something else instead, to explain his mood to her.

'There are so many reasons for the present state of my emotions, Arabella, that I hardly know where to begin,' Darius commented as he came to a halt beneath the lamp in front of Carlyne House. 'I have been treated with icy disdain this past week by at least one of your brothers, and with an equal amount of suspicion by your sisters-in-law. I have also just been forced into a marriage not of my choosing to a woman also not of my choosing.'

'You did not seem to feel that same reluctance a year ago, when you offered for me!' Arabella was stung into defending herself heatedly.

Ah.

Darius's mouth compressed. 'An offer I seem to recall that you did not hesitate to refuse.'

Arabella opened her mouth to protest. And then closed it again. Not only would it be disloyal of her to admit that Hawk had not even consulted her over that offer, but it would also allow Darius to pose the question as to whether or not she would have accepted the offer if she *had* known of it—and she wasn't ready to answer that yet…

She looked up at him haughtily. 'No woman of good sense would have accepted such an offer.' Which meant, perhaps, that Arabella was not a woman of good sense—because she most certainly *would* have accepted a marriage offer from him!

Darius's eyes gleamed coldly in the moonlight as he looked down at her. 'No doubt because my… circumstances were far different a year ago from what they are today?'

'In that you mean you had not yet *conveniently* inherited the fortune of the woman who *was* stupid enough to accept your offer?" Arabella snapped back—only to draw back in dismay as she saw the way Darius's face had darkened ominously.

'This is the second occasion upon which you have voiced such slanderous accusations, Arabella.' His tone had become as icy as his demeanour. 'I would advise, for your own sake, that there not be a third.'

Arabella felt a shiver of apprehension down the length of her spine as she realised she really did not know the man who was now her husband. 'You are right, Darius. This is not the best time for such a discussion. Nerves are obviously frayed, and tempers even more so.'

'On the contrary,' he drawled in a deceptively soft tone. 'It has been my experience that it is exactly when nerves are frayed and tempers roused that the truth tends to be spoken.'

Perhaps, Arabella allowed heavily. But she would far rather her words had remained unspoken tonight of all nights!

She gave a heavy sigh. 'I spoke in the heat of the moment only, Darius.'

'If that is in the nature of an apology, Arabella, then let me assure you that it falls far short of the mark.' Darius didn't know which of them he was more angry with. Arabella—or himself, for actually allowing her words to pierce the guard he invariably kept about his emotions.

In truth, her accusations were not so different from the many others levelled at him over the years. He was a rake. A womaniser. A gambler. A fortune-hunter. A possible murderer.

Hearing them spoken by one's own wife, however, was extremely unpleasant.

He looked down the length of his nose at her. 'Perhaps you even believe that *I* arranged the carriage accident just now, in the hope of ridding myself of my second unwanted wife?'

Her shocked frown showed him that the idea had not even occurred to her until he had voiced it. She recovered quickly. 'Not when you were a passenger in the carriage, too!'

Darius sighed heavily. 'I believe it is past time we went inside.' He curled his fingers about her upper arm and ascended the steps to Carlyne House; if someone was watching them, possibly the perpetrator of the coach 'accident', then they had already lingered far too long outside than was wise.

Arabella had no idea what to do or say in order to dispel the tension that now existed between herself and Darius. A tension that was so at odds with the intensity of passion they had shared in the carriage such a short time ago.

The cold and remote man who swept so arrogantly into the marbled hallway of Carlyne House the moment the door was opened by a footman brandishing a candelabra was not the man who had made love to Arabella either a week ago or earlier this evening. *This* man was a stranger to her. A cold, aloof stranger to whom she was now married and who questioned her belief over whether the carriage accident had even been an accident at all...

'Ah, Reynolds,' Darius spoke to the butler as he appeared in the hallway. 'There has been a accident. No one was injured,' he assured the butler quickly as the man looked alarmed. 'But I am afraid we were forced to abandon the carriage and walk home. It is my intention to return to the scene and check on progress with the carriage. I am sure Her Grace would appreciate being shown to her bedchamber, and then provided with a tray of tea and dainties.' Darius's expression was forbidding as he released Arabella to turn back towards the front door, which the footman instantly swept open once again, allowing a blast of cold night air to swirl about the hallway.

Arabella shivered as that coldness pierced the thin material of her gown in accompaniment to the ice creeping through her veins at Darius's announcement that he intended leaving the house. Leaving her on their wedding night!

'Darius?'

Narrowed lids hid the expression in the deep blue of his eyes as he paused in the open doorway to turn and look at her. 'What is it, Arabella?'

Pride—the St Claire pride so embedded in her own nature, as well as that of her brothers—dictated that she could not demand an explanation in front of the listening butler and footman as to why Darius felt it necessary to return to the broken carriage tonight of all nights.

Yet incredulity at his obvious intent of leaving the house on such a fool's errand, rather than remaining with his bride of but a few hours, dictated that she could not just let him leave the house without some show of disapproval at his actions, either!

On top of which, Darius had absolutely no right to instruct that she be 'shown to her bedchamber' in what was effectively now her own home!

She forced a cool smile to her lips, although the blaze in her eyes as she looked across at him gave the lie to that air of serenity she was projecting. 'Perhaps you would care to join me in a reviving cup of tea before venturing back out into the cold?'

At any other time Darius would have enjoyed taking the time to indulge his wife's request for his company—as he would no doubt have enjoyed even more the consequences of quelling her obvious sparks of temper!

At this moment, however, he had far more pressing matters to attend to—he had to think about her safety above all else, even if she wasn't aware of it.

'I think not, thank you, Arabella,' he drawled. 'It's probably best if you do not wait up for me,' he added dryly. 'I have no idea when I will return, and you are no doubt tired after the excitement of the day.'

Darius could only regret the way her cheeks paled at his obvious dismissal, and he made a mental promise to himself—and her—to make up for the disaster of this, their wedding night, as soon as could be. As soon as they were both safely away from London…

Her dismay did not last long, however, as two bright spots of colour appeared in the pallor of her cheeks. 'What a considerate husband you are, to be sure, Darius.' The sweetness of her tone did not match the anger glinting in her golden-brown eyes.

He could only eye her appreciatively, even as he once again privately regretted his need to leave her. 'I have no doubt that you intend being as considerate a wife as I am a husband.'

'Oh, undoubtedly!' she retorted.

Darius bit back a smile at the promise of retribution glittering in those bright golden eyes. 'Pleasant dreams, Arabella.'

She gave him a sweetly saccharine smile. 'I have no doubt they will all be of you, my dear Darius!'

In that case he very much doubted they would be pleasant dreams, but rather ones of a violent nature, no doubt culminating in some painful punishment dealt him by her for his desertion.

All humour left Darius's expression as he strode back towards the disabled carriage, pondering what he was sure was an attempt on his life. And not just on his life, but Arabella's too. Darius considered himself more than capable of taking care of himself. Indeed he had been doing so for some years now. But endangering Arabella in this way was unacceptable.

Someone would pay for this evening's mischief.

Someone would pay dearly, he vowed grimly.

Arabella ignored the tray of tea things that had been brought up to her as she paced restlessly, agitatedly, angrily, up and down the spacious bedchamber that, as the Duchess of Carlyne, was now her own. It was a graciously appointed bedchamber that had been hurriedly decorated to her tastes in gold and cream this past week, in preparation for her arrival this evening, and it possessed an adjoining door to the room of her husband.

A husband whom, at this particular moment, Arabella dearly wished to throttle within an inch of his life!

Admittedly the broken carriage had to be removed from the street. The grooms must be returned to the house. The horses stabled and calmed after their ordeal.

Yet it was simply beyond Arabella's understanding that Darius considered those grooms and horses more deserving at present of his solicitude than his own wife. Surely a senior member of his household could have sorted out the mess?

How could he treat her in this callous way?

How could he just turn her welfare over to the care of servants after the scare she had suffered such a short time ago?

How *dared* he just abandon her on their wedding night?

Arabella sat down abruptly on the gold brocade coverlet draped over the blankets of the huge four-poster bed that dominated the bedchamber. A four-poster bed in which she was expected to sleep alone.

On her wedding night…

After days, a week, of nervousness as she imagined herself and Darius going to bed together on the night of their wedding, Arabella instead found herself abandoned and alone. It was an unforgivable insult. A humiliation beyond endurance!

Arabella was well aware of the gossip of servants. They would all know that the Duke had not cared to share the Duchess's bed on their wedding night. From which piece of delectable gossip certain conclusions would no doubt be made…

Either that the rumours were all true, and the Duke had already shared his bride's bed before their marriage and so felt no particular compunction to share it again on their wedding night. Or—more humiliating still—having dallied with her and then been forced into a marriage not of his choosing, the Duke felt no inclination to claim what was now his by right.

Darius would pay for insulting her in this way, Arabella vowed fiercely.

He would most definitely be made to pay!

Chapter Six

'You are very quiet today, Arabella.' Darius eyed his young wife across the width of the carriage—the second-best carriage, as the main ducal vehicle was once again safely in the stables at Carlyne House and awaiting repair—as they travelled from London to Worcestershire in the early-morning gloom.

Arabella turned from looking out of the window and returned his gaze coolly. 'I prefer to think of it as being introspective, Your Grace.'

Oh, dear, they were back to the formality of Your Grace! 'No doubt you have much to think on?' he pressed.

'No doubt.' The smile that accompanied her reply did not reach the coldness of her eyes.

Everything about Arabella was cool today. The pale green gown and matching bonnet she wore for travelling. The pristine white lace gloves that covered her tiny hands. The pale, smooth alabaster of her face and throat. The deep, unfathomable brown of her eyes.

Not that Darius did not fully deserve Arabella's coldness after the way he had left her so abruptly the night before—a desertion that had ultimately proved fruitless.

There had been nothing to gain from examining the wheel and axle of the carriage once it had been returned to the stables. Except to tell Darius what he had already guessed: the rivets that held the wheel in place had come loose. Whether by accident or design it had been utterly impossible to tell.

A visit to the home of William Bancroft, recently returned home from Darius and Arabella's wedding celebrations, to continue their earlier discussion in view of this latest 'accident' had been of little help, either. Bancroft had no new information as to the whereabouts of Helena Jourdan, the French spy whose existence Darius had denied to Arabella, following her escape from custody the previous week. If, indeed, it *was* she who was trying to kill Darius. There was a second possibility, much closer to home, that Darius found even more unpalatable.

His younger brother Francis...

Disgraced and banished, could Francis have returned to England somehow and even now be plotting Darius's and Arabella's deaths?

His mouth thinned at the thought of the danger he might have placed Arabella in simply by marrying her. The same danger that Sophie had found herself in the moment Darius had taken her as his wife a year ago...

Was Darius *never* to be allowed any personal happiness?

Last night's 'accident' gave every indication that was the case!

He sighed heavily. 'You are still angry with me because of last night.' It had been very late when Darius had returned to Carlyne House after seeing Bancroft, almost two o'clock in the morning, and as promised, rather than disturb Arabella, he had instead retired directly to his own bedchamber.

Only to remain restless and virtually sleepless for the remainder of the night as he regretted telling her he would not be joining her in her bedchamber. It had been impossible to sleep when he could so easily imagine how beautiful, how desirable, his wife would look as she lay back against downy pillows, with that gloriously golden hair spread out beneath her….

Darius still ached at the vividness of that image!

Arabella raised haughty blond brows. 'What happened last night, Darius? Admittedly, the carriage accident was a little—bothersome, but I assure you I slept surprisingly well, considering.' The dark shadows visible beneath those dark brown eyes gave the lie to her claim.

A fact that Darius was well aware of. Just as he was aware that it was the St Claire pride that sustained Arabella in the face of what she no doubt saw as Darius's abandonment of her after she had been so shaken by the carriage accident, and also his rejection of her on their wedding night.

It was not Arabella that Darius had rejected, it was the taking of a wife at all when his own life was being dogged by someone who wished him harm and did not care if his young and beautiful wife shared that same fate, that caused Darius to guard his thoughts and deeds. But he dared not share that information with her.

'In that case you will have no need of sleep once we have arrived at the coaching inn,' he murmured.

'I do not understand, sir.' But the delicate colour that crept up Arabella's throat and into her cheeks said she understood his huskily spoken words only too well!

Darius sat forward on the padded bench-seat so that his face was only inches away from hers. 'I am sure we will both benefit from retiring to our bedchambers for the rest of the afternoon. In order that we might bathe and…rest after travelling.'

Arabella stared at Darius. Was he seriously suggesting that they amuse themselves in bed all afternoon? Did he really dare to think that she would be willing to participate in the pleasures of the bedchamber after the way he'd treated her?

Her disappointment at Darius's desertion the evening before, followed by outrage as his absence continued long after she might have expected his return, had sustained Arabella through the long night that had just passed. She certainly had no intention of allowing Darius to make love to her for the first time in a coaching inn, of that she was sure. As was the case in most inns, it would offer little comfort and absolutely no privacy!

Arabella's intention to treat Darius with dismissive coldness for the dreary and lengthy duration of their journey into Worcestershire, in an effort to show him how contemptible was his behaviour of the night before, was completely forgotten as she bristled indignantly. 'You may choose to pander to your mistress rather than your wife, Darius, but I assure you that I am not someone who can be discarded and then picked up again when it suits your own needs!'

Amusement darkened the blue of his eyes to

cobalt. 'And what do you know of the treatment of mistresses, Arabella?'

Her eyes snapped with temper. 'You seem to forget, Darius, that I have three older brothers.'

'And?'

'Do not treat me like a backward child, Darius,' she warned tartly, her mouth thin. 'It is well known that the men of the ton change their mistresses as often as they change their linen.'

'Oftener, in some cases,' Darius allowed, and he sat back against the upholstered seat, arms folded across the muscled width of his chest as he gazed at her speculatively. 'And you count me in their number, do you, Arabella?'

She gave an inelegant snort. 'Your own actions have placed you in their number.'

'Indeed?'

Arabella was completely aware of the underlying steel in Darius's tone. But she felt perfectly justified in ignoring the warning in view of his desertion of her the previous night. Long hours which Arabella had spent alone in her bedchamber. Hours when her imagination had provided her with thoughts of whether or not it was actually another woman rather than the broken carriage that had drawn Darius's attention away from his new wife so soon....

It had also occurred to Arabella some time during her sleepless night that when she'd questioned Darius the previous week he had not denied having a mistress at present, only the need to continue to keep one after they were married. Perhaps last night had been the end of their affair? Perhaps the woman had even been a guest at their wedding!

Once the idea had presented itself to her, Arabella had found her imagination taking flight to the extent that she had clearly been able to visualise Darius in bed with the other woman. To imagine the two of them lying naked and entwined, satiated from their lovemaking, as they perhaps laughed together at the thought of Darius's abandoned lonely bride.

The mere thought of that being the case made Arabella's blood boil anew!

She looked across at Darius coldly. 'I take it you feel no desire for me to produce your heirs immediately?'

He frowned. 'Not particularly, no.' He didn't want to give his enemies yet another innocent, vulnerable target!

Arabella nodded abruptly. 'In that case I see no reason to share your bed at the present time.' She turned to once again stare out of the window at the now softly falling rain. The gloomy weather was reflective of her own mood.

Darius continued to study Arabella through narrowed lids and he realised from her remarks, as well as from the things she had left unsaid, that she had drawn her own conclusions concerning his lengthy absence from Carlyne House the night before. He was experienced enough to know that her anger at the thought that he'd visited his mistress was merely a shield for the much deeper hurt she felt at his apparent shunning of her on their wedding night.

The obvious thing to do to put things right between them would be for Darius to offer Arabella reassurances as to his whereabouts the night before. Unfortunately, in doing that he would also have to explain his reasons for having gone to see Bancroft. An explanation that even now Darius would not—could not—share with anyone. Even his young wife.

Eight years ago, in the midst of those bloody years of England's battles against Napoleon, Darius had known that as the second son he was expected to take up a commission in the army. Tired of Society, jaded from his years of drinking and gambling, disenchanted with the women who frequently shared his bed, it had been an action Darius had been only too willing to take.

However, before he had been able to do so he had been approached by a member of the English government—a man who had explained that he re-cruited a widespread group of men and women, both in England and France, who, despite the danger to their own lives, had become spies for their country rather than overtly displaying their patriotism on the battle-field.

The work was dangerous, the man had explained, the rewards few, and the thanks non-existent as the role those people played in the fight against Napoleon could never be made public.

All that was required of Darius was for him to con-tinue to live the debauched and profligate life he was already leading. To lull the public in general, and the ton in particular, into believing he was nothing more than a wastrel and a rake. He would be surprised, the man had assured him, how indiscreet a traitor could be when in the company of a man they considered too drunk or uninterested to pay any attention to their conversation.

They had been prophetic words, Darius now ac-knowledged wryly.

For six years the ton had continued to believe him too lazy or cowardly to fight for his country. During those same six years Darius had become adept at discovering a man's—or a woman's—secret alliances. More so than he could ever have imagined. His success had been such that he had moved quickly up the rank and file of this secret organisation, until he had eventually found himself as the head of one of the networks of England's spies.

Two years after Napoleon's final defeat Darius still headed that network. William Bancroft, Earl of Banford, was only one of their number.

None of which Darius was at liberty to share with anyone—not even his own wife. Not even when the work he had done, and continued to do, might have placed Arabella in that same danger as Darius himself....

There was one thing he *could* make clear to her, however. 'I do *not* have a mistress, Arabella.'

Her expression was scornful as she turned to look at him with hard brown eyes. 'Perhaps not now, no. But only because you probably ended it just last night!'

'Not for some time,' he stated firmly, his expression intent as he leaned forward again. 'Arabella, there has been no woman in my life, or my bed, since Sophie's death.'

Arabella's eyes widened. Did Darius seriously expect her to believe he had been celibate for a whole year? A man who, despite having gained respectability since inheriting a dukedom, was still known for his womanising. For his carousing. For his gambling.

Had he been womanising, carousing or gambling during the week of their betrothal?

Not to Arabella's knowledge. Or that of her brothers, she felt sure. For Arabella had no doubt that one or all of them would have brought it to her attention if he had.

But just because he had behaved himself in the week before their wedding it did not necessarily mean that Darius had remained celibate for this past year.

Then why would he say that he had?

Darius was still very much a puzzle to her, and did many things she could not approve of, but she had no reason to believe he had ever lied to her. More truthfully, Darius was arrogant enough never to feel the need to lie about any of his actions.

Her chin rose challengingly. 'Did you love your first wife so much, then?'

He gave a rueful shake of his head. 'I can always rely on you to ask the unexpected, can't I?'

Her brows rose. 'In that case you will not find me tedious.'

'Far from it!'

'Did you love your first wife?' she repeated determinedly.

'For my sins—no.' Darius grimaced.

Arabella gave a graceful inclination of her head—as if the answer were just as she had expected. 'You have been widowed a year. Even before you became a duke you were considered highly eligible. So why have you not taken advantage of that rank and fortune this past year to secure yourself a mistress?'

Darius mouth twisted with distaste. 'Perhaps because I preferred it when I knew a woman's partiality was only to me rather than due to a title or a fortune.'

Arabella bristled. 'Your implication being that *I* only married you for your title?'

'There can be no other reason,' he pointed out calmly. 'Not when I have been reliably informed by Hawk that you have no need of my fortune when considerable personal wealth became yours upon our marriage yesterday.'

It was true, of course. Arabella's parents had been more enlightened than most, and had considered their daughter to have as much right to financial independence as any of their three sons. Consequently her father had left her a vast fortune in his will, which Hawk had managed for her these past eleven years, and a small estate in Norfolk, which Hawk had also taken care of by putting in a manager. The estate had become part of Arabella's husband's lands upon her marriage, of course, but the fortune would remain in trust for her children, with the interest set aside for her personal use.

Her wedding yesterday had made Arabella an even wealthier and more independent woman than ever she had been before that marriage.

She smiled tightly. She could not—would not—allow this arrogant and sarcastic man to know that she would probably have married him a year ago, whatever his wealth or title, if she had known of his offer.

'How clever of you to guess!'

He looked at her coldly. 'Cleverness has nothing to do with it.'

'If you say so.' She nodded coolly. 'Did you have a particular reason for confiding your celibacy to me now?'

Amusement now danced in those cobalt-blue eyes. 'I was merely trying to reassure you that you may expect my complete fidelity, Arabella.'

Arabella wasn't yet ready to forgive him for leaving her so abruptly on their wedding night. 'Surely that is something any new bride might expect?'

'Expect, perhaps,' he said ruefully. 'But never be truthfully assured of.'

She raised a sarcastic brow. 'In that case I should no doubt consider myself fortunate that you feel able to offer me such assurances.'

Once again Darius was tempted to lift her skirts and paddle her bottom until she screamed for mercy. After which he would enjoy nothing more than making love to her until they were both thoroughly satisfied!

She was a little madam. A minx. And he found her completely enchanting. She was a temptress who had occupied far too many of his waking thoughts—and his dreams—this past week.

Perhaps if she had not Darius might have been more on his guard yesterday. More expectant regarding the sabotage of their coach...

He would not relax his guard again until they were safely ensconced at Winton Hall. Once there, he had the necessary security in place to ensure Arabella's safety at least.

Darius's expression hardened as he once again regretted that he had allowed himself to be beguiled into marrying her. By doing so he had brought her into the web of deceit and danger that had necessarily become his own life these past eight years.

He would not have been so tempted beyond resistance if Arabella were not so beautiful. So delectable. So spirited. And if he had not wanted her so badly in his bed for years...

'I am pleased to hear you are wise to the honour,' he bit out in response to her sarcasm. 'If you will excuse me, Arabella? I believe I might nap for the rest of the journey.' He lowered his lids, deliberately shutting out the vision of loveliness that was his brand-new bride.

Except Darius could still see her and feel her behind those closed lids, as she glared rebelliously across the width of the carriage at him.

The silky gold of her hair was tempting him into releasing it. The pout of her lips was begging to be kissed. The full swell of her breasts was spilling over the low neckline of her gown. A fullness that Darius ached to cup in his hands. To kiss and caress once more as he had that evening a week ago in Hawk St Claire's study.

Dear God, he had no need to fear meeting death at the hands of his enemies when this desire for Arabella was sure to drive him into an early grave!

'I am very tired, Darius. I believe I will retire for the night.' Arabella placed her napkin on the dinner table before standing up.

She had found herself becoming more and more tense, and their conversation had reflected that tension as the two of them dined privately in the warm comfort of the secluded parlour the landlord of the inn had provided for their use. As bedtime had approached, that tension had reached breaking point...

Having suggested that once they reached the inn they might retire for the afternoon together to their bedchambers, Darius had once again busied himself—unnecessarily so, Arabella had felt—in seeing to the stabling of the horses and the securing of the coach.

Leaving Arabella to be shown upstairs to the privacy of her bedchamber and the attentions of her maid, who had been sent on ahead to the inn with Darius's valet and their luggage. Having bathed and changed into her robe, Arabella had lain down upon her bed and managed to fall asleep, waking only when her maid came back into the room to help her dress for dinner.

Darius had obviously found time to shave and bathe, and his hair was freshly washed and gleaming deeply gold as it curled in meticulous disarray about his stunning face. He had also changed from his dark travelling clothes into a tailored superfine the same colour blue as his eyes, his impeccable linen was snowy-white, and his buff-coloured pantaloons moulded to the muscled length of his thighs above shiny black Hessians.

On first seeing him thus, Arabella had had to allow that Darius was the handsomest man in England!

The knowledge that this man was also her husband, and that the second night of their marriage was fast approaching, had made Arabella all the more aware of him as each second of the meal progressed, resulting in her doing little more than pick at the food placed before her. That Darius's hooded blue eyes had settled on her often, and no doubt noted her lack of appetite, had only added to her increasing nervousness.

Darius also now rose from the table. 'I will join you shortly.' He nodded coolly, the expression in those deep blue eyes unreadable.

Arabella swallowed hard even as she eyed him shyly from beneath lowered lashes. 'I…' Her voice sounded reedy, and too high even to her own ears. Completely unlike her usual forthright tone. She drew in a controlling breath. 'I really am exceedingly tired, Darius.'

'I do not see how you can possibly be tired when you slept most of the afternoon and early evening away,' he pointed out as he moved away from the table.

Irritation creased her brow as she raised her chin to look at him fully. 'And how would you know how I spent my afternoon when you were engaged elsewhere?'

Darius did not need the warning glitter in Arabella's eyes to tell him that he had displeased her yet again. This time by the lack of the attention he had promised to her this afternoon. 'I sincerely hope that you are not going to be one of those wives who expects to be told of her husband's every move?'

Angry colour entered the previous pallor of her cheeks. 'Unless I am mistaken, Darius, I am not, as yet, a wife of any kind!'

Now, with Arabella's temper on the rise, was not the time to smile, Darius knew. But it was hard not to do so when she looked so put out, so disgruntled by the fact that he had not yet made her his wife in the fullest sense.

He gave a mocking inclination of his head. 'I assure you, Arabella, that I have every intention of remedying that omission as soon as we are alone together upstairs.'

Her throat moved convulsively at she realised it was Darius's intention to make love to her once they were in her bedchamber. More evidence, if Darius had needed it, of her youth and inexperience.

He did not need it when he knew Arabella had been under the fierce protection of Hawk St Claire these past eleven years. Added to which, while Arabella's ardour had not been in doubt when Darius had kissed her the previous week, her inexperience had been evident to him.

And in equal part arousing…

Arabella's eyes widened slightly as she watched Darius approach her with all the smooth and predatory elegance of a cat stalking its prey, and it took every effort of will on her part not to make herself look completely ridiculous by taking a step backwards. Especially when to have done so would have brought her up against the wall of the shabby parlour!

Darius stood in front of her now, the lean and muscled length of his body only inches away from her own. The heat of his body and the tantalising smell of his cologne caused Arabella's pulse to beat erratically, her heart to pound loudly, and her head to spin. She moistened stiff lips. 'I would rather you waited until we are upstairs before any—any intimacies take place.'

He raised blond brows. 'Surely a kiss from one's own wife cannot be classed as an *intimacy*?'

If it in any way resembled the way he had kissed her—and she had kissed him back—a week ago, then, yes, it most certainly could!

Arabella shook her head. 'I would rather wait, Darius.'

His eyes glittered down at her with amusement. 'And if I would rather not?'

Her eyes narrowed. 'I do not appreciate being played with in this odious way.'

'No?' He reached up to trail a finger down the creamy length of her throat, that finger lingering in the deep and sensitive well at its base. 'That is a pity—when I so much enjoy playing with you!'

Arabella found it difficult to breathe, and her skin

burned where he touched it. 'Stop it, Darius!' She was becoming agitated by his easy arousal of her senses.

'Your skin is like velvet, Arabella,' he murmured appreciatively, his gaze now following the line of his finger as it moved lower still, to skim lightly across the top of her rapidly rising and falling breasts as they swelled over the peach material of her gown.

Breasts that became fuller, heavier, the tips tightening, becoming as hard as berries against the silk of her shift as he stroked her.

'You have to stop, Darius!' Arabella's agitation increased in tandem with her arousal.

Darius looked at her from beneath lowered lids, recognising the rapid beating at her temple, the fever-brightness of her eyes, the flush to her cheeks and the full arousal of her breasts for exactly what they were. Signs of desire. The same desire that thrummed through his own body, hardening his thighs so that his arousal throbbed and ached beneath his breeches.

He stepped back abruptly. 'As you wish, Arabella.' His jaw was tight, the expression in his eyes hidden beneath narrowed lids. 'You may have ten minutes before I join you in your bedchamber.' Darius only hoped that he could control his desire to possess her for longer than that allotted time....

Chapter Seven

Arabella was standing in front of the window, looking out into the darkness below, when she heard the door of her bedchamber softly open and close behind her— evidence that Darius, after the briefest of knocks, had entered the candlelit room.

She had toyed with the idea of already being in bed when Darius joined her, but once beneath the bedcovers had decided she appeared far too much the willing sacrifice. Or at best far too eager!

Having decided earlier that a roadside inn was the last place in which she wished Darius to make love to her for the first time, Arabella now found she wanted him to touch and kiss her with such an aching intensity that she no longer cared where he made love to her, only that he should do so as soon as possible.

'Arabella.'

She turned slowly, her breath catching in her throat as she looked across the warmly lit bedchamber and took in Darius's appearance. He wore a dark and paler blue fitted robe of rich brocade which fastened at the waist with three buttons. The deep vee of the dark blue lapels revealed that his chest was bare beneath, hard and muscled, and covered in fine dark blond hair. As Darius moved to put a tray containing a decanter of brandy and two glasses down onto the table beside the door, before stepping further into the bedchamber, Arabella saw that the long and muscled length of his legs were also bare.

Leaving her with no doubt that Darius was completely naked beneath that brocade robe! 'Did you walk down the hallway dressed like that?'

He regarded her teasingly. 'I believe I am well past the age of climbing up the ivy outside the window in order to reach my wife's bedchamber!'

Arabella felt no amusement at Darius's self-deprecation, only a fierce shaft of jealousy that pierced through her as she imagined one of the other female guests at the inn seeing Darius walking down the hallway wearing so little clothing and looking so rakishly handsome!

He quirked a brow. 'Arabella…?'

'I— But anyone might have seen you!'

He gave a dismissive shrug. 'Anyone did not.'

'That really is not the point, Darius—'

'Then what *is* your point?'

Her point was that if another woman had seen him walking down the hallway wearing only this magnificent brocade robe, then that woman could not have helped but want him. Desire him.

As Arabella desired him.

Her jealousy faded as her earlier nervousness returned with a vengeance. She made an evasive movement with her hand. 'If it does not bother you, then I see no reason why it should bother me.'

Darius looked unconvinced. 'No?'

She glared at him frustratedly. 'Where would you like me?'

Darius raised mocking brows at her bluntness. 'Where would I *like* you?' he echoed with considerable amusement.

Her cheeks burned hotly. 'Well…yes. Lovemaking does not necessarily need to be confined to the bed, does it?'

Darius instantly had visions of Arabella seated on the window as he knelt between her parted thighs and pleasured her with his lips and tongue. Or, once pleasured, draping her over the back of the armchair in the corner of the room as he entered her from behind. Or perhaps against the wall, her fingers clinging to his shoulders and her legs clasped about his waist, as he thrust into her again and again…

But no, pleasurable as any or all of those things might be for him, Darius intended indulging in none of them tonight. Far better that Arabella be introduced to pleasure slowly. With tenderness and care. After all, he had a lifetime in which to introduce his young wife to all the pleasures of her body, as well as his own. He did not need to frighten her before they had even begun!

Although it was a little difficult to turn his thoughts from those vivid and erotic images when Arabella's hair was once again cascading loosely down the slender length of her spine, and she wore only a sheer white silk and lace robe over an equally diaphanous nightgown. The low and rounded neckline of both garments clearly revealed the firm swell of her unconfined breasts.

He swallowed hard. 'I had thought we might share a glass of brandy together first.' He moved to the tray he had brought in with him and poured some of the rich amber liquid from the decanter into the two glasses.

Arabella could have wept with relief at this short respite. Her nerves were so jittery now that her hand shook slightly as she took the glass of brandy from Darius's long and annoyingly steady fingers.

Not one of her sisters-in-law had thought to tell Arabella of the painful nervousness edged with anticipation she would feel when Darius came to her bed-chamber for the first time. No doubt that was because Jane, Grace and Juliet had known they were loved by the men to whom they were married. They had felt re-assured by that love, and secure in the knowledge that their husbands would never do anything that would either hurt or frighten them.

Arabella knew that Darius would be an accomplished lover—his rakish reputation amongst the women of the ton was testament to that—but would he be a gentle and a patient one?

Darius did not in the least care for the way in which Arabella was looking at him over the rim of her glass as she took a sip of the brandy. Almost as if she expected that at any moment he might throw her to the floor and pounce upon her!

Darius was fully cognisant of his scandalous reputation amongst the ton—after all, was it not a reputation he had deliberately nurtured these past eight years? But he was sure he had never heard himself described as a cruel or violent man. Why, then, did Arabella now look at him with such a look of apprehension in her beautiful eyes?

'You—'

'You—'

Both broke off as suddenly as they'd started speaking. 'You first,' Darius invited.

Arabella drew in an audibly ragged breath. 'I was about to say that you must be tired after your disturbed night and this day's travel.'

He hid a smile. 'Not too tired to make love to my wife, I assure you.'

'Oh.' Those golden-brown eyes dropped demurely to the carpeted floor.

This awkwardness between them was intolerable, Darius decided impatiently. Unaccountable, even, when Arabella certainly had enough to say to him out of the bedchamber!

He swallowed down a liberal amount of brandy before trying again. 'Do you want me to make love to you, Arabella?'

Those dark lashes rose sharply as she looked at him once again, heated colour in her cheeks. 'I— What sort of question is that to ask the woman you have been married to for only one day?' she exclaimed, falling back on defensive anger in her obvious embarrassment.

His mouth twisted ruefully. 'A valid one, I would have thought, given the circumstances.'

Arabella looked more irritated than upset now. 'And what circumstances are those?'

'I am sure there is no need for us to discuss the reason for our marriage any further tonight, Arabella. Or indeed any other night,' Darius said as he placed his empty brandy glass back onto the silver tray. 'Either you wish me to make love to you, or you do not. I am not an unfeeling monster. Neither do I intend to force the issue. If you do not want me here, then it is for you to say that you do not.'

'But we are married!'

He sighed. 'Even so, I have never yet made love to a woman who did not wish it, and I do not intend to start with my own wife. No matter what the provocation...' he added huskily.

Arabella swallowed hard. 'Provocation...?'

Darius's eyes darkened. 'Do you have any idea how desirable you look in the candle-light, dressed just so and with your hair loose about your shoulders in that wild and wanton way?'

Until Darius had said so, no—Arabella had *not* known that he found her appearance to be in the least desirable....

She moistened dry lips with the tip of her tongue. 'Do you have any idea how desirable *you* look in the candle-light, dressed just so and with your hair rakishly ruffled in that wildly attractive way?' she returned softly.

Darius's expression softened even as his eyes flashed with admiration. 'You are a woman like no other I have ever met, Arabella,' he said gruffly.

For now that was enough...

It had to be enough. Darius was her husband, and if Arabella did not wish him to turn to the arms of another woman as soon as the honeymoon period could decently be called over—and she most certainly did not—then she must become his wife in the fullest sense of the word.

She took hesitant steps towards him, her courage instantly fuelled by the flare of desire Darius allowed her to see burning in the cobalt-blue of his eyes. Her head went back proudly as she came to a halt only inches in front of him. 'Make love to me, Darius.' Her voice was low and inviting. 'Show me—teach me how to make love to you too.'

Darius had long admired Arabella. Her beauty was all too apparent. Her strength of character was much more subtle.

Looking down at her now, seeing the unwavering courage in the depths of those deep brown eyes as she met his own gaze unflinchingly, Darius knew her to be a woman who was more than a match for him. In every way, he hoped.

His thighs were hard just at the thought of making love to her. 'I need to make love to you first, Arabella.' His voice was a husky, unrecognisable groan. 'I have to!' he muttered achingly as he drew her fiercely into his arms.

It seemed to Arabella, as Darius's mouth claimed hers, that it had been far longer than a week that she had hungered for him to make love to her again. Hungered. Ached. Yearned…

She heatedly returned his kisses, her hands sliding up the muscled hardness of his chest before her fingers dug into his shoulders as he tasted her, gently biting the swell of her bottom lip before sucking it deep into the heat of his mouth.

Arabella was aroused, her breasts full and aching, the rosy tips hard and tingling for Darius's touch. So much so that she offered no resistance as one of his hands moved from about her waist and she felt his fingers untying the ribbon at the front of her robe to slide the silk material down the length of her arms before allowing it to drop to the floor at her feet.

Darius drew back slightly, his eyes intent as he looked down at her standing so proudly before him, so unflinchingly, in the sheer white nightgown that showed more than it hid; her breasts were firm and pouting, tipped by dark, rose-coloured nipples that stood hard and inviting against the soft material of that gown. Her waist was slender, her hips a gentle swell, with a triangle of dark blond curls between her thighs that begged for more intimate exploration.

Just looking at her, aware of his increasing desire, made Darius question the wisdom of his past year of celibacy. Would he be able to hold his own needs in check long enough to give Arabella the attention she deserved?

He absolutely would, Darius instructed himself firmly. He must maintain control. He had to. For Arabella's sake. He had to prepare her. Make her ready. To ensure that she was as aroused as he was, so that when he did enter her, breaching her virginity, he caused her as little pain as possible.

He slid one of the ribbon straps of her gown from her shoulder and allowed the material to slip slightly, baring one of her breasts. His gaze feasted hungrily on that exposed flesh. Arabella's skin was so creamy-white, her breast round and perfect, the rosy nipple unbearably tempting. 'May I?' he prompted huskily.

Arabella stared straight ahead, but Darius could feel the way she trembled slightly beneath the touch of his hands. 'Please,' she whispered.

Darius slowly lowered his head, his tongue flicking lightly, across that rosy nipple in a moist caress, and he was able to feel and see Arabella's response as her trembling increased and her back arched slightly so that her breast thrust against his mouth in a silent plea.

Darius went slowly at first, until his hunger far outweighed his need for caution and his hand moved to cup Arabella's other breast. He captured that second nipple between thumb and finger and began caressing it gently.

Arabella's earlier nervousness disappeared completely as she looked down at that golden head lying so close against her breast, Darius's lashes were resting on the hardness of his cheekbones, his face unusually flushed as he concentrated on pleasuring her.

Emboldened by his complete absorption, Arabella let her fingers became entangled in the thick golden hair at his nape, and she watched in fascination as his mouth moved against her nipple like a thirsty man in a desert as his other hand squeezed and caressed its twin.

There was heat between her thighs, a pulsing, throbbing heat, and Arabella could feel herself blossoming there in a way she never had before. Shockingly, she began wanting to take Darius's hand and place it against her, have him caress away the ache that was growing there.

As if aware of that desire, Darius moved back to swing her up in his arms and carry her over to the bed, before sitting her gently down upon the covers.

Her eyes widened as Darius removed one of the pillows before lying her head back again. They widened even further still as Darius raised her slightly, to place that pillow beneath her bottom and elevate her thighs to a shocking degree before gently folding back the soft material of her nightgown to bare the lower half of her body his heated gaze.

'What are you—?' Her exclamation choked in her throat as Darius gently pushed her legs apart before moving to kneel between them. She voiced her uncertainty. 'Darius…?'

His eyes glittered darkly as looked up at her. 'I will not hurt you, Arabella,' he assured huskily. 'Believe me when I say I will never hurt you.'

Arabella wanted to believe him. To trust in him. It was only that these intimacies were so much more than— 'Ah…!' Her breath left her in a strangled gasp as both Darius's hands moved to touch gently between her legs, just as Arabella had instinctively longed for him to do only seconds ago.

Long and sensitive fingers parted her silky curls, and instead of feeling exposed Arabella instead felt an ache that burned. 'Please…!' Her own fingers dug into the sheet beside her and her head turned restlessly on the pillow. Seeking. Wanting. So desperately needing something she didn't really understand. Arabella gave an incomprehensible groan, her hips rising in sweet surrender as Darius lowered his head and the soft rasp of his tongue touched that part of her that was so swollen and sensitive.

Instantly sending Arabella to both heaven and hell!

Heaven because she had never known such pleasure as this existed. Hell because she thought she might die if Darius should stop!

Darius had not meant to move so fast. He had meant to go slowly. To gently introduce Arabella to this intimacy. But, having once lain her upon the bed, he had not been able to resist baring the softness of her thighs and allowing himself to gaze hungrily upon the silkiness of her naked curls. She was so pretty there. So beautiful. Plump and delicious, and just begging to be touched. To be kissed.

The first rasp of his tongue against her caused her to groan and move restlessly, rhythmically, into that caress. Darius continued until he was plundering her with his tongue—until Arabella hung poised on the edge of release.

Darius moved his mouth and slid one finger inside her moist heat. Slowly. Oh-so-slowly. Stilling once that finger was fully inside her so that she might accustom herself to how it felt to have her sensitive flesh invaded.

'Please, Darius…!' Arabella had lost all sense of where or who she was. Darius was her only reality as she felt something pooling deep inside her, building, growing and growing, until it seemed she might explode into a million pieces. 'Darius, please, I want—I need—' She groaned in protest as Darius slid that finger out of her, only to moan low in her throat as that first finger was joined by a second. He slowly began to thrust them inside her in a rhythm Arabella's hips moved up to meet even as Darius's tongue returned to the swollen nubbin above.

She bit her bottom lip painfully as she felt a need to cry out, to scream and shout at the top of her lungs as the pleasure built to an impossible degree, taking her higher, ever higher, to a place she had never been before.

She sat up, her hair wild, eyes even more so, and the eroticism of having Darius look up at her from between her naked thighs was enough to send her over the edge of that pleasure. She cried out in ecstasy.

Darius ensured that he drew every last vestige of what he was certain was Arabella's first ever orgasm, long after she had collapsed against the pillow to roll her head from side to side in mindless and uncontrollable pleasure.

Finally his caresses gentled, became soothing, as Arabella sobbed ever so softly.

Arabella lay back when Darius finally ceased and moved up beside her, looking for all the world like a wanton, with her hair tangled about her shoulders, one breast bared, and her nightgown thrown up about her waist.

He frowned as he saw that several tears had escaped from beneath her lashes and now lay wet upon her cheeks. 'Arabella?' Darius smoothed those tears away with the tips of his fingers. 'Did I hurt you after all?'

She raised long lashes, her eyes a deep unfocused brown. 'If you did then I believe I wish for you to hurt me in that way every night for the rest of my life!'

Darius laughed at her complete lack of guile. 'We have nowhere near finished this night yet.'

'No?' Her eyes widened with unconcealed interest.

'No,' he promised huskily. 'There is still so much more for us to share, Arabella. To explore together.'

She looked almost shy. 'I am to be allowed to touch you in the way you just touched me?'

'Oh, yes,' he assured her with feeling.

Darius had put his own fierce arousal to the back of his mind as he'd concentrated on giving Arabella pleasure. But it came back with a vengeance now. So much so that Darius doubted he would be able to hold long enough for Arabella to place even one delicate little finger upon his throbbing flesh!

'I—am I still a virgin?' Uncertainty creased Arabella's brow.

Darius sobered as Arabella once again revealed that her bravado of their first evening together had been a fabrication. 'I am afraid so.'

'Oh. Then—touching me—in that intimate way—?' Her cheeks were flushed. 'It did not—it did not—?'

'No,' he confirmed regretfully. 'But I promise when the time comes I will endeavour not to hurt you unduly. Do you believe me—?' Darius broke off, frowning darkly as the sound of shouting could be heard outside in the hallway. 'What the hell…?' He sprang lithely from the bed to scowl in the direction of the closed door.

'Fire! Fire!' The shouts became more audible as someone was heard running past in the hallway outside. 'The inn is on fire!'

Arabella sat up abruptly in the bed, her face pale, her eyes wide with fear as she hastily tidied her nightgown before standing up.

The inn was on fire?

Chapter Eight

'Do you suppose that everyone managed to get out?' Arabella asked worriedly some time later, as Darius joined her where stood huddled in the cloak she had managed to gather up before leaving the inn.

The two of them stood outside the front of the inn, staring up at the blaze that had once been the thatched roof above their bedchambers. The flames were so intense that they lit up the night sky and reflected on the faces of the dozen or so other people who stood gathered together in various states of undress— Arabella's maid and Darius's valet amongst them, thank goodness.

'The innkeeper seems to think so,' Darius replied. 'There were only ten guests, including our own party, and they are all accounted for. Fortunately we were able to prevent the stables from catching alight too,' he added grimly.

Arabella turned to look at Darius, still dressed only in his brocade robe. As were most of the other guests.

There simply hadn't been time for anyone to dress, the fire having already spread to the hallway outside Arabella's bedchamber by the time Darius threw open the door to see what all the fuss was about. Now, in the light from the fire, it was possible to see that Darius's face was blackened in several places from where he had assisted the other men in getting the horses out of the stables, before helping to keep the blaze from spreading to the outer buildings.

'That is good news.' A shiver moved down her spine at the memory of the neighing and snorting of the trapped horses before Darius and several of the other men had managed to go into the stables and lead them out to safety.

The inn itself was beyond saving, several parts of the roof having already fallen in and so adding to the force of the fire as it blazed unrelentingly. The numbed innkeeper had accepted it was a losing battle too, and he now stood speechlessly beside his wife as the two of them looked up at the flames destroying not only their home but also their livelihood.

'Those poor people have lost everything,' Arabella murmured emotionally as she saw that loss upon the elderly couple's faces. 'And all because someone no doubt allowed a candle to fall onto the floor, or left it burning too close to the curtains.' She gave a sorrowful shake of her head.

Yes, Darius reflected grimly, no doubt someone *had* allowed the fire to start. Deliberately…

First the carriage accident the night before, and now a fire at the inn where they stayed tonight. Darius was far too aware of the unlikelihood of two such coincidences to accept that they were completely separate or random events.

If the two were connected, then it would appear that someone had known of his every move these past two days. And that someone had either followed Darius and Arabella to the inn earlier today, or they had already known where the two of them would be staying the night and had acted accordingly.

Neither explanation was acceptable. The former implied that Darius, too preoccupied by his young wife's beauty, had been lax in his usual caution of repeatedly checking to see whether or not they were being followed. The latter implied that one of his own servants had been loose-tongued concerning the movements of their employer. Or possibly been persuaded to be so by monetary reward. The fact that Darius had placed two of his grooms on guard outside the inn after their arrival yesterday only made the starting of this fire all the more suspect.

His past eight years as an agent for the crown had evoked a cynicism inside Darius that had taught him to trust no one. Not even those closest to him. Especially those closest to him!

Darius's gaze was icy-hard as he looked down at Arabella. 'Admittedly it will take time, but rest assured I will ensure that the landlord has enough funds to rebuild. A gift in honour of our marriage,' he added, as he saw the way Arabella had turned to him in surprise at his apparent largesse.

It was only fair to make reparation to the innkeeper, as Darius suspected that the inn had been burnt down with the intention of trapping him inside. Which might so easily have become the case, seeing as he had allowed himself to become so engrossed in Arabella's magnificent charms...

'That is—very generous of you, Darius.' Arabella laid a hand warmly upon his arm.

He gave a hard smile. 'No doubt I have inhaled too much smoke, and will come to my senses come the dawn.'

She gave him a chiding look. 'I do not believe you.'

'But talking of the dawn... Bearing in mind that we now have no inn in which to spend the night, and no clothes in which to dress ourselves come morning, I have ordered that both carriages be made ready so that we might all continue with our journey to Winton Hall tonight,' Darius informed her.

Arabella's eyes widened. 'Tonight? But—'

'You would rather sleep in the straw in the stables, perhaps?' Darius asked. 'With the other survivors of the fire? Along with any number of vermin—and I do not allude to the human kind!—nibbling at your feet in the darkness?'

Arabella repressed a shiver at the thought of the rats and mice, let alone the fleas and lice, that probably inhabited the stables. 'No, of course I would not prefer to do that. It is only—what will the servants at Winton Hall think when, come morning, the Duke and Duchess of Carlyne arrive clothed only in their night robes?'

Darius gave a humourless laugh. 'Personally, I do not give a damn what they think!'

No, Arabella was sure Darius would not care a jot for the censure or otherwise of his servants. He had made it more than obvious during their short acquaintance that he cared little for anyone's opinion concerning his behaviour. Including her own! But Arabella, having had such wonderful imaginings of arriving at Winton Hall as its new duchess, could not help but feel dismayed at the thought of this unorthodox introduction as the new mistress to the servants.

'Or perhaps you had imagined that we might *enjoy* spending a night in the stables, where we might finish what we started earlier?' Darius's eyes glittered down at her mockingly.

Arabella recoiled at his harsh words, the colour first burning in her cheeks and then as rapidly fading, to leave her face pale and her eyes a dark and haunted brown. 'Darius…?'

'Yes?' he snapped.

Arabella stared up at him. Was this really the man who had made love to her so gently such a short time ago? Who had carefully and tenderly brought her to such a state of ecstasy that she had lost all control of her senses?

She gave an inward shudder at the mere thought of allowing *this* cold and cruelly taunting man such liberties with her. 'I assure you I thought no such thing.'

'No?'

'No!' Whatever kindness Arabella might have allotted to Darius earlier, in his concern for the innkeeper, was completely erased by his reminder of how easily she had succumbed to his kisses and caresses.

'Have you been thinking that perhaps *I* am responsible for starting this fire?' he asked roughly.

'I will not even deign to answer such nonsense!' Once again the idea was a ridiculous one; Darius could as easily have perished in the fire as anyone else. Including Arabella. Her chin rose proudly. 'I am ready to leave whenever you are.'

His mouth thinned. 'That would be now.'

'Very well.' Arabella gave a haughty inclination of her head before turning on slippered feet and walking in the direction of the stables situated at the back of the inn.

Darius didn't move for several seconds, but instead stared grimly up at the fire as it continued to rage unchecked.

He realised he'd been overly harsh with Arabella just now, but after this second near miss in as many days Darius had been in no mood to coax and cajole her into continuing with their journey to Winton Hall tonight. They had to leave. They had to reach the relative safety of Winton Hall, where Darius would hopefully be able to put more stringent security in place.

As added security he also intended sending one of the grooms back to London with news of this second accident. Better by far that Bancroft was alerted now to the continuing danger rather than informed later of Darius's and Arabella's demise.

For as surely as Darius knew this inn would be completely razed to the ground by morning, he had no doubt that it had been intended that he and Arabella should burn along with it.

'I shall be busy about estate business for the rest of the day,' Darius informed Arabella as he prepared to take his leave after personally escorting her to the bedchamber at Winton Hall that adjoined his own. 'I suggest you use the time to rest and recover after your ordeal.'

To Arabella's relief there had been few witnesses to

the arrival of the dishevelled Duke and Duchess of Carlyne when they'd reached their home some five hours later; most of the household servants had been still abed, and the few maids who were already up and about had been too busy cleaning and lighting the fires in preparation for the arrival of their master and mistress to be aware that Arabella and Darius had already arrived and gone straight upstairs to their bedchambers on the third floor of the house.

It had been an ignominious arrival to say the least. In all her imaginings of this day Arabella had envisaged herself and Darius arriving with all due ceremony and the servants lined up outside the house so that they might wait in turn to be introduced to their new mistress.

Instead of which the carriage had barely come to a halt and the door been opened before Darius had alighted onto the gravel driveway, leaving one of the grooms to help Arabella down. He had marched up the steps at the front of the red-stone mansion and thrown open the huge front door before striding into the marbled hallway. Somehow managing to display the same arrogance as if he were dressed in elegant finery instead of clothed only in his brocade nightrobe!

Having suffered through a wakeful journey, with the silence between herself and Darius of an awkward rather than a restful kind, Arabella had felt chilled both inside and out. She had pulled her cloak more firmly about her and chosen to follow her husband at a more leisurely pace, taking the time to look at the magnificent proportions of what was to be her new home.

The main house of red stone stood four storeys high, with wings of similar proportions curving the driveway on either side, and so giving the appearance of welcoming elegance.

There was no evidence of that same welcome on the present Duke of Carlyne's handsome face now, though, as he looked down his arrogant nose at his wife!

Nor did Arabella know to which ordeal Darius referred. That of having their earlier lovemaking interrupted so decisively? Or that of the fire itself, including his later questioning as to whether she had believed him responsible for it? Or perhaps he meant the cold and awkward carriage ride that had followed?

Whichever it was, Arabella was not disposed at that moment to spend any more time in her husband's company, and her eyes snapped angrily as she glared at him. 'If you will observe, Darius, you will note that your own appearance is no less…disreputable than my own.'

Darius was well aware of Arabella's displeasure with him—both with his behaviour earlier before they'd left the inn and with his preoccupation during the long and tedious hours of the carriage ride that had completed their journey to Winton Hall.

He wished it could be different. Wished that he might confide in Arabella about his own worries concerning both the carriage accident two days ago and the fire the previous night. But the oath he had made eight years ago dictated that he could not do so, which left him to continue his immediate enquiries without alerting Arabella to what he was doing.

Darius's first task of the morning, once he had bathed and dressed, would be to question all the servants who had accompanied them yesterday. From the grooms to Arabella's maid and his own valet. The thought that one of the servants he trusted, or possibly Arabella's own maid, might have been indiscreet, whether accidentally or on purpose, was highly distasteful to Darius. But the possibility had to be followed up before it could be discarded as an option.

'Perhaps so, Arabella,' he allowed. 'But I am no doubt more accustomed than you are to a night in which I have had little or no sleep.'

Colour blazed in Arabella's cheeks and her hands tightened into fists at her sides. 'You would *boast* to me of such things?'

Darius raised an eyebrow at the conclusion she'd jumped to, and couldn't help but tease her for thinking that he was mocking her by referring to his stamina as a lover! 'I wonder, can it be called boasting when one is only stating the truth?'

Arabella was so tired, so disheartened by the way things now stood between them, that she feared at any moment she might burst into loud and humiliating tears. 'I think it best if you leave me now, Darius,' she said fiercely. 'Before one or both of us says something we might later regret.'

He sighed heavily. 'I assure you, Arabella, I rarely have reason to feel regret for anything I do or say.'

Unlike Arabella, who now deeply regretted the way she had responded to Darius's kisses and caresses the night before! He was a self-confessed rake. A womaniser. A man who cared for no one and had no desire that anyone should care for him.

A fact that Arabella would do well to remember…

The worst thing she could possibly do was to fall in love with her own husband!

'Then you should consider yourself fortunate amongst men, Darius.' Her tone was sweetly insincere.

'Oh, I do, Arabella,' he drawled. 'I most certainly do!'

Arabella did not at all care for the speculative gleam she could see in those sky-blue eyes. 'I will wish you good day.' She placed a hand delicately against her lips as she gave a deliberate and dismissive yawn.

'Not so hasty, my dear Arabella.'

Instead of leaving, as she had hoped, Darius took a step towards her. Making her completely aware of the fact that they were both still wearing their nightrobes. Arabella had already discarded her cloak on entering the magnificently furnished green and cream bedchamber reserved for the Duchess of Carlyne. A mistake, Arabella now realized, as she glanced down at herself and saw that the white nightgown and robe did very little to cover the curves of her body. The opposite, in fact, as the sheer material draped revealingly over the full curve of her breasts and clearly outlined the pouting thrust of their rosy tips!

Arabella felt her cheeks burn as she looked up and saw that Darius's gaze had followed her own. Her body was betraying her awareness of his hungry gaze in a way she had no control over, and she felt the pouting tips of her breasts harden to the fullness of ripe berries that begged to be eaten.

She drew in a sharp breath even as she wrapped her arms protectively about herself. 'I really would like to rest now, Darius.'

Seconds slipped slowly by as he minutely regarded her flustered and overheated face. 'Your body says otherwise, my dear,' he finally said.

Her eyes flashed darkly. 'My body responds to *my* commands, not the other way around!'

'Really?' Darius murmured, even as he took another step closer to her. A move that caused those betraying breasts to pucker in ever-increasing expectation. 'I believe you will find, my dear Arabella, that it is *I* who now has command over your body and not you.'

Her chin rose proudly even as she met his gaze unflinchingly. 'If you believe that then you are a fool, Darius,' she bit out contemptuously. 'Or perhaps just overly conceited.'

Despite the fire the night before—the sooty black streaks still upon Arabella's cheeks were a clear reminder of that event, if Darius should need one—and the long and uncomfortable hours of the night they had spent riding in the carriage, Arabella still managed to look every inch the proud and haughty duchess she now was.

So much so that Darius did not have the heart to taunt her any longer. 'Perhaps,' he allowed curtly, and he stepped away from her to stride over to the door. 'As I said, I will be busy for the rest of the day. No doubt we will meet again at dinner.'

'No doubt.' Arabella nodded abruptly, determined to hold on to her tears long enough for Darius to open the door and leave her bedchamber.

He paused in the open doorway. 'You will inform either myself or one of the servants of your movements if you should decide to go outside to explore when you awaken from your nap.'

She frowned. 'I am to inform one of the servants if I wish to go outside?'

'Or myself.'

'I will do no such thing!'

'Oh, I think that you will.' The steely threat beneath the softness of his tone was unmistakable.

Arabella held on to her temper with effort. 'I have been surrounded by arrogant men all my life, but neither my father or Hawk ever felt the need to tell me what I should and should not do. As such, I am accustomed to come and go as I please in my own home!'

Darius's mouth tightened. 'Then you will have to become unaccustomed, will you not? I am your husband, Arabella, not one of your over-indulgent older brothers,' he said harshly as she would have voiced a second protest. 'You gave me every right to tell you what to do two days ago, when you vowed before God to obey me!'

'Not when it is your intention to make me a prisoner in my own home!' She met his gaze defiantly.

'Obedience is obedience,' Darius snapped, but his expression softened slightly as he suddenly saw the pallor of her cheeks. He said more gently, 'Arabella, I am doing this for your own good—'

'Is that not the claim of all tyrants and despots?'

His mouth tightened at the accusation. 'You do not know the area, Arabella, and have no idea of the pitfalls or—or dangers of the surrounding countryside. And until you do—'

'Considering that Mulberry Hall, my brother's home, is only in the county adjoining this one—'

'You will not argue with me any further on this subject, Arabella!' A nerve pulsed rapidly in Darius's tightly clenched jaw.

She swallowed hard. 'So I am to be subject to your

whim as to whether or not I may so much as walk outside in the grounds?'

It was far from an ideal situation, Darius knew. So far removed from what he had hoped for his marriage to Arabella...

But the carriage accident, and the fire last night, along with William Bancroft's warnings the night of their wedding, had ensured that Darius's suspicions were well and truly roused. And until he apprehended the person responsible some of Arabella's personal freedoms must necessarily be curtailed. Much as she might dislike Darius for enforcing such rules on her.

He nodded. 'That is exactly what I am saying.'

Her eyes glittered deeply gold in her anger. 'I believe you will find that I am your wife, Darius, and not a dog upon your hearth or a horse in your stables! As such—'

'As such you will do precisely what you are told!' Darius cut in forcefully, determined not to be thwarted in this. He dared not. Not when it had been made obvious to him that her own life was in as much danger as his own. 'Do not force me into locking you in your room in order to ensure your obedience, Arabella,' he warned darkly.

Those glittering golden eyes widened in alarm. 'You would really do that?' she gasped.

'If you insist on defying me, then, yes, you will leave me with no choice but to lock you in your bedchamber!'

Arabella stared at him incredulously and she realised by the rigidity of Darius's expression that he meant what he said.

Had she known anything at *all* before today of the man to whom she was now married? Arabella wondered dazedly. Or had she merely allowed herself to be daz-zled by his golden good-looks? Challenged by his arrogant disregard for the women of the ton, who had thrown themselves at him before his brief first marriage and afterwards? Could it be that Arabella had behaved totally recklessly in her determination to ignore all the gossip that had circulated amongst the ton concerning Darius this past year, which should have warned her away from him?

What if that gossip were all true, after all?

As Arabella looked at the cold and remorselessly unbending man who had just threatened to lock her in her bedchamber if she did not obey him, she could well believe that it might be…

Chapter Nine

'Am I going to be subjected to this sulky silence all evening, Arabella, or do you think that at some stage you might indulge me by engaging in a little polite conversation?' Darius eyed his wife down the length of the highly polished table in the candlelit dining-room, with a warm fire crackling in its hearth.

They had eaten their soup, followed by the fish course, and were now enjoying perfectly cooked roast beef—all without Arabella doing any more than answering yes or no to Darius's attempts at conversation.

'I never sulk, Darius.' Brown eyes glittered as Arabella stared back at him.

Darius raised sceptical brows. 'No?'

Arabella took a sip of her wine before answering him. 'From what I have observed one has to feel strongly about something in order to sulk over it.'

'Ah. I see.' Darius sat back to rest his elbows on the arms of his chair to look at her above steepled fingers. 'In that case I am gratified to hear you do not feel strongly enough about anything I have said or done to-day to feel the necessity for such an emotion.'

'You are welcome.' She bestowed on him a sweetly insincere smile.

What a little liar she was, Darius mused ruefully. If there had been a knife handy earlier today, when he had instructed Arabella that she was to stay within the confines of the house unless she informed a servant, then Darius had no doubt he would have found it buried up to the hilt between his shoulderblades as soon as he had dared turn his back on her!

His bride looked absolutely enchanting this evening, in a long-sleeved gown of golden-brown silk which was an exact match with her eyes as they changed colour with her mood, with a ribbon of the same colour threaded through her honey-gold curls. Her throat was bare, as were her earlobes. Arabella's only jewellery was the plain gold wedding ring Darius had placed upon her finger but two days ago.

Deliberately so? Probably, Darius acknowledged ruefully, even as he determined to pierce the frosty politeness with which his wife had been treating him all evening. 'Then you acknowledge I had a perfect right to confine you to your bedchamber earlier today?'

A nerve pulsed in the tightness of her suddenly clenched jaw. 'As I recall, you confined me to the *house*, not my bedchamber.'

Darius would have much preferred to confine Arabella to her bedchamber for the day, and to have joined her there so that they might continue their love-making of last night.

Instead of which he had spent an unsatisfactory day

questioning his grooms, Arabella's maid and his own valet, in an effort to see if any of them had any information concerning the carriage accident or the fire. As was to be expected, all had denied knowing anything.

Darius could only hope that his time had not been completely wasted, and that whoever was responsible would at least now be alerted to the fact that his suspicions were aroused concerning both incidents.

His mouth tightened. 'I trust you are well rested now?'

Arabella looked down the table at Darius from beneath lowered lashes and searched his face as to any hidden meaning to his question—for instance, if she were 'well rested' enough not to be in any immediate need of further sleep!

Arabella had been far too angry to sleep after Darius had left her bedchamber this morning. Instead she had paced the room restlessly for some time as she plotted and planned suitable retribution for his highhandedness. It had been several hours later before she'd come to the conclusion that most if not all of those plans were impossible.

Boiling him in oil was not practical. Throwing all his clothes in the bathtub would no doubt only result in his choosing to walk about naked. As for causing him physical damage... Darius was obviously so much stronger than she that that idea was rendered as impractical as boiling him in oil.

Another plan had occurred to Arabella as her maid had helped her to dress in preparation for joining Darius downstairs for dinner. That of leaving Winton Hall altogether by commandeering one of Darius's own carriages and travelling to her family's home in neighbouring Gloucestershire. Once there, she could claim sanctuary with Hawk and his wife.

Of course it would cause the most terrible scandal if Arabella were to leave Darius so soon after their wedding, and she knew that Hawk would try to talk her out of it once he learnt of the circumstances under which Arabella had left Winton Hall. What had Darius done, after all, but suggest Arabella stay in her bedchamber and rest following the burning down of the inn in which they had been staying the night before?

Hawk would have behaved in exactly the same autocratic manner, and he would not see that Darius had bullied or intimidated her. But Arabella understood it only too well. And she would not stand for it. She would not stand for it at all!

The decision made, Arabella knew she must somehow try to avoid her husband's lovemaking for one more night at least; she wasn't sure she would be able to leave Darius at all once he had fully made love to her…

She placed her knife and fork carefully down upon the virtually untouched food on her plate and now avoided meeting Darius's piercing gaze. 'My nerves are still rather—unsettled by the upset of the last few days.'

'Really?'

Arabella looked up sharply as she heard the sarcasm in Darius's tone. 'Yes, really,' she echoed firmly.

'Perhaps a soothing bath before bedtime?'

'Perhaps.' She nodded coolly. 'Although I believe a night of undisturbed sleep would be more beneficial.'

'You do?' Darius drawled, not fooled for a moment by the demureness of his wife's demeanour.

Arabella was the least demure woman Darius had ever met in his life!

Rather, she was stubborn. Headstrong. Far too outspoken for a man's comfort. Arabella was all of those things and more. But demure? No, he did not think so!

Which meant there had to be a reason for her appearing to be so now. 'I believe we might try the bath first,' he suggested. 'Perhaps followed by massaging a little perfumed oil into—'

'Darius!' Arabella gasped, her creamy cheeks blushing hotly.

'Into your temples,' he completed wickedly. 'My late stepmother certainly believed in its restorative powers whenever she had the megrims. Which was often.' Darius's top lip curled back with distaste at the memory of Clara Wynter, his father's third wife, as she languished upon her bed or a chaise in a pose of deep suffering. Usually as accompaniment to something Darius had supposedly said or done!

Arabella's eyes flashed darkly. 'I do not have the megrims! I am merely fatigued— You have a stepmother?' She frowned down the table at him, suddenly diverted by what he had said.

'No longer, thank God.' he replied.

'She died?' Arabella pressed softly.

'Oh, yes,' Darius murmured without regret. Why should he feel regret at the death of a woman who had made his life hell from the age of five until he was ten? 'My father married three times in his lifetime,' he expanded, as Arabella continued to look at him enquiringly. 'He adored his first wife, my brother George's mother, and was happily married to her for almost twenty years, until her death. I have no idea how he felt about my own mother as she died only hours after giving birth to me. After which I was raised by a series of wet-nurses and nursemaids. George was more than twenty years older than I, already away from home when I was born, and I rarely saw my father for the first four years of my life. So perhaps it is safe to assume that he adored his second wife too, and as such blamed me for killing her.'

Arabella frowned. 'Babies do not kill. God decides these things.'

'Or conversely the Devil.'

Arabella felt a stab of guilt as she recalled it was not so long ago she had thought Darius was the Devil disguised as an angel! 'And did your father adore his third wife too?' she prompted huskily.

'She was certainly beautiful enough,' Darius replied harshly. 'I was five years old the first time I saw her. I thought she was an angel come to earth.' His face hardened into sharp, forbidding angles. 'I was wrong!'

Arabella drew in a sharp breath. This was the most that Darius had ever talked to her about his early life, his childhood, and the picture he painted was not a pleasant one. In comparison with her own indulged childhood it sounded very unpleasant indeed.

Perhaps it explained some of Darius's excesses in his adult life—that devil-may-care attitude that had labelled him both a rake and a wastrel…?

No! Arabella must keep firmly in mind that Darius had treated her most shabbily earlier today, and not allow her softer emotions to be touched by the things he had just told her.

As such, she repressed the impulse she had to rise

and go down to the end of the table where he sat. To put her arms about him. To assure him that he would never be alone again.

An impulse totally at odds with Arabella's decision to leave Winton Hall—and Darius—in the morning!

'Your stepmother ignored you, too?' she said instead.

Darius's eyes glittered deeply blue. 'It would have been far better for me if she had,' he ground out. 'But, no, my dear stepmama enjoyed nothing more than comparing her six-year-old stepson unfavourably with the son she produced within a year of her marriage to my father.' His mouth twisted distastefully. 'I was sly. Deceitful. Utterly wild. Not at all a good example for her own darling Francis to emulate.'

'I had totally forgotten that you have a younger brother!' Arabella exclaimed.

'Most people do—to his extreme annoyance,' Darius commented.

Arabella vaguely remembered Francis Wynter as being a pale, nondescript version of Darius himself. 'But he was not present at our wedding, was he?'

A nerve pulsed in Darius's tightly clenched jaw. 'Francis is currently travelling on the Continent. For his health,' he bit out.

Arabella eyed him knowingly. 'Is that not what a man usually does in order to avoid a scandal of some kind?'

'Is it?' Darius's expression was grim as he lifted his glass and took a sip of the red wine.

'You know that it is.' She smiled reprovingly. 'What did Francis do? Run up gambling debts he could not pay? Engage in a scandalous affair with a married lady? Or perhaps he killed a man in a duel?'

'Nothing so honourable!' The harsh denial was spoken before Darius could stop himself, and it visibly startled Arabella. To the extent that Darius knew he had said too much. Far too much, taking into consideration Arabella's sharp intelligence.

Although her innocence concerning Francis's movements had at least served to confirm Lucian's claim that he had not discussed the events of the previous April with any of his family—least of all his young sister...

Darius forced himself to relax and smile pleasantly. 'There is reputed to be a black sheep in every family, Arabella. Or perhaps you had assumed that to be me in the Wynter family?' He raised mocking brows, knowing by the becoming flush that appeared in her cheeks that that was exactly what she *had* thought!

Arabella was totally unnerved by the guilty flush that darkened her cheeks. She wondered what misdeed Lord Francis Wynter could possibly have committed that was worse than his older brother's notorious and well-noted exploits in gambling clubs and ladies' bedchambers...

She raised her chin challengingly. 'You must admit it is a reputation you have long nurtured.'

'Must I?'

Arabella scowled at his obvious amusement. 'It is not something of which you should be in the least proud!'

Darius laughed softly. 'My dear Arabella, you look so very beautiful when you are indignant.'

'Do not attempt to cajole and flatter me, Darius,' she scorned. 'After your behaviour earlier today, I assure you I am beyond being charmed by you.'

'I thought we had agreed that you did not feel strongly enough about my behaviour earlier to be in the least concerned by it?' he teased.

'I am *not* concerned by it!' Arabella snapped frustratedly. 'But neither do I intend to forget it.' The softening she had felt towards Darius a few short minutes ago had completely disappeared.

'What—never?'

'No!'

'I cannot…*persuade* you into thinking more kindly towards me?' he asked.

Arabella eyed Darius uncertainly, not in the least reassured by the way his gaze had darkened and warmed to the colour of cobalt as he looked at her so intently. Or the way those chiselled lips had softened so sensually. Nor by the languid ease of his muscled shoulders and chest beneath his black superfine and white linen. No, Arabella was not reassured at all!

She became even less so as Darius rose slowly to his booted feet to walk slowly, confidently, down the length of the table until he reached her side. 'Perhaps it is time you retired to bed, after all,' he murmured throatily, as one of his hands moved up to curve warmly against the smoothness of her cheek.

It was all she could do to stop herself from melting against that caressing hand. From purring like a kitten at the touch of his fingers against her skin and moaning softly at the shaft of pleasure that coursed through her traitorous body.

She was still so angry with Darius for his high-handed treatment of her earlier today, and had every intention of leaving Winton Hall—and Darius—come the morning.

Yet her body now responded to his lightest touch. Her breasts swelled, and she felt a fierce rush of heat between her thighs that made her shift uncomfortably against the brocade cushion of the dining chair.

She moistened dry lips, and in doing so felt how their swollen sensitivity betrayed her arousal. 'I believe I am old enough to decide for myself when I wish to go to bed, Darius.' Her voice was sharp with self-disgust.

How could she possibly allow herself to be physically aroused by a man who made her as angry as Darius did most of the time?

Darius didn't answer her immediately. Instead he moved both his hands so that they rested on the arms of Arabella's chair and turned that chair towards him and brought his face down to within inches of her own. 'I was suggesting that we *both* go to bed, Arabella,' he whispered, his wine-scented breath warm against her cheek. 'But I will be just as comfortable making love to you here, if you that is what you wish.'

She blinked nervously. 'The footman will be returning at any moment to remove the dishes…'

Darius smiled. 'I have instructed the footman—in fact, all of the servants, inside the house and out of it—not to interrupt us until they are called for whenever the two of us are alone together.'

Having spent the day in her bedchamber, attended only by her own maid, Arabella had not had the chance to meet any of the other servants at Winton Hall. An oversight Darius had corrected when Arabella had joined him downstairs before dinner. All of the servants, from the cook to the butler, had been lined up in the hallway to be introduced to his duchess.

To say that Arabella had been surprised at the appearance of some of those servants would be an understatement!

All the cooks Arabella had known at the St Claire residences, both from childhood and now, were jolly and plump—usually from tasting too many of their own creations. The cook at Winton Hall was a thin and wiry woman, with a pinched face dominated by a sharply enquiring gaze that seemed to see altogether too much as she stared boldly back at the new Duchess of Carlyne.

The maids were all much older than Arabella would have expected too, and the footmen had the rough and ready appearance of labourers rather than refined household servants.

Even so, the butler, Westlake, had to be the most surprising of all. A tall and burly man, his muscled torso and arms straining the seams of his tailored frock coat, his face pocked and scarred, and his nose looking as if it might have been broken on more than one occasion, he gave every appearance of being a prize fighter rather than the butler of a duke!

Arabella knew that Hawk, as the aristocratic Duke of Stourbridge, would not have countenanced allowing *any* of Darius's servants to step foot inside a single ducal household—let alone be employed in one!

'After all, this *is* our honeymoon, Arabella,' Darius added at her frowning silence.

Arabella's bosom visibly swelled as she drew in an indignant breath. 'How *could* you have done such a thing, Darius?' Her cheeks were red. 'Whatever will the servants think of us? Of me?'

'They will think that your husband finds you so desirable that he cannot keep his hands from you,' Darius assured her huskily.

Arabella shot him a confused glance. 'But that is not true!'

Darius had been amused by Arabella's obvious bewilderment earlier, when he had introduced her to the household staff. She had smiled graciously to each in turn, her smile becoming even more fixed when he at last presented Westlake to her. The man looked exactly what he was: an ex-pugilist—a fact that any of her brothers would no doubt have been able to tell her if they had been present. Big Tom Westlake had been a champion fighter of some repute until his retirement from the ring two years ago.

To Arabella's credit she had not shown by word or deed that she found any of his household staff out of the ordinary. So much so that Darius had found his admiration for her increasing considerably. And his desire to make love to her even more so!

'I assure you it is true, Arabella,' he murmured as he easily held her gaze captive. 'We have already been married for two days and two nights, and I have yet to make love to my wife.' A fact that Darius was all too aware of.

'Yes. But—'

'Which is something I now intend to rectify,' he continued.

Every shred of anger left Arabella, every trace of even a thought of repulsing her husband's advances deserting her as Darius's lips caressed the side of her throat. Arabella gave a low moan of surrender as she felt the hot sweep of Darius's tongue against the lobe of her ear.

Everything else ceased to matter when Arabella felt the nip of teeth against that lobe, and pleasure grew and spread throughout all of her body.

Darius drew back slightly as Arabella whimpered slightly. 'Come with me?' He straightened to hold his hand out to her invitingly.

'Where are we going?' Even as she hesitated Arabella placed her hand in his much larger one.

'Nowhere outside of this room, I assure you.' Darius grimaced as he pulled Arabella effortlessly to her feet so that she now stood in front of him. 'I have no intention of allowing anything to interrupt us this time, Arabella.' His hands moved up to cradle either side of her flushed and beautiful face. 'Not even if the house should burn down around our ears.'

The fact that the latter was more than a possibility at the moment—despite the protection of men like Big Tom Westlake—only made Darius all the more determined in his intentions. He had wanted to possess this woman for far longer than he cared to admit. Least of all to Arabella herself. Darius intended allowing nothing, and no one, to stop him from finally making her his own.

'There is no need to be apprehensive.' He reached up to gently smooth the frown from between her expressive eyes. 'You liked what we did together last night, did you not?'

Arabella's cheeks burned as she remembered how the previous night Darius had touched and kissed the most private parts of her body. 'I—Yes, I liked it. It is only—'

'Would you like me to kiss you in that way again?' Darius prompted intensely.

Arabella felt almost faint as she recalled the touch of Darius's mouth and tongue against that sensitive part of her body. 'Are such things completely natural? Do all married couples engage in such—such intimacies together?' Her curiosity was such that for the moment she did not care that the question betrayed her own lack of experience.

Darius gazed down at her indulgently. 'Are you asking me if your brothers and their wives enjoy those same pleasures together?'

Was she? Did Arabella really want to know of the intimacies between her brothers and their wives? No, of course she did not! She'd had Darius's first marriage more in mind when she'd asked that particular question…

'No,' she answered firmly. 'I merely wondered as to the—the propriety—'

'My darling Arabella.' Darius's interruption was indulgent. 'Any degree of intimacy, as long as it is by mutual consent, is permissible between married couples. Or not,' he added more seriously.

'What do you mean?'

Darius shrugged. 'Many married couples, whilst tolerating each other's company socially, do not enjoy each other in the bedchamber. That is not going to be the case between the two of us, I hope?'

Arabella knew that she should stop Darius's lovemaking now. That not doing so would make her leaving Darius tomorrow so much harder to do.

It was only that she was still so curious, and she ached to know what came next when a man and woman made love together. And if she did go ahead with her plan to leave Darius tomorrow, bringing an end to their marriage, then tonight might be her only chance of ever finding out…

Darius's face darkened as he misread her hesitation for reluctance. 'Be assured, Arabella, that I will never force you into suffering intimacies which you find abhorrent.'

Arabella didn't even want to know what those intimacies could possibly be, let alone experience them! 'I did not for one moment suppose that you would,' she came back tartly. 'Nor would I let you!'

This was more like the Arabella that Darius admired and desired. Most especially desired…

He chuckled softly. 'Allow me to aid you in taking down your hair and removing your gown.' He suited his words to his actions, his gaze holding hers as he removed the pins from her hair before unthreading the ribbon from her curls and fastening it loosely about her throat.

Before this night was over Darius intended for that ribbon to be the only thing that Arabella wore!

Chapter Ten

Arabella stood perfectly still, barely breathing, as Darius moved behind her to push her silky hair forward over one shoulder before deftly unfastening the tiny buttons down the back of her gown.

His fingers felt warm through the thin material of her silk shift, his lips cool as he tasted the heated flesh he had bared, his tongue a fiery rasp against her spine, sending quivers of pleasure down its length to blossom and spread between her thighs.

Arabella's breath ceased altogether as Darius's lips moved back up to her nape before he folded the two sides of her gown apart and allowed the garment to fall down to her ankles. His hands encircled her waist before moving upwards over her ribcage and cupping beneath the fullness of her breasts.

'Look, Arabella,' he encouraged throatily. 'Watch as I touch you.'

She breathed softly as she lowered her gaze obediently to where she could clearly see his hands as they cupped her breasts through her shift. His skin was so much darker than the creamy whiteness of those twin orbs, their nipples deeply red and pouting, straining longingly against the sheer material that covered them.

Even as her gaze focused on those disembodied hands the thumbs shifted, caressing those sensitive and swollen tips, and once again sending rivulets of pleasure down to blaze into a burning need between her thighs. 'Darius…'

'Watch, Arabella,' he instructed again.

She couldn't have looked away from those caressing hands now if her very life had depended upon it. Instead she could only gaze as her swollen nipples were captured between thumb and finger, Darius exerting just enough pressure to increase her pleasure, causing Arabella's back to arch and her head to drop back against Darius's shoulder.

'Watch!'

Her breathing was ragged as she straightened to obey, her eyes widening as one of her breasts continued to be caressed and squeezed and his other hand slowly slid down over her ribcage to pull her shift up to her waist, baring her thighs and the silken golden curls nestled there.

She gasped as his long tapered fingers parted those silken curls to reveal a swollen pink nub Arabella had not even realised was there until Darius had touched her yesterday. Why would she? A lady was not encouraged to explore her own body.

'Touch yourself there, Arabella,' Darius urged.

Almost as if he had read her thoughts! As if Darius had known of her curiosity about these secret and so far unexplored parts of her body! 'I cannot.' She moved her head from side to side in protest.

'Do it for me.'

'You said you would not make me do anything that I did not like!'

'I promise you will like this, Arabella,' Darius murmured indulgently. 'Try it and see.' He kept his fingers against those parted curls as his other hand moved to take one of hers and guide it down to that exposed flesh. 'There.' He placed her finger against the swollen nubbin and moved it gently over it.

Arabella gasped as she felt the same pleasure in her own touch as she had in Darius's.

'It is possible to pleasure oneself,' Darius revealed gruffly as he continued to hold her hand in place.

'I— But— How…?'

'Exactly as you are now doing. Touch, Arabella,' he encouraged. 'Caress. Learn for yourself what gives you pleasure.'

'But you—'

'For the moment I take my pleasure in watching *you*,' he told her.

Arabella's cheeks burned and she glanced quickly over her shoulder at him, assured that Darius spoke the truth as she saw that his face was flushed and his eyes dark and feverish with desire.

'Any intimacy is possible between us so long as we both consent to it,' he reminded her huskily. 'At this moment it is my dearest wish to watch you pleasure yourself.'

Arabella had never dreamed—never imagined… 'I cannot!' She snatched her hand away. 'It is too much!' She buried her overheated face in her hands.

Too much, too soon, Darius realised. A pity—he would have so enjoyed sitting in a chair and watching as Arabella touched and caressed herself. Another time, perhaps. Once she was more familiar with intimacy. More intimately familiar with *him*!

Even as Darius took Arabella gently in his arms he wondered if she knew how completely she had given away her lack of all physical experience. Even self-exploration—something that most young men knew about long before they had a physical encounter with a woman.

It had been almost fifteen years since Darius had first made love to an actual woman. A rather beautiful lady of the demi-monde, and considerably experienced, who had seen it as her duty to tutor him well—both in his own pleasures and that of his bed partner. It was experience that Darius had since brought to all of his physical alliances.

Here and now, with his young and inexperienced wife, was not the occasion upon which to indulge in that experience. At least only in so far as to make this as pleasurable an initiation for her as was possible. Darius had no doubt that making love to Arabella tonight was going to stretch his self-control to its very limits!

'Will you help me out of some of these clothes, love?' he encouraged gently as he began to shrug out of his jacket. 'It seems a little unfair that you are almost unclothed whilst I am still fully dressed.'

Arabella was only too glad to move behind him and help slide the tight jacket down his arms, her cheeks still burning with embarrassment at her own lack of adventure. Darius must think her a complete novice when it came to lovemaking. Which she was, of course. But it was nonetheless humiliating to keep proving it to him time and time again!

He somehow appeared bigger once free of the tai-lored black evening jacket—his shoulders wider, his back more muscled against his shirt and the restraint of his silver brocade waistcoat.

Arabella made no effort to hide her interest as Darius quickly despatched that waistcoat, before removing his cravat and unbuttoning the three buttons on his shirt. The open neck of that shirt revealed a covering of darker blond hair on his chest.

Her eyes darkened avidly as Darius pulled that shirt over his head, tousling his hair, the muscles moving silkily beneath the hardness of his chest.

He was perfectly formed: wide shoulders, defined chest, flat stomach, tapered waist, his thighs and legs clearly long and muscled in the close-fitting breeches.

Darius was well aware of the fact that he was twelve years Arabella's senior, and he felt glad now that he had kept himself fit all these years, with regular exercise using his sword, and also in the ring—some-times here with Big Tom. Arabella's eyes showed her admiration for his muscled form as her gaze moved over him unashamedly.

'Like what you see, little puss?'

She looked up at him quizzically. 'Why do you call me that?'

Darius's grin was feral. 'Probably because before the night is out I intend to make you purr like a contented kitten!'

'I—could we blow out the candles, do you think?' she asked shyly, averting her gaze as Darius's fingers moved to the fastening of his breeches.

'By all means.' Darius left his breeches on as he

blew out the offending candles and left the room bathed only in firelight.

A delicate light that shone on the gold of Arabella's hair and through the thin material of her shift as she stood before that fire. Clearly outlining her slender curves—full breasts, narrow waist, the gentle curve of her bottom—and her legs long and slender through the knee-length shift.

'You are so very beautiful, Arabella,' Darius murmured softly as he moved to stand only inches away from her.

'So are you,' she returned huskily, knowing herself to be completely mesmerised by his unmistakable male beauty.

'Men are not beautiful,' he chided teasingly as his head lowered and his mouth captured hers.

But Darius *was* beautiful. As beautiful as that fallen angel Arabella had once likened him to. As beautiful as—

She could no longer form a coherent thought as Darius deepened his kiss. As lips, tongue and teeth laid siege to her own and he swept her firmly into his arms, moulding the softer contours of her body against his much harder one, making her fully aware of the long length of his arousal as it pressed against her.

Leaving her in no doubt as to what Darius wanted.

He wanted her.

Arabella St Cl—no, Arabella *Wynter*. His wife.

As she surely wanted him. Darius Wynter. Her husband.

Her arms moved up and her hands became entangled in the thick golden hair at Darius's nape as she returned the intensity of his kiss. Following his lead, she nibbled upon the fullness of his lower lip before sliding her tongue into the welcoming heat of his mouth, her tongue duelling briefly with his before Darius drew it deeper inside. Arabella felt hot, so tinglingly, sensitively hot. Each sweep of Darius's hands, as they moved restlessly across her body, ignited tiny licking flames of awareness from her breast to her thigh, and then back again. Cupping beneath her breasts, thumbs caressing her hardened nipples time and time again, until she pressed against him, silently pleading for more.

Darius broke the kiss to slip the strap of her shift down her arm so that he could move to the gentle slope of her breast with his mouth. Tasting, caressing, until he reached her nipple and could take its bared fullness inside his mouth. His teeth and tongue became a dual sensual attack that caused Arabella to moan longingly even as she cupped the back of his head and held him to her.

She wanted more. Wanted— Oh, God, she wanted—

'Help me off with the rest of my clothes, love.'

Arabella stared up at Darius dazedly for several long seconds, until his meaning became clear and she looked down to where his arousal strained so obviously against the material of his breeches. Her fingers were clumsy, trembling as they moved to unfasten the buttons, her breath catching in her throat as the last button came undone and she stared down at that hot and heavy fullness as it leapt free to rest against the palm of her hand.

His arousal was so thick and so long that Arabella doubted she would be able to span the width of it with her hand. She ran her fingers experimentally along its length.

Arabella had never imagined that this part of a man's body would look as it did. So beautiful she wanted to touch it. So silky she wanted to caress it. So responsive to her touch that she longed to kiss and caress it with her lips and tongue in the same intimate manner Darius had kissed her the previous night.

'Yes, I *will* feel that same pleasure in being touched and kissed,' Darius encouraged as Arabella looked up at him questioningly once he had completely removed his breeches.

Although he was far from sure of the wisdom of encouraging that intimacy when Arabella moved down onto her knees in front of him. Darius closed his eyes, his jaw clenching as he fought to maintain control as Arabella began to move her hand, testing, experimenting, as she learnt which caresses gave him the most pleasure.

Everything about having Arabella make love to him in this way gave Darius pleasure. Everything!

Touch. Sight. Smell.

The hand about him felt like velvet. The intense expression on her beautiful face as she watched his response to her caressing hand was like an aphrodisiac to his own roused senses.

He— Dear God…!

Darius's knees almost buckled beneath him as he felt her flicking the moist end of her tongue along the very tip of him. A hot, wet stroke that caused Darius to gasp and clench his fists in an attempt to find some self-control.

He managed to withstand that caress for only a few seconds longer. 'I think not!' he managed to rasp as he bent down to place his hands gently on Arabella's arms and pull her to her feet.

She gazed up at him almost shyly. 'You did not like it?'

'I liked it almost too much,' he admitted gruffly as his hand curved gently about her flushed cheek. 'Another time, love,' he promised as Arabella frowned her disappointment. 'I have waited too long to make love with you to be able to withstand that particular intimacy any more tonight.'

Arabella looked up at him searchingly. Darius had waited too long to make love with her? Did he mean these past ten days? Or longer than that?

She had no chance to ask him those probing questions as he slipped the second strap of her shift down her arm and allowed the silky gown to fall to her feet, resulting in Arabella standing naked before him.

Any awkwardness she might have felt at her complete nakedness was forgotten as she saw the heated admiration in Darius's gaze. He made no effort to hide it from her. Even if he had, the response of his naked body would have given him away as he seemed to grow even larger the more he continued to look at her!

'You are as perfect as a statue of Aphrodite I once gazed upon in Greece,' he murmured throatily.

Her eyes widened. 'You have been to Greece?'

He chuckled huskily. 'I have been to many places. And someday I will enjoy telling you about all of them. Just not now, Arabella.' He ran a finger lightly across her swollen lips as he teased her. 'The only thing I want to do now is kneel down at your feet and worship you.'

'I do not want you to worship me, Darius.' Arabella shook her head, emboldened by his obvious admiration of her nakedness. 'I want—I want you inside me.' Her cheeks burned at the admission. 'I need to know how it feels to have this…' her hand caressed along the length of his arousal '…inside me.'

Darius's breath caught in his throat. He had known many women intimately, but none so honest, so open in her needs, as Arabella. 'And so you shall, love,' he promised softly, and he took her hand and moved the two of them to lie down upon the rug in front of the fire.

Darius leant on his elbow to look down at his wife. Her curls were even more golden in the firelight, her body bathed in that same soft glow. 'You are beautiful, Arabella,' he said gruffly. 'So very, very beautiful.'

Her hands moved up the nakedness of his chest, her fingers becoming entangled in the hair at his nape as she gently pulled him down to her. 'Kiss me, Darius. Make love to me,' she pressed shakily.

He kissed her long and deeply at the same time as his hands caressed her, readying her, making sure that she was prepared to receive him before he moved to lie between her parted thighs. 'I do not want to hurt you, Arabella,' he muttered as he paused and rested his forehead against hers.

Arabella had questioned her sisters-in-law enough to know that Darius could not help but hurt her a little this first time as he breached the barrier of her virginity. It was a pain Arabella welcomed if it meant she truly became one with him. If he felt unable—or unwilling—to take that final step because he did not want to hurt her, then Arabella would have to do it herself…

She allowed her hands to move caressingly down the muscled column of Darius's back before spreading her fingers over his buttocks, able to feel the way he tensed at her touch. Her fingers tightened about him at the same time as she arched her hips in a thrust that brought Darius fully inside her.

He lifted his head to frown. 'What are you doing?'

'I want this, Darius,' Arabella told him determinedly. 'I want all of you!' She thrust again, at once feeling the barrier of her innocence tear beneath that invasion.

The pain was sharp and brief. The length of a sharply indrawn breath and passing just as quickly. To be replaced by the wonder of knowing that Darius was finally inside her.

'Easy, love.' He soothed Arabella into stillness as she arched again in her need to take all of him inside her. 'I want us both to savour this moment.'

He slowly kissed the tips of her breasts, licking the tightness of her puckered nipples, then gently biting. His hand moved between them to touch that swollen nubbin nestled amongst her curls, fingers lightly caressing as he increased Arabella's pleasure.

She gasped, her eyes widening as that pulsing pleasure centred hotly between her thighs. She clung to his shoulders as she moved instinctively to meet the thrust of Darius's thighs.

'Yes, love. *Yes*!' he urged through gritted teeth as he began to move his hips, pulling back slightly before surging inside her, again and again until he was so deep it felt as if he touched the very centre of her, sending Arabella into a vortex of unimagined pleasure.

Darius tried to hold back, fighting to control his own release, wanting this never to end. But as she convulsed around him Darius knew it was a battle he was destined to lose, and he rushed towards his own climax before he collapsed weakly onto her breasts, breathing heavily, both their bodies hot and slick from the exertion.

Arabella smiled in dreamy satisfaction as she ran tender fingers through Darius's hair, loving its silky feel as he lay with his head upon her breasts.

She was no longer a virgin!

She was now officially a woman. Darius Wynter's woman.

It was glorious. Wonderful. Unimaginably delightful.

No wonder her brothers and their wives so often walked about with silly smiles upon their faces if *this* was what they shared in their marriage beds. And Arabella was convinced that they did.

It was like being a part of some exclusive club, its members privy to a secret too special, too excruciatingly wonderful, to be shared by any but themselves.

'Your Grace?' A knock sounded on the dining room door in accompaniment to the urgent demand.

Arabella's movements stilled as she recognised the burly butler's rough tones as he spoke on the other side of the closed dining-room door.

'What the hell?' Darius was scowling darkly as he raised his head to look across at that closed door.

'I am sorry to—to disturb you, Your Grace.' The unlikely-looking butler sounded more than a little anxious.

'He's going to be more than sorry when I have done telling him what I think of him,' Darius muttered beneath his breath. 'Give me a minute, man,' he called out.

'I am sure Westlake would not have disturbed us if

he did not have an important reason for doing so.' In truth, Arabella was having difficulty holding back the bubble of laughter inside her that was threatening to break loose.

She and Darius had been married three days. Three days of constant interruptions, for one reason or another, to every attempt at intimacy between them. And now, when they had at last managed to find some privacy for their lovemaking, the butler at Winton Hall had interrupted them yet again. Even after Darius had assured Arabella that he had instructed the servants to do otherwise!

Darius's scowl deepened. 'Did you hear a shot being fired? Or perhaps a herd of wild elephants, loose and threatening to trample down the house with all of us inside it?'

Arabella giggled at the unlikelihood of either of those things ever happening here in the safety of the Worcestershire countryside. 'You know I did not.'

'Well, I assure you, Arabella, they are the only two reasons I gave Westlake for interrupting us this evening,' he grumbled.

Her giggle developed into a fully fledged chuckle at his disgruntled expression. 'Admit it, Darius, it *is* very funny,' she encouraged, as her husband continued to look distinctly unamused.

'You would not have thought so if the interruption had occurred five minutes earlier,' he retorted.

'No,' Arabella acknowledged, with remembered frustration at the previous interruptions to their lovemaking. Even more so now that she was fully aware of what she had been missing all this time!

Darius gave an impatient shake of his head and gently disengaged himself before standing up. 'I am beginning to think someone is deliberately trying to sabotage even the consummation of our marriage,' he growled as he reached for his breeches.

Arabella made no effort to disguise her curiosity concerning Darius's nakedness.

Her fingers ached to touch him again. To caress and handle him until he was once again hard and throbbing with the need to be inside her. Perhaps this time to be allowed to use her lips and tongue to taste and arouse him.

Darius groaned as he obviously saw the intent in her expression. 'Do not look at me like that when there is no chance I am going to be able to make love to you again—in the next few minutes, at least.' He settled his breeches on his hips before fastening them.

Arabella stretched languidly, feeling and no doubt looking much like the satisfied kitten Darius had earlier promised to make of her. 'I am sure, no matter what the problem, that it will not keep you from our bed all night.'

Darius pulled his shirt on over his head before looking down at Arabella once more, relishing the fact that she obviously did not feel the need to cover herself, but instead seemed completely comfortable being naked in front of him.

'Perhaps you should dress too, love?' he suggested gently, reluctantly.

Damn it, if Westlake had not interrupted them Darius knew he would even now be enjoying making love to his wife for a second time.

Unfortunately, given his specific instructions to the

butler earlier this evening, Darius was nowhere near as sure as Arabella that the reason for this most recent interruption would be dealt with as quickly as he hoped it would…

Chapter Eleven

Despite the unimagined pleasure of their lovemaking the previous evening, Arabella was not feeling in the least kindly disposed towards her husband as she swept down the wide staircase of Winton Hall at nine o'clock the following morning. On the contrary, she felt there was every reason for the frown upon her creamy brow as she crossed the large hallway on her way to the breakfast room.

Leaving Darius to converse quietly with Westlake the previous evening, Arabella had retired to her bedchamber to bathe and dress in one of her prettiest nightgowns. She had then lain awake in her bed, waiting for Darius to join her, sure that he would do so at any moment, as eager for their lovemaking to continue as she was.

Their marriage had got off to a somewhat shaky start, but Arabella had begun to believe that now they were truly one the tension would start to ease between them. She'd certainly had reason to rethink her decision to leave Darius come the next morning!

But as the minutes and then hours had passed, without any sign of Darius joining her in her bedchamber, Arabella's eagerness had turned to uncertainty. Perhaps he had not found their lovemaking as satisfactory as she had? Or had he been shocked by her obvious enthusiasm? Although she somehow did not think it was the latter; Darius had encouraged—no, positively *demanded*!—that loss of control.

That uncertainty allayed, Arabella's anger had returned with a vengeance. So much so that it had been the early hours of the morning before she'd managed to fall asleep, only to awaken an hour ago to find the bed beside her still empty. A glance into the adjoining bedchamber had revealed that Darius had not been to bed at all the previous night—in her bedchamber or his own.

Arabella most definitely required an explanation from him this morning—for the way he had abandoned her so completely the night before. And, if she were not to renew her decision to leave him, it had best be a good one!

Prepared for a verbal exchange with him, Arabella felt her ire only increase when she found the breakfast room empty except for the footman waiting to serve her. 'Has His Grace already breakfasted this morning, Holmes?' she enquired lightly, as the footman served the cup of tea she had requested.

The middle-aged man maintained a stony expression. 'I don't fink—er—I don't believe so. Er…Your Grace.'

Arabella's frown deepened. 'Has my husband been seen at *all* this morning?'

'Not that I know of, Your Grace.'

Arabella's irritation deepened at the man's unhelpful replies. 'In that case, send Westlake to me immediately.'

The footman paused in replacing the teapot upon its stand. 'You wants to see Mr Westlake, Your Grace?'

'Immediately,' she snapped. 'Is there a problem?'

She arched enquiring brows as the man hesitated. She really could not imagine where Darius had found the strange collection of people waiting upon them at Winton Hall. From Holmes's accent and the awkwardness of his demeanour, the footman gave every impression of originating from the backstreets of London!

'Er—I…I believe Mr Westlake is busy this morning, Your Grace,' the man said awkwardly.

Arabella's brows rose even higher. 'Too busy to make himself available to his employer?'

'Oh, no, ma'am,' the man assured her happily. 'Mr Westlake is always ready and willing to 'elp the Duke whenever the need arises.'

Arabella deliberately took a sip of her tea before replying, in an effort to allay the footman's suspicions concerning her increasing interest in this conversation. 'And does the need arise very often?'

'Not as often as it used to do,' Holmes confided with obvious disappointment. 'But often enough, I suppose.'

Arabella's interest was well and truly roused now. 'So, Mr Westlake is too busy to talk to me, and you have no idea where my husband is?'

'Now, I didn't say that, Your Grace,' he protested, his Cockney accent deepening in his agitation.

Arabella held on to her temper with effort. 'So which statement was incorrect? Westlake is not busy? Or you *have* seen my husband this morning?'

'Well…the second one, I s'pose. I 'asn't *seen* the Duke, you understand,' he defended as Arabella's frown returned. 'But I do know as where 'e is.'

'And where would that be?'

''e's in the Blue Salon wiv 'is guest.'

Guest…?

What guest?

The betrothal and wedding of Lady Arabella St Claire and Darius Wynter, Duke of Carlyne, might have taken place with more haste than was usual, but surely it was known here in Worcestershire, as much as in London, that the Duke and Duchess of Carlyne were only recently married and as such not yet receiving visitors?

Could the arrival of this guest be the reason Westlake had felt compelled to knock on the dining-room door, disturbing them yesterday evening? Possibly the same reason Darius had not joined her in her bedchamber the night before…?

From the way the footman was now squirming uncomfortably at the realisation he might have said too much, Arabella felt sure she would receive no further helpful information from him. 'That will be all, thank you, Holmes.' She gave the man her most gracious smile along with the dismissal; all those years as Hawk's sister certainly stood her in good stead for her role as Darius's duchess!

So a guest had arrived yesterday evening? Arabella mused once left alone. Someone important enough for Westlake to dare to disturb his employer, despite Darius's instructions for him not to do so unless it was a dire emergency.

Who could that visitor be?

And what was so urgent about their visit that Darius was still privately ensconced with them hours after their arrival?

'You have received no further word as to his whereabouts?' Darius's expression was grimly determined as he attempted to thrust his sword under the other man's guarded pose.

'We only know he left the house in Paris some days ago.' His opponent parried the thrust to make a lunge himself. A parry that Darius easily sidestepped. 'A coincidence, certainly. But his disappearance does not preclude him being the one responsible for the things that have happened these past few days, either.'

The two men had stripped down to their shirts, pantaloons and boots an hour ago in order to practise their swordplay, and Darius could now feel the material of his shirt clinging damply to his back from the exertion. 'Surely the loose wheel on my own carriage three days ago is too reminiscent of similar tampering with another carriage seven months ago for the two to be unrelated?'

'What of the fire at the coaching inn?'

'Perhaps a new innovation on his part?'

'I believe you once claimed that he did not have an original thought in his head?' the other man drawled dryly. 'Besides, Helena Jourdan is far more likely to be the one who wishes to do you harm,' the other man insisted as Darius would have argued the point.

Darius scowled. 'I should have wrung the woman's neck when I had the chance!'

'That would certainly have been one way of resolv-

ing a—a delicate situation,' the younger man acknowledged ruefully.

'Instead of which I now possibly have a vengeful
woman attempting to harm not only myself but also my
wife,' Darius frowned his displeasure.

'Talking of your wife…'

'Which we were not,' Darius bit out warningly,
temporarily losing his concentration as he allowed his
mind to wander to thoughts of his young wife, and
the memory of how beautiful she had looked naked
in the firelight the previous evening. That lapse was
enough to allow the other man to lunge and press the
tip of his sword directly over Darius's heart. 'Oh, to
hell with this!' He threw his sword disgustedly onto
the chaise and began restlessly pacing the room.
'How can I concentrate on swordplay when I have
some madman—?'

'Or woman.'

Darius paused long enough in his pacing to shoot the
other man an impatient glare. 'Or woman,' he allowed
irritably, 'attempting to do away with me the moment
I step outside the damned house!'

'You are recently married, Darius, and as such have
every reason *not* to step outside the house.' The younger
man gave him a mocking glance as he threw himself
into one of the armchairs.

Arabella had left the breakfast room a few minutes
ago to walk outside onto the terrace with the intention
of circling the house and joining her husband and his
guest in the Blue Salon. Instead, shivering with the
cold, she had come to an abrupt halt as she realised the

two men were talking loudly enough for her to be able to hear their discussion. And what a discussion!

Firstly the coach accident three days ago had apparently not been an accident after all! And then the fire at the inn. Also no accident…?

Arabella had easily recognised Darius's visitor when she peeped in at the window. Lord Gideon Grayson. Tall, dark, and very handsome, a man Arabella knew to be a close friend and peer of her disreputable youngest brother Sebastian. He had also been one of Darius's guests at their wedding.

Although what possible business it could be of the rakish Lord Grayson if some woman were supposedly attempting to harm Darius or herself was totally beyond her.

'A vengeful woman', Darius had called her.

Possibly a discarded lover of Darius's?

It certainly sounded a possibility!

Recalling the intensity of their own lovemaking the evening before, Arabella felt herself bristle inside just at the *thought* of Darius being so recently intimately involved with another woman. A woman who obviously felt strongly enough about Darius having ended their affair to attempt to do him harm.

Dear Lord—could the 'he' Darius and Lord Grayson had earlier referred to so scathingly possibly be the woman's cuckolded and jealous husband…?

Arabella's previous anger with Darius returned in force, and she no longer hesitated outside on the terrace but instead opened one of the French doors to step decisively into the Blue Salon.

To say that the two men were surprised by her sudden entrance would be understating the matter. Darius's already grim expression became even grimmer, his eyes turning a steely blue, and in contrast, Lord Gideon Grayson's handsome face was uncomfortably flushed as he jumped awkwardly to his feet to offer an awkward bow at the same time as he attempted to refasten the buttons at the throat of his shirt.

'Good morning, gentlemen.' Arabella gave them a sweetly insincere smile. 'I trust I am not interrupting anything of importance?'

Darius narrowed chilling blue eyes on his wife, not fooled for a moment by the lightness of Arabella's greeting, nor distracted by her beauty in a pale lemon gown. The challenging glint in her deep brown eyes and the flush to her cheeks were more than enough to alert him as to the true state of Arabella's emotions: she was extremely angry about something.

The fact that Darius had felt unable to share her bed the night before could be the reason for that. Conversely, if Arabella had chanced to hear any of his recent conversation with Gray then she might just have taken exception to something she had overheard...

Exactly how long had Arabella been standing outside on the terrace?

'Not at all,' he answered her smoothly, and he crossed the room to draw her to his side by placing a possessive arm about the slenderness of her waist. 'Is the November air not a little cold for you to be outside dressed only in your gown?' Darius could feel the chill of her body through the gown as he anchored her to his side.

Brown eyes gazed up at Darius in what he was sure was deceptive innocence. 'I stepped outside to take some air before breakfast and decided to come and investigate when I heard the two of you talking in here.'

He nodded abruptly. 'Lord Grayson arrived late yesterday evening.'

Arabella turned to Lord Grayson. 'You rode all the way from London in one day, My Lord?'

Grayson flushed. 'I—'

'What does it matter how and when Gray travelled here, Arabella?' Darius cut in. 'He arrived yesterday evening, and we stayed up far too late last night drinking brandy together.'

Too much information, Darius, he inwardly rebuked himself as he saw the frown darken Arabella's brow. He'd just broken one of the principal rules of being a spy: reveal only as much information as was absolutely necessary. It was not necessary that Arabella be told what he and Gray had been doing last night.

'As you can see by our current state of undress, you have caught us practising our swordsmanship in order to shake off the effects of imbibing too much of that brandy. Poor Grayson is quite mortified with embarrassment,' he added mockingly as the other man still fumbled in refastening his shirt.

'Please do not concern yourself, Lord Grayson,' Arabella assured him dryly, and she neatly extricated herself from the curve of Darius's arm to step further into the room. 'My older brothers never felt any qualms about appearing in front of me dressed only in their breeches and shirt.'

'You are too kind, Your Grace,' Grayson accepted lamely.

'Will you be joining us for breakfast, Lord Grayson,

or are you in a hurry to continue your journey?'
Arabella enquired.

As setdowns went, this one was quite subtle, Darius
acknowledged admiringly as he gazed at his wife. Very
subtle, in fact, and yet it more than made clear
Arabella's displeasure at Grayson's interruption of their
privacy so soon after their wedding.

'I have invited Gray to stay with us for a few days at
least, Arabella,' he informed her.

She raised frosty brows. 'Indeed?'

It was all Darius could do to hold back his smile at
that obvious frostiness, and poor Gray looked as if he
were wishing himself a hundred miles away! 'Indeed,'
he echoed mockingly.

Arabella nodded abruptly. 'It can become so incredibly tedious in the country without stimulating company
to alleviate the boredom, can it not?'

If they had been alone Darius would have almost certainly given in to the temptation he'd had on several
occasions in this past week to place Arabella over his
knee and raise her skirts before spanking her luscious
little bottom!

But then if they had been alone Darius doubted he
would have had reason to feel that impulse. Arabella
was obviously severely displeased at the thought of
having Lord Gideon Grayson as a guest at Winton Hall
for the next few days!

As one of the agents who had long worked for
Darius, Gray had been the obvious choice for Bancroft
to send in response to the message Darius had had his
footman deliver to the Earl following the fire at the
coaching inn.

Now that Gray was rested from his hell-for-leather ride to Winton Hall the previous day, the two men had to discuss the situation further before deciding upon an appropriate course of action, even whilst disagreeing as to the identity of the perpetrator of these accidents. Darius still favoured his brother Francis, whereas Gray believed it to be the traitor Helena Jourdan—the Frenchwoman having escaped from captivity on the day of Sebastian St Claire's wedding to Juliet Boyd by seducing her jailer into releasing her.

Whilst Darius sympathised with Arabella's resentment at Gray's continued presence here, he also knew that the other man would be helpful in preventing any more of those 'accidents' from proving to be fatal.

Arabella's cheeks burned with obvious temper. 'I am sure Darius will appreciate having you for company after I have gone.'

Darius became very still. 'After you have gone where?' He looked across at her with flintily narrowed eyes.

Their lovemaking the previous evening had convinced Arabella into abandoning her decision to leave Darius come the morning. But his avoidance of sharing her bed the night before, and now his desire for Lord Grayson's company rather than her own, only days after their wedding, surely meant that Darius did not feel the same way about their lovemaking as she did. Besides which, Arabella had far from forgotten the existence of that 'vengeful woman' from Darius's past…

She met Darius's flinty gaze unblinkingly. 'It seems an ideal opportunity for me to visit with my family at Mulberry Hall now that Lord Grayson has arrived to amuse you in my stead.'

'Oh, I say!' Lord Grayson protested awkwardly.

Forget temptation, Darius decided grimly. The moment they were alone he *was* going to spank Arabella's bottom until she screamed for mercy!

'Would you mind leaving us, Grayson?' His voice was dangerously soft, his gaze still fixed firmly on Arabella's angrily flushed face. 'It would seem that my wife and I have a few things of our own to discuss this morning,' he added with deceptive pleasantness.

'Of course.' Gray grimaced uncomfortably. 'I should go upstairs and bathe, anyway. Excuse me, Your Grace.' He bowed formally to Arabella and received a cool nod of dismissal for his trouble.

Darius waited only long enough for Gray to shoot him an apologetic grimace and beat a hasty retreat, before crossing the room to stand mere inches away from his wife. 'You were not very polite to our guest, love.'

Arabella's eyes flashed with golden lights as she looked up at him. 'I believe Lord Grayson is *your* guest, not mine.'

'Nevertheless…'

'Nevertheless he is *your* guest and not *mine*!' she maintained with haughty stubbornness.

Darius drew in a sharp breath. 'You will apologise to Lord Grayson when he returns downstairs.'

'I most certainly will *not*!' Arabella eyed him scornfully.

'I believe that you *will*.' Darius's tone once again possessed that deceptive softness that most of his acquaintances and all of his enemies would have warned his young and defiant wife to beware.

Unfortunately for Arabella, none of those acquaintances or enemies was now at hand to administer such a warning!

'You may believe what you choose, Darius.' Arabella gave a dismissive movement of her hand. 'Now, if you will excuse me? I need to go upstairs and pack— *What* do you think you are doing?' She gasped indignantly as Darius caught hold of her wrist with steely fingers to pull her along behind him as he strode over to the settee.

'What am I doing?' Darius mused, even as he sat down on the settee and pulled a struggling Arabella face-down across his thighs. 'You have been rude to a guest in our home, Arabella. A rudeness for which you have refused to apologise. It is now my intention to administer suitable punishment for that refusal.'

'But—Darius!' she screamed in protest as her skirts were thrown up over her back and he revealed the plump cheeks of her naked bottom. 'Darius, if you do this I will—'

'Yes?' Darius prompted, as he administered the first light slap against those shapely orbs.

'I— How *dare* you?' she squealed.

'Oh, I believe when you know me better, Arabella, you will learn that I dare any number of things. Disciplining an unruly wife being the least of them!' His expression was grimly determined as he struck another light blow.

'I swear, I will kill you if you do that again!' Arabella ground out between clenched teeth, her face fiery red as she turned to glare up at him.

'You will have to get in line, love,' Darius drawled ruefully as he administered another slap to her naked flesh, the skin now flushed almost as much as her face.

'Those were for your rudeness and your refusal to apologise to Lord Grayson. Now, explain what you mean by your claim that it is your intention to leave me this morning.'

'You have made it more than obvious that you consider our marriage to have been a mistake—'

'In what way obvious?' he demanded incredulously.

'You abandoned my bedchamber last night in preference to drinking brandy with Lord Grayson. You prefer his company this morning instead of my own. You— Oh, you *monster*!' Arabella screamed as another slap resounded upon her bottom.

'We will get at least one of your complaints settled right now, Arabella,' he declared.

'Which is?' she challenged.

'I have *no* intention—of allowing you—to leave me.' Each phrase was accompanied by another light smack to that delicious little bottom as Darius held Arabella's squirming body firmly captive with his arm across her back. 'Not today. Not the next time you take it into your beautiful head to be angry with me. Not ever. Do I make myself clear?'

Arabella continued to struggle against that grasp. 'You cannot stop me from doing exactly as I please—'

'Wrong answer,' Darius said mildly.

She glared at him. 'It is the only answer you shall receive from me. No matter how much and for how long you beat me!'

Darius caught her wrist as her hand came up to strike him. 'I do not in the least *enjoy* beating you, Arabella—'

'Liar!' she accused heatedly.

Darius's arousal testified the truth of that claim. As

did his giving in to the temptation to fondle and caress that plump and fiery-cheeked bottom. Such a warm and deliciously plump bottom. So soft and smooth and— What was this…?

A light caress between Arabella's thighs revealed that his wife of four days was as aroused as Darius himself!

Arabella could not hold back her groan of pleasure as she felt Darius's caressing fingers exploring her intimately. That groan became a husky moan as one of those fingers entered her, and another found and rubbed the swollen nubbin hidden amongst her damp curls. That moan became a strangled cry as Darius continued his assault upon her senses until she became consumed in a release so long and so achingly pleasurable that Arabella felt a rush of the tears on her cheeks that she had refused to cry when Darius spanked her bottom.

She was instantly mortified at her loss of control, and kept her eyes closed as she felt Darius lifting her up and over him, so that her nakedness now straddled his thighs. Thighs that she could feel were hard and pulsing!

Her lids opened wide in surprise. 'Darius…?'

He smiled down at her. 'I want you just as badly, love.'

Arabella stared at him, not understanding how they could have gone from anger with each other to such arousal in just a few short minutes.

'You are right to feel angry with me.' Darius groaned with self-disgust as Arabella only continued to stare at him. 'I should not have struck you. You—'

He broke off with a strangled groan as Arabella reached down between them to unfasten his breeches and release his arousal.

He was just as beautiful as Arabella remembered

from yesterday evening. Hard. Pulsing. With skin like velvet as Arabella curled her fingers about him.

She watched Darius's face as she slowly began to move her hand up and down his length, noting the flush that appeared in his cheeks and the clenching of his arrogant jaw. His hair was already dishevelled from his sword practice, several tendrils clinging damply to his brow, and the hair on his chest, visible at the deep vee of his unbuttoned shirt, was also slightly damp from his earlier exertion.

'God, Arabella,' Darius groaned weakly as she smoothed her thumb across the sensitive tip of his arousal. 'Are you very sore from last night, love?'

'Not at all,' she assured him as she stroked him once more.

Darius's back and shoulders were tense. 'Then will you just take me inside you and be done with this torture?'

That groan and his words emboldened Arabella, and she realised that the control, the power of this encounter, was now hers. 'How much do you want me, Darius?'

He blinked. 'How much?'

'Mmm, how much?' Arabella slowly leant forward so that she might kiss the smooth column of his throat, and was able to feel his shudder of response as her tongue licked the saltiness she tasted on his skin.

He smiled ruefully. 'Enough to know that if you do not soon take me I may just embarrass both myself and you.'

Arabella laughed huskily. 'How much, Darius?' she persisted, and she sat up to deliberately move forward, so that the slick nakedness of her thighs now pressed against the hard throb of his arousal.

He moistened dry lips. 'What do you want from me,

Arabella? You want me to let you leave today after all? Is that it?' He shook his head. 'I cannot allow that.'

Arabella was no longer convinced that she wished to leave Darius! Yes, she had been angry with him for his desertion last night. Disappointed when she discovered he had invited Lord Grayson to stay with them. Furious with humiliation when Darius had thrown her over his knee and spanked her bottom. But then Darius had touched her, giving her the pleasure that she had been craving since the previous evening—and now he was all but begging her to give him that same pleasure in return.

Arabella realised that she secretly enjoyed their heated disagreements as much as Darius obviously did. And she especially enjoyed the result of those disagreements!

'And if I agree to stay…?' Once again Arabella moved her heat against him, eliciting another groan from him. 'You may do as you wish during the day, Darius, but I *will* have your promise that in future you will join me in my bedchamber every night—'

'*Every* night, Arabella?' he cut in, with a quirk of an eyebrow quickly followed by an indrawn breath as again Arabella deliberately and torturously rubbed herself against him.

'Every night,' she repeated firmly.

'Every night.' He nodded, his jaw clenched once more. 'I really need to be inside you now, Arabella!' His teeth were bared as he clasped her arms fiercely, and his eyes glittered with intense desire.

Arabella deliberately held that gaze as she reached between them to guide the hardness of his arousal inside her, inch by silken inch, until she was fully impaled.

Arabella stilled. 'You are now inside me, Darius.'

'Dear God…!' Fine beads of perspiration broke out upon his flushed brow as he moved restlessly beneath her.

'Is that not enough?' she teased him deliberately, determined not to forgive him too quickly for his high-handed treatment of her just now. 'Is there something else you wish from me?'

'Move, Arabella,' he breathed raggedly. 'I need you to ride me!' His hands tightened about her arms as he began to thrust urgently beneath her.

Arabella's father had placed her upon the back of a horse at the precocious age of four, and as she slowly began to ride Darius, lifting up until his hardness almost slid completely out of her, then moving down to so pleasurably fully impale herself on him again, she recognised that it was not so very different.

At least not initially. Not until she became so very distracted by the force of her own pleasure, her breathing becoming as ragged as Darius's own, her fingers digging into his shoulders as she felt the heat of her own release building for a second time.

Darius reached out desperately to pull down the front of her gown and release her breasts above its low neckline, needing to taste Arabella's swollen nipples. He laved them skilfully with his tongue and finally achieved his own incredible release—only to learn she had far from finished with him!

Arabella took complete advantage of the fact that Darius remained hard inside her, riding him fiercely, wildly, until he reached a second, aching climax at the same moment as she—a release more excruciating and pleasurably powerful than Darius had ever known before.

'Dear God…' Darius rested his forehead damply against Arabella's as she collapsed forward weakly. 'If we make love like this every night, love, then I shall be dead within the week!'

Even with the most accomplished of courtesans Darius had never before reached a second shuddering climax so quickly after the first. The fact that his wife was so inexperienced, her lovemaking completely instinctive and so incredibly erotic, only made Darius's complete lack of control all the more incredible.

Arabella's senses returned slowly, and along with them came a feeling of embarrassment at her brazenness just now. Had she *really* just taunted and physically tormented Darius until he agreed to her terms? Demanding that he share her bed every night? Make love to her every night?

'Oh, dear.' She sighed shakily as she buried her face against his shoulder.

'Oh, dear, indeed.' Darius chest rumbled beneath her cheek. 'I fear I am completely unmanned, Arabella. In fact, I am not sure that a certain part of my body is still my own!'

Arabella raised her head to look at him, reassured a little by the teasing she could see in his expression. 'Was I too rough with you?'

'You can ask that after I beat you?' He gently rearranged her gown.

'You did not beat me.' She eyed him knowingly. 'You used just enough force to arouse me rather than hurt me, did you not?'

Darius gave a rueful grimace at her perception. 'Yes.'

She frowned. 'You intended making love to me all the time?'

'Not all the time, no,' he drawled lazily. 'But I admit the idea did occur to me after you had dismissed Gray with such haughty disdain,' he revealed. Instantly realising his mistake as Arabella's eyes narrowed and her mouth compressed determinedly. 'Arabella—'

'Tell me, Darius,' Arabella bit out, 'who is Helena Jourdan?'

Darius drew in a sharp, hissing breath as she so challengingly revealed that she *had* overheard far too much of his conversation with Gray than was safe. For himself. And for her....

Chapter Twelve

Darius's movements were precise and restrained as he carefully disengaged himself from Arabella before lifting her to the floor, so that she might stand up to rearrange her petticoats and gown while he saw to the fastening of his breeches.

All the time he was wondering how much—or how little—he must reveal to Arabella to stop her from probing further into the subject of Helena Jourdan.

As Gray had pointed out to him earlier, the subject of that woman was an extremely delicate one. In fact, it would have been so much better for all of them if Arabella had not so much as heard mention of the other woman's name.

His eyes narrowed. 'Have you been spying on me, Arabella?' That would surely be an irony: the spymaster being spied upon by his own wife!

Several of Arabella's curls, so neatly arranged by her maid only an hour or so ago, had fallen down about her shoulders in the heat of their lovemaking. But Arabella ceased trying to tidy them as she heard the disapproval in Darius's tone.

Her chin rose defensively. 'Despite your denials to the contrary, the woman was your lover until a few days ago, was she not?'

Darius became very still. 'My *lover*?'

'Mistress. Courtesan. Whatever term you wish to apply to the most recent woman to have shared your bed!' Arabella's top lip curled in disgust.

Darius arched mocking brows. 'I believe *you* have that privilege!'

'So far we have not shared a bed,' she pointed out sharply.

He inclined his head in acknowledgement. 'Indeed— only a rug in front of the fire and a chaise.'

Arabella's cheeks burned as Darius's dishevelled appearance reminded her all too forcibly of the wild abandon of their most recent coupling. 'Exactly.'

'Something I intend to rectify at the earliest opportunity, I assure you.'

She frowned. 'I think not.'

'No?'

'I see no privilege attached to sharing the bed of a man such as *you*!' Arabella snapped.

Darius stilled. 'A man such as me?' he echoed dangerously.

Arabella's cheeks became flushed as once again she heard the steel beneath the softness of Darius's tone. The restrained stillness of his body was a warning that she had overstepped the line with that last insulting remark of hers.

'You have not answered my original question,' she said.

'Neither will I,' Darius retorted. 'We were married four days ago, Arabella. I see no reason to account to you for any of my actions before that time.'

'You see no reason…?' she repeated incredulously, her eyes having become a glittering angry gold. 'One of your ex-mistresses is still pursuing you, has apparently several times intended to do us both harm. but you see *no reason* to explain yourself to me?'

A nerve pulsed in Darius's clenched jaw. 'None.'

'You are an unmitigated rake, sir!'

Darius gave a humourless grin as he made a mocking bow. 'At last we are agreed on something.'

Arabella's breasts quickly rose and fell as she breathed deeply in her agitation, and her hands were curled into fists at her sides. 'I believe I might actually *hate* you, Darius!'

Something else they were in agreement on, then—because Darius hated himself at that moment.

Eight years ago, when Darius had first begun to tread this delicate path of spy for the crown, his life had been completely his own, and as such he had accepted that any repercussions and dangers his precarious career incurred would also be his own. It had never been his intention to place Arabella in that same danger.

In fact, since Hawk St Claire had refused his offer for her more than a year ago, Darius had gone out of his way to avoid showing any preference for Arabella's company. What had occurred between them at Sebastian's wedding had been completely unplanned on Darius's part—a temptation he had no longer been able to resist when the lady herself had so obviously been more than willing.

If they had not been found together in that compromising position in Hawk St Claire's study, by none other than the morally upstanding Lord Redwood, then Darius would have simply walked away after the encounter. With regret, certainly, but nonetheless he would have walked away.

Faced with the choice of exposing Arabella to scandal once their alliance had become public knowledge—which without a doubt it would have done—or marriage, Darius had decided to marry her and be damned.

He should have recognised sooner that his actions were not protecting Arabella but placing her in the same danger as Darius was himself.

No, he *had* realised it, damn it! Had known and married her anyway.

His reasons for doing so were completely selfish, and certainly not something that the currently infuriated Arabella would be willing to hear....

Nor were they something that Darius intended even attempting to share with her until his enemy had been apprehended.

He eyed her mockingly. 'That should add a little spice to our lovemaking.'

The heat of her glare was enough to burn him where he stood. 'You are arrogant, Darius, to believe there will be *any* further lovemaking between us after this!'

'I trust you are not once again entertaining the idea of leaving me, Arabella?' Darius jeered. 'Or perhaps you merely wish me to think that you might in order to...provoke me again?'

Arabella was sure that she had never been this angry in her life before. And since becoming betrothed to Darius Wynter there had certainly been plenty of opportunity for her to be so.

He was so arrogant. So mocking. So superior in every way. So—so wickedly handsome that just looking at him made her knees go weak!

How could she still find Darius so attractive when he made no attempt to deny what he was, or deny that the mistress he had denied having had been so upset at the ending of their affair and his marriage to Arabella that she was trying to do them both harm?

Was it really possible to love someone so much that losing them made you want to destroy the object of that love rather than allow anyone else to have them?

Arabella certainly felt violent enough towards Darius at this moment. She could quite cheerfully have hit him over the head with something painfully heavy!

But she was merely fascinated by Darius and not in love with him. Wasn't she…?

No! She would not even *entertain* the idea that she might be in love with her husband. She would not!

'I repeat my earlier statement, Darius—if you attempt to beat me again I will surely kill you.' Her gaze raked over him scathingly.

He quirked a brow at her. 'I take it you meant your comment earlier concerning lovemaking too?'

'I always mean what I say, Darius.'

'I remind you that so too do I,' he bit out brusquely.

'Meaning?'

'Meaning that if you so much as attempt to leave Winton Hall then I will come after you and bring you back.' His mouth thinned. 'I guarantee you would not enjoy the punishment that would surely follow.'

'Do not attempt to threaten me, Darius—'

'It is a promise, Arabella, not a threat,' he warned softly.

She gave him one last scornful glance before turning on her heel to stride from the room, her shoulders stiff and her back ramrod-straight.

Darius made no move to follow her, knowing there would be little point in his doing so. He could not confide the truth to Arabella—his role as spymaster prevented him from doing that—and as such had no way as yet of explaining his own actions, or Grayson's reason for being here, to his wife.

The sooner Darius established whether it was Helena Jourdan arranging these 'accidents', as Gray seemed to think it was, or—as Darius himself was more inclined to believe—his own exiled brother Francis, the sooner he would be able to attempt to heal the rift that now existed between himself and Arabella.

Attempt to—because Darius was not at all sure he would be successful….

'I had not realised that you and my husband were such…close acquaintances, Lord Grayson.' Arabella arched questioning brows at her guest as she presided over the teapot later that afternoon.

Teatime was a social nicety that only the two of them had bothered to attend, the footman having informed Arabella that the Duke was about the estate somewhere. No doubt with Westlake, as the butler was once again absent from his duties.

'No. Well…' Gideon Grayson looked decidedly uncomfortable at finding himself alone with his hostess in this way. 'We have visited the gambling clubs together a time or two, I dare say.'

Arabella's mouth was tight as she handed him his tea. 'With Sebastian, perhaps?'

His gaze avoided meeting hers. 'I'm not really sure…'

'No? But I had the impression when we were all at Lady Humbers's ball earlier this year that you and Sebastian were good friends.' Arabella eyed the young Lord over the rim of her teacup.

'We are. At least…we were.'

'Were?'

He gave a pained frown as he glanced awkwardly about the drawing room. 'The weather is tolerable for this time of year, do you not think?'

What Arabella thought was that the rakishly handsome Lord Gideon Grayson was avoiding the subject! 'Tolerable.' She nodded coolly. 'Can it be that you and my youngest brother have suffered a disagreement?'

'Not at all,' Lord Grayson denied sharply. 'I— Look, I apologise if my being here is inconvenient.' His expression was anxious as he sat forward in his chair. 'Normally I would not have dreamt of intruding upon a newly married couple in this way. It was only—I felt—'

'Yes?' Arabella prompted.

'Stop browbeating the poor man, Arabella,' Darius drawled as he strolled lazily into the drawing room, his appearance impeccable in a dark green jacket worn over a muted gold brocade waistcoat and snowy white linen, his legs long and muscled in thigh-hugging buff-coloured pantaloons above black brown-topped

Hessians. 'No doubt Sebastian and Gray have fallen out over a woman, and now Gray is too embarrassed to admit to it. It is what we rakes do, you know.' He eyed her sharply and paused beside the tea trolley to pour himself a cup of tea as she made no effort to do so.

It was the first time that Arabella had set eyes on her husband since their disagreement this morning. Disagreement? It could be regarded as much more than a disagreement. The two of them had ended by clearly laying down their rules as regarded the continuation of their marriage!

Even now Arabella could not believe how heatedly they had made love this morning before just as heatedly arguing. Heated on her part, at least; Darius had remained coolly distant throughout. Arabella might feel more inclined to forgive him if he had not…

'Lord Grayson and I were merely engaging in social chitchat,' she dismissed evenly.

'Really?' Darius raised disbelieving brows. 'It sounded distinctly like the Spanish Inquisition to me.'

'You are being ridiculous.' Arabella shot him a venomous glare.

Darius settled himself comfortably in one of the armchairs before stretching his long legs out in front of him to be crossed at his booted ankles. 'A fault of all newly married men, no doubt. Perhaps the reason you have continued to avoid the unenviable state, Gray?' He took a sip of his tea.

Grayson looked more uncomfortable than ever as he obviously sensed the increased tension in the room following Darius's entrance. 'I— Er…'

Darius gave a hard laugh. 'My dear chap, I advise

you not to even attempt an answer; whatever you say is guaranteed to offend either my wife or myself.'

Gray frowned. 'Perhaps in the circumstances it might be better if I were to take my leave of you after all, as soon as we have finished tea.'

'You see what you have done, Arabella?' Darius chided. 'You have made our guest feel unwelcome.'

'*I* have?' She eyed him incredulously.

'There, there, Arabella.' That blue gaze openly jeered at her. 'I am sure Gray perfectly understands that you are not as—as composed as you could be.' He gave the other man a bored glance as he confided, 'Arabella's nerves are understandably still a little jittery from all the preparations and excitement of the wedding.'

In contrast, Darius's own nerves were perfectly calm. With the cold inflexibility of steel, in fact. He and Westlake had just discovered that there had been an un-invited guest in the stables some time during the night. Several of the saddles had been tampered with. Including Grayson's. A fact that seemed to imply the other man's assessment of the situation might after all be the correct one; it had been the two of them who had been responsible for questioning Helena Jourdan following her arrest in the summer, and for ordering the death of her French soldier lover.

The sarcastic pleasantness of Darius's present mood served to hide the fierce anger he was feeling inside. A cold, remorseless anger that promised severe retribution for someone.

'I assure you my nerves are not in the least jittery, Darius.' Arabella answered his previous taunt with sweet insincerity. 'On the contrary, as I mentioned earlier today, I find Lord Grayson's presence a welcome diversion from the tedium of country life.'

'There now, Gray.' Darius's eyes glittered as he looked across the room at the younger man. 'I do not see how you can even *think* of depriving my beautiful wife of your company after she has so eloquently expressed a partiality for it.'

Grayson eyed him warily. 'I am sure Her Grace was only being polite.'

Darius looked across at Arabella between narrowed lids. 'Were you?'

Arabella shifted uncomfortably under that coldly direct gaze, not fooled for a moment by the mildness of Darius's tone; beneath that calm exterior he was obviously furiously angry. With her, no doubt. 'I hope that I am always polite, Darius,' she replied noncommittally.

He gave a hard and humourless laugh. 'Oh, I believe all of the St Claire family can lay claim to being *that*, Arabella—even when they are stabbing you in the back!'

Arabella's eyes widened at the slight. 'You dare to accuse any of my family of such a cowardly act?'

'Nothing so obvious, I assure you, Arabella,' he drawled dismissively.

She bristled with indignation. 'Then what *did* you mean?'

He shrugged. 'Nothing of import.'

'I do not care for your tone, Darius.'

'No?'

'No!'

He gave an uninterested shrug. 'And perhaps I do not care to have you state your preference for another man's company in my own home.'

Arabella stood up abruptly. 'It is *our* home!'

Darius looked up at her coldly. 'As you assured me this morning, only for as long as it suits you.'

Arabella's hand itched to slap the arrogant mockery from his handsome face. 'I have reconsidered, Darius,' she snapped, 'and I have decided that I no longer intend giving you the satisfaction of leaving you.'

'I am glad to hear it.' He took another sip of his cooling tea.

She eyed him sharply; he did not *sound* pleased! 'Are you?'

'Of course.' He sounded bored by the subject. 'Now, perhaps you might benefit from resting in your room before dinner?'

'I am not in the least tired.' Arabella stared down at him in frustration. The only reason she did not give in to the inclination she felt—to knock the cup of tea from Darius's long, elegant hand—was that they had surely already provided enough of a show of marital disharmony in front of Lord Grayson for one day.

'You will have to forgive us, Gray.' Darius turned to the younger man. 'My wife and I have not yet worked out the finer nuances of marriage.' He looked at Arabella. 'My dear, my suggestion that you retire to your bedchamber was my way of stating that I wish for you to leave us now, so that Grayson and I might talk in private.'

Arabella gasped. The insult she had felt at Darius's disparaging remarks concerning her family was now overtaken by how hurt she felt at the coldness of Darius's tone; he could not have stated any more plainly his desire to be rid of her company!

Her cheeks flushed with the humiliation she felt at his dismissal. 'No doubt so that you might reminisce over old times and old mistresses!'

'Or current ones,' Darius pointed out wickedly.

Arabella felt that heated colour leave her cheeks as rapidly as it had entered them. 'How *dare* you?'

'As I recall, Arabella, *you* were the one to introduce the subject,' he pointed out.

Only so that Darius might deny the accusation! She had not expected him to react like that!

'If you will excuse me, Lord Grayson?' Her manner was stilted as she gave him a stiff bow. 'I believe I might go to my room and rest before dinner after all.' She had to escape from this room. Before Darius's attitude forced her to do something they would no doubt both regret.

Although Darius did not look in the least as if he regretted treating her so cruelly in front of a guest. On the contrary, he seemed to emit an icy satisfaction at the thought of her going. Leaving Arabella with no choice but to depart.

'I will see you both at dinner this evening.'

'No doubt,' her husband said as he helped himself to a dainty from the tea tray.

'I shall look forward to it.' Lord Grayson, at least, remembered his manners enough to stand up.

Arabella gave Darius a pointed stare, and received only a challenging one in return as he made no effort to emulate the other man's politeness but instead bit into his chosen creamy confection with obvious enjoyment. Inflicting yet another insult upon Arabella before she turned and left the room with an indignant rustle of her skirts.

How she hated him!

Loathed him!

Detested him!

Desired him still…

Arabella's legs almost failed her as she climbed the wide staircase to her room, necessitating in her having to grasp the dark mahogany banister in order to stop herself from sinking down weakly onto one of the stairs. She breathed deeply in an effort to calm her rapidly beating heart and the trembling of her body.

What sort of man was Darius, that he could make love so heatedly to her earlier this morning and then treat her and her family with such disdain just now?

And what sort of woman was Arabella, that she could still want Darius to make love to her like that again?

Chapter Thirteen

'W̲ere you not…a little hard on her?' Lord Gideon Grayson looked reproving.

'I advise you not to attempt to tell me how to treat my own wife, Gray.' Darius put down the creamy dainty that threatened to choke him if he should attempt to eat another bite. In fact, the single bite he had taken, in an effort to convince Arabella of his uninterest in her or anything she did, was already making him feel ill.

'But—'

'It is for the best, Gray.' Darius stood up restlessly, his expression grim. 'Evidence leads me to believe that someone in my own household is hand-in-glove with the saboteur.' How it galled him to admit it, but he could think of no other explanation for how the stables had been broken into during the night.

The servants at Winton Hall had all been hand-picked by Darius months ago. Their obvious lack of manners showed he had not chosen them for their skills as household servants, but as men and women capable of fighting and thieving. Damn it, even the cook was Westlake's sister, and had once been taken into custody under suspicion of picking people's pockets!

'One of your own servants?' Gray frowned his uncertainty at the claim.

Darius nodded, before going on to explain the break-in of the stables during the night. 'If I am right about it being one of my own servants, then it would be as well that all of them believe I have little interest in my wife.' A nerve pulsed in his tightly clenched jaw at the lie; if Darius became any *more* interested in Arabella then he would have no choice but to take her to bed for a week. Longer! 'The charade I am playing might perhaps succeed in safeguarding her more than I have so far managed to do.' His expression was bleak.

'I can see how you might think that...' Gray still looked troubled. 'But is such a course wise? Are you not seriously in danger of alienating your wife to the point of no return? Your remark about her brothers, for instance, was so far from the truth as to be laughable. Hawk St Claire is a duke and a member of the House, a man much respected and admired. Lucian St Claire is revered as a war hero, and Sebastian proved this summer that he is a man loyal to king and country.'

'I am well aware of all the admirable traits shown by my brothers-in-law!'

Darius was also aware of the risk he was taking with Arabella's affections. If his young wife had ever felt *any* affection for him, that was. Which Darius seriously doubted. Responding to his lovemaking merely showed Arabella's curiosity on the subject, not a personal preference for Darius himself....

'What else do you suggest, Gray?' he demanded as he paced the room impatiently. 'When my promise eight years ago to king and country, as you put it,' he bit out scathingly, 'precludes my revealing the truth to Arabella?'

'Perhaps *I* might have a word with her?'

'You are bound by the same promise,' Darius reminded him harshly. 'We all are, damn it. No.' He ran an agitated hand through his hair. 'For the moment my wife will simply have to go on believing me to be the worst kind of insensitive blackguard.'

Darius would just have to hope and pray that when this mess was finally over it would not be too late to try and salvage something of his marriage....

'Yes?' Arabella did not turn from finishing tidying her appearance in the mirror on her dressing table, but instead glanced at her husband's reflection in that mirror as he leant against the open doorway that connected their two bedchambers.

Far from having forgiven Darius for his rudeness to her earlier, Arabella willed herself not to be affected by how handsome he looked in the candle-light in his dark evening clothes and snowy white linen, with his hair shining a deep gold and his eyes appearing the clear deep blue of a summer's sky.

He straightened, the expression in those deep blue eyes guarded. 'I have brought you a gift.'

Arabella stilled as she frowned her uncertainty. 'Something for me...?'

'A wedding gift.' Darius nodded as he stepped fully into her bedchamber to cross the room in strides as graceful and silent as a cat.

Arabella swallowed hard as he came to stand behind her, overwhelmingly aware of his hard and muscled body. She moistened lips that had become suddenly dry. 'Is it not a little late for that?'

'I sincerely hope not.'

Arabella raised blond brows. 'Why would you want to give me a wedding gift when you never cease reminding me that this marriage was forced upon you by circumstances?'

Darius drew his breath in sharply at the challenge, knowing how well he deserved Arabella's ridicule—and wishing that he did not. Knowing how much he wished things could be different between them. He had hoped that in the privacy of their bedchamber at least, well away from curiously interested eyes, perhaps they could be...

He shook his head at his own maudlin thoughts. 'When you know me better, Arabella, you will know that I never allow myself to be forced into doing anything I do not wish to do.'

'Really?' she said dismissively as she stood up to turn and face him, her expression aloof as she looked down her pert little nose at him. She was wearing a blue high-waisted gown this evening, her breasts full and creamy above the low neckline. She possessed a long and slender neck that, Darius noted with satisfaction, was bare of jewellery.

He reached into his jacket pocket to pull out the huge diamond pendant that hung upon a simple gold chain. 'It is my wish that you wear this tonight.'

Arabella looked down at the heart-shaped diamond pendant where it lay across Darius's callused palm, furious with herself as she felt a sting of tears in her eyes at its simplistic beauty. It was exactly what she would have chosen for herself.

And it was surely what a man would choose to give to the woman he loved...

Except Darius did not love her. He had shown by his treatment of her earlier today during afternoon tea that he never would love her.

'It is my intention to wear my mother's sapphires and diamonds this evening.' She moved deliberately to open her jewel box and take out the diamond-and-sapphire necklace her father had given to her mother—most assuredly with love!—on their tenth wedding anniversary.

She only realised once she held up the jewels in the candle-light how much the sapphires reminded her of the colour of Darius's eyes when he was aroused. And that her new gown was of that same intense colour...

Was Darius aware of it also? The expression she could see in those eyes as he gazed down at her seemed to imply that he was.

Arabella's mouth firmed. 'Perhaps you might give the pendant to Helena Jourdan instead? As an apology for your marriage to me? I am sure that any woman might be persuaded into forgiving you anything when presented with such an expensive bauble.'

Darius's gaze was flinty, his jaw set inflexibly as he laid the diamond pendant down upon her dressing table. 'Just not you?'

'I am not any woman, Darius.' Arabella eyed him scornfully before turning away to view her reflection in the mirror as she raised her arms to fasten the clasp of the glittering sapphire-and-diamond necklace about her throat, all the time aware of a similar glitter in Darius's narrowed blue eyes as he stood behind her.

'No, you most assuredly are *not* just any woman,' he acknowledged harshly. 'What would you say if I were to tell you that Helena Jourdan was not, is not, and will never be my mistress?'

Arabella raised her eyes to meet his reflected gaze. 'I would say you are a liar. Let me go, Darius!' She gasped as his hands came down heavily on her bare shoulders, squirming as his fingers held her in place. She glared furiously at him in the mirror as her efforts to free herself came to nought.

Darius had never regretted more than at that moment the promises he had made eight years ago, and the profligate and rakish reputation he had so deliberately nurtured since.

Until his betrothal to Arabella Darius had had no problem with people believing the gossip whispered about him amongst the ton. He knew that he was considered a rake and a gambler. A man who had been married to an heiress for only one month before she was thrown from her horse and died, leaving Darius in possession of her fortune. The man who had inherited the title of Duke following his nephew's death two years ago at Waterloo and his eldest brother's premature and unexpected death seven months ago. Indeed, Darius had no doubt that it was that very reputation that had caused Hawk St Claire to turn down his offer for Arabella last year!

Darius had been furious at the time, but in view of the fate of the woman whom he *had* married Darius had decided Hawk's refusal had been for the best. He doubted that he could have borne it if it had been Arabella thrown from her horse to her death.

As he could not bear her obvious scorn now... 'Whether you believe me or not, Arabella, Helena Jourdan has *never* been my mistress,' he said evenly.

Her gaze was uncertain as it met his in the mirror. 'Then what is she to you?'

His mouth thinned. 'Nothing.'

'If your conversation with Lord Grayson is to be believed, then the woman has tried to kill you—both of us—on several occasions!'

Darius drew in a sharp breath. 'It is suspected that she might have done so, yes.' He nodded tersely. 'But we have no tangible evidence that she is the one responsible.'

Arabella's eyes widened. 'You mean, there is *more* than one person who wishes you dead?'

He quirked a quizzical brow at her. 'Now that we have added you to that list, you mean?'

Arabella recoiled at the suggestion she had ever wished Darius's death. To have him horse-whipped by one of her brothers, perhaps. Rendered helpless at her feet as he claimed undying love for her. But dead? No, even now, when Arabella felt so hurt and confused by him, she did not wish her husband any real physical harm.

Because she was, after all, in love with him?

It had been a question that had plagued Arabella all day as she paced restlessly in her bedchamber.

Most of the time she was so angry with Darius, for one reason or another, that she could cheerfully strike his arrogantly handsome face. At other times she was so physically aroused by him that she could neither think nor be aware of anything else.

Was that love?

Once again Arabella shied away from giving herself an answer to that question. If she never admitted to having feelings for Darius—even to herself—then perhaps they would not exist!

She shook her head. 'It is surely your own fault if Helena Jourdan's husband also wishes to kill you.'

Darius gave her a considering look. 'Is that the best reason you could come up with for someone wishing to kill me?'

Arabella felt stung by his derision. 'It is one of the reasons, yes.'

'Except that Helena Jourdan is not married.'

Arabella frowned her frustration. 'Then perhaps it is her father, or a brother, or another lover who defends her honour?'

'No father. No brother. No lover, either.' Not any more, Darius inwardly grimaced. Helena Jourdan's French soldier lover had been apprehended and quietly killed two weeks ago, whilst Helena herself was being held in London and questioned by Darius and Gray. It was a death that Darius did not doubt she held him responsible for...

'But earlier I am sure I overheard you and Lord Grayson mention that a man may be involved. Darius!' She gasped as his fingers involuntarily tightened around her shoulders.

'I apologise.' Darius removed his hands altogether to turn away, his expression grim; it seemed Arabella had overheard far too much of his earlier conversation with Gray than was good for her. Neither did their lovemaking after Gray had left them seem to have lessened her memory of that conversation… 'It is time we went down to dinner,' he said curtly. 'Gray will be wondering what has become of us both.'

Arabella's brow darkened with irritation. 'It is totally unacceptable that he should be here at all!'

'I thought you found your sojourn in the country tedious and boring and that his presence relieved that?'

She shot him a reproving glance. 'You know that I only said those things because you annoyed me.'

Darius looked at her. 'So am I to take it that you do *not* find my company tedious and boring, after all?'

'Not all the time, no.' Brown eyes glittered with repressed emotion. 'You can be…amusing when it suits you to be.'

Darius laughed huskily. 'As can you.'

'You—' Arabella drew in a calming breath. 'I wish you would send Lord Grayson away, Darius.'

He sighed. 'I could not be so rude, love.'

'Oh, yes, you could,' she disputed knowingly. 'If it suited you to do so.'

Darius shrugged broad shoulders. 'Then obviously it does not suit me.'

Arabella eyed him frustratedly. 'Perhaps we should make this into a Winton Hall house party? We could invite Hawk and Jane and baby Alexander over from Mulberry Hall. Lucian and Grace from Hampshire? Sebastian and Juliet from Berkshire. The Dowager Duchess from the Dower House. Perhaps your younger brother might even return from the Continent—'

'That is enough, Arabella!' Darius cut in harshly, his eyes glittering in warning. 'Your brothers are once again busy about their own lives,' he said, 'and my sister-in-law Margaret has not yet returned from London. It occurred to me to send her an invitation to join us for dinner this evening,' he added dryly, 'until I remembered that Margaret had said she would stay in town after the wedding, to visit George's lawyer and do a little shopping for Christmas. I thought that you might appreciate some female company to help alleviate the tedium of dining alone with two men whose company you find so boring.'

Arabella did not find Darius's company in the least boring or tedious. The opposite, in fact. As had been her hope when she'd decided to accept Darius's offer, he was far too mercurial in his moods for her ever to be bored in his company. Under other circumstances, she would not find Lord Grayson's company tedious, either. She knew from meeting him in the past that he was an amusing, as well as an entertaining companion with whom to pass the time. Just not days after her wedding to Darius, when she wished to be otherwise occupied…

'In that case perhaps we could invite your brother Francis to come and stay? Having missed the wedding itself, perhaps he would appreciate an invitation to stay at Winton Hall?' She looked a query at him.

Darius looked down his long, arrogant nose at her. 'My brother Francis is not welcome at Winton Hall. Or indeed at any of the Wynter family residences.' His mouth had hardened into a grim line.

Her eyes widened. 'Why not?'

'It is a private family matter, and as such does not concern you.'

Her cheeks flushed with temper. 'I am now part of this family!'

'That does not entitle you to know every family scandal.'

'Why bother to keep that particular one a secret when your own indiscretions are such public knowledge?'

Darious drew in a deep and controlling breath, knowing he had gone as far with this present conversation as he was prepared to go. Further than he had meant to, in fact.

Arabella showed her intelligence in every conversation the two of them had together, and intuition on more than one occasion. If she should once get it into her head to solve the puzzle of Francis's banishment to the Continent almost seven months ago he would be undone… To continue their present conversation would surely only pique that interest even further.

'I could always ask my sister-in-law Grace about him, I suppose.' Once again Arabella displayed her intelligence. 'After all, he is also related to her by marriage, is he not? As are you…'

Darius had momentarily overlooked the fact that the niece of his sister-in-law Margaret had married Arabella's brother Lucian some months ago.

His eyes shot sparks at his recalcitrant wife. 'You will refrain from discussing all private family matters outside of this house!'

'Which means I should invite Lucian and Grace to visit us here sooner rather than later.'

His mouth tightened grimly at Arabella's continued stubbornness. 'Will you just leave the subject be, Arabella?'

'And if I do not?'

Darius drew in a harsh breath. 'I will not allow your interference in matters that do not concern you.'

Discerning the cold determination in Darius's expression, Arabella could not doubt the serious intent of his warning. Even so... 'I do not recall asking your permission,' she pressed.

A nerve pulsed in his tightly clenched jaw. 'Someone should have taken you in hand long ago and put an end to your rebellious ways.'

Arabella gave a humourless smile. 'Perhaps someone did—and failed utterly.'

'*I* would not fail!'

Arabella inwardly quivered at the determination in Darius's expression. A trembling she had no intention of allowing him to see. 'You are right, Darius. It really is time we went downstairs and joined our guest for dinner.'

Darius could hardly conceal his frustration as he glared at her. 'Arabella, why will you not accept that you are meddling in things best left alone?'

'How can I know that when you refuse to discuss them with me?' Her eyes were innocently wide.

An innocence that did not fool Darius for one second as he narrowed his own glacial blue gaze on her. 'Do not attempt to defy me on this matter, Arabella.'

'Oh, I never *attempt* to defy, Darius,' she assured him dryly. 'On the contrary, I have always found it is best to just do it rather than waste precious time arguing about it.'

Given the circumstances, it was not surprising that dinner was a tense and awkward affair, with Westlake stumbling about serving the food with his usual ineptitude—Arabella really would have to talk to Darius at the first opportunity concerning the lack of ability for given tasks in all the servants he employed—and poor Gideon Grayson left to supply the lion's share of the conversation as his host and hostess glowered at each other from either end of the table.

Not that Arabella did not enjoy herself. There was a feeling of intense satisfaction to be found in being able to shake Darius's usual air of mocking amusement at those about him.

An intense and delicious satisfaction that made Arabella slightly regretful when it came time for her to excuse herself from the dinner table so that the two men might enjoy their brandy and cigars.

'As there seems little point in retiring to the drawing room alone to drink my tea, I believe I might go straight upstairs,' she announced as Westlake, belatedly remembering his manners, hurried forward to pull back the chair so that she might rise. 'I will wish you a goodnight, gentlemen.' Arabella deliberately made no attempt to look at her coldly glowering husband and instead bestowed a graciously warm smile on the now standing Gideon Grayson.

Darius rose more slowly to his feet. 'I will join you very shortly.'

'Really?' Her brows arched coolly, despite the underlying threat she heard in Darius's tone. 'I had assumed that you and Lord Grayson would once again discuss…private matters once I had left the room.'

'Let's not embarrass our guest by arguing in front of him for a second time in one day,' Darius drawled dryly, not fooled for a moment by Arabella's supposedly pleasant demeanour, having been left in no doubt throughout dinner that his young wife was still spoiling for a fight.

He should not have reacted so strongly earlier,

Darius now realised, and he would not have done so if Arabella had not touched a little too closely to the truth for comfort when she had threatened to invite Grace and Lucian here, in order to quiz them further concerning the matter of Francis's banishment.

Very few people knew the truth behind Francis's abrupt dismissal from England this past summer. Unfortunately, Lucian was one of them. And possibly his wife too, now. Lucian had assured Darius only days ago as to his silence on the true events behind Francis's banishment earlier this year, but even so it could have been a promise the other man did not feel extended as far as his wife.

Darius had come to the same conclusion concerning his own wife during the excruciatingly long dinner that had just passed. He had all but decided that perhaps he owed it to Arabella to share Francis's behaviour with her, at least. After all, what Francis had done had nothing to do with the life Darius had necessarily led these past eight years. He would be breaking no confidences by sharing it with Arabella.

It might also serve to divert her from pursuing the dangerous subject of Helena Jourdan any further…

'I will join you upstairs shortly,' he repeated mildly.

Arabella eyed him frowningly. 'I assure you that I perfectly understand if you would prefer to do as you did last night and stay downstairs and talk to Lord Grayson.'

'Ah, what it is to have an understanding wife,' Darius drawled. 'Be sure to ascertain that it is a quality your own wife possesses, Gray, when and if you should decide to marry!'

'What a flatterer you are, Darius,' his wife came back sharply.

'I only state the truth, Arabella.' His gaze easily met the challenge he could see in the dark glitter of her eyes. 'A patient and understanding wife is surely to be valued above—'

'Diamonds?' Arabella put in tauntingly.

Darius's mouth tightened as he recalled the way in which Arabella had refused his gift earlier this evening. Forced to sit through this long and boring dinner, Darius had amused himself by imagining Arabella wearing *only* that diamond necklace later tonight when he made love to her…

'Most assuredly.' He gave her a mocking bow.

Arabella's mouth thinned. 'I have always preferred emeralds to diamonds.'

Darius raised one arrogant brow. 'And yet this evening you chose to wear sapphires…'

She shot him an irritated glare. 'I have no idea why."

'Perhaps they reminded you of my eyes…?'

Her scathing snort was less than elegant. 'I fail to see the connection.'

'Little liar!'

Arabella glanced pointedly in Gideon Grayson's direction. 'We are once again embarrassing our guest, Darius.'

Darius gave an unconcerned shrug. 'Leave a candle alight for me, love.'

Her chin rose. 'I believe I am still so tired from our travels that I may fall straight to sleep as soon as my head touches the pillow!'

Darius gave a soft laugh. 'In that case I shall very much enjoy waking you up again.'

Arabella could find no suitable reply to this comment, instead addressing Westlake as he hurriedly crossed the room with a candle to light her way. 'Please inform Mary that I will not be needing her this evening,' she instructed the butler, and he held the door open for her to leave; if she had to turn Darius away from her bedchamber then Arabella certainly did not need her maid as witness to it!

How dared Darius call her 'love' in that casual way? As an announcement that it was his intention to make love to her, it was far from subtle.

Perhaps if she really *were* Darius's love she would not mind the endearment so much?

No, she would not mind at all. In fact, she might like it more than she ought! But, as that was never likely to happen, it simply irritated her to hear Darius address her with such insincere familiarity.

Her husband was an unrepentant rake who stead-fastly refused to explain another woman's role in his life, and if he thought for one moment that it was Arabella's intention to go up the stairs and meekly await him to join her in her bedchamber, then he was going to be disappointed.

Arabella held the lighted candle aloft as she entered her bedchamber, turning to close the door behind her before she felt a silencing hand placed across her mouth at the same time as an arm curved in restraint about her throat...

Chapter Fourteen

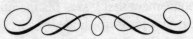

'Arabella?'

Darius was not the least surprised to enter his wife's bedchamber some twenty minutes later to find that she had not left the requested candle alight for him. But the moonlight shone so brightly through the window, the curtains having not been drawn, that it was possible for him to see that the bed was empty and the bedclothes unruffled—evidence that she did not await him there, either.

'Let us not be childish about this, Arabella.' Darius gave a weary sigh as he moved to open the door into her dressing room; it had been a long and tiring day, and the last thing he wanted was yet another fight with his wife.

Where was the peace and ease one was supposed to find in marriage, he wondered ruefully? The calm? The wifely concern? The warmth and affection?

If Darius had truly required those things from his wife then he should not have married a woman as fiery and rebellious as Arabella St Claire!

Darius came to a halt as he entered the dressing room and found that also empty of her presence. Had he so infuriated her earlier that she had decided to leave him after all? Despite his warnings that he would come after her? Or possibly *because* of his warnings that he would come after her?

He moved back wearily into the bedchamber to sit down upon the bedside. Where would she have gone? How would she have left? The answer to those two questions was all too obvious; Mulberry Hall, Hawk's home, was but a short horse-ride into the neighbouring county of Gloucestershire.

Damn it!

Darius's hands clenched into fists at his sides. He was going to throttle Arabella—strangle her with his own bare hands when he caught up with her! How dared she just take off into the night in this way, leaving no word as to her destination?

Arabella would dare do anything she chose!

The question was, did Darius follow her tonight or should he wait until morning? His instinct was to go after her now—and when he caught up with her he would do much worse than throw her across his knee and paddle her backside! That was his initial instinct. Inner caution advised against it. Warned against the wisdom of following her until his own temper had cooled. If it ever did!

Darius dropped back onto the pillows to stare up at the pale canopy above the bed, groaning as he realised that her leaving him was all his own fault. If he had but explained Francis's banishment to her, given her at least some of his confidence, then she might not have felt compelled to take the drastic action of leaving him only days after their wedding.

He stilled as he smelt her perfume on the pillow beneath him, turning his cheek to breathe it in; erotic femininity overlaid by a light floral scent. Darius knew he would always and for ever associate it with Arabella.

His anger returned with a vengeance and he sat up abruptly, his expression grim as he looked about the empty bedchamber. Damn it, how *dared* she do this to him?

Then Darius frowned darkly as his gaze was caught by the moonlight reflecting off something that glittered and sparkled near the leg of the dressing table. What was that?

He stood up to cross the bedchamber on soft and silent booted feet before bending to pick up the object, recognising it instantly as the sparkling sapphire-and-diamond necklace that Arabella had worn earlier instead of the one he had given her. A necklace that Arabella had informed him had belonged to her mother….

Even with only the moonlight to see by Darius could tell that the clasp of the necklace had been broken rather than carefully, lovingly unfastened.

Darius accepted that Arabella had been angry enough to have accidentally broken the fastening of the necklace as she removed it, but to leave it discarded upon the floor was surely not something she would ever have done to a piece of jewellery she valued so affectionately.

Darius's fingers tightened about the necklace and he looked up sharply, his narrowed gaze grimly searching the shadows of the bedchamber. All was tidy—not a comb or a glove out of place…

Not so. There was something else on the floor, near the door. Something Darius had missed stumbling over when he entered the bedchamber because it had been pushed aside by the opening of the door.

Darius placed the necklace down distractedly on the dressing table and then quickly lit the candles in the candelabra on the bedside table, his frown darkening thunderously as he crossed the room and saw that the object on the floor was the single candle Arabella had carried upstairs earlier, in order to light her way.

Another quick glance about the room showed that the gown Arabella had worn this evening was not in evidence, either. Which it surely would have been if she had prepared for bed without the help of her maid. Darius seriously doubted that the blue silk evening gown was what she would have chosen to wear on a cold midnight ride on horseback.

Darius picked up the glowing candelabra to carry it through to the adjoining dressing room, flinging open the doors to the wardrobe to hold the candle aloft as he searched quickly through the many gowns hanging there for the blue one that Arabella had been wearing this evening. Searching a second time, just to make sure.

It was not there!

Darius stepped back abruptly, his hands shaking slightly as he accepted the possibility—the absolute horror—that Arabella had not departed Winton Hall voluntarily!

Arabella's initial fear at having something dark thrown over her head so that she was unable to see, before being dragged from her bedchamber along the hallway to what she believed was the servants' stairs at the back of the house, and then outside into the icy cold wind—all totally against her will as she repeatedly tried to kick her assailant—had turned to indignant disbelief in the last hour or so.

Once outside, Arabella had been tied up and thrown down into what she was sure was the straw of an empty stall in the stables. Several of the horses who shared her captivity had given her enquiringly friendly snorts as they sensed her presence.

She was trussed up like a chicken ready for roasting, with her hands tied behind her back and her ankles bound together, and the cowl had been raised slightly and a piece of rag tied tightly about her mouth before she was once again plunged into darkness. Arabella had been left to lie on the mound of what she could only hope was *clean* straw. Several pieces of it stuck into her uncomfortably in various places through the thin silk of her gown.

Why she should have been dragged from her bedchamber and then abandoned here in the stables was totally beyond her comprehension. But the why was not really important at the moment; it was when Darius would decide to come looking for her that concerned her the most!

Surely he must have gone to her bedchamber by now and realised that she was not there? Unless, of course, Darius had taken her at her word after all and decided to let her sleep undisturbed tonight? It would be just her luck if he should choose tonight of all nights to show her some husbandly consideration!

Arabella stilled, her thoughts frozen, as she heard the

sound of voices outside the stables. Was it her abductor and a cohort returning? Or could it be that Darius had come looking for her at last? Until she had confirmation one way or the other Arabella had no intention of drawing attention to herself.

'I tell you, Gray, we have searched the house from top to bottom and back again, which means Jourdan has to have taken Arabella away somewhere!' Darius rasped harshly as moved across the cobbled yard towards the stables with the younger man trailing behind him.

'We do not know that for certain,'

'I am well aware of that!' Darius turned on the other man fiercely, his eyes glittering dangerously in the moonlight. 'I warn you, if she has harmed one hair on Arabella's head—'

'There is no way Helena Jourdan could have kidnapped Arabella on her own,' Gray reasoned, for what had to be the dozenth time in the past hour. 'Your wife is young and healthy.' He grimaced awkwardly at the unflattering description. 'She is also not a woman to be taken against her will without protest.'

Darius smiled grimly at how true a statement was that. That smile faded as he recalled the broken necklace and dropped candle in Arabella's bedchamber. As he thought of the last frantic hour of searching the house for her. Unsuccessfully.

'I have already told you that someone in the house has to be helping Jourdan.' He glowered at the thought of any of the people he had hired to protect them actually being involved in such treachery. Cut-throats and thieves they might be, but after employing them for many months Darius had believed them to be loyal cut-throats and thieves.

'Riding off into the night without any idea of your destination has to be the height of folly.' Gray followed him into the stables. 'Much better to wait until morning and see if we cannot find a trail to follow. You—'

'Quiet, Gray!' Darius ordered as he stilled, listening intently. 'Did you hear that?'

'Hear what? I—' Gray broke off again as there came the sound of a second muted thud. 'I heard it that time.' He nodded. 'One of the horses moving, perhaps?'

'Perhaps. Perhaps not!' Darius bit out as another, louder thud was heard.

'Careful, Darius,' Gray warned softly, and he raised the pistol he carried.

Darius's expression was watchful as he raised a similar pistol. One he had carried about the house with him for the last hour as he searched from attic to cellar in case Arabella was being held prisoner somewhere. All to no avail. The house was empty of all sign of her. Only the broken necklace Darius had placed in the pocket of his waistcoat confirmed his belief that she could not have left Winton Hall willingly.

'It came from over there.' He pointed the pistol in the direction of the furthest stall. 'Light one of the lamps and bring it with you,' Darius instructed the other man tersely, waiting until Gray had done so before moving silently down the length of the stables.

The lit candle inside the lamp wavered behind Darius in the darkness, sending eerie shadows down the stables and onto the back wall, giving him the appearance of a monster ten feet tall.

His movements were soft and stealthy, his heart pounding loudly in his chest, and he raised his pistol in readiness as he rounded the end stall—and saw the tiny figure in a blue silk dress lying in the straw, hands and feet tied, face covered by a dark sack.

'Arabella!' Darius hurried forward to pull the sack from Arabella's head—only to find himself the focus of a pair of angry brown eyes that glared up at him indignantly from beneath the untidy tumble of her golden curls.

Darius ignored that glare as he threw his pistol down in the straw before pulling his wife up into his arms. 'My God, Arabella!' He crushed her thankfully against his chest.

Arabella allowed herself to fall into that comforting embrace for several seconds, so relieved to see Darius again that she happily ignored the discomfort of her tied hands and feet and the horrible gag across her mouth.

Except Darius continued to hold her in his crushing embrace long after she had ceased her trembling. 'Mmumph!' she finally muttered frowningly against the suffocating material of his jacket. 'Mariush, unnie ne!'

'What, love?' He moved back slightly to look at her.

'Unnie ne!' she repeated around the confining gag.

Darius frowned darkly. 'I'm sorry, love, I cannot under—'

'I believe your wife wishes for you to untie her, Darius,' another voice suggested dryly.

Arabella looked up to see Lord Gideon Grayson leaning against the wall of the stall. 'Neth!' she encouraged impatiently before turning back to her husband. 'Unnie ne, Mariush!'

'Oh, God…' Darius groaned as he realised what an idiot he was being; of *course* she wished to be untied. He had been so relieved to find her, apparently unharmed, that he simply hadn't given a thought to untying her. He hurried to do so now, removing the gag from about her mouth first.

'Well, at least *one* of you has some intelligence!' Arabella rebuked the instant her mouth was free. 'Honestly, Darius.' She gave a disgusted shake of her head as she glared up at him. 'How could you not have realised that I needed to be untied?'

Her curls were in complete disarray, there was a smudge of dirt on one of her cheeks, her lips were slightly swollen and red from the piece of material tied about her mouth, and there were pieces of straw struck to her gown. To Darius, however, she had never looked more beautiful.

Although her ordeal did not seem to have affected the sharpness of her tongue!

Darius gripped her shoulders. 'What happened, Arabella? How did you get out here? Did you see who did this to you?'

'Could you finish untying me so that we might go back into the house before I answer any of your questions, Darius?' She looked up at him imploringly. 'I have been out here for some time dressed only in my gown, and I am so very cold.' As if to prove her statement she began to shake uncontrollably.

As reaction to her ordeal began to set in, Arabella was not sure whether that trembling was from the cold or the relief of being rescued at last. The latter, she thought.

She was barely aware of Darius untying her hands and feet before he rose to lift her up into his arms. 'I am perfectly capable of walking,' she protested awkwardly.

'I am fully aware of all you are capable of doing,' he replied, his eyes glittering silver in the lamplight. 'For once in your life will you just be silent and allow someone else to take care of you?'

Arabella was instantly cowed by the obvious fierceness of his anger; Darius looked perfectly capable of wringing someone's neck at this moment—and for once it did not appear to be her own!

'I suggest you stay here and check out the rest of the stables, Gray,' Darius instructed the younger man, before turning to stride down the stables with Arabella held securely in his arms.

She was glad of those arms about her as Darius stepped outside into the cold and windy night. She had overheard one of the servants predicting this morning that there would be snow before the night was out, and from the icy chill in the air she could well believe it.

She closed her eyes and snuggled deeper into his embrace as the warmth emanating from his body began to melt some of the chill that seemed to go right through to her bones. She had absolutely no idea who had abducted her. Or why. She was just pleased to be safe once again. So much so that she could feel the prick of hot tears behind her closed eyelids.

She must not cry. It would be most unbecoming of a duchess to show such weakness. For Arabella St Claire—no, *Wynter*!—to show such weakness.

Even so, to her mortification, Arabella felt the hot

burn of tears as they began to cascade unchecked down her cheeks.

Darius's arms tightened about her as he entered the house and saw the wet tracks of tears falling down the pallor of her cheeks. 'Bring some brandy into the Blue Salon, man,' he told the hovering Westlake before taking Arabella into the room where they had made love only that morning.

The heated fierceness of their lovemaking seemed so long ago now, and Darius's emotions were not in the least carnal as he laid her gently down upon the chaise before sitting down beside her to take both her cold little hands into his own and trying to instil some warmth into their chill. And all the time the tears continued to trail down through the dirty smudges upon Arabella's cheeks, as evidence of the fright she had so recently suffered.

Darius's mouth thinned grimly as he thought of the things he would like to do to the person who had taken her. 'Did you see who did this to you?' he asked again.

'No.' She released one of her hands, attempting to wipe the tears from her cheeks but only succeeding in smearing those dirty smudges further. 'He attacked me from behind. Put a hand over my mouth and an arm about my throat.' She shuddered delicately. 'I was so frightened, Darius,' she admitted shakily as she looked up at him with huge brown, tear-wet eyes. 'So very, very frightened!' She sat up to throw herself against his chest, fingers clinging tightly to his waistcoat as the tears fell in earnest.

Darius's thoughts were murderous as he held her tightly in his arms and rested his cheek against the softness of her hair. Arabella always gave the impression of independence. Of being able to take care of herself and needing nothing and no one. Most especially not a man to take care of her. The fact that she sobbed so brokenly against his chest now told him just how very frightened she must have been earlier tonight. How frightened she still was.

He glanced up as Westlake quietly entered the salon with a tray containing the decanter of brandy and two glasses. His expression was telling as he gave the other man a fierce glance.

Westlake's face was just as grimly drawn as he glanced down at the sobbing Arabella in Darius's arms before giving a firm nod. Telling Darius that, although she had only been at Winton Hall a matter of days, she had nonetheless managed to creep into the affections of the hardened pugilist. Reassuring Darius that Westlake, like himself, would leave no stone unturned in his search for her abductor.

Darius reached down to put Arabella away from him before he stood up to pour brandy into the two glasses, allowing Arabella to take a reviving sip from her own glass before questioning her again. 'You must have seen something, Arabella.' He frowned. 'Could you tell if it was a man or a woman who—?'

'It was a man, of course.' She looked up at him indignantly over the rim of her glass. 'I would not have been taken at all if it had been a woman.' Her free hand clenched into a fist at her side.

Darius did not doubt her ability to defend herself for a moment. Unfortunately, the fact that she believed her abductor to be a man did not help in the least in identifying him. It could have been Francis, of course. But, as Darius had told Gray earlier, it could just as easily have been a man working for Helena Jourdan. Someone in his own household, who could easily get in and out without suspicion…

Darius's mouth tightened. 'Do you remember anything about this man? Was he tall or short? Fat or thin? Did he have a distinctive smell of some kind?' It was a sad fact of life that servants did not wash as often as they ought.

Arabella took another sip of the warming brandy before closing her eyes as she tried to recall in detail those few moments in her bedroom when she had had that hand placed over her mouth and the arm about her throat. 'He was tall, I think. As he stood behind me his arms came up easily over my shoulders to hold me so that I could neither move nor shout for help. Neither fat nor thin, I would say, but muscled—like you,' she continued. 'As to smell? I *do* recall something… Something slightly floral, I think. Which is no help at all.' She gave a disgusted shake of her head as she opened her eyes again. 'That could be either a man or a woman.'

'Not quite, love,' Darius drawled. 'Did the muscled chest have any breasts upon it?'

Colour warmed her cheeks as she answered. 'No.'

'A man, then.' Darius nodded his satisfaction. 'The jacket of the arms that came about your shoulders—was it made of a soft and expensive material, or something rough, like a labourer or servant might wear?'

'It was…soft.' Arabella nodded eagerly as she recalled the fabric. 'Like a velvet or fine wool.'

'Good.' Darius praised her with a small smile. 'Did he speak at all? Even once?'

'I am afraid not.' Arabella sighed her disappointment before taking another distracted sip of the reviving brandy. 'There is one thing that puzzles me, though…'

'Yes?'

'Why do you suppose that someone went to all the trouble of abducting me from my bedchamber only to leave me trussed up like a chicken in the stables?'

Once again Arabella showed the intelligence that Darius both applauded and feared. He could not have borne to be married to a stupid woman, but her obvious intelligence was making it very hard for him to continue hiding the truth from her.

Recalling his earlier decision to tell Arabella about his brother Francis, Darius knew that, with her abduction tonight, the time had come to confide *that* truth to her, at least….

Chapter Fifteen

Arabella held out her glass for Darius to refill it with brandy even as she stared up at him in disbelief for the things he had just related to her. 'You are saying that Francis was responsible for the death of both your first wife *and* your brother George?' she repeated breathlessly.

Her husband looked severe. 'That he caused Sophie to fall from her horse to her death and George to have a fatal seizure of the heart? Yes, that is exactly what I am saying, Arabella.'

She stared up at him wide-eyed. 'I— But— You—'

'I am well aware that most of Society believes *me*— to be guilty of killing my wife—as Francis intended that they should—and a few even whisper that I had a hand in causing George's death too,' Darius said simply. 'They are wrong.' His arrogantly handsome face hardened noticeably as he looked down at her in challenge.

Arabella took another hasty sip of brandy, wondering if it could be the alcohol, along with her earlier ordeal, that was causing her to have hallucinations. Darius could not *really* have just informed her that his own brother had maliciously killed two people and deliberately implicated Darius as being responsible for those deaths.

People—*gentlemen*—did not just go around randomly killing other people….

But of course they did! For years gentlemen of the ton had been known to 'go abroad for their health' after they had committed some crime or other punishable by law. Had not Arabella herself made some such teasing remark to Darius when she'd learnt of Francis Wynter's banishment to the Continent?

'*You* were wrong, Arabella,' Darius added softly.

Arabella looked at him from beneath lowered lashes, feeling guilty as she recalled that in a fit of temper she had more than once accused Darius of being involved in the death of his wife.

Yet since coming to know Darius better—since becoming his wife, since making love with him—Arabella had known there had to be some other explanation for those rumours. She could no longer believe Darius guilty of killing anyone, but she had not dreamt the true explanation would somehow involve Darius's younger brother!

She moistened dry lips. 'It has been some time now since I believed you capable of doing anything like that.'

'Oh?'

'Yes.' Arabella was not in the least daunted by the disbelief she could read in Darius's expression. 'Since our marriage I have come to realise that you are every bit as arrogant as my own brothers, and that if you had truly killed someone then you would feel no qualms about admitting you had done so.'

Darius raised an eyebrow. 'Even at the risk of imprisonment or worse?'

'Yes.'

'I am unsure as to whether that is a compliment or yet another of your insults!' Darius's mouth twisted ruefully.

'It is a simple statement of truth,' Arabella assured him briskly. 'You say it was always Francis's intention that you be thought responsible for the deaths?'

'Yes.' Darius sighed heavily. 'I realised how neatly that guilt was to be laid at my feet last summer, when it became obvious that Francis intended to kill me too and make it look as if I had taken my own life because I could no longer live with the guilt of what I had done.'

Arabella gasped. 'That is truly terrible! He is a monster, Darius! How could you have simply let him escape to the Continent? Tacitly accept the blame for the death of your wife and brother when the guilt really lay elsewhere?'

'He is my *brother*, Arabella.'

'He is a *murderer*!' she retorted hotly.

'Yes.' Darius frowned darkly.

'And now you think he is back in England and once again attempting to kill you?'

'Perhaps,' Darius allowed. 'Which is why we have to now discuss why his actions, both past and present, are of import to you.'

'To me?' Arabella echoed sharply.

'You are now my wife,' he pointed out gently.

'I fail to see what that has to do with—' She broke off, her eyes widening even as her face paled. 'You are believed guilty of those two crimes because the death of your first wife left you in possession of her fortune, and the death of your eldest brother left you as heir to a dukedom…' She spoke softly, deep in thought, for the moment ignoring the look of distaste upon Darius's arrogantly handsome face. 'When in reality the fact that your first wife was already dead when you became Duke of Carlyne—'

'*Conveniently* dead, remember?' her husband drawled dryly.

'Stop it, Darius!' Arabella gave him an irritated frown as he reminded her of her own accusation.

'I apologise.' He grimaced ruefully. 'Please proceed.'

Arabella shot him a narrow-eyed glance. 'Because you had been widowed by the time George died, you had no wife with whom you could provide a legitimate heir. And so if you were also to meet an accidental death then Francis would inherit the title…'

Darius revealed none of his admiration for his wife as he looked at her from beneath hooded lids. Which was not to say he did not admire her—very much. In only a matter of seconds, it seemed, she had managed to grasp the motivation behind Francis's causing the death of two completely innocent people. For also, possibly, being the cause of the most recent 'accidents' involving Arabella and Darius.

'Until you remarried you were not in danger,' she continued slowly. 'But now our marriage once again allows for the eventual appearance of a legitimate heir…'

'I am not sure that I altogether like your repeated references to a "legitimate" heir, Arabella,' Darius said. 'I have already assured you that to my knowledge, I have no illegitimate heirs, either!'

Once again she felt the warmth enter her cheeks. 'It was only a figure of speech, Darius.'

'One I do not care for,' he muttered.

'You are grasping at irrelevancies—'

'It is *not* irrelevant to me!'

'Very well.' Arabella gave a cool nod. 'Is the rest of my theory a factual one?'

She could see that Darius's jaw was clenched and his teeth gritted as he obviously fought back his temper. Although why he should be so annoyed by it Arabella had no idea; Darius's numerous affairs over the previous ten years had become legendary—so was it not logical to assume that there might have been one or two unwelcome consequences to those alliances?

'It is,' he said curtly.

'Why did you tell me—? Why did you deliberately lead me to believe that you were responsible for Sophie's death?' She eyed him reprovingly.

'Because I *am* responsible,' Darius snarled. 'If I had not married Sophie then Francis would not have felt the need to be rid of her.'

'That does *not* make you responsible—'

'I disagree,' he cut in, that coldness back in his expression. 'I did not know it at the time, but I placed Sophie in danger just by marrying her.'

Arabella eyed him guardedly. 'You have already indicated to me that you were not in love with her. Why not?' She drew her breath in sharply, uncertain whether she would be able to withstand hearing that Darius *had*, in fact, been in love with his first wife after all…

'We…respected each other for the honesty of our…needs.' Darius's jaw was set tensely.

'I do not understand.'

Darius placed his clenched hands behind his back. 'It was a marriage of convenience. Sophie wished for a title, and I was obviously in need of her fortune.'

Arabella frowned.

Darius looked rueful. 'Unpleasant, is it not?'

It had not been a love-match, certainly, but many a match was made amongst the ton for far lesser reasons. Except… 'Was it for financial gain that you also offered for *me* last year?'

Darius lowered heavy lids to hide the expression in his eyes. 'I do not believe this conversation to be of any relevance to the here and now.'

'It is relevant to *me*!' Arabella insisted.

'Why is it?' Darius eyed her quizzically. 'What do you wish me to say, Arabella? What do you wish to hear? That I offered for you prior to offering for Sophie because I had need of *your* fortune? Or that I offered for you because I have loved you, been obsessed with you, since the moment I first set eyes on you?'

Arabella felt a painful twisting in her chest. 'We both know that the latter is not true.'

'Then it must be the first, must it not?' Darius rasped harshly.

Arabella's heart felt heavy. 'You are right. This conversation is not helping our present situation.' She drew herself up proudly. 'If my abductor tonight *was* Francis, then why do you suppose he only took me from my bed-chamber before leaving me tied up in the stables? Surely the death of a second wife in little over a year would have sealed your guilt in the eyes of the law, as well as the ton?'

Darius should have felt relieved at this sudden return to the events of this evening, but what he really felt was a cold and icy shiver down the length of his spine at the thought of Arabella being at Francis's questionable mercy. 'Perhaps he did it to show me that he could?'

He had thought that by banishing Francis to the Continent he had solved the dilemma of his younger brother's despicable actions. But these last few days of 'accidents', to Arabella, as well as himself, and then her senseless abduction, served to convince Darius that if Francis were the one responsible for these things then the mental sickness that so obviously held him in its grip must be worsening; his brother was becoming a danger to himself, as well as to others.

Unless, as Grayson preferred to believe, Francis was not the one to blame, but rather it was the vengeful Helena Jourdan?

Darius had to admit that the fact that Arabella had been taken from her bedchamber this evening to be left in the stables, tied up but unharmed, did not seem like something that Francis would have done. Surely once Francis had got his hands on Arabella he would have arranged for her to die whilst he had the chance?

'Perhaps he did,' Arabella agreed distractedly now. 'But just because Francis is your brother it does not seem sufficient reason to me for you to continue to allow the ton to believe that you are the one guilty of these awful deeds!' She looked up at him searchingly.

His mouth twisted ruefully. 'Believe me, Arabella, my reputation is well able to withstand the scandal.'

'But—'

'It really is better left as it is,' Darius insisted firmly.

'Better for whom, exactly?' she shot back.

'For everyone.' His expression was bleak. 'Have you forgotten the existence of my sister-in-law, Margaret?'

Ah. The Dowager Duchess of Carlyne. George's widowed wife.

Arabella's gaze sharpened. 'You prefer that she continues to believe that *you* rather than Francis may be guilty of killing her husband?'

Darius stood up impatiently. 'Margaret does not believe me responsible for killing anyone.'

'I appreciate that she has remained here at the Dower House since her husband died, but surely once she returned to town for our wedding she would have heard the gossip about you.'

'If she did then she will have dismissed it,' Darius said, his gaze glacial. 'My sister-in-law knows me, you see, Arabella. She knows unequivocally that I would never have harmed George in any way. He was my brother, Arabella.' His voice deepened emotionally. 'I have already explained that he was older than me by twenty years and more. What I did not tell you is that he and Margaret effectively became parents to Francis and myself after our father died. We grew up here with their own son, Simon, and we were all treated exactly the same by them. As such, I loved both Margaret and George. I deeply respected them, and would never, ever have wished George harm. Margaret may very well have heard the gossip whilst in town for our wedding.' His expression was grim. 'But I assure you that she will have dismissed those rumours as the mere tittle-tattle that they are.'

Arabella cheeks flushed uncomfortably as she

heard the underlying accusation in Darius's tone. 'But the truth would exonerate you completely in the eyes of Society—'

'I do not give *that*—' he snapped his finger and thumb together dismissively '—for what Society thinks of me!'

'And my family? Should *they* not be told the truth?' Arabella looked up at him in frustration.

Darius looked haughty. 'Why?'

'Because—well, because—'

'Because you do not want them to think badly of your husband?' he taunted. 'Or because you no longer want them to think badly of *you* for marrying the man Society believes me to be?'

Arabella flinched. 'You are deliberately twisting my words, Darius.'

'Do you not think that Margaret has already suffered enough, with the death of her only son two and a half years ago, followed by that of her husband but seven months ago? What good would it do now to start the gossip all over again by publicly claiming my innocence of any wrongdoing? For Margaret to learn that, although George was ill, he still need not have died when he did? That but for Francis's actions she would almost certainly not be alone now and widowed?'

Once again Arabella felt the prick of tears behind her lids as she thought of all that Margaret Wynter had suffered.

Her expression softened as she looked up at her husband. 'Why do you choose to keep your kindness to your sister-in-law, your love and loyalty for your family, hidden behind a social mask of arrogance and coldness?'

'Because I *am* cold and arrogant, damn it!' Darius glared down at her fiercely. 'The fact that I choose to avoid even more of a family scandal by not revealing the truth does not make me any less the selfish man Society believes me to be.'

Arabella knew Darius was often arrogant and mocking. That he could be cold and hard, too. But he was *not* selfish. Far from it.

Once again Darius seemed to have overlooked the fact that she had three older brothers who were just as outwardly arrogant, and who could also be cold and hard. But as their sister, Arabella knew there was so much more to them than the faces they chose to show to Society.

Just as there was so much more to her husband....

Darius's determination to protect Margaret Wynter from the truth more than proved that. Making her curious as to what else he chose to keep hidden. And why...

'No,' she accepted softly. 'But your kindness as regards your sister-in-law does allow for there being another, softer side to your nature that you choose not to share with Society.'

Darius grimaced. 'Arabella, please do not attempt to bestow virtues on me where none exist.'

Was that what she was doing? Perhaps. And yet...

'As for your own family being privy to the truth,' Darius continued, 'I believe you will find that Lucian, at least, knows I am not guilty of killing anyone.'

Arabella gave him a startled glance. '*Lucian* does?'

Darius had meant only to reassure her, but as he saw the way her eyes darkened with suspicion he accepted that he would have to share *all* the events of seven months ago with her.

'Grace is Margaret's niece, and she and Lucian were here at Winton Hall in April when I confronted Francis,' he explained. 'Lucian is sworn to secrecy over the matter, but…' He gave a rueful shrug. 'I doubt, as with most men, he has managed to keep all of the truth from his own wife.'

'Can that be the reason, do you suppose, that Lucian did not disapprove of our marriage?'

'Perhaps.'

'Only perhaps?' she teased.

Darius shrugged taut shoulders. 'Lucian and I have been acquaintances for many years. He and my nephew Simon were at school together. As such, Lucien stayed here often at Winton Hall when we were all children. We have also passed many an evening together at our clubs, or elsewhere, since we became adults,' he added dryly.

She had no wish to know the details of this 'elsewhere'—either in regard to Darius or her brother! 'In other words, even if Lucian had not been present last April when you confronted Francis, my brother knows you well enough to realise you could not have been responsible for killing either Sophie or George?'

'As I have said, Arabella, do not bestow virtues on me where none exist!' Darius insisted. 'I assure you I am more than capable of killing if I feel that any member of my family, or myself, is being threatened.'

Arabella felt a shiver down the length of her spine as she saw the icy determination in his expression. 'Perhaps we should not discuss this any further tonight?' She stood up to cross the room to his side, the slenderness of her body almost touching his much harder one.

'I need you to hold me, Darius,' she encouraged gruffly. 'To hold me close so that I know I am once again safe.'

Darius knew he was lost the moment he looked down into the depths of her warm brown eyes. Her gaze was both direct and vulnerable—a combination guaranteed to captivate. And it certainly did captivate Darius, ensnaring him into experiencing an instant aching sensuality that made even continuing to breathe difficult.

Arabella's lips were so full and pink, so soft and succulent, and the swell of her breasts moved gently above the low neckline of the blue silk gown as she breathed shallowly. Expectantly. As if waiting for, anticipating the intimacy that would surely follow.

Darius's gaze moved to the pale creaminess of her throat. Her pulse was a wild flutter just beneath the surface of her smooth and silky skin, that same pulse beating at the delicacy of her temple as his gaze moved slowly across her face. Even as he looked at Arabella her lips parted expectantly, a pouting encouragement that instantly caused his thighs to harden.

'If I were to hold you now, I cannot guarantee that is all I would do.' His voice sounded harsh in the tense and expectant silence that now surrounded them.

Her answer was to move closer still, an inviting smile curving those full and swollen lips as she did so. It was a warm and totally trusting smile that cut right to the heart of him.

'You have already been through so much tonight, Arabella, and I may not be able to be as gentle with you as you need me to be,' he warned her as his hands reached out to grasp the bare tops of her arms to hold her slightly away from him.

She had suffered a terrifying ordeal this evening, but Darius knew that he felt that fear on her behalf no less sharply. As such, his own emotions were raw and fierce, and he was not sure he would be able to control those emotions if he took her into his arms.

Once the dropped candle and broken necklace had convinced him that she had not left her bedchamber willingly, Darius knew he had behaved like a madman as he'd searched the house from top to bottom in an effort to find her. That heated anger had turned to an icy fury in his chest the moment he'd realised she was no longer in the house, but somewhere outside in the darkness, most probably the prisoner of someone who wished to do her harm. At the very least in the power of someone who thought to wound Darius by taking her from him.

To now have her back, obviously shaken but un-harmed, was almost more than he could bear, and if he started making love to her he knew that he was in danger of losing all restraint. Of possibly frightening her with the depth of his need to possess her in an effort to keep her safe from further harm.

She shook her head now. Several of her silky curls had fallen loose about her shoulders during her captivity. 'It is not gentleness I require from you tonight, Darius.'

His breath caught sharply. 'Then…what?'

The boldness of her gaze met his unflinchingly. 'I wish to *feel*, Darius. To experience…everything. Every kiss and every caress.' She moved to press the softness of her body against him, her breasts a voluptuous crush against his chest. 'I want to feel all of those things and know that I am truly still alive and safe in your arms.'

A nerve pulsed in his clenched jaw. 'You may find yourself less safe with me than you would wish!'

She looked totally confident. 'I do not believe you would ever do anything that might hurt me.' She lifted one of her hands to trail her fingertips down the hard hollows of his cheek. 'Take me upstairs and make love to me, Darius. Please!'

He swallowed convulsively, knowing he was not strong enough to withstand her pleading. Yet also knowing, no matter what the cost to himself, that he would do everything in his power to show her the gentleness she needed from him.

He swung her up into his arms and carried her out into the hallway—to find Gideon Grayson standing there, talking to Westlake. Arabella's arms tightened about his neck and she buried her face against the hardness of his chest as she also saw the two men. The fierce expression on Darius's face was warning enough for neither man to attempt any further conversation with him tonight.

'What will they think of me?' Arabella groaned in embarrassment as Darius carried her effortlessly up the wide staircase.

'They will think, as I do, that you are a very brave young woman who at the very least deserves to be carried upstairs to her bedchamber,' he said indulgently.

Her arms tightened about his neck. 'Your own bedchamber, please, Darius. I cannot—I do not wish to go back into my own room tonight.'

His mouth tightened grimly as he thought once more of the fear Arabella must have suffered when last in her bedchamber. His eyes glittered fiercely as he recalled her mention of that silencing hand placed across her mouth and the restraining arm about her throat. That she was still alive and safe here in his arms was almost enough to bring Darius to his knees.

As it was, his arms tightened about her as he carried her down the hallway. His own bedchamber was bathed in a golden glow from the single candle that his valet had left burning on the bedside table. A glow that bathed Arabella in that same golden light as Darius placed her carefully on top of the bedcovers.

Her arms remained tightly locked about his neck as she pulled him down with her, his fully clothed body half lying across her own as she raised her mouth to his invitingly.

It was an invitation Darius had no will or desire to resist, and his mouth gently claimed hers, that gentleness blazing into fierce desire as her lips parted beneath his and Darius felt the soft, encouraging stroke of her tongue against his own.

Their kiss was urgent, hungry as they tasted each other. Darius's hands moved up to cup either side of her face, his body above hers pressing her down into the bed.

Arabella could feel the hard need of Darius's thighs pushing against her as he kissed her long and deeply. Her hands tangled in the heavy thickness of his hair as she returned the heat of that kiss. There was only the heavy sound of their increasingly ragged breathing to break the silence as they began to throw off their clothes, both of them needing, aching for even closer contact.

Arabella gasped as Darius returned the heavy weight of his naked body to her own. He was burning hot.

Searing. Her nipples hardened like berries against the heat of his chest. Her thighs undulated against the hard length of his arousal and her legs parted in immediate invitation.

'Yes, Darius!' she pleaded as he would have pulled back slightly. 'I need you so very badly.'

'You are not ready yet, love—' he broke off with a strangled groan as she thrust her hips upwards to take an inch or two of him inside her.

'I need you inside me now,' she moaned urgently.

Her need was enough to send their lovemaking into a wild frenzy as they kissed and touched, caressed, devoured. Arabella felt at that moment as if their hearts and minds were joined in the same way as their bodies, the pleasure rising higher and higher, and then higher still, until they reached the pinnacle together in a hot burst of blinding pleasure.

Darius blew out the candle before falling back onto his pillows with a groan. He took Arabella with him, his arm firmly about her waist as he held her tightly against his side, her head resting on his shoulder as she continued to run a lightly caressing hand across the heated dampness of his chest.

Their silence was companionable, satiated, and as Darius heard Arabella's breathing start to slow, to deepen, and felt that caressing hand become still against his chest, he knew that she was falling asleep.

Darius wondered if he would ever sleep again. If he would ever again feel able to relax his watchful vigil. His determination to keep her safe was so strong that he knew he wouldn't be able to fully rest until their enemy was caught. He could not—

'Darius?'

He glanced down in the moonlight at the pale oval of Arabella's face, surrounded by those wild golden curls. The heavy weight of her lashes against her cheeks showed him that her eyes were still closed. 'Yes, love?'

'Westlake is not really a butler, is he?' she murmured sleepily.

Darius chuckled huskily before relaxing completely against her and allowing the darkness of sleep to claim them both.

Chapter Sixteen

Arabella was pale but composed as she walked lightly down the staircase of Winton Hall the following morning. Darius had not been beside her when she woke in his bed an hour or so ago, but feeling the warmth of the sheets beside her Arabella realised he had not been gone long, that he had probably left her sleeping so that she might rest as long as possible after her ordeal the previous night. She was also aware that he would want to be up and about early this morning, wanting to see if he could learn any more of her abductor now that it was daylight.

'I trust you are feeling better this morning, Your Grace?'

Arabella turned to smile at the butler-who-she-was-sure-was-not-a-butler as he appeared in the cavernous hallway below. 'I am, thank you, Westlake.'

'His Grace told me to inform you that he will be outside with Lord Grayson for a time.' The man's battered face was creased into kindly lines of concern as she stepped down to join him in the reception hall.

She smiled up at him warmly, more than ever convinced—even if Darius's laughter the previous night had not already confirmed her suspicion—that this man was not what he pretended to be. In fact, she now believed that he had been hired to act as an extra protection against any attacks.

The almost guilty look on Westlake's battered features as he continued to look at her told her that he was less than pleased with himself at this moment. 'Would you care to join me for a cup of tea in the breakfast room, Westlake?' she invited.

He looked stunned. 'Your Grace?'

'Please do come,' she encouraged as she tucked her hand into the crook of his arm and smiled up at him mischievously. 'I am simply longing to know what profession you enjoyed before my husband persuaded you into coming to Winton Hall!'

Darius came to a stunned halt in the doorway of the breakfast room as he beheld his young wife and his butler sitting down at the table, drinking tea together as they chatted like old acquaintances.

Having spent the last two hours unsuccessfully scouring the cobbled courtyard, the stables, and the grounds of the house for any sign as to how last night's intruder might have got inside, the last thing Darius had expected to find when he decided to join his wife for a late breakfast was Big Tom and Arabella sitting together as if they were the best of friends!

As if sensing Darius's presence, Arabella ceased talking to glance towards the door. The warmth of the smile she bestowed upon him revealed no lingering shadow of the fear and distress she had suffered during the previous night's ordeal.

'Darius!' She stood up to cross the room to his side and link her arm companionably with his. 'Do come and join us. Tom has been regaling me with wonderful tales of his experiences in the fighting ring.' Her eyes gleamed up at Darius teasingly as he glanced across the room to where Westlake had just risen uncomfortably to his feet.

'Stay where you are, man,' Darius urged as he walked further into the breakfast room.

The ex-pugilist gave a self-conscious shake of his head. 'I'd best be about my duties now that you've come back, Your Grace.' He shot Arabella an awkward grimace before beating a hasty retreat.

Darius smiled. 'Arabella?'

Her laughter deepened. 'And to think I had decided yesterday that I must needs talk to you about the unsuitability of the household staff you have employed here!'

Darius shook his head ruefully as he sat down at the breakfast table. 'I do not believe you will in any way help with the disciplining of that staff when you invite them to take tea with you.'

That laughter still gleamed in the deep brown of her eyes as she strolled over to join him at the table. 'But Tom has led such an interesting life.'

'A life the details of which your brothers would all be deeply shocked to learn you have been made privy to,' Darius groaned.

She chuckled softly. 'Did you know that Tom won his first fight when he was only thirteen? That he—?'

'Arabella, please.' He winced. 'I assure you, as soon

as this—this situation is resolved, we will see about replacing the servants now presently in our employ with others more suited to the task.'

Arabella paused in sipping her tea. 'You cannot be thinking of replacing Tom?' she protested. 'He confided in me but a few minutes ago that after years of fighting for a living he actually enjoys the work here.'

Darius did not miss the determined light in her eyes. 'But he has proved time and time again that he has no idea how to be a butler—'

'Oh, please, Darius!' She looked across at him imploringly. 'He is far too old to return to the ring, and I am sure that with a little advice and guidance from me he will soon learn all he needs to of how to be butler in a ducal household.'

Darius had absolutely no doubt that she was well up to the task. That she was capable of doing anything she set her mind to. Their present conversation was also succeeding in keeping her attention diverted from the previous night's events. He set himself to be deliberately provocative…

'And what will we do when your brothers visit—especially Hawk, as he surely will, if only to assure himself that I have not done away with his sister!—and they all recognise Tom for who and what he is?'

'What he *was*,' Arabella corrected firmly. 'I think you underestimate my family, Darius. I am sure they will all come to appreciate Tom as I do. Even if they do not, it is of little real import; we are at liberty to choose our own household staff, I trust?' She looked effortlessly proud—a true duchess.

Darius gazed at her admiringly from between narrowed lids. While she was a little pale this morning, she otherwise appeared delicately lovely in a gown of buttercup-yellow. Yet it was a delicacy that Darius knew to be totally deceptive!

'We will talk on this subject again some other time,' he said briskly. 'For the moment we must decide what to do next. I believe it best if you depart for Mulberry Hall after breakfast so that you might stay with Hawk and—'

'No.'

He quirked one arrogant brow. 'No?'

'Absolutely not.' Arabella met his narrowed gaze unwaveringly, her back and shoulders very straight. 'I will not be forced into running away, Darius. Into leaving what is now my home.' She gave a firm shake of her head, blond curls dancing at her nape and temples.

'And if I insist?'

Arabella looked at Darius speculatively, knowing by the grim set of his face—narrowed eyes, unsmiling mouth, clenched jaw—that he *was* insisting. 'Then I will have no choice but to try to persuade you otherwise.'

'Only *persuade*, Arabella?' Darius's mouth twitched. 'That does not sound at all like you!'

'Yes. Well.' Arabella's gaze dropped from that probing blue one. 'It is not always necessary for us to engage in an argument in an effort to make my own views known.'

Darius gave a disbelieving snort. 'This is the first I have heard of it.'

She frowned her irritation. 'Is it any wonder I so often feel the need to disagree with you when you are always so sure you are right?'

He chuckled softly. 'That is more like the Arabella I have come to know!'

Her cheeks flushed hotly. 'You are not taking me seriously, Darius.'

'On the contrary, Arabella, I am taking your involvement in this situation, and in what happened last night, *very* seriously.' Darius sat forward, his expression once again grim. 'Hence my suggestion that you travel to Mulberry Hall later this morning.'

'A suggestion I have already informed you I find totally unacceptable.'

Darius scowled as he saw her stubborn determination in the tilting of her little chin and the firming of her mouth. 'I am endeavouring to keep you safe, you stubborn baggage.'

'And if I prefer to remain here with you?'

'Then, as last night has already proved, you will *not* be safe.' He stood up to pace the room restlessly. 'Do not be so ridiculously mulish about this, Arabella. Once I know you are safely ensconced at Mulberry Hall I will be able to concentrate all my energies on apprehending your abductor.'

'Are you saying that I am a distraction to you?'

He shot her a knowing look. 'I am saying your presence here is a distraction.'

'Is that not the same thing?'

No, it was not, Darius acknowledged with a frown. Worrying about Arabella's safety was a total distraction for his mind. Her presence was a distraction to his body, as he found himself desiring her both day and night! 'I cannot concentrate on apprehending your abductor if I constantly have to worry that it might happen again. With less satisfactory results.'

'You mean, that if I am taken again I might be killed?'

Darius had fallen into a satiated sleep the night before, only to awaken suddenly in the darkness minutes later. His arms had tightened about Arabella and they had remained about her all night long as he had lain there awake, holding her safely against him. He'd spent the night imagining someone somehow taking her from him again. Finding her broken and lifeless body after searching for her not just for hours, but for tormented days and nights…

'It is a risk I am unwilling to take.'

'But it is not *your* risk, Darius.' Arabella spoke softly.

His hands clenched at his sides. 'Of course it is my risk! No matter what our reasons for marrying each other, you are still my responsibility. Mine to protect!'

How awful that Darius should only consider her his 'responsibility'. His 'to protect'.

Arabella was aware of exactly what he meant by 'no matter what our reasons for marrying each other'. Knew that he had to be referring to his belief that she had only married him because he was now a wealthy duke rather than a penniless lord. As for his own reasons for marrying her…

'Why did you marry me, Darius?' She looked at him searchingly.

He shot her an irritated scowl. 'This is hardly the time—'

'There may not be another time, Darius.' She shook her head sadly.

A white line of tension appeared beside his thinned lips. 'That is precisely the reason I am insisting you leave here today.'

'I have said no.'

'Arabella—'

'I will not go, Darius, so you may as well cease repeating yourself. You—'

'I am sorry to interrupt…' An uncomfortable Gideon Grayson stood hesitantly in the open doorway.

'What is it, Gray?' Darius turned to the other man with considerable thanks for interrupting his disagreement with Arabella; she would leave here later this morning if he had to tie her inside the carriage to achieve it!

Gray winced. 'A rider has just arrived with a letter. From London. He refuses to give it to anyone but you,' he added tellingly.

Darius looked concerned. 'Did he say who had sent it?'

'He refused to tell me that, either,' the other man revealed.

'Very well.' Darius nodded tersely as he walked to the door. 'Stay here and keep Arabella company, would you?'

'I am not a child who needs to be watched every minute of the day,' his wife commented dryly as she overheard his muttered comment to Gray.

Darius turned to look at her. 'Would you deny our guest the opportunity to eat breakfast?'

Her cheeks flushed at the rebuke. 'No, of course not.'

'Then I am sure Gray will be only too happy to keep you company whilst you finish eating your own meal.' The glittering intensity of his gaze challenged her to defy him again.

'I had not realised until recently, Lord Grayson, how tedious husbands can be,' Arabella remarked lightly as she resumed her seat at the breakfast table.

Darius scowled darkly as he saw that Gray was having trouble holding back a smile at his expense. 'If she tries to leave, Gray, you have my permission to tie her to the chair!'

The younger man looked scandalised. 'I could not possibly—'

'I believe my husband is playing with you, Lord Grayson,' Arabella cut in, taking pity on him. 'With us both.' She shot Darius a glare that warned of retribution for his high-handedness.

'You cannot be so sure of that…' Darius drawled mockingly, before taking his leave, leaving an awkward silence behind him.

Arabella found herself the focus of the embarrassed gaze of Gideon Grayson. 'Please do sit down, Lord Grayson.' She indicated the chair opposite her own that Big Tom had so recently vacated. 'Darius does so love to tease,' she remarked casually as she poured him a cup of tea, all the while wondering precisely why this man was still here… 'You stopped here on your way elsewhere, I believe, Lord Grayson? Will your hosts not be concerned by your delay?'

'Oh, no! Well—I—'

'You were not on your way to anywhere but Winton Hall, were you?' Arabella's shrewd gaze pinned him where he sat.

Gideon Grayson gave an uncomfortable start. 'I really cannot talk about it, Your Grace.'

'Call me Arabella,' she invited. 'And of *course* you may talk about it. I am Darius's wife now, and any business that you have with my husband you may also discuss with me.'

The young Lord looked even more ill at ease. 'I am afraid I cannot. No.'

Exactly as Arabella had expected. Just as she suspected there was much more going on in Darius's life than he had so far confided in her. 'Then perhaps you would prefer to discuss the weather, as we did yesterday?'

'I would, yes.' His Lordship looked much relieved by the suggestion.

'Did you and my husband find any evidence this morning of how the intruder could have entered the house yesterday evening?'

'But— That is hardly the weather, Your Grace!' He shifted restlessly in the chair.

Arabella gave him a sweetly saccharine smile. 'I merely asked if *you* would prefer to discuss the weather, Lord Grayson. I did not say *I* intended doing so.'

He gave a reluctant laugh. 'It is easy to see now that you are indeed Sebastian's sister!'

Arabella's smile deepened. 'You find my youngest brother as amiable as I?'

'I find he is as full of surprises,' Lord Grayson contradicted wryly. 'The most recent, of course, being his marriage to Lady Boyd.'

'No doubt you will miss Sebastian's company about Town?'

'Your brother and I have not been as…close of late as we once were.' He looked less than comfortable with the admission.

'So Darius has remarked.' Alerting Arabella to yet another mystery; her brother Sebastian was outwardly the most charming of men, and he and Gideon Grayson had been friends for years. She no longer believed

Darius's hint that Sebastian and Lord Grayson had fallen out over a woman, either. As far as Arabella was aware Juliet had been the only woman in Sebastian's life for some months now. 'Perhaps you were also present at the Bancroft house party in the summer?'

Lord Grayson stiffened, his expression now wary. 'Perhaps.'

'Either you were or you were not?'

He gave a slow and reluctant inclination of his head. 'I was.'

'I see... Darius has been rather a long time, has he not?' Arabella frowned her concern as she realised it must be ten minutes or more since Darius had left them. She stood up abruptly. 'I believe I will go and see if—'

'Carlyne expressed a wish for you to remain here.' Lord Grayson also stood up.

Arabella raised haughty brows. 'I trust you are not about to attempt to physically restrain me from joining my husband, My Lord?'

'Of course I am not.' His face flushed uncomfortably. 'I just think it wiser if you remain here until Darius comes for you.'

Arabella shot him a derisive glance. 'You have known Sebastian for some years now, and during that time you must surely have come to realise that the St Claires are not always wise?'

Grayson grimaced. 'I have found that to be the case on occasion, yes.'

'You see my point, I hope?'

'Yes. But—'

'There is no *but*, Lord Grayson. I intend to go and look for my husband now. My advice to you is that you continue with your breakfast until Darius sends for you.' Arabella gave him one last challenging smile before turning on her slippered heel and leaving the room to go in search of her husband.

Darius sat behind the desk in his study, his face pale as he attempted to accept the significance of the note he had just received from William Bancroft.

'Darius…?'

The contents of Bancroft's note were so disturbing that Darius was not in the least surprised he had not heard Arabella open the study door and enter the room before quietly closing it again behind her. Nor was he surprised that she had not done as he had asked and stayed in the breakfast room with Grayson; Arabella had not obeyed any of his suggestions to date, so why should he have expected that she would obey that one?

'What is it, Darius?' She glanced at the note that lay open upon the top of his desk. 'Have you received bad news of some kind?'

His laugh was completely lacking in humour. 'Not just bad, Arabella, but earth-shattering!'

'What is it?' Arabella's concern deepened as she took note of the pallor of his face. 'Darius, what has happened?' She crossed the room to his side.

He did not answer her with words, but instead held out the note for her to take.

'Read it, Arabella!' He stood up abruptly to move away from her and stand in front of the window, his hands gripped tightly together behind his back, his expression as grim as the cold and frosty weather outside.

Arabella's hand shook as she held the note, her emotions too disturbed for her to immediately be able to focus on the words written there. She had never seen Darius like this before. So bleak. So utterly lost to all hope, it seemed.

Her heart sank as she read the note signed by Lord Bancroft. Helena Jourdan was dead. She had been drowned over a week ago, when the ship taking her back to France had floundered and sunk in a storm off the Normandy coast. The bodies of those who had died were only now being washed ashore and identified.

Darius looked so bleak, so helpless, because Helena Jourdan had died…?

Arabella crumpled the note in her hand to stare across the room at her husband. 'You cared for her after all, then.'

'Do not be ridiculous, Arabella!' Darius exclaimed as he turned impatiently back into the room, his eyes ablaze with emotion.

She shook her head. 'But you are so upset—'

'Of *course* I am upset.' Darius began to pace the small confines of the room. 'Do you not see what this means, Arabella? Can you not see that if Helena Jourdan has been dead this past week then she cannot be the one trying to harm us? It must be Francis after all.'

Now that Darius had pointed it out to her, of course Arabella did see. But it was not that realisation that made her face pale as she stumbled to the chair placed in front of the desk and sat down abruptly. No, that was for quite another reason entirely.

Even the thought of Darius being in love with another woman, of his being devastated at learning of that woman's death, had been almost enough to bring Arabella to her knees in aching anguish.

She *was* in love with Darius!

She had known herself to be fascinated by him during her first Season. Had imagined herself to be slightly infatuated with him, and been infuriated rather than saddened when he'd married Sophie Belling the previous year. But Arabella had not known, had not realised until this moment, that she had really been in love with him all along.

Even when he had felt himself forced into offering for her she had fooled herself into believing that she was only accepting him because he would make her a much more interesting husband than any of the other men she had met during her two Seasons.

How could she have been so stupid? So blind to her own feelings?

'Arabella?'

She looked up to find Darius frowning down at her, and was at once engulfed in feelings of panic. Darius could not know how she felt about him! He must never learn that she had been foolish enough to fall in love with him when he was a penniless lord, and that she was still in love with him now that he was a wealthy duke!

She drew in a deeply controlling breath. 'I realise this must be disturbing for you, Darius. But surely it is as you imagined?'

'Imagined, perhaps. But I never gave up hope it would not be the case.' He sighed heavily. 'We will, of course, both have to return to London immediately.'

Arabella blinked at the sudden change of subject. 'We will?'

Darius nodded. 'Immediately.'

'But of course I shall come to London with you if you think I can be of any help to you—'

'It is not *I* who is in need of your assistance, Arabella, but your newest sister-in-law, Juliet.'

Arabella looked bewildered. 'Juliet?'

'Of *course* Juliet,' Darius confirmed impatiently. 'Your sister-in-law will need the support of all of her family to help sustain her through this difficult time.'

'I had not realised that anyone but close family yet knew of Juliet's…condition.' Arabella was completely at a loss as to Darius's train of thought. Perhaps having confirmation of his brother's perfidy had unhinged him slightly? No, Darius was not a man to become unhinged by anything, and she had no doubt that when he finally apprehended Francis he would deal with his brother in the same calm and collected way he had dealt with him seven months ago.

Darius looked confused. 'What condition?'

'Why, she and Sebastian are expecting…' Arabella trailed off into silence. She knew by Darius's blank expression that he'd had no idea Juliet was with child. 'Darius, why exactly do you think that Juliet needs her family around her at this moment?'

Darius had been so weighed down by the evidence of Francis's guilt that he had spoken without thinking. Without practising his usual caution. Arabella, being Arabella, was now starting to draw her own conclusions from that slip. No doubt they would be the correct ones!

No matter. Darius had thought long and hard as he'd lain awake the previous night, holding her safe in his arms, and the conclusion he had come to from all that thinking was that as a married man it was now time for him to withdraw his services from the crown. He had enough to occupy him in being Arabella's husband and the Duke of Carlyne. Most especially in being husband to the wayward Arabella!

Darius had never known another woman like her. Her beauty was all too apparent. But she was also self-confident. Self-willed. So high-spirited. A young woman, in fact, who refused to be cowed or frightened by anything or anyone. Even her scare the previous night—something that would have reduced a lesser woman to tears and hysteria—had only shaken her momentarily before she returned to being her normal stubborn self. As for the way she had sat down this morning and drunk tea and gossiped with Big Tom Westlake…

No, Darius had never before known a woman quite like her…

He grimaced. 'Arabella, have you not wondered why William Bancroft should be the one to inform me of Helena Jourdan's death?'

'Well, I… That *is* rather strange,' she agreed. 'What is the Earl of Banford's connection to her?' Her gaze was suddenly sharp with suspicion.

'I will explain that in a moment.' Darius sighed. 'Arabella, Helena Jourdan was Juliet's cousin and companion.'

Arabella gasped.

Darius nodded. '*And* a French spy.'

A frown appeared on Arabella's creamy brow, and her eyes widened before just as suddenly narrowing again. Her beautiful pouting lips thinned indignantly as she glared up to at him. 'The same French spy arrested at

Lord and Lady Bancroft's house party this past summer?'

Having made his decision to leave off working for the crown, Darius knew the time for prevarication as regarded his young wife was over. 'Yes.'

Arabella went from being indignant to blazingly angry in a matter of seconds, and she stood up with an impatient ruffle of her skirts. 'Why did you not tell me before? Why did you not explain?'

'I could not, love.'

'Do not "love" me, you—you—'

'Diverting as this conversation no doubt is to the two of you, I find that I am becoming rather bored by it!' a contemptuous voice suddenly interrupted.

Darius turned sharply to stare into the shadowed corner of the study behind him, his eyes widening with disbelief as he saw the man standing there, looking back at him so disdainfully.

His brother Francis!

Chapter Seventeen

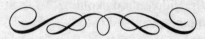

Arabella turned to frown at the man who had somehow joined them in the study without either of them
having been aware of it until he spoke to them. She recognised him instantly, of course: young and handsome,
with golden-blond hair and pale blue eyes, Francis
Wynter really was a weaker-looking version of his
brother.

'How convenient that I should find the two of you
alone here together,' Francis remarked mildly as he
stepped out of the shadows to reveal that he held a
raised pistol in each hand. 'Recognise these, Darius?'

Darius nodded tersely, a nerve pulsing in his tightly
clenched jaw. 'They are our father's duelling pistols.'

'One for each of you, yes.' The younger man gave a
mocking inclination of his head. 'I apologise, my dear.
We have not as yet been introduced.' He turned that bold
blue gaze upon Arabella. 'I am—'

'I know who *and* what you are.' Arabella looked
back at him scornfully.

'Oh, dear, Darius, what *have* you been telling your young wife about me?' Francis gave his brother a taunting look.

'Darius did not need to tell me anything about you,' Arabella assured him disdainfully. 'I know from your previous actions what a monster you are, and your cowardly behaviour of last night only confirms that belief.'

'Arabella—'

'Oh, please, do let her continue, Darius.' Francis Wynter calmly interrupted Darius's words of warning. 'I am all agog to hear what the haughty Lady Arabella St Claire thinks of me.'

Arabella drew herself up to her full height. 'I am Arabella *Wynter*, Duchess of Carlyne, and as such you will address me as Your Grace!'

Those pale blue eyes narrowed with dislike. 'Not for very much longer, my dear,' he assured her evilly.

Arabella felt a shiver of apprehension run down the length of her spine. 'You, sir, are—'

'Arabella, please!' Darius stepped forward to push her behind him in an attempt to shield her with his body, all the time keeping his steely gaze fixed firmly upon his brother. 'How did you get in here, Francis?' He asked one of the questions that had been plaguing him these last few tense minutes as Arabella had kept Francis occupied in conversation and Darius's mind had raced as to how he was to reach his own loaded pistol hidden in the top drawer of his desk.

Francis gave a humourless smile. 'Because you and our cousin Simon, and frequently Lucian St Claire—' he shot Arabella another look of intense dislike '—chose to habitually exclude me from joining in your diversions outside, I was left to stay indoors and fall back on my own devices. In the process of doing so I discovered several secret passageways that had obviously been installed in the house when it was first built. In order to aid escape if the inhabitants of the house were ever attacked, one presumes. You see?'

He balanced one of the pistols so that he might reach out and touch the rose design in the centre of one of the panels on the wall, resulting in the whole panel silently opening.

'Ingenious, is it not?' He pressed the rose and closed it again before resuming his previous position, having both pistols levelled on Arabella and Darius. 'God knows what our ancestors got up to that they needed such an escape, but I have certainly found those passageways helpful for my own plans.'

It explained how Francis had managed to enter the house the previous night undetected, at least. Without, as Darius had previously suspected, the aid of one of his own servants. That was something, at least. 'What do you want here, Francis? Have your past actions not already caused enough unhappiness to our family?'

'My dear Darius, I have not even begun!' his brother said coldly as he pointed one of the pistols directly at Darius's chest. 'Now, for this to work properly, I am afraid you will have to step aside.'

Darius felt his heart turn to ice. 'What do you mean?'

Francis smiled. 'First you will shoot your wife in a fit of temper, and then you will take your own life.'

'A fit of temper?' Arabella was the one to repeat it incredulously as she stepped out from behind Darius.

'I assure you Darius is far too much in control of his emotions to resort to anything so childish as a fit of temper!' she dismissed contemptuously.

At that moment Darius wished that his wife were a little less outspoken and more in control of her *own* emotions! 'Would you please allow *me* to deal with this, Arabella?' he asked mildly.

'"This" being your disgrace of a brother, I presume?' She shot Francis another contemptuous glance.

Darius winced as he saw the murderous glint that had now entered Francis's eyes. 'Arabella—'

'No, please allow her to continue, Darius.' His brother continued to look venomously at Arabella. 'It will make it so much easier to shoot her when the time comes!'

That lump of ice in Darius's chest became even heavier. 'You will never get away with this, Francis. No one will believe that I shot my wife of but a few days before taking my own life.'

'But of course they will.' Francis gave them a confident, insane smile. 'Once the rumour is circulated that your wife and Grayson were involved before your marriage, and that she invited Grayson to be with her here as early as your honeymoon, I have no doubt that the ton will believe every word of it!'

Darius's eyes narrowed to icy chips of blue. 'Lord Grayson has a perfectly legitimate reason for being here.'

'I'm sure,' his brother drawled knowingly.

This was not going well, Darius realised frustratedly. Not that he expected Francis's story to be believed for a moment; too many people of influence knew of his true relationship with Grayson. But if he and

Arabella were already dead it really was going to be of little interest to either of them what anyone believed! If Darius could only get to his own gun in the drawer of his desk. Perhaps if he could distract Francis?

'Have you been hiding in the house this whole time, Francis?' he enquired lightly, only to receive a frowning glance from his wife. He once again managed to move so that his body acted as a shield for hers.

'At the Dower House, actually.' Francis smiled. 'The few servants that Margaret retains apparently do not talk to the lower class of servants you have engaged here since becoming Duke of Carlyne, and conveniently saw no reason to enlighten anyone as to my presence there.'

His brother really was insane, Darius realised heavily. Completely. Utterly. Which was not going to make the slightest difference when Francis pulled the trigger on his pistol and killed both him and Arabella!

'Can we not sit down together and talk about this?'

'How magnanimous of you, Darius.' Francis gave him a derisive glance. 'I seem to recall that as a child you were always one for doing the right thing. I made sure my mama never believed it of you, of course,' he added. 'Young as I was, I still remember her talking of how I would make a far better duke than either George, Simon or you could ever be.'

Arabella now understood the need Darius felt for caution; his brother was obviously not in his right mind. Had not been so for some time, from the sound of it. No doubt he had been helped along in that insanity at a very young age by the ambitions of a mother who had proved herself to be vicious and unforgiving to the young and vulnerable little boy who had been her stepson.

'Margaret is expected back tomorrow.' Francis gave a contented smile. 'I have decided it will be more convenient for all if, when she arrives, she is able greet me as the new Duke of Carlyne. If you would kindly step aside so that I have a clear shot, Darius?' He made a waving motion with one of the pistols.

So that he had a clear shot at *her*, Arabella realised with horror. This man, Darius's own brother, intended to calmly and cold-bloodedly kill both of them! As he was the only one of them holding pistols, Arabella could not see how they were going to deflect him from carrying out that plan, either.

Perhaps if she were to pretend to faint? No, Arabella doubted that would ruffle the obviously deranged man in the slightest; he would probably just take advantage of her prone position and shoot her where she fell.

Francis gave an impatient sigh as Darius continued to shield Arabella with his own body. 'I really would have preferred for you to see your duchess die before your eyes,' he said in disappointment. 'But ultimately it is of little import which of you dies first.'

Once again he levelled the pistol at Darius's chest.

'No!' Arabella screamed as she saw that finger about to squeeze the trigger, moving to grab Darius's arm in order to pull herself round in front of him. She clung firmly to both his arms as her hungry gaze ate up every handsome inch of her husband's angry face, and then she heard the sound of breaking glass and the loud report of the pistol being fired…

'Arabella! Arabella, for God's sake open your eyes and speak to me!'

Her first thought was that she had failed and Francis

had succeeded after all. That she and Darius were both dead. How else could he now be talking to her? Her only consolation—if it could be called such—was that she and Darius were still together.

'Arabella, I *know* you are awake because I saw your eyelids move just now. Now, open your eyes, damn it!' Strong hands clasped hold of her arms and she felt herself being shaken.

She had never given particular thought to what it would be like in the afterlife. There would be angels, of course. Celestial music, perhaps. But never in any of her imaginings on the subject had Arabella thought to hear Darius cursing at her. Or that she would still be able to feel his strong fingers around her arms…

Her lashes flickered before she opened heavy lids to gaze upwards, blinking dazedly as she found herself looking at the canopy above the bed in her bedchamber. Was this what heaven was like? she wondered dreamily. Did the same life continue? With the same surroundings…

'Arabella, *look* at me!' The pale yet fiercely angry face of her husband moved into her line of unfocused vision as he bent over her. 'Do you hear me, Arabella?'

'I hear you, Darius,' she managed to croak out between stiff lips. 'I imagine that the whole of heaven can hear you when you are shouting so loudly.'

'*Heaven?* Damn it, you are not dead!' He scowled down at her darkly. 'Although God knows how you are not! How *dare* you place yourself in front of me in that way? How *could* you deliberately put yourself in danger?' He shook her once again, before just as suddenly pulling her up into his arms, his expression anguished. 'Oh, Arabella, I thought he had killed you! I thought you were— Oh, God…' He buried his face in her golden curls and began to shake uncontrollably.

She was *not* dead!

She could not be dead when Darius felt so solid and warm against her. When she could feel his body shaking as he held her so tightly against him.

'Darius?' Arabella reached up a hand to wonderingly touch the soft golden reality of his hair and the hardness of his jaw. 'Darius, you are not dead, either!' She buried her face against the warmth of his jacket as she clung to him.

'Neither one of us is dead, love.'

As if to prove the point Darius began to kiss her throat, her earlobes, her cheeks, her eyes, her nose, and then finally her lips. They kissed hungrily, desperately, deeply, for long, wonderful minutes.

'Why did you do that, Arabella?' Darius finally pulled back slightly to glare down at her fiercely once again. 'Why did you deliberately put yourself in the path of danger?'

His eyes were dark and pained with the memory of that few seconds in time when Arabella had moved in front of him to place herself directly where Francis had been aiming the pistol.

'You really are alive, Darius!' Arabella's eyes glowed as she looked up at him wonderingly. 'You—' She broke off as he gave a pained wince. Her fingers had tightened on his arm. 'You are hurt!' Her eyes widened in alarm as she removed her hand and saw blood darkening the material of his jacket.

'It is unimportant. A flesh wound only,' Darius dismissed. 'Arabella—'

'I wish to see this flesh wound.' Arabella pushed him gently back so that she might sit up on the side of the bed. 'Take off your jacket.'

'Arabella, you will not deflect me from my chastisement of you by attempting to change the subject,' Darius warned her harshly. 'You will explain yourself.'

'Take off your jacket immediately and let me see your arm.' She ignored his rebuke as she concentrated on trying to peel his jacket from his shoulders.

Darius's expression softened at her concern. 'It really is only a flesh wound, Arabella, and can easily be dealt with later.'

She looked up at him uncertainly. 'How is it that we are both still alive?'

He grimaced. 'Because Francis is the one who is dead.'

'How?'

'Grayson,' he told her. 'He went outside after talking with you, and as he passed the study window he saw Francis in here, pointing the duelling pistols at the two of us. He shot him at the same time as Francis pulled the trigger on his own pistol, jerking Francis's aim and so deflecting the bullet into my arm instead of your back.' Darius's face was ferocious at the memory of what had so nearly occurred.

Arabella remembered the sound of breaking glass that she had heard a mere fraction of a second before the loud report of Francis's pistol. 'Then the danger really is over?'

'Francis's death has brought that whole sorry business to an end, yes.'

'I am so sorry, Darius.'

'I am not.' His jaw was rigid with tension.

Her eyes were wide. 'But what will happen now? How will you explain Francis's death?'

Darius shook his head. 'I have not had a chance to work out the details as yet, but I think perhaps it might be arranged in a few days that my brother has met his death by contracting influenza whilst travelling abroad.'

Arabella frowned. 'Arranged how?'

'I have said I have not worked out the details as yet—I am sorry, Arabella.' He sighed as he saw how hurt she looked at the harshness of his tone. 'It is only that at this moment I am more interested in why you threw yourself in front of me in that reckless way.' Darius looked down at her searchingly.

Those few seconds, when he had held the limp Arabella in his arms, had been the worst of Darius's entire life. A moment of utter and complete despair. Before he'd felt the pain of the wound to his own arm and realised that Francis's bullet had not struck and killed her after all. Then had come the most euphoric moment of his life...

'Tell me why you did something so stupid? So unbelievable? So utterly selfless!' His eyes glowed down at her fiercely.

She swallowed hard, her gaze not quite meeting his. 'I could not stand by and let that monster kill you.'

'Why not?'

She looked up sharply. 'You would rather I *had* let him kill you?'

Darius gave a rueful smile. 'I would rather that you answered my question, Arabella.'

Tiny white teeth worried at her lower lip. 'Will you not just accept that—?'

'Arabella, it is time that you knew how much I have always loved you,' he cut in. The time for prevaricating about his feelings for the courageous young woman who was now his wife was as over as his career spying for the crown. 'I have loved you, been obsessed by you, since the moment I first set eyes upon you eighteen long months ago.' He sincerely repeated his statement of the previous evening, which he had then said mockingly in order to put her off the scent of the truth.

Her eyes widened. 'Is that true, Darius?'

'Impossible to believe, is it not?' His mouth twisted.

'I—but you married Sophie Belling!' She frowned her confusion.

'Yes,' he confirmed harshly. 'And all I have been able to selfishly think since then is that if I had married you in her stead a year ago then it would have been you that Francis killed!'

'You loved me even then?'

'Long before then.' Darius admitted stiffly.

'Then I do not understand why you married someone else.'

'Sophie was not all that she seemed. Besides…' Darius's expression became bleak. 'What did it matter whom I married once you had refused me?'

'But I did not—what do you mean, she was not all that she seemed?' Arabella looked even more confused.

Darius stood up abruptly, knowing that he had to put some distance between himself and Arabella while he told her of his years working for the crown whilst deliberately fooling the ton into believing he was nothing more than a fortune-hunter and a rake. Besides, Arabella had not yet told him that she returned any of the feelings he had just confessed for her, so perhaps she did not…

'Sophie was an agent for the crown. As am I,' he added softly. 'Our marriage was one of convenience, as I have already explained. But it was a convenience meant to confirm my own apparent desperate need for a wealthy wife, and Sophie's need for a titled husband, whilst allowing us both to continue our work for the crown without alerting the ton or anyone else as to those less public activities.'

Arabella appeared to have been rendered speechless by his revelation. Although, characteristically, she did not remain so for very long! 'Your *apparent* need for a wealthy wife?' she questioned.

Darius shrugged. 'The rumours of my bankruptcy were vastly over-exaggerated, I am afraid.'

'Deliberately so? By you?'

'Yes.' He sighed. 'I have always been in possession of rather a large fortune, love,' he assured her dryly, as still she frowned.

'I— But you— How long have you worked as an agent for the crown?'

'Eight years,' Darius told her bleakly.

'*Eight years!*' Arabella gasped, shaking her head in disbelief. 'And the Earl of Banford and Gideon Grayson?'

'Also agents for the crown. Obviously ones who have been allowed a more respectable reputation than I,' he added with a humourless smile.

'All this time—all these years—you have *deliberately* allowed Society to think the worst of you!'

He grimaced. 'I did not deliberately allow them to

think anything; eight years ago, when I was asked to work for the crown, I was very much the rake everyone believed me to be.'

'And in the years since?'

Darius gave a rueful shrug. 'Once a rake always a rake, you know.'

Except he was not, Arabella realised. Darius was no longer a rake, or a gambler, and had never been a fortune-hunter, or responsible for the death of his wife and brother, or indeed any of the awful things that Society had believed of him for so long. Instead he was as much a hero if not more, as any of the gallant soldiers who had publicly taken up arms to fight for their king and country.

'How can you bear it, Darius?' she choked emotionally. 'How can you stand the gossip and sneering of people who should instead be thanking you for their very freedom?'

He shrugged wide shoulders. 'I have never much cared for Society's opinion of me, Arabella.'

'And my own opinion of you?' Did *that* matter to Darius?

Only minutes ago he had told her that he loved her. That he had loved her for this past year and a half! Arabella stood up slowly to cross the room so that she stood only inches away from him. From the heat of his body. From the warmth of the arms he kept firmly behind his back.

'Darius, I have loved you, been obsessed by you, since the moment I first set eyes upon you.' She met his deeply searching gaze unblinkingly as she repeated his own words back at him and allowed him to see her love shining in the depths of her eyes.

A nerve pulsed in his tightly clenched jaw. 'You refused my offer for you over a year ago.'

'No.' Arabella knew there must be absolute truth between Darius and herself now. 'I did not even know of that offer,' she explained at Darius's questioning look. 'I had no idea of it until Hawk told me of it on our wedding day.'

Those blue eyes narrowed. 'Your brother did not even *consult* with you that first time before refusing me?'

'No.'

Darius drew in a harsh breath. 'What would your answer have been if he had told you of it?'

Arabella smiled. 'I have no doubt, no matter what my feelings for you, that I would have considered long and hard before aligning myself with the disreputable Lord Darius Wynter. But ultimately…' Once again love glowed in her eyes as she gazed up at him. 'Ultimately I know I would have said yes!' She put a hand on his arm. 'I love you so very much, you see, Darius. I always have. And I always will.'

Darius closed his eyes briefly as he attempted to take in the wonder of Arabella having loved him all along. 'Do you think that perhaps we *are* both dead and gone to heaven, after all?' he murmured wonderingly as he took her into his arms to hold her tightly against him.

Arabella gave a husky laugh as she pressed into the warmth of those arms. 'If we are then I hope we will both stay here for ever!'

For ever with Arabella.

It was all that Darius had ever wanted and more.

Chapter Eighteen

Mulberry Hall
Seven weeks later.

'Come along, Arabella, it is Christmas Day and all of your family will be expecting us to join them downstairs for breakfast some time before lunch!'

Arabella stretched sleepily as she lay naked in her husband's arms, realising they both must have dozed off for several minutes after having indulged in some rather wonderful lovemaking.

'I have not given you your Christmas gift yet.'

'No?' Darius grinned down at her.

'*That* was not your Christmas gift.' Arabella returned the warmth of that smile as she moved up on her elbow to look down at him. 'I thought that since you have now given up spying you might appreciate having some other diversion with which to keep busy.'

'You are not enough?' Darius teased indulgently.

'Perhaps,' Arabella allowed huskily. The past seven

weeks of knowing how much they loved each other had been more wonderful than she could ever have imagined. 'But I would not wish you to become too bored at Winton Hall with just me for company.'

Darius sobered, his gaze intense as he assured her, 'You could never, ever bore me, love.'

'Does that mean you do not want your Christmas gift?' Arabella swirled the hair upon his chest with the tip of her finger, instantly reigniting Darius's desire for her.

He eyed her speculatively, noting the teasing glow in her eyes and the secretive smile that curved her kissable lips. 'What mischief have you been up to now, love?'

'Have *we* been up to,' she corrected. 'Although I am afraid I will not be able to properly place your gift into your arms for another seven and a half months…'

Darius frowned his confusion. 'I do not understand—Arabella?' His voice sharpened as she took hold of his hand and placed it against the flatness of her stomach.

Her smile was one of complete happiness as she announced. 'I am with child, Darius!'

'I— But— Are you sure?' Darius sat up abruptly to look down at her in utter disbelief.

'Jane's physician confirmed it only yesterday. Do not look so concerned.' Arabella laughed indulgently at his look of stunned disbelief. 'I believe it is a perfectly natural occurrence when couples make love as often as we have this past seven weeks!'

Those weeks had been blissfully happy ones for Arabella, as she knew herself well and truly loved by Darius. It was a love she returned just as deeply.

Darius had resigned from spying. After a suitable time Francis had reportedly become 'ill in France', and then been buried in the family crypt—a necessary fabrication for both Margaret Wynter and Society.

Arabella's family had been wonderful throughout, Hawk having had a quiet conversation with Darius some weeks ago in which it had been revealed that Hawk's new position in the government had finally allowed him access to knowledge of what Darius had really been doing this past eight years. Darius had been rendered speechless by the other man's apology for any heartache he might have caused Darius or Arabella by refusing Darius's first offer, and for his disapproval of their marriage two months ago.

Altogether, it had been as if those first few dangerous days of their marriage had never been. And now they were to have a baby. A child they had made together with the deepest of love.

'Is it not wonderful, Darius?' Arabella glowed up at him.

'*You* are the one who is wonderful, my darling Arabella,' he said huskily. 'I love you so very, very much,' he murmured gruffly, and once again he took her in his arms.

'As I love you,' she assured him fervently as she threw her arms about his neck and drew him down to her.

Breakfast, Christmas Day and her family could all wait….

* * * * *